The Butcher's List

By

Roger S. Williams

The Butcher's List

ISBN: 978-1-257-84484-5

The Butcher's List

Cover and Headers
by
Helen McManus

Forward and Back Cover
by
Daveda Gruber

Editing
by
Joree Williams
and
Helen McManus

All Interior and Exterior Formatting
by
Daveda Gruber

Dedication

"For my lovely wife, Bette, who patiently put up with hours, days, weeks and months as I tried to accomplish this work. Thanks and I love you."

Also, for Shannon and Jodi, our twin grandaughters, whose encouragement and teenage advice helped bring the characters in this story to life.

The Butcher's List

Foreword

What would happen if you lived in a nice quiet community and terror started to erupt? Children have started to be murdered and chilling torture happened to the bodies. If this isn't horrific enough, rape seeps its way into the picture. Could it get any worse?

Is it possible that no one can determine who the killer could be? Is it likely that the slayer can be caught? After an investigation, was the right killer put in a jail cell? Who else could have possibly done these horrific murders? Will this unsettling killing spree stop? What will it take to find a man who is so excited at the prospect of murder and blood?

Someone has made a list of victims. That list continues to grow. A man, a serial killer, is at large. Who will be smart enough to gather clues to these vicious attacks and not be caught in gathering information? Or maybe they will find themselves on a list of murders to be carried out?

Roger S. Williams has a way of intriguing his audience with spine chilling action that takes his readers into the ghastly mind of a serial killer. Williams has a way of letting you peek into a step by step vision of a man who is fixated on murdering certain victims.

Find out the answers to some very alarming questions and more in this terrifying story that will have you on the edge of your seat as your read chapter to chapter of 'The Butcher's List.'

The Butcher's List

CHAPTER ONE

They found the body. Actually, Mark's best friend, thirteen-year-old Ollie Frazier, found the body. The two boys from Dalton, a small town in Central California, were riding their bicycles on top of a flood control levee when Ollie needed to relieve himself. He left the trail to scramble down the bank where he could use some of the junipers and scrub oak as a screen. "Oh my God," he cried. "Oh my God!" The tone of his voice rather than the actual words sent an unexpected chill all the way to Mark's stomach.

"Ollie? What'cha got?"

"Oh my God!"

"What?"

"Oh my God!"

"Well crap, Ollie. I'm coming down."

Mark Goodwin used the heel of his western boot on the kickstand then parked his silver ten-speed bicycle next to Ollie's beat-up old red one. There was an ominous silence in the air. No insects were stirring, not a bird in the bushes as he turned to follow the same precarious path his buddy had used.

"Mark," Ollie choked, the words seemed as though squeezed from his throat. "Don't come!"

"What do you mean, 'don't come'?" His friend's broad back was already in view blocking whatever was holding him so spellbound. Mark stumbled when a shelf of rocks gave way and he slid the last six feet, leaving a trail of yellow dust, forcing him to use both hands against Ollie's solid frame to halt his progress. A peculiar feeling gripped his gut as Ollie turned to face him. He realized there was a dark stain on Ollie's khaki shorts, so he asked, "What the heck is going on?"

"I peed all over my friggin shorts." It was practically a sob.

1

The dust cleared, revealing a pinkish gray lump protruding from behind a sage bush. "God, Mark, don't look."
Mark looked. "What the heck is that? It looks like . . . ."

"Oh shit Mark, I pulled the bush aside to get a better look. She's dead. It's Laura. It's your little sister."

The sound began someplace deep inside, roiling at first, coming out as an expanding moan, turning into a heart wrenching, keening screech. "Oh my God!"

CHAPTER TWO

The Man parked his dark Lincoln Navigator in the garage then reached to pull down the door, looking up and down the street. In the small farm community of Dalton, California it was early in the morning. There was no one in sight, only the windows of the four houses in a row staring blankly back at him. In the kitchen he found his refrigerator nearly empty; only a part of a carton of milk, a saucer with half a cube of oleo covered with brown toast crumbs and three peaches, which were beginning to mold. The freezer compartment held nothing except ice cubes. The nearby cabinets held little in the way of food. The Green Spot is about due to open, he was thinking; I'll take a run down there. Taking a deep breath, he slowly let it out with a long hissing sound as he moved into the living room where he settled into his recliner.

Lying back he closed his eyes, wondering how one could feel so many things at once, hatred, fulfillment, happiness, guilt and excitement . . . and hunger. Placing both his hands up to cover his face, he breathed behind his palms, pressing the tips of his fingers tightly against his throbbing forehead trying to force his mind under control. Crazy brain seems to be slipping in and out of gear.

Sniffing several times he wondered at the strange smell. Better take a shower before going down to The Green Spot. There were streaks and splotches on the backs of his hands and between the fingers that were a deep crimson in color. Blood, he thought, smiling in satisfaction as he remembered the source. Dried blood.

* * *

Candy perched on a stool next to the kitchen counter pondering over the crossword puzzle in the Sunday Montgomery, Alabama Advertiser, one of those things at which she was very good. She was finding it hard to concentrate since the little town of Dalton, California was on her mind. Aunt Helen and her mother were sitting at the dining room table sipping at their coffee. Candy glared at the two women, somehow blaming her mother over the prospect of moving to California.

With a movement like the snake he was, her ten-year-old brother snatched the pencil from her grasp. "Michael," Candy screeched, "gimme my pencil." Leaping from her chair she caught a handful of T-shirt only to have it slip from her fingers as he slithered into the space under the breakfast nook. Aunt Helen was in the process of cleaning out the kitchen cabinets so both benches were piled with pots and pans and boxes. To reach him she'd be forced to crawl under.

She heard her mother say to her sister, "Helen? I can't tell you how much we appreciate you putting up with us for three whole days. The kids are having a ball. Too bad your three are at that church thing this afternoon and in school tomorrow. They get along so well."

"Michael, gimme me that pencil. Right this minute."

"For heaven's sakes, Candice," her mother snapped. "Find yourself another one. Leave your brother alone."

As she tried to reach under the tabletop, he called out, "Fatty, fatty two by four. Can't get through the kitchen door."

On her hands and knees, she could see him scribbling on the wall, pressing so fiercely the lead broke deep inside the pencil. "You little turd."

"Candice, don't you dare use that kind of language around your brother."

The phone rang. Aunt Helen stood so abruptly she slopped coffee onto the table. Throwing her napkin onto the spill the portly woman grumbled, "Excuse me, Bette. I'll catch it in the den. I've been expecting an important call."

"Since you broke it, you can have it." Candy made her way down the hall heading for the bathroom, pausing when she overheard her aunt's side of the conversation.

"Mom, I don't mind helping out but these three leaches have about eaten everything in the house. Thank goodness only one more day. That . . . turd, Michael, has been responsible for about two thousand dollars worth of damage to my furnishings. On top of that I have to listen to that whining, smart mouthed redhead.

. . . "Did you say 'high strung', Mom? A little brat is more like it.

"No they haven't. You'd think with the big check Bette is picking up tomorrow for her house she'd at least spring for a few groceries.

"Candice? Okay, I'll tell her.

"Oh, that sounds great. We'll all be there. What time?

"Okay. Talk to you later. Bye Mom. Love ya."

Candy moved on into the bathroom. When she was through she washed her hands, merely glancing at the mirror. The reflected image looking back at her wasn't what she saw. Here she was, thirteen years old and continued to visualize the person from a year ago, fat, and freckled and with a mop of carrot colored hair. In the past year it had been her fate to shoot up an unbelievable inch every month, her body slimming considerably. She was developing a bust-line and the unruly hair had turned a burnished copper. She glanced at herself in the mirror. Unlike her teenage friends, she felt no interest in staring at her reflection. However, she did like the changes.

When she returned to the kitchen Aunt Helen was saying, "By this time next week you guys will be settled into your new home in California."

"Pretty much," her mother answered, "but there are so many things we need to do it'll be like starting over. One of the first things we have to do is look for a new car. Vince sold my old Firebird. Practically gave it away. Insisted it wasn't worth driving to California."

"From the pictures Vince brought back of that old boarded up monstrosity I wouldn't think you'd feel very much at home. Michael, don't swing on the refrigerator door. That is not a toy."

Candy was disgusted that her mother paid no attention to what Michael was doing. Instead she was saying, "Vince and the moving van should be almost to Dallas. Said they'd be in California by noon Tuesday. We're flying out that afternoon, by evening we'll all be in Dalton."

"Dalton?" The red headed teenager groaned. "Don't you mean Dulltown? I hear nothin' ever happens there, no rock concerts, not even any crime. They close the whole dang town down every day at six o'clock. I'd like ta hear what a person is supposed to do to with their time?"

"Make some friends, Candice. I'm sure the local kids have plenty of activities to keep them busy."

"Oh sure, 'make some friends'. That's easy for you to say."

"I realize making friends might be a novelty to you, but take some lessons from Michael. I assure you, he won't have any trouble."

"I hope they got some place there where I can keep up my karate lessons. At least I found something I'm good at."

Aunt Helen chuckled. "Probably due to the fact you've always been such a tom boy."

"She's that," her mother agreed. "I wasn't happy about having to stay behind to finalize the escrow, but it turned out to be a blessing in disguise for me since I didn't relish the thought of riding all the way to California in a U-haul truck pulling a car."

"I'll tell ya what was good luck," Helen let her sister know. "Selling that old house the way the market has been."

"Brick two stories like ours always seem to be in demand. Vince was good at keeping it in excellent shape."

"You are so fortunate to have married someone so handy. As you can see, Harold is a total klutz when it comes to fixing things up. Been wanting to get this shabby linoleum replaced and those horrible green cabinets redone for years."

"Decent places to live in Dalton were so scarce we took a lease option on that house until we can find or build something to our liking. Our old house took . . . "

"Oh, by the way, Candy, that was Grandma Swanson on the phone. She wants us all at her place for dinner tonight. At the moment she wants you to walk on over there for a few minutes."

"Whatever for? Why do I gotta go over there? I don't need any more lectures?"

Bette Swanson pointed a finger at her daughter. "Candice, it's going to be quite a while before you will be seeing your grandmother again so the least you can do is get your fanny over there and politely say good-bye. I don't want to hear another word."

"Oh Mom." She would have stomped her feet if she thought it would help.

Her mother was shaking the finger at her. "Don't 'Oh Mom' me. Do as you are told and I mean right this instant!"

* * *

Friday nights and Saturdays were their busiest times so Marion Montgomery worked the weekend, taking Monday and Tuesday off. She doubled as the clerk/dispatcher for the sheriff and public information clerk for the court. With a two-man police department in the quiet town, neither agency kept her very busy.

She was finishing her lunch when Frank Martinez, the sheriff walked in. Her eyes were asking if they'd found Laura Goodwin. The question was answered as the sheriff shook his head.

"I'm pretty much in a daze," he told her. "Was up all night. Need to rest up for a spell so I turned the search parties loose and put Ralph and a couple other men in charge. Been at it long enough to know what they're doin." Pretty sure that damn little twerp has run away again."

"If she has, it'll be her third time." Marion found it rather surprising. "With teenagers you have to expect it, but Laura is only eight."

"Yeah. First time we found her hiding in the Baptist church. Second time she'd been taken in by Mrs. Brubaker, who has a daughter the same age. I'm beginning to wonder if there isn't some truth in what the kid has been telling us. She keeps claiming she runs off every time her father whips her for something or the other she'd done."

"Who knows, Frank? Kids have been known to make things up when they are angry or don't get their own way. The Goodwin's declare up and down all they'd done was scold her."

"Well, two times in two months, makes a guy wonder if they are abusing her. Should have called Child Protective Services and have them check it out. If she has the same story this time when we find her, by God, I'm gonna."

"Being a parent myself, I kind of lean toward the Goodwin's"

"We shall see. In the meantime, I believe I'll try to catch me some shuteye."

He sat in his chair; his fat frame bulged through the wooden arms, his hands rested in his lap, his chin on his chest and his eyes closed.

Marion smiled, shaking her head. Why he didn't go back into the lounge she couldn't imagine. The shrill ringing of the phone interrupted her thoughts as well as Frank's attempt for a snooze.

She snatched it up on the first ring . . . and listened. "Ollie, would you calm down," she nearly shouted at the phone. "I can't understand one word you're saying." Her tone was loud enough to cause the sheriff to stir but he didn't look up.

"Say that again. You're where? . . .

"You and Mark found a what? . . .

"A body?"

Frank, all at once alert, saw her looking toward him as he snatched up his phone, trying to punch the buttons but his pudgy finger pushed in two and he had to stab at it again.

"Where is this body? Is it anybody we know?" Marion continued.

The sheriff looked at her. She was clutching her chest like it ached.

"Who is this?" The sheriff roared. "And what's this about a body?" The boy's answer brought him totally out of his chair and he heard Marion repeat it.

"Laura Goodwin? Oh my God!"

"Where are you callin' from, kid?"

Ordinarily once she'd turned over a call to Frank she'd hang up. Not this time.

The big man frowned. "From Mrs. Maxer's place, huh? Then you're out on Quarry Road, right? So how do I find this body?" Frank was yelling into his phone. After listening to the boy's directions he turned to her and told her, "Get a hold of Ralph. He's probably hanging out at the Green Spot as usual. Tell him to meet me out there. 'Bout three miles out on Lone Pine Trail. Knowing that Goodwin boy, this could be these teenagers idea of a sick joke. I'll let you know if we need the County Coroner."

"Right Frank." She squirmed in her chair. "Uh . . . are you going to call the Goodwin's?"

8

"Well? . . . Not 'til I check this thing out."

"I hope you're right . . . I mean . . . about it being a joke."

* * *

The redheaded teenager took her time, trudging the long six blocks to her grandmother's house feeling as though she were heading for her execution. She tried to smooth down her always-unruly hair but a swirling breeze didn't make it any more presentable. Stopping for a moment, she looked down on the view of the city from in front of the ancient antebellum style home. Even though she'd never been the type to attract friends, she was gonna miss Montgomery. She was thinking about the Karate lessons. It was the first thing in thirteen years her mother had okayed without making a big deal out of it.

Looking up at the six white columns supporting the roof over the huge porch, she wondered what the old gal would say if she rushed in and said, "Hi Grandma. Goodbye Grandma. Gotta run," and lit out? Grandma had been like the rest of the family, always coming up with that, 'Why can't you be more like your brother?' The usual crap. Why would the old gal want to see her? She had never been among her grandmother's favorites, so why this command performance? Was she dreading this visit? Like, you got it.

* * *

The Sheriff could see the Frazier boy from a half mile away. Lone Pine Trail ran for several miles alongside a twelve foot high dike built by the Corps Of Engineers thirty years ago. Behind it was a dry flood control basin that protected several thousand acres of farmland from the Sandstone River if it reached flood stage. Been living here going on twenty-three years, he was thinking. I ain't seen it even come close. That's the government for ya, always finding ways to waste our money.

Pulling to a stop fifty feet directly even to where he could see the two bicycles on top of the dike, he opened the door, struggling to extract his ample stomach from behind the wheel. Look at the size of that Frazier kid. Damned near as big as I am, and he's what? Thirteen? Off in the distance he could hear the siren from Ralph Powell's cruiser. His deputy was always looking for some excuse to run Code 3. Must be driving all the way out here wide-open. Frank waved his hand in front of his face as the black

9

and white cruiser came to a stop in a cloud of dust.

Ralph, whose police uniform always looked as though it was brand new, came out panting like he'd been running. "Comin' on duty an hour and a half early," he smirked. "Do I get time and a half?"

"You get paid by the month, Ralph, same as me. Let's see if we can crawl up that slope. Shit, I ain't built for mountain climbing." By sliding along at an angle he was able to scale the incline. Standing at the top, he turned to look at the big lad and frowned. Kid was panting like mad. Oh that's right. Called from Mona Maxer's place so he musta barely beat us here. "Whatcha think, Ralph? Looks like the kid dumped his coke on his shorts. I'll say this for him; there ain't any fat under that striped shirt. Nothin' but muscle."

The Frazier boy moved to the edge of the slope, pointing, "d-down there, under the bushes."

Frank looked down to where the Goodwin boy was sitting atop a huge granite boulder. "You know what, Ralph? I think these clowns are being cute, calling us out here for nothing."

"That's what Marion suggested. We may as well make our way down there for a look see."

The far side was mostly rocks and loose gravel. The climb down turned treacherous for someone as fat and out of condition as the sheriff. He ended up losing his footing, landing on the seat of his pants, using his broad bottom as a sled all the way down to where the Goodwin boy was sitting. Ralph was laughing like some kind of baboon as he easily made his way down the slope. Frank glared at him. "Stuff it Ralph. I fail to see the least bit of humor in this. So where's this body supposed to be?" He moved directly to the correct mesquite bush.

The kid on the rock was looking right at him but didn't move a muscle, not even an eyelash. Darn right spooky. "Get this kid," he told his deputy. "Leather jacket, all in black with a piece of chain running from his belt loop to his wallet, cowboy boots and long hair. I'm telling ya Ralph; I'm about convinced this is going to turn out to be a prank. It's the type of thing you learn to expect from some wannabe gangster. If it is I'm gonna fry his ass."

Ralph crowded in beside him pulling a sizable branch to

one side. The brittle wood snapped leaving him holding it in his grasp, making sounds as though he might heave up his lunch.

* * *

Grandma Swanson had lived in Alabama all her life. The woman was in her late fifties but to Candy she seemed to be closer to a hundred with her totally white hair and lots of wrinkles on her face and the backs of her hands. Thank goodness grandpa wasn't home. Fishing up at Lake Martin with some of his cronies. Candy wasn't sure, but she ventured a guess the lady was five foot four and a hundred sixty pounds. Even her flower print dresses looked old. To her surprise, when she made her way through the leaded glass entry, Grandma King was also there. Oh boy, whatever was coming, she was in for a double dinging.

Grandma King lived in Florence, way up in the northwest corner of Alabama. Unlike Grandma Swanson, she looked to be in her early forties. Was always smartly dressed in skirts and blouses or, as she was today, in a business-type suit. Her hair looked naturally brown but Candy knew it was dyed. Looking young and attractive seemed to entice a host of men friends and Candy overheard her mother telling Dad that grandma slept with them. What the heck? Ain't nobody's business. Grandma owned a beauty salon up in Florence. It had been seven or eight months since Candy had seen her.

When she'd entered the house she was so busy working up a defense for what she feared she'd be facing that she didn't realize how much her appearance took Grandma King off guard. She knew her body was changing for she spent considerable time at the sewing machine altering her clothes and she was aware that she had a degree of baby fat around her waist and about her face. She was also aware that other people did remark about what she considered her most striking features; her spun copper hair and her eyes, which ranged from bluish gray, to blue green, to a deep emerald depending on the weather, the lighting or her mood. She simply didn't feel any different.

Candy had no idea that Grandma King and Grandma Swanson had been planning this meeting via telephone for several weeks. Both women had come to an agreement, that as adults, they were very wrong in their treatment and judgment of a young lady who was forced to grow up without parental guidance and without love. She had never felt that she was part of the family so didn't know the two women thought she needed help and had formed a pact.

The first recognizable indication that things were changing began the moment she walked in. Grandma King exclaimed, "Holy armadillo, would you look at this!" What has happened to our fat little carrot top?"

"What did I tell you?" Grandma Swanson smiled.

"I swear, that gal has grown a foot, and you're right, Clara, she is turning into a lovely young lady. I do believe she looks like a young Maureen O'Hara."

Who the heck is Maureen O'Hara, Candy wondered? She sniffed. The house was filled with the aroma of something baking.

"In my opinion," declared Grandma Swanson, "she looks more like Ann Margaret. Same mouth, same green eyes, same hair. Remember the way she looked in Picnic?"

"Kim Novak was in Picnic. You mean Bye Bye Birdie."

"Whatever."

Candy thought they both had gone off their rockers. She knew who Ann Margaret was, the gal that played in Grumpy Old Men. There was no way in the world she would ever look like that beautiful lady. Not ever.

* * *

The sheriff stooped to examine the body. "Darn it Ralph, don't you go puking all over potential evidence."

Ralph jammed the broken branch into the bush. "Sorry boss. I got it under control. Guy cut off one of her legs. What kind of sicko does it take to do something like this?"

"I aim to find out." "Looks to me like only part of it. Her leg is laying right here next to her head." He picked it up with no more emotion than he might show had it been a piece of wood. "The perp musta cut a hunk of her thigh off and kept it. Figure that one." The Goodwin boy hadn't moved and Frank could feel his penetrating blue eyes as he reached down and rolled the small naked form onto its back, dropping the leg beside it. "Holy shit, what a mess."

"Well Frank, guess that solves the run-a-way child case."

The sheriff snorted, turning to where Mark continued to

stare directly at him without seeing. "Come on boy," he ordered. "I want you down off that rock. Get your ass up there with your friend while Ralph and I conduct an investigation. When we're done I'm gonna want to talk to you." Reaching out, he grasped him by the ankle and tugged.

Mark seemed startled and looked at the man as if in a fog. "Oh. Sheriff? Oh my God!"

Damn creep in his gang-banger outfit, coming right to this spot. Pretty suspicious I'd say. "Did you hear what I said, boy? I want you to get up there with your friend. Stay put till we're through down here."

Frank watched Mark making his way up the slope. The kid was shaking his head as he moved next to where Ollie stood. The big kid draped an arm about his buddy's shoulder and asked. "You okay?"

"No I ain't okay. I'm thinking about what happens when they tell my mom. I'm not feelin' okay, I'm feeling sick"

* * *

The two boys turned to watch as the sheriff and his deputy spent fifteen minutes wandering about the surrounding brush looking for evidence. "I can't believe what those two jerks are doing to the crime scene," Mark told his friend. "I've seen enough cop shows on TV to know they aren't supposed to touch anything until the Medical Examiner has done his thing.'

"Man you're right, Mark. They ain't takin' any photographs or nothin'. All they're doin' is trampin' all over everything."

Mark stood, practically numb, looking down at the two men.

"Killer didn't leave any clues, I'll tell you that," Frank grumbled. "And even if he did, those two kids walked all over the place destroying whatever evidence there might have been."

"Sure looks that way. Nothing around here but some trash blown in by the wind." Ralph picked up and discarded various pieces of junk. "Guess we may as well go back up and call the coroner. Probably take that jerk an hour or so to get up here from Clarksdale."

"That's okay. I want to talk to these boys. Think it's mighty strange how they happened to ride their bikes out to this exact place. Mighty strange. Grab a roll of crime scene tape. Run a piece from this mesquite bush here to that tree over there."

"Got it covered."

The sheriff had a more difficult time climbing back up the gravel side of the dike, slipping and sliding until he in the end accomplished the task on his hands and knees. "Damn it all to hell. Ruined a perfectly good pair of slacks. Tore the knees right out of 'em." He didn't try to be macho about going back down to the squad car, sitting on his rear, using his hands and feet to inchworm his way to the bottom.

Picking up the hand mike he made the call into the office. "Marion, this is Frank. This thing turned out not to be a joke after all. Need you to call for the coroner and medical examiner. And uh . . . turns out it is the little Goodwin child. Since I'll have to stay out here till the county guys arrive I'd appreciate it if you'd give the Goodwin's a call. . . .

"Damn it Marion you gonna have to handle it. Also might give Frazier down at the newspaper office a call. Let him know what's going on. Tell him I'll give him a statement the minute I get back. . . . Okay, that's a 10-4. I'll send Ralph back in to cover things there. . . .

"Yeah . . . me too. See ya when I see ya. Over and out." Turning to his deputy, he told him, "That about winds it up for us, Ralph. Told Marion you'd high tail it back into town so we'll be covered there."

"Wait!" Mark called out, seemingly quite alert, making his way down the embankment to where the sheriff stood. "Aren't you going to bring in some professionals from Clarksdale? You know. They could bring their mobile crime lab."

"Well, look who decided to wake up," Frank snarled. "What do you think we are chopped chicken liver? You're looking at a couple of professionals."

"Bull! Professional what? You ain't never been involved in anything like this." Ollie came sliding down to be with his friend.

"Don't get smart with me, boy. We don't need any big city jerks sticking their noses into local business. Me and Ralph know how to handle these things better'n any of those high paid, college educated, baby cops. What I want is to have a chat with you two boys. I have an idea you know a heap more about this than you are telling me."

"Based on what?" Ollie's eyes looked twice as large as normal.

Mark was cowering which filled Frank with self-satisfaction. Had the boy's attention.

"Why are you jerking us around?" Mark asked. "Do you think we did it?"

"Let's say I'm reserving my opinion on that."

"I can't believe . . . You brick-head. We're probably gonna have to solve this case for you."

"Very funny, wise ass. All I can say is I got my suspicions."

* * *

The Man was relishing the wonderful feeling of satisfaction he felt after dumping the body out in the middle of nowhere. Knowing it would probably be found, he was wondering what the medical examiner would think, what the people in Dalton would think, when they discovered she had not been sexually molested. First thing that pops into people's minds when a child disappears . . . and they find the body, is that it is some psychosexual pervert. Well, guess what folks, this has nothing to do with perversion. Nothing at all.

CHAPTER THREE

Jodie Frazier was lying on her stomach on the couch watching TV. She heard the doorbell. A few seconds later her mother called, "Jodie that Tarmen boy is here. You want to come in for a minute. Buzz?"

"Naw, Mrs. Frazier. I'm all grimy you know what I mean? Been picking up a few bucks cleaning out people's garages. Doing Mrs. Champion's today."

Hearing her mother laugh, Jodie rolled off the couch and moved into the living room. Lookin' at Buzz's sleek brown skin, which was virtually shiny, she could see that his blue coveralls were smudged with dirt.

Her mom told him, "When you finish up over there you can start on ours. Been trying to get Ollie off his duff but he and Mark seem to always have more important things going on."

"Hi Buzz. What's up?" Ollie's twin sister, a tiny girl, used both hands to flip her long, ash blond hair off her shoulders. At eighty-seven pounds she was less than half Ollie's size. Hardly anyone who saw them side by side believed for a minute they were twins.

"Did Mark or Ollie say when they were going to get back? I need one of them to give me a hand lifting some heavy junk." The boy had the clean-cut good looks prevalent among so many of the blacks whose ancestors migrated from the Caribbean.

"I don't have a clue Buzz. He mentioned something about riding out to the quarry. Ollie ran in right after church, changed his clothes and headed out. Want me to come help?"

"Are you kidding? You couldn't lift a paper sack full of air. Know what I'm sayin'? I'll mosey over to Mark's."

"Hey Buzz, you might be surprised. I'm a heck of a lot

stronger than I look." The phone was ringing. She wondered why her mom didn't get it. "You know how Mark and Ollie are, always got something extreme going down. If they come back here I'll let them know you stopped by." She heard her mother answer the phone.

"Hello? . . .

"Oh, hi Hon. How's our big time newspaper editor doing today?

"You've had a what? . . . . .

"Oh . . . oh my God! Who?"

* * *

"Sit down, honey." Grandma Swanson placed a towering plate of warm, chocolate chip cookies on the coffee table. From the cozy kitchen other smells were drifting, something baking, something cooking. "Help yourself to the cookies while we chat for a spell. Your Grandma King and I have been talking about your family. About you in particular."

Ignoring the overstuffed furniture, she sat on an antique straight-backed chair. She didn't want to get too comfortable since she wasn't staying. "Yeah, right." Candy grabbed a handful of the cookies, looking at the two ladies curiously. A slight glow remained following their assessment of her looks. She was resigning herself to the coming lecture but her face was showing outward signs of a young mind closing itself off so Grandma Swanson let her have it.

"You are a loud mouthed, nasty dispositioned, sassy little brat!"

Candy's mouth was hanging open, a cookie poised an inch from her lips, but she managed to blurt out, "Grandma!"

Both of her grandmothers were smiling. "Got your attention, didn't I?"

"First," Grandma King told her, "we want you to know both Grandma Swanson and I agree with you. It is not your fault that your mom and dad haven't treated you fairly."

"That's right," Grandma Swanson added. "And that's why we want to talk about your problem while they're not around."

"Which problem? Looks to me like we're 'bout ready to leave them all behind." She looked around at all the antiques and collectables her grandmother had amassed over the years. In

17

spite of her tenseness, the house felt comfortable.

"Candy, you cannot run from your problems, they always follow you."

"Okay then, 'stead of being the loneliest kid in Montgomery, Alabama, I'll be the loneliest kid in Dulltown, California." What's with Grandma? She actually called me Candy.

Grandma King smiled. "I believe that's Dalton, dear."

"Whatever. But I don't see why Dad couldn't stay put. He had a good job here. I've spent my whole life right here. I don't know anybody out there." Things are bad enough here but they're sure to be worse in this Dalton place.

"Your father has to go where opportunity takes him. The new job is a better position and a great deal more money."

"I know . . . but gee whiz."

"Do you want a glass of milk, dear?" Grandma Swanson hauled her bulky frame into the kitchen, returning with a huge glass of ice-cold milk. "I can tell by your looks that you're anticipating some sort of a lecture. Candice honey, when I suggested, 'Let's talk', that is exactly what I meant. We want this to be a three-way conversation. Let's discuss your past, your present and your future. Whatever you say here today is strictly between us."

What are they up to? Candy wondered. I don't think I need this. "What y'all want me to say?"

Candy took the glass of milk and Grandma Swanson told her, "We aren't going to preach to you or make light of your concerns. We realize that your family hasn't always been there for you."

"Tell us, dear," Grandma King leaned toward her. "How do you feel about your folks?"

"Rotten," she replied straight away. "Just 'tween you and me, right?'

Both ladies nodded.

"They all wanted a boy. Look what they got. Always called me fat, and ugly, and freckle-faced, and carrot head. All I ever wanted was for my Dad to like me but he totally ignores me or calls me stupid or 'That dummy' or 'that fat pig'. I've had thirteen years of total misery." She stopped to stare at the two faces, waiting for them to disagree with her.

Grandma Swanson lifted the platter. "Have some more

18

cookies. This is exactly what we want to hear, Candy. Your problems haven't helped you attract friends. Oprah had that on her program this very morning, about how sad it is when there's no father/daughter bond."

"Candy, what we want to do," Grandma King told her, "is to give you some advice on how you can make things better. How you can take control of your own life and future. Use our advice . . . or ignore it. Up to you. But please listen. Okay?"

"You know what my biggest problem is? I've got me a ten-year-old brother, who is 'Perfect in every way'. That's all I hear. 'Why can't you be more like Michael? Michael gets straight A's. Michael has so many friends he can't even count 'em. Everybody loves Michael. Michael has the lead in the grade-school play. Look how lean and trim Michael is. You're nothing but a slob.' Well, I could tell them a thing or two about Michael. Michael is a turd."

Grandma King smiled and nodded. "It has always been obvious he is their favorite. I notice he doesn't hesitate to rub it in. How are things between you and your Mother?"

"Oh, not too bad. She pretty much leaves me to shift for myself." Candy sat for a minute in silence, wondering if she should tell the next part. "Did I say shift for myself? Get this. My period started a few months ago. Isn't my mother the place I am supposed to go for advice?"

"I'd say," Grandma Swanson spoke as though it were confidential, "that is one of the most important moments in a young woman's life. So what did she say?"

"My Mom told me, 'another damn problem. That means I have to buy Kotex for two.' That's what she said. I had to learn what it was all about from some of the gals at school."

Both Grandmothers were making clucking sounds. "My daughter," Grandma Swanson sighed, "never has been high on parenting skills."

The three-way conversation went on for a long time. Candy discovered she needed to talk. Listening to their advice was tougher, but what impressed her most was the fact both grandmas, for the first time, actually seemed to care about what she felt and thought. And they constantly called her Candy . . . or Honey.

* * *

Mark didn't understand why he didn't have an overwhelming sense of grief. What he felt was numb. He could see the horror of her body in his mind, so he was annoyed in view of the fact it could have been any one's sister and he would have felt the same.

There was another problem that concerned him at the moment. He didn't say as much to the sheriff, but he had his own suspicions. Frank thought he was spaced out when he was sitting on the rock. He was, sorta, but in truth he was watching every move the two men made. It pissed him off at how indifferently the sheriff handled Laura's body and her severed leg. However he wasn't surprised.

While he was waiting for the police to arrive, he'd been thinking about something that happened last year at the 4th of July picnic. He remembered his dad had driven the whole family down to the fairgrounds so they could watch the parade, take part in the festivities then hang around for the fireworks. Dad couldn't find a place to park but found enough room to squeeze in between the sheriff's car and a fire-truck. Didn't even get out of the car when here comes Fuming Frank bellowing at the top of his lungs. "Goodwin! You can't park there. That's a fire lane." He and Dad got into a battle of words since there was no way it could be a fire lane. There was a fence across in front of 'em. Frank told him to either move it or he'd call Louie's Towing.

They moved, but he remembered his father yelling back at the sheriff, "Typical. Give a man a dab of authority and it goes right to his head." To his family he snorted. "Man's nothing but a big fat pig."

Half an hour later Mom practically ordered him to take Laura on the pony rides. So he did. As they were leaving Laura accidentally kicked a big pile of pony manure. Guess what? There stood Frank watching his own kids ride. Most of it went all over Frank's polished boots. He went ballistic like Laura did it on purpose. Called her all kinds of names. Words he shouldn't even use in front of a six year old.

Laura had shrunk back against Mark's legs and yet as Frank started to turn away she stuck out her tongue.

"Better pull that f'n tongue in, Missy, or I'll take out my knife and slice it off." To Mark he snapped, "tell your folks they'd better teach this little witch some manners or I'll do it for them." The worst thing I remember is when he informed me, "The world would be a better place without your kind." Everybody in town knew how much the sheriff hated kids, which was strange considering he had some of his own.

Explain this. Frank had wondered how he and Ollie happened to come directly to this spot. So okay, with all this wild brush growing here what made the sheriff walk directly to the exact bush where Laura's body was hidden? He was sure of it, Frank was the man responsible. But what could he do? That's why the man doesn't want any outside help.

Mark didn't say anything, turning to look up at his bike, knowing there was no way he could ride it back to town. The fact it was he and Ollie who found the body was beginning to tear him up inside. The terrible horror yet to come, when his folks found out, was starting to make his guts churn and there was another growing sensation. Anger.

* * *

It was the middle of the afternoon in Dalton where another thirteen year old was busy with her sewing. Shannon White, who lived on the corner across the street from the Goodwin house, wanted to have at least five items ready in time for the fair, that was due to start a week from Thursday. Last year she won a blue ribbon for a clogging outfit plus two whites for third on a dress and a blouse in the teen category. This year she felt she had at least three winners. The outfit she was presently creating was a western jacket cut from powder blue denim. It was to have white suede fringe, nail heads surrounding silver, red, green and gold glass studs. In the recesses of her mind she heard the phone ringing but ignored it. Mom was in the kitchen. It was probably one of her church ladies anyhow.

"Shannon!" Her father, a tall, broad-shouldered man, stood in the doorway holding the portable phone along side his dark face. His being the pastor of the local AME church made him feel he should wear his suit all day Sunday. "It's for you, that Frazier kid again. I'm expecting a call so make it quick."

The tall teenager moved to the end table and picked up the tan instrument. "Okay, Dad, I got it. Hi, Jodi. What's cooking?" Ollie's sister sounded frantic.

"Did you hear about Mark's sister?"

"Yeah, I heard. She ran away again last night."

"No, no, get this. Dad called us from the newspaper office. She didn't run away, they found her body."

"They what?"

"They what?" Echoed Mr. White who was listening in. "Where?"

Ordinarily his constant nosiness ticked her off, but this time what Jodi was telling her upset her so completely her mind went blank.

"Some place out on Lone Pine Trail near as I could make out. I guess Dad didn't have all the details yet, except that she was murdered."

"Oh my God," Shannon cried. "Does Mark know?"

"I don't think so. He and my brother went someplace on their bikes right after church. This is too awesome for me. I know I'm not about to be the one to break the news."

* * *

"Candice." The well-worn couch sagged under Grandma Swanson as she sat a second plate of cookies between Grandma King and herself.

There it was again. They knew she despised the name Candice but being desperate for any kind of attention she found herself listening as the conversation wound down.

"You need to look at this move to California, not as a nightmare but as an adventure. I remember, in years past, when you used to play a game where you were an Indian Princess."

Candy grinned. "You 'member that? I played something that doesn't exist, an Indian Princess Warrior. But what the heck? It was my dream."

"And that's my point. Set your mind to it and you can be whatever you want to be."

"Oh yeah? Where do I start?"

"Listen to me, Honey," Grandma King took over. "It's time for you to recognize that you are a special person, one of a kind. You need to start doing things that will make you proud of who you are. You are turning into a very lovely young lady, the sort of person who should have a bubbly personality and be surrounded by friends.

Candy was thinking, come on grandma, I don't need this. In her heart, she was listening. "Everybody hates me. Nobody wants me for a friend."

Grandma Swanson leaned forward, looking directly into her eyes. "Nobody hates you. This is something you have created as an excuse due to your attitude that drives people away. When you get to Dalton, and meet a student at your new school, compliment her on something. Her hair, the way she is dressed. You'd be surprised how they love to hear that stuff. How wonderful they will think you are for telling them. I can't tell you how precious a dear friend can be since it is something you need to experience. This sounds simple. I can't explain it, nor do I know whom I'm quoting, but it goes like this. 'Need a friend, be a friend. Want some love, give some love.' Don't you think it is worth a try?"

"I understand what you are trying to tell me, Grandma. I'm not as dumb as my folks think I am."

"Of course you're not," Grandma King agreed. "You are turning out to be a very smart young lady."

"Of course she is," Grandma Swanson smiled, her eyes sparkling. "Takes after the Swanson side of the family."

Grandma King rolled her eyes. "The retarded side?"

Oh yeah, Candy was thinking. This smart kid would die for grandma's deep violet eyes.

"One more thing," grandma King looked serious, leaning forward to place her hand on top of Candy's where it rested on the arm of the chair. "Use your smarts, Honey. Instead of criticizing people, think of nice things to say. Anything. Their eyes, their hair, their clothes. Be honest, and listen when they talk. Everyone loves a good listener for the reason that it makes them feel important. Makes them want to get to know you."

"Grandma King is right." Grandma Swanson added. "One more thing. You have always been a rather pushy, 'let me get mine first' type of person. Try taking a new path, one where you say, 'please, thank-you, yes ma'am, that's very nice of you. Please help yourself. I'm after you.' You will be amazed at how people will react. Are we getting through to you, Honey?"

She nodded, unsure how she felt about all this. "You guys act like this is a matter of life and death."

"It's a matter of life . . . your life and how good it can be."

Candy sighed deeply, "It can't be any worse than it is now." She stood, preparing to leave. "I gotta go. Uh . . . thanks for the advice . . . I guess."

"Candy," Grandma King reached out to take her hands. "Honey, it has been very hard for me and Grandma Swanson to get close to you, but it's actually our fault for not understanding. Sweetheart, you are a very dear part of our family. We both love you very much."

For the first time in her life, as she made her way to the door, she hugged and kissed them both, tears streaming down her cheeks. Going through her mind was a phrase she had never heard before. 'We both love you very much.' There was another phrase she overheard as Grandma Swanson closed the door, which wormed its way into her mind and nested there. "By God Ethel, that is one smart little gal. I'd make a bet that she's going to surprise us."

* * *

The Man was amazed when the body was discovered so soon. In a town like Dalton where only about 3500 people lived, the grapevine spread the word about the murder to nearly every citizen in a matter of hours. At first he had planned to bury it some-place out there, but after giving it some thought decided to dump it in the bushes. Wait for some hikers or hunters to stumble across it. Best of both worlds. Let the Goodwin's agonize over her disappearance then receive a second whammy once she was found. The fact it was the little kid's brother who located the body was an added bonus. All in the family. He snickered. Yep. All in the family.

CHAPTER FOUR

There were no direct flights from Montgomery to any location near Dalton, California. The best Candy's family could manage was a flight to Phoenix on Arizona Clipper then a transfer to Vanguard Air, which took them to Las Vegas. Once they arrived at this desert oasis, they faced a nearly two-hour layover before they caught the shuttle flight to Clarksdale.

The weather was clear all the way. Candy, on her first flight, was constantly leaning across her mother to see the scenery from thirty thousand feet. Michael was busy annoying the passengers by working his way up and down the aisle on his hands and knees pushing a plastic dump truck into various people's feet. One of the stewardesses already had to chase him out of the galley. Another admonished him about swinging on the bathroom door and throwing toilet paper all about. Her mother, caught up in one of her romance novels, was out to lunch.

Candy had been mulling over some of the things her grandmothers had tried to plant into her mind but she made no effort to be nice to Michael. Be a total waste, and kissing her parent's ass wouldn't help either. "You want to have people like you," Grandma King told her, "then learn how to listen instead of blowing off steam. Everybody loves a good listener. When you do talk, think before you speak." And what was it Grandma Swanson told her? "When you are having a conversation with someone, try to think of something nice to say about them . . . without being phony." She shrugged. Easy for them but how do I go about it? Sounds like so much barf to me.

She pulled her elbows in tight against her stomach and and cringed. I ain't happy about this move, she thought. Got this bad feeling inside that what she'd soon be facing would be far worse than her life in Alabama.

Midway, during the flight leg to Arizona, Candy's mother made a trip to the restroom. A stewardess, pushing a cart loaded with goodies, paused next to her seat. Candy wondered. Would this be a good time to try out grandma's ideas?

"Would you like a soft drink or a package of nuts?" The lady asked.

"Thank you ma'am. I'd like one of each if that's okay."

"It certainly is. I have Coke, Sprite, root beer, orange and grape."

"A root beer, please. Golly, Ah surely do like your hair. It's beautiful. Wish I could wear mine like that."

"Well . . . what a lovely complement. You made my day. I had it done yesterday and my boyfriend didn't say squat. Only I wish mine was the color of yours and your eyes are to die for."

Candy felt warm all over. Grandma King's eyes are to die for. Mine are a crummy green. "I've never had my hair done in a beauty shop," she grinned. "On my allowance Ah cain't afford it."

"You'd be a knockout with the right style. Have boys fighting over you at school. Know what I'd do if I were you? I'd make a deal with my mother . . . you know; a trip to the beauty shop in return for doing dishes for a month or something. Give it a try. A new hairdo makes you feel like a new woman." She glanced up the aisle to where Michael was bothering some passengers. "Your little brother sure is a livewire, isn't he?"

"Michael? He's a turd."

The stewardess grinned then bent to whisper in Candy's ear. "I would have said that but Arizona Clipper frowns on us expressing ourselves in bad language. Hang in there. I have some other passengers who are getting antsy, so I'll talk to you later."

Candy watched the stewardess move toward the front, considering what a glamorous life the pretty lady must lead.

In a few minutes the smiling attendant returned. "Here, try a couple of these cream filled cupcakes. By the way, I love your accent"

Then she was gone again. The redhead marveled over what had taken place and how good it made her feel. Grandma Swanson, Grandma King, you guys are okay.

* * *

Ollie decided to drop by Mark's place after school on Tuesday. This was one of the times he was glad there was a side door into Mark's pad. He sure didn't relish facing his buddy's folks. They were all staying home until after the funeral which was scheduled for Wednesday.

"You okay, dude?"

"I feel like a real butthead. She was my sister. I treated her like dirt."

"Yeah . . . well . . . it's . . . " Ollie didn't know what to say. There was no way he could handle this sort of thing the way he wanted to.

"We were so sure she had run away again. Last time we found her hiding down at the church. The house seems kinda empty not having Laura around. I can't believe she's gone . . . forever."

"I know . . . and you and me finding her was the pits."

"She was always such a pain. She was a tattletale and she bugged the heck out of me, nevertheless she was family. I loved her, only I never once told her so. You know what, Ollie? She died thinking I hated her." There were tears seeping from his eyes and he tried to squeeze them off. "I never once . . . I never even hugged her." He tried to shake it off but couldn't. He began to sob.

Ollie placed an arm about his friend's shoulder and left it there. It gave him a peculiar feeling given that he couldn't remember ever crying like that himself. Probably did when he was a kid, but that was so long ago. He didn't know why, but he was thinking about how Mark always had this fascination for Superman. They would take turns with first one then the other playing the Caped Crusader or the villain. Now that they were older they occasionally played the game, but with a guilty feeling at the prospect of being caught. So did that mean that today he was Superman or did the Man of Steel ever cry?

Mark cried openly for quite a while. Ollie kept his arm where it was for several minutes and then asked again, "You okay, Marcus?"

There was a long pause. "Yeah, Ollie, I'm okay." He brushed at his eyes with the back of his hand. "I'm okay, but I promise you this. If I find the psycho who did this he sure as heck ain't gonna be."

"Saw in this morning's paper where the sheriff is promising an early arrest."

Shaking his head as though to clear his thoughts, Mark told him, "what wires me is, I got this thing bouncin' around in my mind which bothers me. I don't remember if it was something I saw or something that I heard, but it's like a puzzle with a piece missing. I'd sure like to have that piece."

Ollie shrugged. "I can't help you there. The funeral is to-morrow, huh?"

"Sheriff is so stupid he even suspects I had something to do with it. Well, let me tell you something, Ollie. When you start thinking about who could have done it, who would have a motive for doing it, and somebody who has never liked me . . . or Laura, who we got? Sheriff Frank Martinez, that's who."

"You're kiddin'. Never thought of that. Guy always treats kids like they were . . . insects or something."

"Right. And he would have had the opportunity cruising around town in his black and white. I'm mad as hell that he and Ralph say they are gonna handle this thing all by themselves. I wish there was something I could do. I gotta notion to call the county sheriff's office in Clarksdale.

"What? And tell them you suspect Frank?"

"Naw, not that. I'd like to let themknow that nobody here thinks Frank and Ralph can handle something like this. Maybe tomorrow, after the funeral."

Ollie was looking out the window, deciding to change the subject. "Looks like somebody's moving into the old Clayton place."

"Yeah, I saw them but haven't paid much attention. Doesn't seem too important at this time. Moving van's been parked out there all afternoon." Mark moved to the window, placing his hands on the sill.

"Don't know why anybody would want to move into our haunted house." Ollie started to laugh but choked it off. "Wonder if they have any kids?"

"Looks to me like at least two."

"Oh yeah? How can you tell?"

"See the two bikes leaning against the porch. Looks like a small boy's bike and a full size ten-speed. Old like yours."

"I wonder if he's around our age."

* * *

Vince Swanson was not aware of the tragedy involving his neighbors across the street. He was directing the placement of furniture by the movers, knowing Bette would change it all, his mind filled with visions of what he could do to the house. The old run down, two-story structure, had in years past been a Riverview Drive showplace. He was making plans to restore it to its former glory as he had done to the Montgomery house, a challenge he enjoyed. Finding this house was very nearly an accident. Homes for sale or rent in Dalton were scarce. Nothing the agent showed him turned him on.

In desperation the realtor had suggested, "Let's drive up to Sandstone Lake. It's about eight miles north on highway 61. I have several very attractive homes for lease or sale right on the lake."

"Right on the lake? That would appeal to my son. Michael's ten and he truly likes fishing. That's where I'm staying, up at Lakeland Village. Didn't think about looking around there. Let's do it. It's obvious there is nothing here in town."

Vince snapped his seatbelt, turning to look past the agent at three impressive homes on Riverview Drive. "Too bad none of these houses are for sale." Then he saw it. "Stop! Stop, stop, stop." He was out of the sedan looking up at a huge antebellum style home. His eyes focused on the four pair of columns, two stories tall, supporting the porch roof and attic gable. The windows and doors were covered with plywood but ornate trim showed from around the edges. The siding was gray and weathered, the paint long gone. Due to it's location, an exquisite stained glass window in the gable had never been covered.

"The old Clayton house," the agent told him. "Been vacant going on thirty years," he laughed. "Some of the locals claim it's haunted. Uh . . . we'd better head on up to the lake. Gets dark here around seven thirty this time of year."

"Do you know if this place is for sale? I have a knack for restoring old houses. This one has some possibilities." His mind formed a picture of the rehabilitated building befitting his new position as vice-president and general manager of Dalton General Foods.

The salesman frowned. "I'd certainly be glad to check into

it."

Here he was, a month later, every once in a while walking out into the middle of the street to look back at the imposing structure, sensing the grandeur, the elegance behind the unsightly condition. Right out of Gone With The Wind. The inside was in surprisingly good condition. If this house had been in Montgomery, vandals would have destroyed the place.

At the same time he was thinking about his new position, his new adventure. When Montgomery Grocers parent company, Blue Ribbon Foods of New Orleans, bought out Dalton General Foods, they offered him this position at a salary twice his previous income. The capper was when they agreed to pay all moving expenses. He was walking in tall cotton.

* * *

"Hey Mark, I gotta go. Promised Mom I'd wash the windows of all things."

Mark actually grinned. "I don't do windows. Thanks for stopping by, Ollie." His room at one time had been the den before the house was remodeled a few years ago so a door remained to the side yard. Mark walked out as far as the driveway with his friend, gazing curiously at the tall man standing in the street, his arms folded as he stared at the old building. One of the movers closed and latched the rear doors then ran around to climb up into the driver's seat. The diesel growled and snorted, actually shaking the ground when it started.

The new neighbor seemed to sense their presence, turning to face them. Apparently impressed with what he saw he moved their way. "Hi men. You guys like to make a few bucks?"

Taken by surprise Mark combed his long hair with his fingers, frowned, then asked, "Doin' what?" He didn't feel that he should even be outside, considering, and he certainly shouldn't be doing what ever this guy wanted. Ollie stood with his hands thrust deep in his pockets.

"Give you twenty bucks apiece if you'll give me a hand unloading the U-haul. It's full of power tools and building materials. Need to get the truck down to the One Way Rental place and drop it off before I drive down to Clarksdale to pick up the rest of the family.

Why the heck not, Mark was thinking? Take my mind off

things. "Twenty bucks each? You got a deal, buddy. Right, Ollie?" Ollie's eyes were shining as he nodded.

"Okay. I'll unhook the car and back the truck up to the garage. By the way, I'm Vince Swanson."

Mr Swanson extended his hand. Mark shook it, wondering if the guy could tell he'd been bawling. "I'm Mark . . . uh, Goodwin. I live here. This is my buddy, Ollie Frazier. He lives downtown."

"Nice to meet you boys. We better get with it. Running out of time."

* * *

As he backed his Lexus off the tow dolly, Vince again glanced at the fine home next-door to his left and then at the imposing structures on the right. The first one, the judge's house, was impressive, but the home on the hill, the one the agent had called, 'The banker's mansion' was awesome. Looking back at his decrepit building he was thinking, doesn't look anywhere near as foreboding as it did all boarded up. Or did it merely appear ominous after the agent jokingly mentioned it was haunted. Be interesting to know the history of the place. Find out exactly why people thought it might be possessed. A murder, a suicide, or perhaps a demented monster? But it was good in a way for the run-down condition made the price very attractive.

Once he had the truck backed up to the garage, the two boys didn't waste any time. I'm lucky to find a couple of high school kids that actually want to work. Bet that big one is a football player. Tall blond kid looks like trouble. Maybe, maybe not, most likely its all for show.

All he had to do was convince Bette to like California, even though Dalton wasn't what one pictured when California came to mind. It was more like a mid-western country town surrounded by crops and greenery. If it wasn't for the mining company, and some tourist trade attracted to the area by Sandstone Lake, without DGF the town would dry up and blow away.

She had better like the place because he'd closed a deal on the purchase rather than a lease. Going to be a heck of a lot quieter spot to live than Montgomery and a heck of a lot safer. Wonder if this town even has a police department.

* * *

The Man sat in his automobile for a long moment at the

31

corner of Washington and Riverview Drive. Looking past the banker's mansion, easily the biggest and finest house in town, he saw the large truck. "I'll be damned," he mumbled aloud. "Some-one's moving into the old Clayton place. Thought it was tied up in a legal dispute among the heirs."

Making the turn to the left he decided to cruise by. See if he could spot the new owner. Directly across the street from the moving van was the Goodwin place. It was the first time he had driven down the street since Saturday night. It gave him an eerie feeling as though people were looking out the windows, watching him, suspecting him. No way they could know. The Goodwin's got exactly what they deserved.

Two teenagers were busy unloading the U-haul. He recog-nized them both. Goodwin and the Frazier kid. As he passed the old residence, he was aware of the tall Italian looking guy, hands on his hips, studying him as he passed. Averting his gaze he in-creased his speed. No use giving them a chance to get suspicious.

* * *

Candy continued on a high when her father met them up at the Clarksdale airport. "Guess what, Dad. We had a two-hour layover in Las Vegas so we took a shuttle bus to the Excalibur Hotel. You should have seen it. Man was it ever cool."

Dad looked at her mom and asked, "Oh yeah? So how much did you lose, Bette?"

"Hah! Gotcha there. While the kids played video games upstairs, I won forty some dollars on a quarter slot machine."

"You would have liked the place, Dad. It was so bad. Whole town is nothing but lights even in the daytime. Wish we could have stayed till dark. Michael got busted for climbing on top of a pinball machine. He broke the glass." Candy simply had to get in a dig.

"Oh my gosh. Are you all right Michael? You didn't get cut did you?"

"Naw, and it was Candy's fault. I was standing on a stool and she pushed me."

"You little fibber. I did not."

"Did so."

"I might have known," her father snapped.

"Did not. Mom tried to pay the guy with the money she

32

won."

"I insisted but they refused to take it," her mother shrugged.

"I see your daughter has been wasting her allowance on junk clothes again."

Rearing back her shoulders she displayed the white castle on a black background under the silver letters 'Excalibur'. "Isn't it bitchin'?"

"Candice," her mother snapped, "don't use that word."

"Awww. Anyway, we found a T-shirt shop that had them three for ten dollars. Look at Michael's. It says, 'Busted in Las Vegas.' I don't even know how they can afford to sell them for that."

"Advertising, most likely. How's this for a typical California night? Full moon. Sky filled with stars. Temperature's about seventy."

Michael was excited. "Look at the big river, Daddy." The moon glistened on the slight ripples turning it into a broad silver ribbon.

"Yeah Mike. That's the Sandstone River. Runs right along this road all the way from Clarksdale up past Dalton to the lake."

"Looks deep and yucky," Candy grumbled.

"Not actually. I understand it is only three to four feet deep. Moving about a mile an hour. Makes it look deep."

A few miles south of Dalton, Candy could clearly see two old men in a small motorboat heading upstream toward town. The light from the full moon was so brilliant it was possible to see the fishing gear lying in the bow so that it hung over the side. The two men were drinking, probably beer she thought. The one wearing a straw hat covered with fishing flies and lures waved as they passed.

"See that Michael?" Her father was pointing. "You and I should be able to get in some fishing. Good fishing is what the real estate man told me. You're gonna like that, buddy."

It isn't fair, Candy thought. Dad spends a great deal of time with Michael. Fishing was one of their favorite pastimes. Me? I don't even exist.

"Oh boy. Tomorrow?" The boy was pounding his hands on the back of his father's seat.

"How come you never take me fishing?"

"Candice, you wouldn't know what a fish was if it bit you on

33

the ass. Not tomorrow, Michael. We have to get settled in first."

Michael began imitating motorboat sounds, keeping it up for the next several minutes. Candy tried to shut him up but he merely became more obnoxious.

As they left the cover of the huge cottonwood, sycamore and oak trees they crossed a bridge. Candy got her first look at the small town. Her heart sank in total dismay. The moon moved behind a cloud and darkness seemed to suck them into another world. Windows like curious yellow eyes were already peering from many houses. It was worse than she had imagined. The houses were old, the streets narrow. At seven o' clock on this Tuesday evening, it appeared most of the place was already closed for the night. The only spots open seemed to be two gas stations and the neon sign, 'Lucky Lady Bar'. There were streetlights, as old as the town itself, so dim that to Candy, Main Street seemed to be deserted.

"I kinda like the downtown area," her father told them. "Looks like an old western movie set. That three-story sandstone building with the white dome is the city courthouse. Dalton used to be the county seat before it was moved to Clarksdale."

Across the street she could see a three-story brick structure housing a combination TV, Appliance and Jewelery store. Next to it was a well-kept, white painted building with a small black sign lettered in reflective gold, 'R.L. Snyder MD'. That has to be a comfort for my always-ailing mother, Candy thought. On their left they passed the general store, which was dimly lit inside while totally dark on the exterior. A small sign under one dull spotlight stated, 'STEVEN'S GENERAL MERCHANDISE'.

"This town is an armpit," Candy groaned. "No Wal Mart, no K-mart, no McDonalds. Where are we supposed to eat?"

Her father drove another two blocks where at the corner of Palm and Main, was a restaurant, The Green Spot Café. Diagonally across the street was another eatery, The Burger Pit. She could see a number of vehicles parked at the café but felt a rush of excitement for it looked like a whole bunch of kids were at the fast food place.

"We may as well stop here for dinner. I didn't have time today to see about the utilities so all we have at the house is water and candles. Other than that hamburger joint and I guess

34

the bowling alley, this is the only place in town to eat. Ate here a couple of times on my last trip. It's not too bad. There are other restaurants in the area but they are up by the lake. That's where all the motels are. We will either have to drive up there or throw a couple of mattresses on the floor and rough it. We can use the bathroom. Cold water that is."

"Didn't I see a motel as we came off the bridge?" Her mother asked.

Her dad snorted. "The Ez Inn. I hear it's a dump. DGF put me up at the Ramada Inn in Lakeland Village when I was out here last month. Come on you guys, let's see what they have that's good to eat."

"I certainly hope their food is not too greasy," her mother was looking across the street at Kelly's Burger Pit. Candy knew what she was thinking . . . food at that place would be plenty greasy.

"I don't wanna eat here," Michael bellowed. "It looks yucky."

"Michael," his father explained, "we have to eat here. There is no other choice. Maybe we can get a steak or some fried chick-en."

"I wanna hangaburger. I wanna hangaburger."

"I'm sure they have hamburgers here," his mother informed them.

As soon as they were seated Candy found herself glancing about. It felt like everyone was looking at them. She squirmed, feeling uncomfortable.

* * *

The Man was sitting in his favorite booth as he watched the family enter the restaurant. No idea who they were. Probably heading up to the lake. Bet that Guy's wife is something to see in a bikini. Couple of bratty looking kids though. Boy and a girl.

"Table or booth?" The waitress, wearing her usual saucy smile, met them with menus.

"Got anything good to eat here?" The father asked. Oily looking guy. Slicked down hair and pencil moustache. Jerk can't take his eyes offa Peggy's chest. "I believe we'd prefer a booth," was the guy's answer.

The Man watched Peggy pass around the menus then she told the group, "tonight's special is country style pot roast in gra-

vy over homemade noodles. Just had some myself. It's wonder-ful."

"Don't want no dumb noodles," the little boy whined. "Wanna hangaburger . . . and lots of catchup with French fries."

"Hi there young man. What's your name? You came to the right place. We make the best hangaburgers in town."

"His name's Michael," the lady answered. "We're the Swansons. We arrived in Dalton today."

"Well. welcome to Dalton and welcome to the Green Spot Cafe. My name's Peggy and if you need anything give me a whistle."

The Man had to smile when he heard the little redheaded bunny ask, "You got catfish and hushpuppies?"

Peggy smiled. "Not tonight, honey. The closet thing we have to country vittles is country fried steak."

"Guess I'll try the special."

Swanson? The Man was thinking. Oh yeah, the new general manager out at DGF. Okay, I remember. He was the guy I saw in the street in front of the old Clayton place. What a jerk. Sits there and gives Peggy a wolf whistle right in front of his wife. Red headed teenybopper is cute as hell when she smiles. Jailbait, that's for sure. Wonder what her name is? He chuckled. Not that I have any quarrel with these folks, but I might want to add hers to my list . . . after I've done all the others. Just a thought.

* * *

Frank Martinez left the Green Spot Wednesday morning wearing a dribble of egg yolk on his brown shirt directly above the beer gut. Sliding behind the wheel of his patrol car he was thinking he would check in at the office for a couple of hours then make one last tour of the town before the funeral, which was scheduled for two o'clock. He could see his clerk through the glass door leading into his department. The gold lettering stated, Dalton Police Department, but he preferred to be called Sheriff.

Marion was waiting as he came banging in, hanging his western hat on the clothes tree before he sat down. "Frank, a copy of the preliminary report from the Medical Examiner's office came by courier." She pointed at his stomach. "You got dab of egg or something on your shirt."

He wiped it on his palm. "Let me see that sucker." She

36

hadn't opened the brown, clasp envelope even though he knew she would be dying to see what was inside. This gal's never been involved in anything like this so no way she would understand the report. He made a face. Of Course . . . neither have I.

Frank scanned the sheets of paper then sat shaking his head as he tried to decipher its contents. "This whole danged thing is written in Greek as far as I'm concerned. Where is that package of pictures Ralph took of the body? I'm gonna wander across the street to Doc Snyder's office and see if he can explain this thing."

* * *

Doctor Snyder was busy conducting a pelvic examination on Mrs. Jacobs, a teacher from the Middle School who was having her first child. Unaware that his nurse had left the patient room door open about an inch he whirled in alarm as someone came barging in.

"Good God Frank!" Both he and the nurse, who let out a shriek, grabbed at the green sheet in an attempt to cover the patient whose feet were up in the stirrups. "What in the heck are you doing in here?"

As though his actions were the most natural thing in the world, Frank told him, "need to talk to you Doc, 'bout something important."

"Frank, get your fat ass out of here. I'll be finished with Mrs. Jacobs in about ten minutes."

"Okay, but make it snappy." Frank tipped his hat. "Nice to see you again, Miss Jacobs. I guess I better wait out here."

Hurrying the examination as much as he dared, which was no problem since Mrs. Jacobs was progressing admirably; he made his way out to where Frank waited. He knew there was no reason to say anything to the sheriff about the unwelcome intrusion since the thickheaded jerk was impervious to criticism. Frank handed him a brown medical parcel along with a white envelope containing a dozen graphic pictures of the body. The Doc was slightly miffed that he hadn't been called to at least pronounce the youngster dead.

"Doc, this dumb jackass writes everything in some foreign language. Maybe you can decode it for me."

"Horrible thing, this killing. Absolutely horrible." Reading

37

the entire report before he tried to explain item by item what it contained, he looked up as the fat man drummed his fingers on his desk. A sheriff who can't even read a medical report, what next? "According to the M.E., he sets the time of death at between seven and eleven Saturday night. He feels the murder took place at another location and the body was probably dumped out on Lone Pine Trail early Sunday morning. It was one of those freak coincidences you hear about from time to time that those boys stumbled onto her Sunday afternoon. If they hadn't, she could have laid out there for years."

"Some coyote probably would'a found the corpse and dragged it out into the open. I been wondering about this 'coincidence' though. How did she die?"

"Mmmm, let's see. It seems your assailant introduced a sharp foreign object into her vaginal canal." He read only part of the medical details aloud."

"In plain English, what's he saying?"

What am I going to have to do, draw the sheriff a picture? "She was raped with a foreign object. Worse, Doctor Gainsworth states, she was alive at the time making her very much aware all the while he was making all the cuts and slices in her flesh. The ME doesn't make any assumptions, but I'd guess the killer wanted it that way." He was looking at one of the pictures, which clearly showed the hundred plus small slices but his eyes were focused on the child's face, which was relatively unmarked.

"Some sort of torture, huh?"

"In a way. I'd say it was meant as a form of punishment."

"Punishment for what?"

"I have no idea. It's simply a thought. Anyway, that's not why she died. Perhaps that's why he taped her mouth shut."

"What a sick bastard! Perp ended up slashing her throat. Guess that's what killed her."

"Negative. That was done post mortem. She died of nasal asphyxiation."

"A fix a what?"

"Since her mouth was already sealed, he held her nose until she expired."

"No shit? Does the Medical Examiner give any hint as to what this sharp instrument was?"

"No. He thinks it was metal, approximately 12.7 millimeters in diameter. That's half an inch. He also states the piece removed from her upper thigh was severed, first with a sharp instrument, possibly a razor blade or a scalpel then the bone was cut with a fine tooth saw such as a hacksaw or a physician's bone saw."

"Not a whole lot to go on, is there? Sharp instrument? Could be any number of items. Duct tape? Everybody has a roll of duct tape. Most everybody has a hacksaw."

Doc Snyder could darned near feel Frank's eyes pricking him when the sheriff asked, "every doctor has scalpels and a bone saw, right Doc? I need to find some clues to not only nail this culprit, but to put him away forever."

"Don't include me in your list of suspects. I got plenty of people who can vouch for my where-a-bouts Saturday night. Are you getting anywhere with the investigation? Saw in the morning newspaper that you my have some suspects."

"I got a couple of ideas. Something I'm not free to discuss at the moment. First, I got me a funeral to attend. Should be done by three. You coming down to The Lucky Lady later?"

"Mrs. Jacobs was my last patient for today since I'm also going to the funeral. Might drop in after I take the wife home. Sorry I couldn't be more help."

"Yeah, me too. He's gonna be one hurtin' mother as soon I get my hands on him."

The doc was shaking his head and thinking, hope your right Frank, but I doubt it.

* * *

The Man was gloating. Today is the funeral. Sitting at the table in his tiny kitchen he was doodling on a yellow tablet. Some of the doodles were just that, merely scribbles; boxes, circles, triangles; each one outlined a dozen times. Three of the drawings were more than doodles. Each was a crude depiction of a young female. A malevolent smile creased his face as his eyes squinted. He continued adding items to punish each figure. Ice picks, knives, a keyhole saw, a pair of vise-grips. Under each drawing was a name: Heinz, Morris, Goodwin. Grasping the pen in his fist as though to stab someone he drew an X across the one labeled Goodwin so forcefully it tore the paper, then made a circle around a second figure. "You're next," he said aloud. "Yes, you are next as soon as I work out all the details. I got a few things to take care of then I'm going to a funeral people are dying to attend." He began laughing, slapping his open palm over and over on the table. "Yeah . . . just dying to attend."

CHAPTER FIVE

Wednesday morning Candy's father ran downtown early and returned with donuts and coffee; milk for the kids.

"Candice," her mother told her, "I want you to go with me this morning. I have to run down to get all the utilities turned on, today if possible. After we finish with that we'll drive over to the Middle School. Need to get you enrolled. I want you back in class tomorrow."

The teenager turned to frown at her mother, who was wearing a high-necked burgundy blouse and tan slacks. "Mom!" Tomorrow's Thursday already, why can't I stay home to help unpack 'til Monday?"

"This is not open to discussion."

"I wanna go too," sitting on the floor eating his donut; Michael was leaving chocolate icing on the leg of her slacks.

"Michael, your daddy is going to take you down to your school this afternoon. He wants you to stay here and help him get things unpacked. With her grades your sister can't afford to miss any more school." Her mother was digging into her purse for the keys to the Lexus.

"You guys had better plan on walking," her father told them. "I told you I need the car this morning."

Her mother slapped the top of her head with both hands. "You know I'm not into walking."

"Good grief, Bette. It's all of three blocks to the utility companies."

"I'd like to walk," Candy ventured. "We can check out the town."

Her mother sighed. "Damnit. One of the first things we are going to do is see about getting me another car. Come on Candice. Let's get this over with."

As if on cue, Candy and her mother stopped on the sidewalk then turned to look back at the house. It was the first time they'd seen it by daylight. Bette Swanson had her arms folded and was shaking her head. "What a wreck. That man must be out of his mind."

Candy, wearing acid washed blue jeans, a shirt; dark blue, buttons down the front, looked up at the sky where a few clouds were gathering. "Probably belonged to The Adams Family." She'd never admit it but she rather liked the old house, especially her room from where she had a nice view of the Sandstone River.

"All this talk of hardwood floors under the shag carpet and cherry wood railings on the stairs under all that white paint. We're going to be living in chaos for the next year." She let out a long disgusted sigh. "Well, let's get going. We've got a bunch of stops."

Their first destination was to each of the utility companies two blocks from the house where they signed up for gas and electric. They were assured these would be in service today. From there they walked three blocks down Cedar to the phone company. Candy was relishing every minute of this. The only time she had ever walked with her mother was shopping for clothes in the mall. When they were finished at the phone company, she felt like skipping as they did the three additional long blocks along Lincoln to the school.

Candy registered and selected her classes. Unlike Montgomery, there were not many electives. "I gotta be here tomorrow," she grumbled to the school secretary. "My brother gets to wait 'till Monday."

At the moment they entered the corridor a noisy bell rang signaling a class break. Several doors opened and students poured into the hall. She paused to study her future classmates curiously. A few glanced her way but most of them were so busy gabbing with friends they didn't notice her. Most were wearing shorts or jeans but her attention was drawn to a student who was dressed in tight, black, leather shorts, calf-high boots, a vest at the top that showed a bare midriff. Her black hair was spiked.

"Biker Babe," she muttered more to herself than to her mother. "Guess they don't have a dress code."
"Well hello there."

42

Unaware of the large Mexican influence in California farming communities, Candy assumed the Latino man, complete with black hair and moustache, was most likely Cuban.

"You folks must be the new family from Alabama."

"Yes we are. I'm Betty Swanson. This is my daughter, Candice. Wanted to get her registered for school. She will be here tomorrow full time."

"I'm Roberto Hernandez, the principal. Welcome to the community. And to answer your observation, Miss Swanson, we do not have a dress code. The young lady is Carmelita Hoover, one of our harmless rebels. We only have a couple."

Candy eyed the dark complexioned man suspiciously, feeling his syrupy voice and goody goody attitude was not the real face of Mr. Hernandez.

"All we ask is that you dress comfortably and modestly. You look very nice exactly the way you are today."

Cool," she said. And you look very handsome, she was thinking.

Once they were outside they paused for a moment on the sandstone steps. Looking up at the, threatening black and gray clouds, her mother told her, "It sure does look like rain. If it does and I get my hair ruined it's your fault. You're the one who insisted we walk." Together they headed down Main toward the Post Office.

Candy shrugged. "Wonder if there is any place in this dumb town where they teach Karate? That's what I wanna know."

"Oh my, look what we have here. Wonder what they call that color?" They were in front of the Deiter Ford Agency where her mother was admiring a cherry red SUV. She moved to walk around it and Candy trailed behind.

"Think it's called Candy Apple, Mom." They were both studying the information sheet on the passenger side window. Candy couldn't remember, ever, having her mother treat her like a person. She didn't want it to end.

"'Wild Cherry Metallic,'" her mother read. "I need to get your dad down here . . . perhaps later this afternoon. What do you think, Candice? Do you like it?"

"It's okay, I guess, but look at the price. Costs as much as a house."

Glancing toward the showroom her mother insisted, "Let's move along before some fast talkin' salesman spots us."

Candy was plotting. "When we were down at the phone company you said something about needing to find a beauty shop." She jerked her thumb toward a building across the street. Dalton Beauty and Barber were the words on the gold and black sign.

"You're right. That's something I must see to." Her mother looked both ways then crossed in the middle of the block. "Need to set up a monthly appointment."

"Uh . . . Mom? Do you think it would be all right if I had my hair done . . . in a beauty shop I mean?"

"Whatever for? With your rats nest it would be a total waste of money. Do you have any idea what a perm costs?"

Grandma King had told her, 'Think about what you intend to say before you open your mouth.' Hmmmm. Mom has already told me I'd be doing the dishes until Dad got a washer installed . . . so, "Yeah Mom, I do. I'd be willing to work around the house for it. Whatever y'all want done. Please Mom, could I? I thought maybe . . . you know . . . yours always looks so nice."

Her mother smiled ever so slightly. "I certainly hope so. It costs a small fortune to keep it that way. Pretty strange sort of deal coming from you." She looked back at her daughter, her hand on the ornate door handle. "I think it would be a big waste of money but I'd be happy to make out a list of things for you to do."

"Can I get it done today?"

"That's not the way it works, kiddo. We'll see if they can work you in sometime next week."

The shop was tiny, perhaps twenty feet wide and thirty feet deep. There were two operators, a young man and a grand-motherly woman. The guy was placing rollers in the hair of an attractive blond woman Candy guessed to be somewhere in her thirties. The other operator, who turned out to be the owner, was sitting at the receptionist counter watching a small TV. Candy heard the tail end of a conversation but it didn't register.

" . . . scary is all I can say. Don't let my daughter out at night anymore," the blond woman said.

"The bad thing is," the young man told her, "I don't think

the sheriff has anything."

"Excuse me," her mother interrupted. "I'm Bette Swanson. We moved to Dalton from Alabama so I need to find a new hair dresser who can take me once a month."

"No problem, Mrs. Swanson. No problem at all." The lady leaped up to began leafing through her appointment book. "Any particular day better for you?"

"I had it done last week so what do you have three weeks from today?"

"Ummmm . . . I have a Wednesday, the twenty-forth at ten o'clock."

"Wonderful. Then pencil me in for that time slot every fourth week."

"Good as done. Oh," she spoke, extending her hand. "I'm Gloria Shipman and this is my son Jeff. He is very good, by the way. I'd like to introduce you to Carolyn Deiter. She and her husband own the Ford Agency."

"Nice to meet you." Candy's mother offered her hand. "My husband is the new CEO at Dalton Foods." She smiled. "I intend to have him down to your place to look at a new car for me. Maybe yet today."

Candy felt Mrs. Deiter staring at her as the lady brought her hand out from under the protective sheet to take her mom's. "How nice. Ask for Bernie . . . that's my husband. Tell him you talked to Carolyn. Next year's models are coming in this week so we're offering huge discounts on this years stock. What grade is your daughter in?"

"Eighth," Candy replied.

"Another eighth grader? You'll be going to school with my Heather. What a pretty color your hair is."

"That's what I was thinking," Gloria added. "I've heard the term 'Copper Penny' but this is the first time I've seen it. However, young lady, you should consider having it styled."

Everybody seems to mention my hair. Here I've never liked it because I look like a freak. "Yes ma'am. Mom told me if you guys could work me in . . . "

"Well lucky you. I had a cancellation so I can do it right now if you have the time."

"Cool," Candy grinned, heading for the vacant chair.

Her mother heaved a sigh. "I'm going to go ahead and take care of some other errands. An hour and a half?" she asked the beautician.

"An hour and a half will be fine. How would you like it, dear?"

"Anything you do will be an improvement," she giggled. "I don't suppose you could make it look like Ann Margaret's in Bye Bye Birdie?"

"I'll have to use some straightener. Strange you should ask that. I've seen every film that gal's ever made right up to Grumpy Old Men II. I don't recall how she had it in Bye Bye Birdie but I do remember how it was in State Fair."

"Cool," Candy nodded. That'll work.

* * *

At Dalton Middle School many of the students gathered in the grassy area next to the athletic field for lunch. Ollie and his sister, Jodi were perched out in the sunshine while Shannon and Buzz were sitting together under a sycamore tree. In months past the boys wouldn't be caught dead having lunch with the girls. Then Buzz got a crush on Shannon and began to disappear at noon to seek her out. From there Ollie couldn't remember what had happened. Shannon wouldn't abandon Jodi. The next thing he knew he and Mark joined them. Ollie knew that Mark didn't care much for the ladies but that was his problem. He was sure beginning to notice 'em.

A slender gal with long blond hair walked by, staring wistfully at them. "Hi you guys. Hello Ollie."

"Hello Ollie," Jodi mimicked when the blond was out of earshot. "Heather Deiter," she sneered. "Can you imagine? She's sweet on my brother. Ain't that extreme?"

"Maybe we ought'a ask her to join us," Shannon joked.

In the grassy area of the baseball diamond two huge black crows were doing their stilt-walking dance as they searched for worms.

"You kiddin'?" Ollie threw his apple core over the fence where the two birds frantically pecked and squawked, wings flapping as they dueled. His eyes followed the blond girl in fascination until she sat on the stone-dividing wall between the athletic field and the gym. "Wow, ain't that awesome? Hair is so long

46

she can sit on it. Too bad she's such an airhead. Cries over every little thing."

Shannon was also watching the tiny classmate. "You know, she' so sweet and outgoing, wonder why she doesn't have any friends. Doesn't seem to be the least bit shy."

Buzz was sitting behind Shannon with his hands on her shoulders. "Man is she ever white. She ought'a get some sun."

"Can't," Shannon insisted.

"Why not," Ollie asked.

"She's an Albino. You ought to see her in the showers after cheer leading practice. Every hair on her body is white."

"Every hair?" Ollie smirked.

Shannon giggled. "Yes even that."

Ollie grinned. "Thought Albinos had pink eyes. Her's are blue."

"Trust my brother to notice." Jodi teased.

"I'm kinda surprised she is into so many things. Like you know, softball, swimming and cheerleader. Guess she has asthma pretty bad."

"Well, I like her," Jodi told them. "Got her in a couple of my classes."

"How is Mark holding up?" Shannon asked.

Ollie grimaced, lying back on the grass to look up at the darkening sky. "Gonna rain." He sighed. "Not real well, I'd say. He's got this bug that he's somehow to blame. I was over there last night."

Shannon was moving her shoulders in circles under her boy friend's fingers. "I sure couldn't handle it if it was one of my sisters. Heard on the news that the sheriff has a couple of suspects."

Ollie snorted. "That's a laugh. Get this. He suspects Mark."

Buzz stopped rubbing Shannon's shoulders. "You're kidding. Mark's the last . . . That guy has a head fulla hot air. You know what I'm sayin'?"

"Not any more wild than Mark's idea. He thinks the sheriff did it."

"The sheriff?" Shannon made a face. "What makes him think that?"

"No idea. Hey! There's a new family moving in across from Mark's place. You know. The old Clayton house."

"Now way! Into our haunted house?" asked Jodi. "They

got any kids?"

Ollie was nodding. "They'll probably ruin the place by painting it and fixing it up. Remember when Mark and me pried the plywood off a window and we all went inside to check out the ghosts? Pretty darned spooky and Marcus thinks they have two. One young boy and another guy about our age."

Jodi instantly perked up. "Happen to know that one of them is female. Did you see the guy? What did he look like?"

"Nobody has seen him yet. Guess they're movin' in from outta of state."

"We didn't see the guy," Shannon told them, "but I saw his sister."

"Oh yeah?" Ollie asked. "Where'd ja see her?"

"Gal about my size. Right here in school."

"Oh yeah," Jodi remembered. "Saw her at break out in the hall with her mother. Has red hair that looks like Little Orphan Annie."

"That bad, huh?" Ollie laughed. "Here I was thinking maybe I could find me a gal." All of a sudden he was somber. "Only a couple more hours till the funeral."

"I know," Shannon nearly whispered. "I wanted to take off this afternoon and go. Mom said it was okay but Dad nixed that real quick."

"How come?" Buzz asked.

"Dad doesn't like the Goodwin family. 'You don't even know the little brat so what do you care?' Was what he said? I told him it wasn't for her it was for Mark. Man that set him off. He tells me, 'I want you to stay away from that kid. He is nothing but trouble.' I told him that Mark is nice even though he sometimes dresses weird. He told me to 'mind what I say and as for his sister, she was nothing but a smart mouthed, spoiled little brat who had no respect for anybody. The world is better off without that kind.' Can you imagine anyone saying that about a murdered child?"

"I can," snapped Buzz. "A narrow-minded hypocrite."

"Boy, you can say that again."

"At our house it was different, Jodi told them. "Mom thought Ollie, being Mark's best friend, ought to be there."

Shannon cocked her head in curiosity. "So, how come you

aren't going?"

Ollie struggled to his feet, standing with his back to the group. "Funerals bring me down. Anyway, Mark understands."

"He was afraid someone would see Mr. Macho Man bawling," Jodi chided.

"So?" Ollie was defensive. "I got feelings. There is nothing wrong with a man crying. Heck, even Mark did yesterday evening when I was there."

The group sat in silence . . . staring toward the east . . . toward the cemetery.

* * *

Nearly two hours passed before Candy's mother returned, which was fortunate as it took that long for the beautician to make something out of her unruly hair.

"What in the world did they do to your hair?" Her mother asked as they proceed on down Main past the Pawn Shop and the newspaper office.

"I think it looks fab, Mom." They were in front of Kelly's Burger Pit. "Hey Mom? Wanta stop in the Burger Pit for a sandwich? I'll buy." Running her fingers through the new hairdo, she told her, "Grandma Swanson told me it's the way Ann Margaret wears her hair."

"Ann Margaret? Oh please! You'll buy? So what did you do wrong?"

"Nuthin'. Saved some of my allowance case I find something I want. I believe I got enough left."

"You want to buy me to a hamburger? Will wonders never cease? But why this place? You have any idea how greasy fast food is?" She continued to the door.

They pushed into the cozy interior. At the counter Candy told the clerk, "Two cheeseburgers, please."

"Double-double?" she asked.

Candy checked the menu, calculating the price. She nodded. "Cool."

"And two chocolate shakes," her mother added.

Candy checked her money. "Uh . . . can I borrow a couple dollars? I'll pay you back."

"Not necessary. Shakes were my idea." Once they had their food and seated themselves in a booth, her mother asked,

"How come you're treating me?"

"Well gee Mom." Thinking again about her grandmother's words, she considered very carefully what to say next. "Not very often I get a chance to pal around with my mom. I want to make it last as long as I can."

Her mother actually choked on a sip of her milkshake, seeming to be unusually flustered. "This place makes a lot better burgers than I expected."

Once they left The Pit, as the teenagers called it, they moved on past the Furniture Mart and the Thrift Store on the corner of Main and Cedar. They were forced to stop for a hearse that was turning off Cedar onto Main heading for the bridge, followed by two-dozen automobiles with their headlights making gloomy eyes in the overcast daylight.

"Looks like somebody died," Candy sounded surprised.

"It happens."

The funeral didn't interest to Candy but she was enjoying one aspect of her first day in the new town. She couldn't remember ever spending so much time with her mother who was civil for a change. She was doing her best to put some of her grandmother's advice into practice by being polite to the people they met; by being a pal to her mother rather than an antagonist. Although at that moment, as she looked up and down the bleak deserted streets, in a voice filled with disdain, she expressed her thoughts aloud. "If this is the start of my big adventure, they can stick it."

"Incidentally Candice," as they walked toward home her mother actually reached out and took her hand. With three words her mom changed the teenager's entire outlook for the day. "Thanks for lunch."

* * *

After a lengthy tear-filled service at the Baptist Church, the mourners gathered across the river at Calvary Cemetery for the interment. This was the older part of the cemetery where the size and height of tombstones was used as a measure of a family's wealth.

The sheriff hated funerals, but the thing going through his mind, which he had learned from watching TV, was that the murderer was quite often drawn to these events. He was watching

50

each man, looking for a sign, watching each pair of eyes, particularly the Goodwin boy. What was his name? Martin? No, it was Mark. The boy was the same as he had been at the scene of the crime, staring blankly into space. There were no tears, no emotion. Not a sign of remorse. Sheriff Martinez found this extremely curious.

* * *

The Man squinted, his eyes so dilated from excitement they were nearly black; as he watched the four men slide the small casket from inside Hallie's Cadillac hearse. They slowly carried it past the mourners and placed it on the rigging spanning the open grave. The Goodwin's were in the front row obviously overcome with anguish. A smug smile replaced the slight sneer on the Man's face.

"How does it feel?" he asked silently. "Payback is a wonderful thing, don't you think? A wonderful thing. Yeah." He drew his eyes away from the anguished faces of the child's parents. What a heady feeling to see them suffer. That's what this is all about. Before he took the girl from them, they had no idea what agony was. Agony was what he knew best. It's their turn to learn about agony. Next to the Goodwin's he could see the Kraut family. Heinrick Heinz. Foreign bastards. Jackass and his woman . . . Ingrid, wasn't that her name? They're hovering over their little brat like a pair of vultures.

A light rain began to fall, turning the asphalt street shiny. Everywhere he looked umbrellas popped open. Here and there a brightly colored one amidst the somber blacks, grays and maroons. "Can't have a funeral without rain. Unwritten law."

Over the sound of a breeze rustling the leaves of the huge oak under which the crowd was gathered he could hear the voice of Reverend Johnson telling everyone what a wonderful person the little Goodwin kid had been. How sorely this beautiful flower would be missed. "What a crock. The truth was, she's like the little Heinz kid, rotten, disrespectful, and out of control. Spoiled brats."

Unless something unexpected pops up with one of the others, the Heinz kid is next. Yep. He licked his lips then grinned. "Wouldn't it be a kick-in-the-ass to snatch her right out of this crowd? I can dream, can't I? Guess I'll have to bide my time.

51

* * *

It was over and the mourners began to depart. Mark's hair glistened with drops of water but the rain had stopped. Hey Dad, "I'm going to sit here for a while . . . if that's okay."

"We understand, son. I need to get your mother and grandma home. Doc Snyder gave her a shot to control her nerves so she's about ready to collapse."

"I'll walk home when I'm ready."

Mark didn't sit a while as he stated, but instead wondered about aimlessly among the headstones reading the dates and the inscriptions unaware the sheriff was quietly keeping pace some thirty feet away. Why he didn't feel more hurt, more sadness over his sister's death he couldn't understand. What he felt instead was an intense anger at whoever did it and for what they were doing to his mom and step-dad. Laura was their baby. At the moment it wasn't even important that his step-dad ignored him. Laura had been robbed of a chance to grow up.

He had a crazy thought. She'd never get to go on the big rides at Disneyland. What ticked him off was, he had been robbed of being more of a big brother.

When he reached the mausoleum he decided to check it out. Inside it was damp and cool, nearly cold. He shivered. It turned nearly dark as someone stood in the doorway. Mark whirled and started in surprise. The sheriff was standing behind him. He realized the big man had him pinned in a corner.

"Need to talk to you, boy."

Mark didn't feel like his usual cocky self. "I uh . . . yeah, sure. What about?" His knees felt like they were made of jelly. The sheriff stood, his right hand resting on his gun. Mark cringed as the huge man placed a plump hand against his chest to push him rather roughly against the wall.

"I've got a gut feeling you know more 'bout your sister's death than you're lettin' on. Isn't that right boy?"

"Wha . . . "

"Been watching you. You ain't even sorry she's gone. Not one bit."

"The heck I ain't! How come you're getting on my case?"

"I'll tell ya why, kid."

He shoved him again. Mark was thinking, you're starting

to piss me off, fat boy. Got this guy figured out, he's trying to turn my suspicions away from him?

"I think you did it, or . . . know who did."

Mark cringed away from the sheriff's horrible breath. "Man, you're way off base." Think this guy's had too much to drink. Looking down at a pair of highly polished boots he glanced about to see if there were any impressions showing on the damp floor. There weren't. Frank's left wrist was bare. Didn't the sheriff always wear a watch? Of course he did. "You gonna read me my rights?"

"A wannabee gang banger ain't got no rights."

Mark grinned, repeating a phrase he'd heard somewhere. "Then whatever I might say is not admissible in court."

The sheriff shoved him back against the wall again. "You been watching too much TV boy. What I want to know is, why did you kill your sister?" His face was so close to Mark's his foul breath was nearly overwhelming, a broken tooth made the incisor next to it appear to be a fang.

"I can't believe you are asking me that."

Holding Mark against the wall, he snarled, "I have a sworn statement that you hated her."

"Hey, I hated her but I didn't hate her. She was my baby sister for crying out loud. Sometimes I say that I hate my Dad too, but I sure don't want to kill him."

"Sometimes in a fit of anger . . . "

"Hey man! I'm no pervert. I saw my sister's body. Whoever did it wasn't angry. He was a psycho. You better get off my case and start looking for the retard that did it."

"Okay smart ass, suppose you tell where to look for this retard."

"I don't have a clue." Mark was visibly relieved. This jerk was doing exactly what he suspected, trying to cover his own ass. He didn't dare accuse the sheriff. Frank might shoot him. Claim he got me to confess and that I went after him. "It's time for you to quit jerking me around and start doing your job."

"Listen to me, you little wart, I never have liked you."

"Does that mean you want to kill me?"

Frank cocked his fist like he was going to hit him, but he didn't.

"I've had about enough of your smart mouth. Get the hell out of here but keep this in mind. From here on boy I'm going to be keeping my eye on you."

Mark moved to walk out of the mausoleum then turned back, knowing he should keep his mouth shut. In any case he felt compelled to say something. "You know what, Frank? As much as you hate kids it wouldn't surprise me if you weren't the one to kill my sister. I'm going to be keeping my eye on you."

* * *

The Man was sitting in his Chevy wondering what the Goodwin kid was up to? Looks like he's wandering around reading the tombstones. "I don't believe this. That dumb sheriff is tailing him around like he thinks he has a suspect. That fat jerk doesn't have a clue. Not a clue. Going around town asking questions from everybody like he thought he was a big time investigator. All he is doin' is chasing shadows. What was it he heard Frank tell the editor of The Dalton Union? 'Expect to make an arrest very shortly, perhaps as early as tomorrow.' He probably will arrest somebody, but the Goodwin kid? That's gotta be a classic. Punk tries to act like Mr. Tough Guy. Probably puke his guts out at the sight of some blood."

The Man watched the sheriff go bumbling along like some hick Inspector Clouseau. "He'll never be able to figure out who did it. Not in a million years. I'm way too clever; way too smart for that dingbat and there is gonna be a great deal more suffering before the score is even. That's a promise."

CHAPTER SIX

Even though he was gripped by an unrelenting agony, Eric Goodwin returned to his job at Dalton General Foods on Thursday. There was no way he could stay home since there was a nagging concern about this guy who was taking the job he wanted. Lucky for him, his wife's mother had flown in from Phoenix for the funeral, agreeing to stay as long as Julie needed her.

The loss of his baby was all Julie's fault and she knew it. Laura had been their child. Mark was her kid by a previous marriage. Of course, being aware that she was responsible, she was doubly suffering. The worst thing that night was his telling her, "Better run over and pick up Laura. She shouldn't walk all the way home from the church in the dark."

"It's only two blocks," Julie insisted. "She's done it a dozen times. Walks with the Anderson kids."

Could kick myself for listening to her. Should have dragged myself away from the TV and picked her up.

As plant manager he had his own reserved parking space. When he pulled into the parking lot he screwed up his mouth when he spotted the out of state license on a gold Lexus, parked in George Dalton's old spot. The new Vice- president and General Manager was due to start today. "Oh boy," he muttered. "Not looking forward to this." When Swanson was being shown around last month he felt an immediate dislike, partially based on the fact the promotion he had expected was given to this stranger from Alabama.

As he entered the main office, wearing his usual pastel colored sweatshirt and worn Levis, everyone he passed looked up in surprise. Elaine Garcia, his secretary, hastily hung up the phone. Probably one of her sneaky personal calls. "Morning," he growled.

"Mr. Goodwin. We didn't expect you back today."

"Aaaaaaah. No way I could stay home. Thought I'd come in to make sure everything is in order before I have to deal with the new Commander-in-Chief."

"He's here," she whispered.

"Yeah, saw his car outside. A frown creased his forehead when he saw a maintenance worker carry a packing box out of his office and place it on the floor next to the door. "Is he up in Dalton's office?"

"No, he's in your office."

"Why do I have a bad feeling about this?" Curious, Eric looked into the open box. His heart practically stopped. On top of a pile of manila folders was a picture from his desk, one he'd taken last summer up at Sandstone Lake. It was a smiling picture of Julie and Laura. Feeling violated he turned abruptly and charged right in. Sitting behind Eric's desk was the slick haired, mustachioed guy who looked more like a gangster from an old Mafia movie than management. Even his clothes, tan slacks, firmly creased, tan suit coat, diamond stickpin in a blue silk tie, spit shined shoes. Salvador Hoover, head of maintenance, stood next to the desk.

"Mister Swanson, I'm Eric Goodwin. The uh . . . plant manager. We met last month."

"So you are. Sal, get a hold of a good floor covering outfit. Have them bring by some samples. Some of that glue down wood planking would look nice in here. Didn't expect you back until Monday, Goodwin. Sorry 'bout your daughter, but these things happen you know."

Eric could tell by Swanson's eyes that he didn't approve of his casual dress. These things don't just happen, asshole, especially not to people like the Goodwin's in a quiet little town like Dalton. Chalk up another reason for not liking this jerk. "What's going on?"

"I was going over some changes with Mr. Hoover. Thought I'd set up shop in here so I could be closer to the action. I've arranged to have your things moved in with Thornburg's."

Eric choked. "I thought you'd want to take Dalton's old office. It's twice the size of . . . " The worker was carrying a second

56

box out the door, placing it on top of the first.

"Which reminds me, Sal, send one of your men upstairs with a handcart. Bring me the filing cabinet containing personnel records. I personally want to review each one. Need to make some changes down the line. Tell you what, Goodwin. If you're impressed with that dump, go ahead. Move your things up there. I'll have a couple of clerks go through everything. That old man kept records that go back a thousand years but we'll dump ninety percent of it."

Eric's eyes were boiling, his cheeks slightly pink. How much lower can things go? "I'll start getting my personal things out of the way. I will use Dalton's office."

"Sal is going to have his maintenance crews in here this evening as well as Saturday and Sunday. Some fresh paint, new floor covering, new furniture. Monday you won't recognize the place. Do you want your desk and chair or will you be using the old man's?"

Eric puffed out his cheeks and blew a long breath through his lips before he replied, "I'll take my chair."
"Incidentally . . . I'll be using Miss . . . " he indicated with his thumb, "whatsername out there. In addition to her other duties, I plan to make her the receptionist."

"Elaine?" It came out automatically. She's my personal secretary."
Swanson merely shrugged. His expression proclaimed, "so what?"
* * *

Candy was out of bed before her alarm went off. Looking down at her rumpled pajamas where a hundred yellow happy faces grinned back up at her. "You guys can smile," she scolded. "I'm the one who has to go back to school in the middle of the week." Glancing about the room she nodded her head. It was decorated the way she wanted it. Rock group posters on the walls, the Bullwinkle quilt grandma Swanson had made for her several years ago. Perched at the foot of the bed was a stuffed Smoky The Bear that due to its buckteeth she called Bucky.

She had to share the hall bath with her brother but that was no problem. She'd be long gone by the time he got up. In the past it had always been the lick and a promise then out the door, but this morning she spent quite a while in front of her mirror before leaving for school. Who is this stranger looking back at me? The airline stewardess was right. Getting her hair done truly did make her feel like a new woman. What a bitchin' job that gal had done. Took out most of the kinky curls. Turned it into a cool shape. If I only had the face to go with it. The dumbest thing was the feeling her hair would help her face the kids in this new school.

Certain she was arriving early enough there would be few students about she received a surprise that there were several dozen in the hall. Unlike the thirty-foot wide, tan painted, concrete halls in her school in Montgomery, Dalton's were narrow, covered with a shiny, waxed Congolium. Candy stopped next to the locker assigned to her, eyeing the short, plump gal who was fumbling with the combination lock on the door next to hers.

"We didn't have lockers where I came from," she told her. "Took 'em all out 'cause of vandalism." Candy felt herself tighten up, feeling a pair of deep blue eyes checking her out.

"No kidding? Principal Hernandez would crack some skulls if any of the kids trashed these. You must be the new eighth grader."

"Ummm, let's see. That was right to four, left past four to eighteen, then right to zero . . . walla. It works. Yeah. Name's Candy. From Montgomery, Alabama."

"My name's Leora. I'm in the seventh grade. Don't even know where Alabama is. Think you'll like it here. Golly, you're pretty."

Candy grinned as she took off the knapsack containing all her books and school essentials. She stuffed it into her empty locker. "Have you had your eyes checked lately? Hey, any idea where I go from here?"

Pulling a black binder and a book from her locker she told her, "History for me. What's your first class?"

"Got English my first period."

"Mrs. Turner. She's a real cool head. Come on. I'll show you where the homeroom is. That's where we all meet before first period to study or whatever."

Midway down the main hall were the open double doors to a large room filled with desks. Feeling nowhere near as confident as she was acting she tried to walk in like she owned the place, again surprised to discover it was nearly half full. The students were milling about in groups. Her first thought was, oh my Gawd, what am I supposed to do? She'd only caught a glimpse of the kids yesterday so was unsure what most of them wore to school. For her first day she had chosen black slacks, slightly flared legs, a forest green-and-white striped top, black shoes with two-inch platform heels.

Wouldn't you know, totally out of place? The uniform of choice for the girls she could see seemed to be every conceivable color of denim shorts and various tops imprinted with advertising. The boys wore baggy shorts, the legs ending three or four inches below the knees with T-shirts showing off sports logos or witty sayings. Sure different from what she was used to at home. Everyone in the room was looking at her. She wondered what they were thinking. Not even a hello. Would they shut her out like the kids in Alabama?

Glancing at the vacant desks with no idea where she was supposed to sit, she randomly picked one and plopped down.

A girl at a nearby desk called out, "hey you with the hair, that's Carmelita's desk."

Candy shrugged. "I'll move when she comes."
Home-room, huh? In Montgomery students met between classes in a number of smaller rooms. Both the seventh and eighth grades gathered here in one big room. Counting the number of desks across times the number of rows she came up with one hundred fifty. In her old school this room would seat about a quarter of the eighth grade.

"Hey! You're in my desk."

Candy looked up into a glowering face. Cuban or one of those Spanish types, she thought. Ummm, hard eyes that spell T-r-o-u-b-l-e. The same spiked black hair she had seen yesterday. Short enough, and with her square jaw, high cheekbones and bushy brows, make her come across like a good lookin' boy. Even dressed like a boy. "Oh. Sorry." Standing, she discovered she was nearly a head taller than the stocky student. "I'm Candy Swanson. We moved here from Alabama." Boy! She thinks she's somethin', doesn't she? Wonder what's with the shit kickin' boots?

"Well, move it Swanson or it'll be Swan Song."
"Hey, chill out. I was warming it up for you. Waiting for whoever

it is that tells you where to park it."

"Why don't you park it back in Alabama?"

"In a minute if I could. In a minute."

As she turned away from the dark haired girl Candy heard someone say, "Hey Mark. You're back."

"Hi Ollie." The two guys did a slapping, grasping, bumping sort of secret handshake.

"Hey man, good to see ya. Thought you'd stay out till Monday."

With her arms crossed in front, she surveyed the two guys who were the center of attention. One was huge, all muscle, probably two hundred pounds. The second boy was obviously from a street gang. Black Raider's hat with the bill to the rear, medium long, blonde hair, dark leather jacket, a chain to his wallet, black Levis, western boots . . . and you can tell that he thinks he's God's gift. Several students called out, "Hey Mark," but they seemed to be holding something back. There was considerable whispering and pointing. Guy had probably been in some kind of trouble if he wasn't expected back until Monday?

"Oooooeee, look what we got here," the big guy was loud enough everyone in the room turned to see where he was looking. "Wow! That's what I call a fox. The boy named Mark glanced her way then shrugged, telling his friend, "Hey, when Lois Lane is your dream woman, a freckle-faced kid can't hold a candle to her. She's nothing but another dumb girl."

Oh yeah? 'Nothin' but another dumb girl?' Man what a freak. From a guy in love with Lois Lane.

"Hello. You're Candice Swanson, right?" A tall, thin woman spoke as she stopped next to where Candy waited. She seemed to be one size from chest to waist to hips. Wore a thin, light green, cotton dress that hung to her ankles. "I'm Chelsea Dickerson, today's study hall proctor." She offered her hand and Candy took it. "My how nice your hair looks"

My hair again? Guess I must be a new woman. "Had it done yesterday down at Bernice's"

"She's good isn't she? If you'll follow me, I'll show you to your assigned seat."

* * *

For a long, boring quarter-hour Candy fidgeted at her desk

60

in the homeroom while the other students crammed for tests. At last a buzzer announced the start of the first class. Looking frantically about, she spotted a student with an English book like hers. No problem. I'll go where she goes.

When Mrs. Turner, the English Teacher, entered the classroom she spoke briefly with the boy named Mark who sat in the last row. Candy couldn't fathom why but he seemed to be a hero to the others, but she heard the teacher say, "Kinda surprised to see you here, Mark. Can't tell you how badly I feel for you. Such a sweet child. Are you doing all right?" Shaking her head, she reached out and removed his hat, placing her other hand on his upper arm.

"I'm okay. Rather be here than hanging out at home."

Her fingers trailed down his arm until she touched his hand. "If you need someone to talk to my door is always open."

Candy stood about halfway down the right side, uneasily waiting to find out where she was supposed to sit. Watching the exchange she wondered if the old gal with the fantastic shape had the hots for Mr. Tough guy. She's really old. At least forty.

Moving toward the front, the teacher came directly to her, smiled, and then faced the class. "Students, I want you to meet your new classmate from Montgomery, Alabama. I understand her family moved into the old Clayton house. We want to do everything we can to make her feel welcome. First, I want Candice to come up front and tell the class some things about herself and her family. Then it would be nice if each student will stand and introduce themselves." A chorus of groans.

Looking out over the expectant faces, she stood twisting the bottom of her blouse wondering what she was expected to say. Her heart was going a million beats a second. "Hi y'all. Uh . . . Name's Candice Swanson. We moved to Dulltown from Alabama. Ah usta live in Montgomery. My mom takes care of the house and my dad is the new head guy out at the Dulltown Food place. Gotta ten year old brother who is a smuck."

There was a smattering of guffaws from the class. The teacher smiled. Candy could tell she was wondering if it was her southern accent or did she actually say 'Dulltown'? She didn't know what else to say. Everyone was staring at her.

"How big was your school?" A student in the back saved

the moment.

Candy made a face. "Heckafire, in Montgomery we had at least a half dozen junior highs. That's what they call them there. Not middle schools. Had three grades 'stead of two. Over two thousand students where I went."

Someone whistled.

"Mr. Hernandez said y'all have a hundret and nine here. A hundret nine, 'cluding me . . . " She looked about. "And only forty-seven in the whole dang Eighth Grade. We had six hundret-twenty."

"Ye'all wear shoes down there in Alabamie?" Someone asked with a phony nasal twang.

It was the jerk dressed all in black. "Only when we're 'round some wannabe tough guy who likes to throw a lotta B.S., let alone bein' a hoodlum ta boot."

More chuckles, some rather pronounced, and another smile from Mrs. Turner, who urged, "All right students, we'll start in the front row with Heather Deiter and introduce ourselves to Candice. Heather?"

"Hi. I'm Heather Deiter and you sure talk funny."

So? You look funny, thought Candy. Pretty thing though. Totally white hair, white eyebrows, white lashes, pink skin. What do they call em? Albinos?

"My folks own Deiter Ford over on Main Street. I have an older brother who is also a schmuck."

One after another the students introduced themselves. What a complete waste, she was thinking. I have this total mental block rememberin' names.

"We've met," the stocky gal from the study hall was speaking. "I'm Carmelita Hoover. My mom works at Steven's Store. My old man is head of maintenance at Dalton General Foods. And I got two older brothers who definitely are not smucks."

When the big guy's turn came he stared in her direction. "Hi good lookin'. I'm Oliver Frazier, but you can call me Ollie."

She smiled, remembering that the big guy had called her a fox. She kept her eyes right on his until he squirmed next to his seat.

"My dad runs the newspaper," he finished.

She felt some tension when the guy called Mark stood. Actually the guy was a hunk, if you like someone from a motorcycle gang. So what was the problem? Something about him rubbed her all wrong.

"Hi Red. I'm Mark Goodwin . . . "

With her eyes spitting green fire she snapped, "don't call me Red. My name is Candice. C-A-N-D-I-C-E! My friends, who I never expect to count you among, call me Candy." Crossing her arms in front she hugged herself, waiting for him to finish."

"Well la de da. Who pulled your chain? Little short on the temper there ain't we . . . Red?"

"Mark." It was obvious Mrs. Turner wasn't one to put up with any nonsense. "That will be enough."

"What the Hell? She's the one being the crappy bitch."

"Mark Goodwin! I want to see you in the principal's office. Right this instant!"

"Yes ma'am."

Even though he smirked at her when he turned to go, Candy could feel the coldness from his piercing blue eyes. Dang it. What's the matter with me? She chewed on her lower lip, aware of the faces of the other students. It was written in plain English, 'You blew it'. Opened my mouth without thinking. What the heck? They could stick it.

"How could you?" With a voice that sounded like a whip cracking, a pretty black student with shoulder length black hair glared at her. "Look what you did."

"Why are you coming down on me? He's the one . . ."

"You idiot! Mark's little sister was murdered last Sunday. Funeral was yesterday."

Candy stood with her mouth open, one hand extended in a helpless gesture, unable to speak.

* * *

As Mark left the room he heard the teacher apologize to the class before following a few paces behind him into the principal's office. He was thinking fast, deciding to forego his usual, "Hi Bobby, what's happening?" The principal's standard reply was, "That's Mr. Hernandez; Mr. Goodwin. Please show some respect." The result of this earlier exchange had half the kids in school calling the principal, Bobby. This wasn't his first trip to the principal's office and this time could be . . . who knows? Stay after school for a couple of nights.

"Alright Mr. Goodwin," Mrs. Turner snapped, "I'd like a full explanation for your rude actions. Is that any way to welcome a newcomer to our school? Your use of the words 'Hell, crap' and 'bitch' was totally uncalled for, and I don't want to hear them used again in my classroom. I'd like to hear what you have to say?"

"Well I . . . "

"I'm waiting, Mr. Goodwin." The teacher was tapping a steel edged ruler on her palm.

"We are both waiting, Mr. Goodwin." Principal Hernandez stood glaring, his arms crossed.

Mark shuffled his feet for a few seconds then a fat idea leaped into his mind. His gaze moved toward the ceiling, his expression pained. "I uh . . . I'm sorry, ma'am. You see uh . . . I haven't been myself the last few days. You know; Laura's funeral was yesterday and I guess I ain't been handling this whole thing too well. Wanted to stay home for the rest of the week," he lied. "My dad thought it would be better if I came back. Thought I wouldn't have as much time to think about it." By the looks on their faces he knew he had their sympathy all over the place.

"Oh Mark!" Mrs. Turner cried, "You poor boy. If you'd like to go home, I'll write up a forgiveness slip."

"Naw, that's okay. I've made it this far and I'm sure I'll be alright. If only he could change into Superman, he'd snatch up that red headed Swanson bitch, fly her right out into the middle of Sandstone Lake and drop her in.

* * *

Frank, Ralph and Doc Snyder sat in a window booth at the Green Spot Cafe having donuts and coffee. Ralph carried on his usual one-sided flirtation with Peggy, the slightly overweight but attractive waitress.

"Making any progress on the Goodwin case?" the doctor asked.

Frank could tell that Doc was pissed that he didn't call him when they found the body. "I swear, Doc, with that bushy white hair on each side of your bald dome and those half-inch thick glasses you look more like a professor than a doctor."

"Yeah," Ralph snorted. "Einstein."

Frank tasted his coffee, made a face then added more

cream. "Me and Ralph are hitting nothing but dead ends on this one. Couldn't find a damned thing out where the body was. Obvious to me he killed her someplace else. Been combing the whole town. Perp had to leave plenty of blood somewhere. Keep hoping somebody may have seen someone around."

"Always a possibility." Doc waved his empty cup toward Peggy. "Givin' any thought as to why he cut off a piece of her leg?"

"No idea. Never can tell what one of these weirdoes has in mind." Frank leaned back as the waitress filled his cup.

"I ain't gonna burn ya," she teased.

"Maybe he ate it." The deputy joked.

"Ralph," Peggy cried. "You're sick."

"Love sick," he patted her on the hand holding the coffee pot.

"You mentioned you had some suspects. Is that going anywhere?" Doc was busy with a huge apple fritter.

"Nothing concrete. Got some ideas." Jelly filling slid down Frank's chin like a slug, dropping into his coffee. He smeared at his face with his palm. "However," he shrugged. "Might be wrong. Could be it's one of them dope heads. You know, from down Clarksdale way. Even some hobo passing through."

Ralph was nodding. "Got the railroad and the main highway runnin' right through town . . . and we ain't got nobody here in Dalton that would do a vile thing like that."

The doctor kidded, "Ralph agrees with whatever you say, Frank, right or wrong. You can never actually tell about people. Sometimes a mild mannered preacher can go off the deep end when it comes to sex. Or even some kid who is high on dope and has his juices flowing."

"That's why I've been keeping my eye on the Goodwin boy. Not that he is mild mannered by any stretch of the imagination. Sure has been acting weird ever since the murder. I been wondering how come he and that Frazier kid knew exactly where to find the body."

"The Goodwin kid? Somewhat wild like you say, but I don't think he's into dope. As far as them finding the body, probably one of those freak things you hear about every once in a while."

"Not so sure, Doc. Well known fact of law enforcement is when a child is killed the immediate family are prime suspects."

"Interesting thought," Doc again motioned to Peggy indicating he wanted his bill. "Happens sometimes." He lowered his voice an octave. "Evil lurks in the hearts of all men?"

* * *

"I hate Phys Ed," Candy muttered as she headed for the gym. She was aware all the students were psyched at her over what happened in class. How was she to know the tall kid . . . Mark whatsisname . . . Goodhead or whatever, had just faced something that bad? He sure didn't show it. In any case, she recognized the fact all the other kids in this little hick school thought he was some sort of a God. Kids like him were a dime a dozen in Montgomery. Most of them weren't in school. In Juvie maybe. Probably into dope and gangs and petty theft. Some things she didn't need because that stuff was dumb. He could stick it too.

In the locker room everyone pretty much ignored her. Once she had on her gym outfit she made her way out into the auditorium. To her surprise, Mrs. Turner was also the girl's Phys Ed Teacher. About two-dozen students showed up for class.

"Okay ladies. Want you to choose up sides, four teams; two teams in each court. Shannon and Carmelita will be team captains for this end. Patty and Stacy in the far court. Shannon, you choose first."

"Jodi." The slim black teenager who spoke was the same one who had jumped on her case in class. She was wearing black shorts and a white top. Nearly all the students wore shorts, but man, were her shorts tight. The straight hair was as dark as her clothes, the bangs cut low over the largest eyes Candy had ever seen. A tiny wisp of a gal, that looked all the smaller near the tall black girl, bounced over to stand beside her. The little one looked like she was ten years old.

Candy had been through this sort of thing many times before. Never been any good at sports. Always the last one picked and since they all hated her . . . "

"Joyce," Carmelita called out.
Going the way I figured. Names were called until four girls remained. The Albino gal stood next to a tiny gal with half-inch thick glasses. They were chosen next. That left her and a fatso, four foot tall, four foot wide. Candy stood glaring at her finger-

66

nails. Could use a new coat of polish. Boy, am I being ignored. Didn't matter. Never cared much for athletic crap anyhow.

"I'll take Miss Alabama there," Shannon joked. "At least she's tall."

There were six girls on each team and they all played. The teacher gave Shannon's team yellow, sleeveless T-shirts to pull on over their gym clothes. The black gal jumped center against Joyce in the free throw circle, easily tipping the ball to one of her teammates. The game was underway.

After several minutes Candy realized her teammates were playing as if she wasn't there. Not once did anyone pass the ball to her. Worse, she had to guard Carmelita. Tough job. She played like a boy. All muscle and elbows, several times faking Candy out of position, shoving her aside for easy baskets. She was obviously the spark plug. Had to give her that, she was good. The yellow team fell half-dozen points behind.

Candy, a complete novice, began to notice some things about the game. Carmelita had a habit of holding the ball in front of her body in both hands before she dribbled or took a shot. It was as though she was teasing her defender. "Your mistake," Candy thought as she simply snatched the ball out of her hands. Glaring at Candy, Carmelita moved from offence to defense, raising her arms to guard, then she took a step back, daring her to shoot. Candy looked down. She was well beyond the three-point arc. Could she even throw it that far? Making a one-bounce dribble she took a one-handed shot. To her surprise, and everyone else's, the ball swished through the net.

"Right on," someone shouted.

The next time down the floor, the little one called Jodi passed her the ball. What the hey she thought? Can't do any worse than they've been doin.' Dribbling toward Carmelita, who with her quick hands tried to slap the ball away, Candy made her move. With a head fake, a quick spin like she'd seen pro players do on TV, she was around and past her defender. Pushing up a scoop shot with Carmelita hanging all over her, she missed. She could hear the shrill whistle; foul on Carmelita. Candy made both free throws.

Shannon sprang forward with a high five. "Awesome! You're pretty good."

On the next possession Candy again stole the ball and as the game progressed, twice more she swiped it away when Carmelita was dribbling. Three times she blocked the stocky girl's shots. The gal was becoming furious. Cool, Candy thought. Get her mind all addled. She continued to play and to learn.

She'd always been so awkward, she couldn't believe it when she began to get the feel for handling the ball. Several times driving into the lane, making a shot or drawing a foul. The other players began to sag in on her. When they did she'd locate an unguarded teammate and pass off. The yellow shirts easily won the game and Candy had scored twelve points.

As she headed for the showers Mrs. Turner remarked, "nice game. You're a natural."

Candy felt a warm glow.

Carmelita, her eyes fierce, brushed against her. "You really think you're something, don'tcha?" She snarled.

Not wanting to make waves, Candy shrugged. "Dumb luck. What can I say?"

In the showers five teammates were heaping on the praise. "Man, you're something else." Shannon told her.

She'd never been the center of attention before, and knew in her heart it wouldn't last. "I'm . . . uh, thanks."

"Too bad you got started off on the wrong foot in class. Getting somebody like Mark Goodwin busted your first day isn't any way to win friends and influence people."

"One of my talents. Had no way of knowing 'bout his sister. Someone said she was murdered. Y'all know what happened?"

"Happened last Sunday. Mark and Ollie, Jodi's brother, were riding their bikes out in the country. Accidentally found her body."

"Oh my Gawd." Candy swallowed. "What a downer. Sure couldn't tell it by the way he acted."

"Think he was trying to cover up his feelings. My God. Can't even imagine how horrible that would be?" She shuddered, then continued, "Oh, by the way, I'm Shannon. This is my best friend, Jodi. She's a twin."

"Hi." The tiny girl's attention seemed to be elsewhere.

"She's Ollie's twin sister. Ollie's the big guy who was sitting next to Mark. Would you believe, Ollie tips the scales at something like two ten, and here we have little Jodi who tops out at eighty seven pounds."

"Twins? You're jerking my leg."

"Well I am," Jodi insisted.

Candy was having funny feelings about Shannon. She did most of the talking while Jodi simply stared. Since her father always insisted blacks were inferior, in Alabama she rarely connected with blacks.

"If you're looking for a couple of friends . . . unless you, being from Alabama and all, find my color a problem."

Candy started to make some comment about the blacks in Alabama but some of her grandmother's remarks popped up and she smiled slightly and then grinned as broadly as her face would permit. "That's pretty funny. Way I was brought up, it truly should. Would for sure bug my dad. He's a full-fledged Red Neck. Not only doesn't bother me, but you are the prettiest girl I've ever seen."

Shannon blushed profusely even though it scarcely showed. "Gee whiz. I better take back what I said about you in class. Heck, you don't do too badly in the looks department. I'd die for that drop dead hair."

"Awww," her face glowed. "It's all right, I guess. Grandma thinks I look like Ann Margaret."

"No way. You mean the old gal who played in Grumpy Old Men II?"

"Get real," Jodi, cocked her head. "Well, maybe in a way, when the gal was a lot younger."

Candy squirmed, feeling uncomfortable at the attention. Friends? Could it be possible? Getting back into her regular clothes, she looked curiously at Jodi, the small one. Never sat still, kept fussing with her hair and was forever looking about like she was expecting somebody. If Shannon wants to be my friend, I'd better jump at it. They were outside the gym, heading for their next class.

Shannon was walking backwards in front of the others. "So? You wanna hang out with us. Already know how it feels to be the new kid on the block. Went through it last year."

"Cool. What's your last name, Shannon?" She looked at Jodi who seemed to be off in another world. The big kid's sister, huh? "Yours was Frazier, right?"

"Frazier the Blazer, that's me." The small gal placed a hand in her long blond hair and flipped it forward over her face then used her head to flip it back as two boys walked past.

Candy frowned for the boys were eyeing her. She was all mixed up about what was going on. This was a whole different world.

Shannon grinned. "Last name's White. Don't ask me why so many black people are named White, 'cause I haven't a clue. Jodi doesn't talk much but you're gonna find out once you get her motor running you have to tape her mouth shut."

' What's with this guy Mark? Is he the school Godfather or what?"

Shannon grinned. "Never thought of him quite that way. Whoops! That's the buzzer for next period. We better hit it." She offered her hand for a high five and Candy gave her one. "I've got a feeling that the three of us are going to be best friends."

Candy nodded, desperately hoping it would be true. So far today she had learned a couple of valuable lessons. Everything grandma suggested works.

* * *

Vince Swanson looked up, leaning back in his chair, as the Garcia woman came in with some checks for him to sign. "Incidentally, uh . . . Elaine, when we both have a free moment or two I'd like to talk to you about your position." He saw the sudden look of concern cross her face. He smiled. "I believe you'll like what I have in mind. Goodwin will have to find another secretary since you'll be working directly for me."

"Oh, I see. Does Mr. Goodwin know about this?"

"Not very happy about it, but he knows. Got a feeling the man pretty much resents my being here."

"Disappointment mostly. I guess he thought the position of General Manager would be given to him."

"Tough cookies, Goodwin. Best man got the job. I'll have these checks ready for today's mail."

Elaine nodded and walked back out to her desk. He watched her through the window as she stood there talking on the phone. Instead of sitting at her desk, she turned and slipped back into his office. My, my, that's nice, he was thinking. What a fine looking woman and not married.

She stood in the doorway. "Excuse me sir. George Martinez is on line one."

Wondering why she hadn't buzzed him on the intercom he replied, "Martinez? Name sounds familiar. Take a message. I'm waiting for an important call."

"Mr. Martinez is the Mayor."

"Oh oh, I'd better take that one." Looking at the blinking light on his phone he picked up the receiver. "Hello Mr. Mayor. Vince Swanson here. What can I do for you?"

"Vince. You can call me George but not Georgie Porgie." He was chuckling like it was the funniest thing he'd ever said. "Wanted to discuss a civic matter with you."

"All right, what's on your mind, George?"

"This is in regards to one of your executives there at DGF; Eric Goodwin. This community wants to do whatever they can to help apprehend the man who killed Goodwin's daughter. Dalton Union and a group of concerned citizens are putting together a reward package. We already have commitments from several businesses. Steven's Market is putting up a thousand, Turner Lumber is offering two and Deiter Ford has kicked in five. I feel, since he is one of your own, and as a matter of civic duty, DGF should offer to put up a substantial amount."

"Substantial? You have a figure in mind?"

"With what we already have pledged, fifteen thousand would round it out to twenty-five grand. What do you think?"

"Well . . . uh . . . George, I'll have to get back to you. Need to clear it through the head office, but I'm sure they'll go along."

They exchanged a few pleasantries then Vince pushed the intercom button.

"Yes sir." Elaine acknowledged.

"Would you please call the head office? Ask for Tony Minelli. If he's not available have him call me back." Glancing out through the plate glass window, again he was thinking, what a fine looking woman. Come on Vince, keep your mind on business.

"Yes sir." She was dialing.

Vince was surprised when the call to his boss went directly through. "Hello Tony. Need to discuss something with you."

"Some sort of a problem?"

Tony sounded relieved when he told him, "Nothing like that." Explaining the situation, he asked for twenty-five thousand.

"Did you say murdered? Knew he was off on bereavement leave for a death in the family, but this is news. Stuff like that doesn't make the local media. Twenty-five?"

"It's our duty, Tony. Since most of these crimes are solved by diligent police work, very rarely is a reward paid out. Use this thing right and we can get a million dollars worth of free publicity."

"Ummh. See your point. Actually Vince, that's good thinkin'. I'll have the funds earmarked for that purpose transferred to DGF's bank today. Glad you called."

Me too, thought Vince. Let Goodwin think it was all my idea. He pushed the intercom button again. "Elaine, put me through to the Mayor's office."

* * *

On the way to history class, Candy passed Mark in the hall. Maybe she should stop him and apologize for her short fuse. He flipped her the bird. She stuck her tongue out at him.

"Candice! I'd like a word with you." Mrs. Turner stepped out into the hall.

Candy had already decided the old gal was well into her forties, yet she wore minis and casual tops like a teenager. Uh-uh, she was thinking as she waited without turning to face the woman, knowing she was going to get a good butt chewing for what happened between her and the class hero. She needed to explain that she didn't know 'bout the guy's sister.

"Candice, two things. You did an outstanding job in gym class. You're gonna fit right in. I am also coach of the pep squad. One of the members of our team has been dropped for academic reasons, so I was hoping you might fill the position.

Candy was so taken aback she found herself stuttering. "B-b-but . . . you mean m-m-me?"

"Since we're such a small school, we don't play football at Dalton, but the pep squad performs at band events, and you know; parades on Memorial Day, Christmas and the Fourth of July and all winter long at basketball games."

"Well . . . I mean, I've never done anything like that."

"You'd pick it up in a minute. What do you say?"

Candy was speechless. This is too good to be true.

"This will also give you a chance to become involved in what we call, 'The Spirit of Dalton Middle School.' We meet to-night right after school. I'm going to add your name to my list."

What could she say? Was this Fatso Candice Swanson the lady was talking to? "Well . . . I guess. Cool. Oh man! I'd like that so much. I'll be there, and uh . . . thanks, Mrs. Turner. This is awesome."

* * *

The Man pulled into the City Parking Lot, kitty cornered from the elementary school. He sat there for a while watching a group of kids screaming and cavorting on the playground equip-ment at Palm School. The car was in the shade of a huge cot-tonwood tree. Didn't dare park in the open sun. Metal attracts heat like a magnifying glass. Be a 200-degree oven in fifteen minutes. All the little tots fascinated him but one held his interest more than any of the others. Who else? At last I found out her first name and it was Gretchen Heinz; next one on his list. She was supposed to have been the first. Try as he might an opening never presented itself but at last he had a plan.

The Goodwin brat was actually number three on the list. What's a man to do when the opportunity pops up? The Baptist Church always had something going for the kids and all of a sud-den there she was, bigger than life, in the dark, trotting along Washington Street. All he had to do was stop around the corner. Hide behind the bushes next to the theater parking lot on River-view. Had been damned near too easy.

That evens the score with Goodwin. Got four more names on my list. One thing for sure, the order doesn't matter, as long as he punished them all. "And that my friend is what I'm gonna do. Punish them all."

CHAPTER SEVEN

For Thursday's eighth grade gym class, Coach Ed Donnelley was acting as referee. He pitted his first string basketball players against the rest of the class. As he watched them work out he could hardly take his gaze off the Goodwin kid. Like his fellow teachers, he was surprised to see the boy at school the day after his sister's funeral. Yet he understood. It was the kid's way of escaping.

Kinda wish the lad didn't have such a tough guy . . . bad boy, reputation. Kid seems to be constantly doing mischievous things that keep him in hot water with school officials and with the sheriff. He found himself smiling at the idea Halloween was coming in a couple of weeks. What would the boy come up with this year? Last year he convinced a group of about fifteen seventh and eighth grade boys to help him push Miss Johnson's old Volkswagen Beetle from her driveway, across the street, then lift it up to carry it through the double doors and set it down crossways in the school lobby. Took Louie's Towing darned near two hours to get it out.

I'm as bad as the sheriff. Here I'm saying, 'He' without any proof. Of course the Goodwin boy was the chief suspect, but no one saw anything, no one heard anything, no one squealed.

On the other hand, this tough guy, bad boy could be exactly what the doctor ordered. After all, I'm the adult here. Blowing his whistle he stopped the action. "Okay men, hit the showers. You! Goodwin. Wanna com'mere a minute?"

* * *

Mark frowned as he looked at Ollie who shrugged. "What could I have possibly done?" he muttered as he turned to move toward Donnelley, who was the math teacher, boy's phys Ed teacher and also coach of the Dalton basketball team. He glanced back but Ollie was on his way to the showers.

"Let's talk a minute. Might not be a good time considering what you've been through this week, but I've got a problem. Was hoping you might be able to help me with it. I'm very sorry about your sister."

Mark liked Ed Donnelley. Scuttlebutt had it the coach had been a superstar for some national championship college team; Michigan State, think it was. Someplace like that. Had a knee injury destroy his chances of being picked up by the NBA. "I'm hangin' in there okay. Was worse yesterday with the funeral and all."

Donnelley placed a reassuring hand on his shoulder as he told him, "I understand what you are going through. I actually do. Uh . . . hey Mark. I realize that last year you had that broken leg that kept you out of commission but . . . "

"Yeah, pretty stupid. Took a spill. Got my leg tangled up in my bike." He didn't mention he was riding someplace he wasn't supposed to be.
"I've been watching you in gym class the past few weeks, so I was wondering why you didn't try out for the team. I hate to see all that talent go to waste."

"What can I say? Didn't want to show up all those other pansies." It was an opinion Mark was pretty sure the coach shared.

Donnelley made a face. "What we have here is, a coach who needs twelve guys to make up a team. This guy has only a couple of dozen boys to pick from in the entire seventh and eighth grades. Most of the seventh graders can't cut the mustard. Got five or six other boys who wouldn't know a basket ball if they were sitting on one and when three or four others don't even try out, my collection of talent is rather pathetic."

Mark shrugged feeling that Donnelley could read his thoughts.

"I'm going to be straight with you, Mark. Due to your reputation, I wasn't even sure if I wanted to take a chance on you. You're a pretty tough guy, right?"
Mark shrugged again.

"I notice everyone comes down on you about the way you talk, the way you act, how you dress, even the way you wear your hair."

"Hey man, that's their problem."

"It's nobody's problem. It's a statement that says, 'this is who I am. This is what I can do,' but it needs to go much further than that. Inside this tough guy is a real man who wants to prove what he is by what he does. But you've been doing ill-advised things that you think they will get you recognition. And they do. You want recognition? What I would like to see you do is channel some of your tough guy attitude onto the basketball court." He smiled. "Only not tough to a point you keep fouling out. You're the tallest boy in school. How tall are you, six feet?"

"'Bout that. Guess I've grown six inches the last six months."

"Here's my problem, Mark. I desperately need your height and your play making ability. Citrus has a guy about six one. So does Clarksdale. I would like to see you prove what you can do. Take Superman for example. He doesn't jump into his cape and say, 'Hey, look at me. I'm the Man of Steel'. He goes out and proves it."

It was impossible for Mark to grin more broadly. The expression on Donnelley's face told him the coach was wondering what he'd said.
"Are you psychic?" Mark asked. "You like Superman?"

"Always been my idol. That's what I want to see you do. I want to see you fly with a basketball. I want you to prove what you are capable of. We have practice right after school today so what would it take to get you to play?"
Mark chewed on his lower lip, making a face as he considered the proposition, watching the coach who seemed to be holding his breath. "Me and Ollie and Buzz go as a team."

The coach snorted but grinned. "Oh boy Mark, I don't know. Buzz Tarmen is somewhat on the small side although he is exceptionally quick. But Ollie? Football maybe, but isn't your friend kinda beefy for basketball?"

"You'd be surprised. For his size, Ollie's faster than greased lightning. Down under the basket he's unstoppable. Heck, you got a couple of pretty good guys already in Romero and Shorty

Carr. Put them with the three of us. We couldn't be any worse than last year's mess."

Donnelley was grinning as he shook his head. "I'd have to see how you guys work out. I doubt if I can get you ready in time for our opening game next week with Citrus, but we'll see. Does that mean you're in?"

"In the end, do I get Lois Lane?"

"I can guarantee it." He offered a high five.

"Man, you got me wired." The boy slapped the outstretched hand. "And coach . . . "

Donnelly had turned away and then he looked back.

"We'll be ready for Citrus."

* * *

"Candy, I can't believe it. You're trying out for cheerleader?" She and Shannon were on their way to the day's final class. "What a trip. I didn't know we had an opening."

"Hoover gal got cut 'cause of her grades. School policy I guess. 'C' or better or you're history."

"Awesome! Couldn't happen to a better person. None of us liked her anyhow. She thinks she's so cool, but most of it's makeup. Half the time she looks like a gangbanger, rest of the time like a streetwalker."

"Me and her have already crossed paths," Candy told her. "She acts pretty tough."

Shannon nodded. "Runs with a rough crowd. Hey, we're having practice tonight. Can you make it?"

"Planning on it."

"Alright! See if you can come over to my place after dinner. We can study together. I'll call Jodi to see if she can come. I live in the yellow house on the corner of Washington and Locust. Right behind Mark's place."

* * *

At the end of the school day Candy headed for the exit filled with excitement at all the things that happened on her first day at school. Good things, so she had been told, came in threes. Of course, so do bad things, but she was wondering what the third good one could possibly be. Making friends with Shannon and Jodi was the first. The invitation to try out for the pep squad was number two. She didn't feel that the basketball game was important enough to be rated number three. Walking toward the double doors, she peered about, wondering why her new friends were nowhere in sight. Neither of them was in her Spanish class. She was looking down at the floor not paying attention to where she was going and collided with a male teacher as he left his classroom. She had forgotten to zip her backpack and everything inside scattered about the hall.

"Excuse me," he was stooping to help her pick up the books and papers. "Ahha! You're the new student aren't you?"

He made her feel uncomfortable when he stared and stared. All she managed to say was, "Sorry, I'm such a klutz."

"I'm the klutz," he told her. "I was wondering, can I get you to say something for me?"

"Say somethin'? What'cha you want me to say?"

He reached up to tug at his ear then told her, "say . . . uh . . . say, 'I declare Muriel, you don't know anything at all about men.'"

"Well . . . that's weird."

"Please. Go on say it."

She shrugged. "Ah declah Muriel. Y'all don't know . . . uh . . . the first dang thang 'bout m-en."

The teacher stood with his mouth open. "You are perfect, absolutely perfect. Have you done any acting? I mean in school plays or church pageants?"

"Only acting I ever done is during pretend games when I was a kid."

"What did you say your name was?"

"Candice . . . uh, Candy Swanson."

"I'm Brad Kelly, the music teacher. Candy Swanson, next Wednesday after school I want to see you at the drama club meeting in the music room. I need a Southern Belle in this year's school play, The Golden Harvest,. With that copper hair and your accent, I've got just the part for you."

"You gotta be kidding. 'Causin' ah don't know a dang thang 'bout actin'."

"It happens that I do and I'll coach you. Have we got a deal?"

"I'm willing to try," she told him.

He handed her the rest of her books. She stuffed them

78

into her bag, this time zipping it up. Slipping her arms through the strap, it hung down her back.

"See ya Wednesday then," he spoke over his shoulder.

"Oh my Gawd," she squealed, clasping her hands on top of her head. "This is so totally awesome." Heading for the exit she was wondering where her friends were. She could hardly wait to share everything that had happened.

Once outside she saw her new friends next to the athletic field gate. "Hey. Shannon, Jodi; hold it up."

They both stopped, turned and waited for her to catch up.

And that's three, she thought. So when do the three bad things start?

* * *

The Man continued working on his plan. A few minutes after two that afternoon he took a cruise out Highway 61 a couple of miles north of town. There was a five hundred foot high mound of earth and rock that the townspeople called Mount Dalton. Up on top was a rambling ranch style home where the Heinz family lived. The house was surrounded with huge granite boulders. The whole thing looked as though it had been piled there by some gigantic dump truck.

He used the winding drive all the way up to the house. He'd already checked and was sure nobody was been home. Heinz would be at work and Ingrid taught fifth grade at the elementary school. So there was no way for him to be detected. As he walked around he was thinking, no dog. That's kind of a surprised considering where they live. They do have a nice barn. Walking all the way around the dwelling he peered in window until he located the one he wanted. "Her room; stuffed animals and all kinds of girlie crap," he told himself. "Nice big window." He had moved to where he could look down the back side of the hill, standing there considering that it should be an easy task for someone in good shape to climb up from boulder to boulder. Use the barn for cover. That's pretty much everything I wanted to know. Everything is falling into place.

* * *

"Hey, Connie, wait up." As Brad Kelly left the music room he spotted Mrs. Turner near the exit. With three giant strides he was beside her in time to open the door. "Walk ya to your car."

She tilted her head and smiled. "What's up, Brad? You look like the proverbial cat that ate the canary. Did you win the lottery?"

He liked her. Even though both were happily married, they carried on a harmless, mutual, flirtation. "I wish. Gloating you might say. Talked to that new gal . . . you know, the little red-head."

"You mean, Candy Swanson?"

"Yeah. She's something else. I'm considering her for the lead in the school play. I'd say the acting gods are looking out for me. I needed a Southern Belle and the gods sent me one."

"Excellent choice, Brad. I can already tell that little cutie has a great deal of hidden talent."

They were walking alongside the fence next to the outdoor basketball courts. A group of boys was involved in a pick-up game. The couple stopped to watch for a few minutes.

Brad let out a long sigh. "Most of the time, at this grade level, these uh . . . dramas are merely a learning experience for these kids rather than an actual production."

"Might be true at most schools." She nudged him in the ribs with an elbow. "But most schools don't have a Brad Kelly as a director. You have the ability to take ordinary children and make these things a wonderful adventure for your students and an audience."

He grinned, embarrassed. "I've got a problem though. I was going to use Raymond Collins for the male lead but he is turning out to be impossible. Thought maybe he'd matured since last year but he goofs up every scene. I need a tall, handsome lad who looks the part of our hero."

"Like that one?" She nodded toward the group of boys. One stood a head taller than the others. As they watched he faked out a defender, did a 360 turn around him and flipped the ball into the basket his momentum carrying him nearly to the fence where Brad and Carol stood.

"Nice shot," she called out loud enough for the boy to hear.

"Thanks, Mrs. Turner. I try." He gave her a thumbs up and returned to the game.

"Well?" She turned and made a face.

"Goodwin? Hmmm. Kid looks as though he doesn't belong

in the eighth grade. Man, has he changed since last year."

"There's your hero, tall, handsome, muscular, obviously talented. Doesn't he also fit the picture you have in your mind of how the lead character in Golden Harvest should look?"

He wondered. "Kid gets involved in a great deal of devilment. Not actually a bad kid per se, merely creative. Wonder if I'd be able to tame him? What's so funny?"

She grinned. "Some of this so called devilment is actually comical. Remember last summer when Mark and a group of his followers went up on top of The Swiss Dairy? Painted the life-sized cow a deep purple?"

"How could I forget? Drove by it every morning. Fortunately the dairy manager took it in good spirits. Maintenance guys painted some white here and there so it looked like a purple Holstein. I'm also remembering the T peeing of the open trusses in the gym . . . or the food fight in the cafeteria. I can think of a number of other wicked little pranks both the sheriff and our principal blame on the kid . . . whether or not he was the instigator. Seems like he always has an alibi. No one can ever prove anything."

"Mark's problem is he has a great deal of energy, ambition, intelligence. The boy is clever . . . but . . . he has a stepfather who ignores him so he lacks something important; male bonding. You spoke of taming him. Maybe you're that male bond, Brad. Give the boy an outlet . . . like acting. Why don't you go talk to him?"

"Okay. You talked me in to it." He opened the gate and looked back at her. "But you'd better be right."
She turned to move toward the parking lot then looked back over her shoulder. "I generally am. See you tomorrow."
* * *
"Hi Candy. You ready?" Shannon asked.

"Man am I ready. You're not going to believe this. On my way out, Mr. Kelly stopped me in the hallway and asked me to be in the school play."

"Far out." Shannon offered a high five. "Heather Deiter and I are both trying out for parts."

"Hey you red headed bitch!"

Candy stopped, turning slowly. The person speaking was

81

the solidly built Spanish student named Carmelita. Shannon's words from yesterday echoed in her mind. Her brief skirt displayed fabulous legs and a tight black, scoop neck, sweater let everyone know she was developing a shape. Candy muttered toward her friends. "Streetwalker."

"Yeah, that's Carmelita," Shannon told her quietly then whispered. "Watch it Candy. She's a wildcat. Comes from a bad family. I wouldn't be surprised if she isn't carrying a knife. Know what I mean?"

Candy shrugged her friend off. "You got a problem, Carmelita?"

"You're my problem, Frog Face."

Candy watched as three of the angry girl's friends moved around anticipating being part of a showdown. Other nearby students, also sensing the prospect of a potential fight, began to move in close. She'd never been in a fight and was trying to think of something to say to avoid one.

"First day you come to school, you walk in and take over," her antagonist snapped. "What makes you think you're such hot stuff?"

Candy tried to laugh it off. "Gosh, I don't know. Speed, endurance and coordination." She was calmly watching the stocky girl's eyes while at the same time wondering, why me?

"Bull shit. Mrs. Turner's Pet." She practically spit with the word pet. Then today you steal my cheerleading spot. You go after the most popular boy in school. I know how your kind works. What'cha gonna try for next?"

"Class President." Lacing her fingers together behind her head she tried to stare her down. "Come on, Carmelita, don't get so addled. I didn't steal your spot."

"Well, what'cher gonna get is a knuckle sandwich." She moved forward, a ferocious glow in her eyes. "When I get done kicking your ass, you'll have to open your mouth to go to the bathroom.'"Better get some help. I ate bimbos like you for breakfast in Montgomery."

Lowering her head she didn't hesitate, coming at Candy with hands balled into fists, throwing a punch very much like a man would. At the last instant, Candy dropped into a Karate stance, ducked under the flailing arm with a spin move and then grasping a wrist she used her hip. Carmelita did a complete flip, landed on her feet, but out of control, reeling backward for several yards before she ended up on her rump, skidding in the damp grass, eyes like two black olives.

"Come on, Carmelita, let's talk about this. I'm not looking for a fight."

Carmelita came springing up, cursing in Spanish and Candy felt a sudden anxiety. With three friends behind her they all seemed to be charging her way, hands outstretched like angry animals. The redhead stood her ground. At the instant of contact she again did a three sixty, planting her foot directly into the girl's chest. Carmelita staggered backwards, taking two of her friends with her. She was on her hands and knees, gasping, choking, coughing, tears streaming on her cheeks.

"Oh wow," cried Shannon. Carmelita's other friend was backing away while students stood looking on in awe.

"Man that was extreme," Jodi was dancing in circles around Candy. "That's called Karate, isn't it? You gotta teach me how to do that."

"Later," Candy was feeling something she'd never had. Power. "It's time for us to go get us some practice."

* * *

Walking through the open gate Brad stood along the baseline watching the boy make his moves. Dynamic, was the word. One of the smaller boys took a long shot that missed. The rebound came right at the music teacher. He hauled it in, standing with the ball in both hands.

"Hey Kelly," Mark shouted. "Let's see whatcha got. Your shot."

Brad had been a pretty fair athlete in his own high school and college days. As a result he surprised the eight boys when he took one bounce, stepped back behind the three-point line and put it up. There was a satisfying swish.

"Outta sight," one of the boys exclaimed as the teacher moved directly to Mark.

"Hey Goodwin, can we talk for a minute?"

Mark frowned, flipping the ball toward Ollie. "'Bout all the time I got. Waitin' for Coach Donnelley. Wants me on his team so I gotta practice tonight."

They walked over next to the fence where Brad stood

studying the tall lad for a time, wondering why he was in school the day after his sister's funeral. Wondering if he should say anything about it.

"Hey teach it's your nickel. What's going down?"

"Mark, how would you like to have a part in the school play?"

"The school play? Are you kidding? I can't act." He shook his head like a wet dog. "What the heck is going on here? Why am I, out of the blue, in so much demand?"

"Everybody can act. Everybody does, everyday, without even knowing they are doing so. The secret to being a good one is when you know it's an act, but you know how to live the part. I have a role in Golden Harvest that was made for you. It happens to be the lead and you strike me as having the ability and the smarts to pull it off."

"Boy," Mark grinned, "I don't know. Don't have much time since the coach wants me to play basketball."

"Mark, kids who are talented, kids who are smart, also learn how to manage their time. What I'm saying is, this is something you could do and do well. Come on, give it a try."

Mark shrugged, his palms up, thinking about the many times he and Ollie had played Superman. "So I'd play the hero, huh?"

"You'd play the hero."

"Does that mean I gotta kiss the leading lady?"

Thinking that Mark wanted to, Brad grinned in return. "There is a kiss in the final scene."

"Yuck," Mark groaned. "When do I have to let'cha know?"

"We're having a short meeting next Wednesday right after school in the auditorium to talk about the play and pass out the scripts."

"Got a ball game Wednesday evening against Citrus."

"Oh, I forgot about that. Look, all I need is about ten minutes. Think you could manage that?"

Mark laughed. "Gee Kelly, I hope you know what you're letting yourself in for."

* * *

Candy simply had to tell somebody about the sudden changes in her life. She knew her dad wouldn't give a hoot.

84

Barely inside the door she called out, "Mom, got something to tell ya."

Her mother was involved in a mystery novel. Didn't even bother to look up. "How come you're so late getting home?"

"That's what I wanted to tell ya," Candy continued as though she didn't notice the lack of response. She could see Michael sitting in front of the TV playing with his Gameboy the volume nearly shaking the house as usual.

"This school isn't going to be so bad after all. I met two gals who want to be my friends. And guess what, Mom? The drama coach wants me to try out for a part in the school play." Does Mom even care? "Guess what else? Mom? Are you listenin'?"

"Michael, honey, could you turn the sound down. I can hardly hear what your sister is saying."

Candy glared at the boy's back when he didn't respond. "Reason I'm late is, they asked me to be a cheerleader. We were practicing. Gonna have to buy a cheerleading outfit; right away. We got a game next Wednesday. Man what a trip. Okay if I go over to my friend's house after supper to study?"

"Slow down there a minute, kiddo. You any idea what a cheerleading outfit costs?"

"Mrs. Turner told us Simon's Clothing carries what we need. I'll pay you back out of my allowance."

Her mother actually snorted. "We're talking about more money than your allowance would cover in several years."

Candy felt like she'd been slapped. "But Mom . . . "

"As awkward as you are, I don't see how you expect to learn cheerleading moves. I'll bet they feel sorry for you and the fact you're new. In any case I'll have to discuss it with your father. Why don't you make supper? There are some chicken patties in the freezer. You can make some macaroni and cheese and a green salad. Maybe throw some mixed veggies into the microwave. By the way, I posted a list of chores on the bulletin board. Don't you have homework to do?

"Yeah, that's why I wanted to go over to Shannon's house. She lives right around the corner." Candy was looking at the list. There were two pages. "Oh my Gawd," she complained. "Mom? All of these?"

"You're the one who made the bargain."

* * *

At this time of year the Dalton coach would have his team members go home right after school to do their chores, or whatever, then have them return for practice. That way he wouldn't feel so pressed for time. The middle school gymnasium was cold and drafty but Coach Donnelley hardly noticed the conditions as he tried to conceal his elation when the three boys showed up for practice. Using Mark at center due of his height was okay, but he couldn't keep him in the high or low post after that. The boy was all over the court with moves like an NBA guard. This could work out for it would be confusing to the other team's defense. This kid is not only an excellent ball handler but also a deadly shooter. He seemed to have an uncanny sense of where a rebound was going and his reputation caused all the other boys to idolize him.

But, he was thinking, there is mustard on my hotdog. Mark had been right about his friends. Ollie raced up and down the floor as fast as his smaller teammates. His moves under the basket were not only quick, but as graceful as a huge NBA forward. As Mark had promised, his size made him unstoppable. With the two other boys he had been counting on and the speedy little Tarmen lad, he had the nucleus for a presentable team at Dalton Middle School for the first time since he'd taken on this responsibility.

* * *

When Mark arrived home following practice, his stepfather jumped him the second he walked in. "Where the heck have you been? I thought we had an agreement that you would paint the garage door right after school. You know I can't handle that too, I'm trying to cope with your mom. She's been damn near a basket case all week. Thank God grandma's here."

"Well gee dad, I was at basketball practice. Coach Donnelley wants me and Buzz and Ollie to play on the team this year. I'll take care of the garage door, like you know I got it wired for Saturday. I'll have more time then. Be able to do a better job. Where's Mom?"

His father was standing at the kitchen stove stirring a pot of spaghetti sauce. Dressed in Levis and a Lakers Tee shirt, he didn't bother to look back at his stepson. "You better not come up with some lame excuse for not doing it Saturday. Your mother's lying down until dinnertime. Grandma Bishop is taking a nap. How did things go at school? Kids ask you many questions? I've been keeping myself busy so I don't have time to think about it."

"Most of the kids at school chilled out 'bout it. All of the teachers told me how sorry they were. Good thing 'cause I'm not in the mood to talk about it." Mark was looking at his shoes. "Been keeping myself busy too.

"I'll tell ya Mark, this thing has hit me pretty hard. That's why I had to go to work today. I realize how horrible it's been for you, but somehow, together, we'll get through it. What's this crap about basketball practice?"

The conversation gave Mark a strange feeling and the word, 'together' came as a surprise. He was used to being ignored by his step-dad but in this case, his father's words seemed man-to-man. "Oh! Coach is trying to get us ready by next week. We're gonna play Citrus Wednesday evening. Can you come?"

Lifting the wooden spoon to his lips, he mumbled, "Needs a touch more Basil. Did you say Wednesday? Not a chance. I have Lion's Club at the Green Spot that night."

"Bummer. Couldn't you cut out this once?" Mark, trying to hide his disappointment, already knew the answer. His stepfather could care less.

"Are you kidding? I'm running for president this year so I have to be there. Anyhow, you don't have a chance against Citrus."

* * *

Candy flopped down on her bed, staring at the ceiling, mumbling aloud, "this is the pits." Grandma Swanson had told her, "anytime you have a problem . . . big or small . . . you call me . . . collect. I'll be here for you." Okay Grandma, I have a problem. Without considering the three-hour time difference she dialed the number and waited . . . and waited.

"Clara Swanson speaking."

Operator was saying something about a collect call. She interrupted. "Hi grandma, it's me, Candy."

"Yes. Yes, I'll accept the charges. Candy? Is everything all right?"

"Oh grandma, this is soooo baaad. My first day at school and I've already made a couple of friends. Then this afternoon the drama coach offered me a part in the school play. We're going to be doing The Golden Harvest."

"Slow down a minute, would you dear. I'm trying to take all this in. This is wonderful."

Thank goodness, Candy thought, she didn't say 'I told you so.' "Oh, and guess what?"

"You and Michael are good buddies?"

She snorted. "That'll be the day. No. They want me to try out for cheerleader. And do you know what else? Yesterday I had my hair done in a beauty shop. It looks exactly like Ann Margaret's."

There was such a long pause Candy asked, "Grandma? Are you still there?"

"Yes honey, I'm still here."

"I had to call and tell somebody. Nobody at our house gives a hoot. All I can say is, thank you, thank you, thank you for your help." Grandma sounded like she was crying, so very softly she told her, "I love you grandma, and I miss you."

There was another longer pause. When she came back on the line her grandmother asked, "Sweetheart, would you call grandma King . . . collect? Tell her everything you told me?"

* * *

The Man was was cruising up and down the quiet streets of Dalton going over and over the details in his mind. Man has always got to be totally prepared. He prided himself on preparation and never making a mistake. Heiny bowls in a league every Wednesday night. Seven till eleven. Leaves the misses and the little brat up there by themselves.

What I need to do is create a diversion. Maybe a fire. Not big enough to be seen from the highway. Bale of hay should do the job. Someplace out by the barn. Stick a couple of cherry bombs inside the bale to make some noise and a fire big enough to get the Kraut woman to come outside. That way the door's unlatched and I'm inside. I can use a rag with chloroform on the little brat's nose, snatch the little monster out of her bed, then out the back door and down the slope to my car that'll be hid in Sandstone Park before she even comes back in. Probably won't even check the little brat's room until it's time for momma to go to bed. In fact, probably not until old man Heinz comes home

88

from bowling. By that time . . . .
*   What the Hell, it's only fair. Another family will learn as much about agony as I have.*

CHAPTER EIGHT

Eric, always an early riser, snatched the phone from its cradle before it could disturb Julie. Ever since her mother had arrived she'd been staying in bed until Grandma woke up, usually after ten. "Good morning," he mumbled.

"Oh, hi Mr. Goodwin. This is Ollie Frazier. Is Mark up yet?"

"It's ten till six so I doubt it. Doesn't usually roll out until half past. What's up?"

"Have you seen this morning's paper?"

"Usually get the coffee perking first. Was on my way out when the phone rang."

"They're offering a reward to catch whoever killed Laura."

Eric felt his chest tighten at the mention of her name. "DGF is putting up twenty-five thousand. Other businesses have added another ten."

"Well, that's a surprise. Have to rethink my opinion of that guy Swanson. Okay Ollie, I'll let Mark know."

"No, no. Dad printed up a hundred reward posters. Mr. Swanson gave me twenty bucks to go out early this morning before school, wants me to staple them to telephone poles all over town. I thought maybe Mark would like to help."

"Mark's been somewhat withdrawn ever since . . . .. Hmmm. That's a good idea, Ollie. I'll wake him. You coming by here?"

"Naw, have him meet me at the Green Spot in about twenty. Tell him I'll spring for a couple of donuts."

"For a couple of donuts I might come myself. I'll tell him, Ollie.'"

"Oh, tell him to bring his bike."

* * *

Mark's was startled awake when his dad shook his shoulder. His first thought was, oh oh, must have done something wrong?

"Hey buddy. Roll it out. The Frazier kid called."
"Ollie? What does he want? Is he on the phone?"

"Guess he wants your help putting out a bunch of posters. The city and DGF are offering a reward. Thirty-five grand. I'd rather you don't mention anything about it to your mother."

Mark was out of bed, heading for the bathroom. Over his shoulder he asked, "Is Ollie at home?"

"I don't think so. Wants you to meet him at the Green Spot. He did mention springing for the donuts."

Mark didn't waste a second and was into his clothes in record time and as he headed for the front door he could see his stepfather pouring a cup of coffee.

"Hey Mark? Grab the paper on your way out and toss it in here."

"Sure thing, dad. Leaving the front door wide open he slipped out to pick up the morning paper. He stopped short. Mrs. Swanson, in a green robe, was walking down their drive to retrieve their paper. Something unusual for him; thinking about how good-looking she was. What held his attention was the bright red Ford in her driveway. "Wow!" he spoke loud enough for her to hear. "That's awesome." It was obviously new for it had the paper Deiter logo in the license frame.

"Good morning," she called out, looking pleased. "What do you think?"

Continuing across the street he walked around the SUV, his eyes filled with admiration. "It's awesome," he repeated. "Man. I'd give my right leg to have one like it. What do they call this color? Candy apple?"

"That's what it cost," she joshed. "an arm and a leg. Vince can have his old Lexus. This one is all mine. They call it Wild Cherry Metallic."

"It's bitchin'," he told her.

"Knowing how men are about cars, I'll take that as the ultimate compliment." She bent to pick up the paper then squinted as she checked him out. You must be Mark?"

"Yes ma'am." Something about her made him uncomfortable.

91

"You certainly don't look like the young man Candice has been telling us about. She seems to see you as some sort of a bad boy. 'Big trouble', I believe was her description."

Mark grinned sheepishly. "That's me. Bad to the bone."

She laughed with him. "Well, Mr. Bad to the bone, it's been a pleasure meeting you."

"Here too," he replied. Nice lady, he thought. Too bad Red isn't more like her.

* * *

The Man made his usual morning stop at the café about six, the morning paper under his arm in its plastic wrapper. "Thanks," he told the big kid who held the door for him. Nice boy that Ollie Frazier.

Once he was situated, his order in and a steaming cup of coffee waiting, he heard the waitress say, "I swear, the amount of sugar you dump in there, that's gotta taste like syrup."

"Same way I like my women, hot and sweet."

"And black?" She teased and moved away.

Sliding the paper out of its protective cover he spread it out on the table. "I'll be damned," he muttered, surveying the large headline. DGF OFFERS $25000 REWARD

Reading further he discovered pledges by other merchants brought the total to thirty-five thousand. His face creased in a crooked smile. Is that all I'm worth? Well, we'll see. He frowned when the Goodwin boy sauntered in heading directly to where the Frazier kid was sitting. Weird. Kid gave me the strangest look. He can't possibly suspect something? I can't even imagine why. Glancing at the two boys, he wondered. What's the Frazier kid holding up for Goodwind? I'll be damned. He's got a stack of posters. He could see the large print from where he sat. Big black letters: REWARD and below that, $35000. Once I get through with this town they'll up the ante to a million or more. He smiled again but it was more nearly a sneer.

* * *

"Man we darned straight earned our money." Mark was dressed entirely in black. Raider's T-shirt, Levis, black boots and cap. They parked their bikes in the metal rack and headed for the school. "Waste of time though."

"Why a waste of time?"

92

"What we should have put up was a poster with Frank's picture on it. 'Wanted for murder'."

"That's funny!" Ollie laughed and gave him a high five.

"See ya in a minute. Gotta hit the John." Mark was in the bathroom for some time. When he came out he went directly to his locker. Opening the door his skateboard fell out. Locating his English book he wedged the skateboard back into the jamb packed opening and then looked about for Ollie. A frown creased his forehead when he saw him down the hall. Red was next to her locker surrounded by a half-dozen seventh and eighth graders . . . and Ollie.

"Hey Ollie," he called, "C'mere a minute." Everyone looked his way then back at the redhead. Ollie said something to the bimbo who giggled as he moved away.

"What's up, Marcus." For the benefit of onlookers, they did their peculiar handshake.

"So Dude, what's going down? Saw Butch in the restroom. Tells me that his sister told him a wild story this morning. I guess the new gal and Carmelita Hoover had a run in? Somethin' 'bout Hoover going after her with a switchblade but I understand Red kicked her butt. Nutt Traster was in there too. Way he heard it was, Red kicked the crap outta Carmelita along with three of her buddies. Any idea what the real skinny is?"

"Actually I do. Didn't mention it this morning 'cause you were kinda opening up for the first time since we found your sister so I figured you needed to talk. My kid sister was there when it went down." Ollie turned toward the group of students. "Hey Jodi." The tiny girl glanced his way. He motioned for her to come, and she did in her usual animated fashion.

"Hi Mark. Did you hear about what Candy did?" She was clutching the top of her head with both hands. "You'll never believe it." Jodi was wearing white bib overalls over a paint splash T-shirt.

"I heard she and Carmelita had a showdown."

With her right arm in the air she pointed toward Candy waving a finger up and down. "Hoover was blaming Candy for taking her cheerleading job."

"Red's gonna be a cheerleader? Come on Jodi, get real.

"God's truth. Carmelita's grades took a dump so Mrs. Turner asked Candy to take her place."

"So what happened?" Jodi was so excited in the telling Mark thought she was going to wet her pants. She's nearly as bad as Ollie.

"Oh! Oh! Get this. Carmelita came right at her. Turns out Candy knows some karate stuff. Grabbed Hoover by the wrist and flipped her on her butt."

"Man, that blows my mind. Never guess by looking at her."

Jodi was waving her hands in front. "Wait. That's not all. The dummy didn't know enough to stay down. Went right after her again. Candy did some sort of spin. Gave her a karate kick right in the belly that put her in the dump. Carmelita's not even here today."

"So the new kid's turned into Sheena; Queen of the Jungle. Maybe we should send her out to find my sister's killer." As soon as the words left his mouth, Mark was thinking, what a dumb remark. He'd always liked Carmelita although not as a male/female type of thing. Didn't understand why this incident upset him so much.

* * *

Candy was back at school for her second evening of cheerleader practice. She understood that they generally practiced right after school so they'd be through by the time the basketball team came to do their thing, but tonight the gym was being used for something else so they were told to go home and return at six. Mrs. Turner had talked Mr. Donnelly into doing a half court practice so they could use the other. As she had promised Mrs. Turner, she was awkward and self-conscious, mostly due to her inexperience and nervousness.

"Candy, Candy, Candy. What I'm going to do with you. Would you loosen up?"

She sighed deeply, looking down the floor as Mark took a shot from way out by the center circle, astonished when the ball hit nothing but net. "Ah'm trying to, ma'am. I tole ya I wasn't very athletic." Candy was worried. Was she about to lose her spot on the squad? She had been so surprised to get it she wanted to keep it.

Mrs. Turner gave her a smile of encouragement. "Why are you so graceful playing basketball but here you look like a stick figure jumping around." She squinted and did something with her lips. "From what I'm hearing about this morning, I believe you've had some karate lessons."

"Yeah, bummer. Don't teach karate anyplace 'round here. Learned a couple of things when I usta live down in Montgomery."

"Very well. Much of karate is similar to dancing. Do you dance?"

"Of course. Doesn't everybody?"

"All right then, properly executed, even cheerleading is done to a rhythm. Listen to some music in your mind . . . like uh . . . the Notre Dame fight song."

The rest of the girls we're more or less faking practice moves and it was obvious they were watching the boys.
"You mean the one that goes, 'Be kind to your web footed friends?'"

"Ummm. Don't you mean Stars and Stripes Forever? The last time I heard that version I was in school. Hum it to yourself then turn your movements into a dance. Okay ladies, let's all try it. For our next session I'll bring my CD player."

* * *

As the boys came out of the shower, Mark told his buddies, "Coach sure rides us hard, don't he. An hour and a half, full bore. Dark already and I got to head straight for home."

"Bummer," groaned Ollie. "See ya sometime tomorrow, I guess." They high-fived and the big lad turned to look at Buzz. What do you say Buzzard? Want to head over to the Pit? Me? I'm aching for a malt."

"Don't have to ask me twice."

"I'm gonna have to eat and run," Buzz told Ollie. "Told my folks I'd be home before eight."

"Yeah. I'd better hurry it up too." Ollie stretched out so that the two boys took up an entire booth. "I wanted to check out what you thought about Marcus. I can't figure the guy out. Seems to me like he's blocking what happened to his sister out of his mind. Talked to him this morning when he and I were out putting up all those posters. But other than that . . . "

Buzz shrugged, the malt leaving a pale, tan moustache on his black lip. "I don't know how I'd handle it if it was me. Saw the posters offering thirty-five big ones. Wouldn't it be something if you or me could find out who done it?"

95

"Sure glad the Pit hasn't put in one of those stupid soft-serve machines. These old-fashioned malts are super. Mark is dead set that the killer is sheriff Frank."

"I know he does, and I say, no way. Frank isn't the type. Only thing is, can't convince Mark who simply doesn't want to talk about it."

"Crap, Buzz. I've tried and tried to get him to talk about it. Keeps evading the subject. Did dump on me while we were riding around this morning. Talks kinda wild. You know, like he wants to be the one to catch the guy who done it. Even Miss Bailey, the school counselor, flagged me down. Suggested I try to get him to open up about it. I guess she had him in for consultation but as soon as she mentioned Laura's name he cut out."

"I reckon she thinks since you're his best friend, you probably have the number one shot of dragging him out of his shell."

Both boys were tipping their malted milk containers above their upturned faces to try and get the last drops. "Maybe. Got a couple of problems though. Something like that takes some special training. And number two, I've been having my own nightmares ever since I found her." He looked at his Mickey Mouse wristwatch then out the window. "Geez, its dark already. Come on, let's boogie, I'll walk with you as far as the power company."

* * *

Mrs. Turner had been right, Candy was thinking as she headed for home. I've started to get into it. She had planned on walking with Shannon for her mother thought if there was any chance this killer remained in the area, girls should always walk in pairs. I mean, like you know. That guy is long gone. But Reverend White picked his daughter up right after practice so she was on her own. Heather had been waiting for her mother to pick her up so she'd stayed for a while with her blond friend and Jodi to run through some of the moves a few more times. It was about fifteen minutes later that Mrs. Deiter showed up and they'd all left.

It was about six blocks home and she was heading down Forest drive to the alley that ran between the city parking lot and the Dalton Bank where she stopped. What a week this has been so far. Man, was I ever wrong, she thought. Moving to Dalton has been the best thing to ever happen to her.

Staring into the murky passageway she very nearly didn't turn into the alley. It was filled with sinister shadows and gloomy recesses. Her mother's remark about the danger of girls walking alone had her thinking about Mark's little sister and her unknown killer. She made the turn intending to use the alley as a short cut. From what she'd heard, guy had to be a real sicko. She shuddered and glanced about uneasily and it felt like the hair on her arms was sticking straight up. There was the feeling that she was being watched, being followed. She increased her pace. It was dark all the way to Cedar Avenue but she could cut across the City parking lot and once she was by the Power Company the whole block was lit up. No problem; cut through there and be a block from home.

Sensing a movement to her right she tensed, peering into the shadows of an oleander bush, steeling herself, ready to run. A scruffy black cat launched itself past her legs. She yelped, leaping back in return. "Phew! Just a dumb ole cat."

Her heart was racing and she was unaware of the two guys who moved from within the dark depression created by a pair of dumpsters behind the thrift store. Before she could react one stood at each side, grasping her by her arms.

"Right on!" Came the sound of a voice.

Candy peered into the shadows toward the voice that sounded as though it was coming from a bucket of gravel. Straight ahead was the leering face of Carmelita Hoover.

* * *

Getting dark earlier and earlier, Frank thought. Instead of going home, he headed for the Lucky Lady. He'd called his daughter, Joyce, and told her she'd have to fix dinner for the troops. Told her he'd catch a bite downtown. Something had been festering in his mind all day and he was pondering a remark the Goodwin kid had made out at the cemetery.

Pushing through the double doors of the Lucky Lady he wanted to grab a quick bite to eat and then maybe a brew or two before heading for home.

"Hey Frank, how's it goin'?" Paul Traster, six foot ten and skinny as a telephone pole, called out to him. He could see that Traster, Doc Snyder and Curly Ferguson were eating chilidogs and having a couple of cold ones.

"Got things under control," he let them know, the fourth chair creaking in protest as he sat, leaning with his elbows on the table.

"How's the Goodwin case coming?" Doc asked.

"Me and Ralph are working on it full time. 'Spect to make an arrest any day." He'd never been involved in any type of murder investigation but he'd seen enough of how it was done on TV shows to at least steer him in the right direction.

"Does the little woman know you're out honky tonkin'?" Curly asked.

"Had to go over to Cotton. Her mother's sick. Some kinda virus, I guess."

"You been bragging all week about how you got suspects and all that crap." Traster emptied half his mug of beer in one big gulp. "This town wants to see some action."

"Frank," Doc Snyder's eyes were drawn to mere slits under his white brows. "I think you should bring in some help. I keep tellin' you, you're in over your head."

"Bull pucky," the sheriff snapped, holding his thumb and forefinger about a half inch apart. "I'm that close. Police work ain't sittin' behind a desk, you know. There's a lot of legwork and dozens of people to talk to. Man's gotta have ironclad proof before he makes his move." He ordered a couple of chilidogs and a beer while thinking how much these guys were getting under his skin. Fortunately no one asked how he could carry on such a thorough investigation from his three favorite hangouts, The Green Spot Cafe, Dalton Bowling Alley or the Lucky Lady Bar.

In an unusual move for him he finished his chilidogs and one beer and then left. He'd made a decision. As far as he was concerned his calculations had been quite conclusive. There was someone who might provide some answers. He located Walter Jordan, the town retard, at the bowling alley. Placing a hand on the boy's shoulder, he squeezed, "Walter, I want you to come down to the station with me. Like to ask you some questions."

"Sure Mr. Frank. Oh boy! Do I get to ride in the police car?"

Walter was thirty-two and it seemed the boy had been roaming the city streets forever. If anybody hung around the kids more than Walter did, it certainly wasn't obvious. The Sher-

98

iff was happy that Marion had asked for the afternoon off for he didn't want her to hear him interrogating the man. Walter nearly stumbled when he shoved him in the back as they went through the glass door. The office was empty. Ralph must be out on patrol, he thought.

"How come you push me, Mr. Frank? I ain't did nuttin', you know."

What was it Doc mentioned about Walter? The kid was spastic or something. Sometimes passed out and would fall down. Seemed to always hit the same spot on his head. Had a permanent goose egg on his right temple. "Walter, I am sure you killed that little girl." He thought no such thing but he was hoping Walter might have seen something or someone. All he needed was to jog his memory.

"Oh no, Mr. Frank. Laura was my friend, I would never hurt someone as nice as Laura."

"Yeah?" His voice was filled with sarcasm. "I'll just bet she was." Again he shoved the smaller man roughly into a chair then grabbed a handful of his Dodger's sweatshirt. "Where were you Saturday night?"

"Saturday? Oh, you know, tomorrow be Saturday, Mr. Frank."

"I mean Saturday night a week ago, stupid."

"Uh, you mean like last Saturday."

"That's exactly what I mean. Tell me where you were last Saturday night."

"Oh . . . sure. I 'member. Went to the show. That's why I' member last Saturday. Saw the Ninja Dalmatians. Did you see it? Boy! It was cool. Fire department had this dog . . . "

"Where did you go after the show?"

"After the show? I was walking. I like to walk, you know."

"Did you happen to see anyone?"

He had to ponder on that for a while. "I seen Miss Maxar's dog. Pookie likes to walk with me, you know."

"Miss Maxar? Then you were walking out by Quarry Road, right?"

"Yep. I mean, yes sir, Mr. Frank. You're pulling my shirt, Mr. Frank. It hurts."

"Sorry Walter. This whole thing has got me kinda tense."

He released his hold on the cloth. "I'm trying to help you remember. If you keep going down Quarry Road it leads to Lone Pine Trail. Were you walking on Lone Pine Trail Saturday night?" My God, he thought, where is this leading?

"I walk out Lone Pine sometimes. It's close to three mile."

"Were you out there Saturday night?"

"I don't think so. I don't rightly 'member. Doc Snyder says I be sick sometimes."

"I want you to listen to me Walter, this is very important. Did you get sick Saturday night?"

"Uh . . . I don't 'member. When I get sick I don't 'member what I done."

"Oh my God," Frank whispered. "Oh my God." He couldn't believe what was happening. "Walter, Saturday night you got sick, didn't you. And while you were sick you killed Laura Goodwin, isn't that right."

"Oh no!" Walter declared. "Oh no, Mr. Frank. You gotta help me 'member."

The boy was beginning to shake like some sort of fit was coming on. Frank stood with open hands. Then Walter began to bawl.

* * *

"Let me go," Candy snapped, trying to jerk her arms free but the two boys tightened their grips. Carmelita Hoover had moved forward until her nose touched Candy's chin.

"I wantcha ta meet my brothers. Husky one they call Duke. Short one is Bugsy. They gonna hold ya while I rearrange your face. See how Miss America looks without any teeth."

Candy's mind was racing. Did she know enough Karate to get her out of this jam? All her training had been one on one. The thought of being hurt terrified her. She cringed as her rival drew back her arm, the hand balled into a tight fist. Okay. Use the grip on her arms for leverage. When she lunges, pull up then plant both feet in her mid-section. The momentum should make it possible for her to catch the big guy between the legs on the way back. As she began her move she tried to turn her head in case the fist connected. She couldn't for at that moment the one called Duke laced his fingers in her hair.

"Wha . . . Who?" asked Carmelita as her wrist was caught

100

in mid-swing by a large hand.

Candy could see Buzz Tarmen and Ollie Frazier standing behind Carmelita.

"You punks better let go of our sister," Duke snarled pulling at Candy's hair until she winced.

"You let go of the redhead," Ollie told him, "unless you two dorks think you can take me and Buzz."

The eyes of the one called Bugsy betrayed what he thought as he looked at the small black boy. In his hand was a small but menacing knife. Candy felt her right arm come free as Bugsy stepped away with both hands up like someone was pointing a gun at him.

Carmelita kicked out catching Ollie in the shin with her heavy boot. He danced about on one leg while managing to keep his grip on her wrist. Twisting fiercely he pulled down until she was forced to her knees. "What do you say, Duke? A couple of high school big shots, you should be able to take a pair of eighth graders."

"Aw come on, Frazier." He too let Candy go. She rubbed at both her arms. "We weren't gonna do nothing. All we wanted to do was to put the scare on her."

"In a pig's eye. You best not touch her again, if you get my meaning. And that goes for you too, gangster babe. Now vamoose." The trio was gone. "You okay, Candy?"

"Yeah, Ollie, I'm fine. Thanks for your help. Was just about ready to take all three of 'em out." At least it sounded good. She was in fact trembling.

* * *

"No! You are not going over to Ollie's first thing in the morning."

Mark was flaked out on the couch to watch TV. He tilted his head back to look up at his step-dad who was glaring at him.

"You promised to paint the garage door in the morning and I'm holding you to it."

"Well gee whiz, won't take that long. I've got all day."

"Tomorrow morning!" The phone rang. Mark glanced toward the sound. "Don't try to weasel of it," his step-dad snatched up the instrument. "Hello!" . . . "Yeah Ollie, he's here. Mark, it's for you." Placing his hand over the mouthpiece he told him, "If this is about tomorrow, tell him you'll see him after lunch. Must be important, kid can hardly talk."

Making a face, he took his time getting unwound from the couch pillows, taking the phone from his dad's hand as he turned to move into the den. Mark glanced at the clock. Seven after eight. Knowing how Ollie was, he grinned. "Hey Dude. What's up?"

"I just this minute walked in. Dad just got a phone call."

"Gee guy, thanks for sharing that with me."

"W-w-wait. Too late to be in tomorrow's paper."

"Calm down, Ollie. What's gonna be in the paper?"

"I didn't want to tell your dad 'cause you better do that. They arrested Weird Walter."

"Arrested Weird Walter? Whatever for?" It wasn't hard to figure out why.

"Guess he's the guy who killed your sister."

Mark was speechless. After a long-long pause he replied, "No way!"

* * *

The Man was frantically going through his house. Where in the Devil did I put my good watch? Usually leave it on my dresser but it isn't there. Would have missed it earlier but I only wear it when I'm going out on Saturday, like I am today, and of course always on Sundays. Let me think back. Last Saturday? When I was hauling the body out Lone Pine Trail I'm sure I wasn't wearing it then. Think! Think! If I did, maybe I took it off in the SUV. Yeah, probably did, knowing there was going to be blood. Maybe dropped down in between the seat and the console. I'll back it outside so I can get a good clear look.

Moving toward the garage he was thinking, stupid sheriff has arrested Weird Walter. Isn't that a crock? Man has cottage cheese instead of a brain. Weird Walter? As if he could plan anything as clever as this. It was bad enough when he suspected the Goodwin kid. That fat ass has about as much business in the sheriff's boots as I would being the Pope. If it wasn't that his brother is mayor he wouldn't even have that job. Oh well, Weird Walter serves a purpose. Makes Frank feel good thinking he's a big time criminal investigator. Wrong man, Frank. And you'll know soon enough. And I mean soon. Wednesday night. Is that soon enough for ya, Frank? Won't even bother to tell Walter

102

he's sorry when he finds out he's wrong. He backed the black SUV out into the drive to begin searching. He was on his hands and knees, peering under the seats and into any cavity where it could have hidden. Sure don't see that watch. Man, I've lost it somewhere. Wonder if it could have fallen behind the dresser? I'd better go in and take that bedroom apart. It's a loose end and I don't like loose ends.

CHAPTER NINE

Mark was high up on the ladder putting a few additional dabs of paint into the nearly inaccessible corner of the eaves where the hip rafters met.

"Man that looks awesome," Ollie told him as he stood in the driveway with a paintbrush in one hand.

"Damn betcha. Dad's gonna flip when he sees we did all the trim too. You got a big smear of blue paint on your right cheek."

Picking up a wet rag Ollie daubed at it. "Gotta admit the whole garage looks better with the tan door and the blue trim, only you may have dug up a can of worms. Next he'll want you to do the house."

"For a price, dude, for a price."

For the first hour, while they were painting, they yakked and yakked about the arrest of Weird Walter and about how Mark's dad and mom had reacted. Mark could think of a hundred reasons why Walter wasn't the one. It was hard to tell what Ollie believed but even his folks didn't seem to accept it. Ollie was one of those guys who always took the opposite side of every argument, so Mark had the feeling he hadn't been able to convince his friend.

"Oh! By the way, you'll never guess what happened last night."

"You won the Lottery?"

"Don't I wish?" Ollie, in his usual excited, animated fashion told him about the encounter with Carmelita and her brothers.

Mark took off his cap, ran his fingers through his long blond hair, then told him, "That stupid redhead is gonna end up with knots on her head. Even I know better than to mix it up with the Hoover family. They don't take these things lying down. You know what I'd like to do, Ollie?"

"I don't know about you, but I'd like to ask that little red-head out to a movie or something."

"You gotta be kiddin'. Wouldn't take that twerp to the city dump."

Ollie shrugged. "I like her. Anyway, I'd kinda like to get me a girlfriend. Heck, Bad Frank has a gal, Rubin has a gal, Buzz is going with Shannon. I mean, man, Candy's pretty darned cute. Like Jodi was saying, she looks like Ann Margaret. Heck, she's better lookin' than Ann Margaret and she's got the best lookin' legs in the world."

Mark made a face. "Yeah, great legs. Reach all the way to the ground. And Ann Margaret? Isn't she the old redheaded gal who played in Grumpy Old Men? Get real! No way she looks like her. Only Ann Red looks like is Orphan Annie."

"I don't mean the way she looks today. Annie was a real fox when she played in flicks like Bye Bye Birdie and State Fair."

Mark was busy washing out the paintbrushes. "Never heard of either one of those movies. Before my time, I reckon."

"Yeah! Hundred years ago. Jodi's the one who brought up the subject. Anyway, like I was sayin', I like her."

First it was Buzz getting the hots for Shannon and now Ollie is getting the itch. Don't understand what the big deal is. Not only that but the redhead pissed him off. Like to find a way to get back at her. "Not me baby. If you are so intense for a girlfriend why don't you hook up with the Deiter gal? She's got the hots for you. Starts drooling every time she sees you."

"Heather? She's . . . Are you nuts? She's being friendly. I don't think . . . you really think so? You know what? She does kinda turn me on. Maybe I'll check her out too. Man can't have too many women. Hey man, let's take a ride down to the Pit and grab a burger and a coke."

"Hey Dude, cool; only you gotta quit reading my mind."

They rode their bikes up the same alley where Candy had her encounter the night before. It would take them to The Burger Pit's back entrance. "You ain't spoke two words all the way down here," Ollie jerked up on his bike so that it jumped a pothole. "What's on your mind?"

"Been thinking 'bout my sister's murder a lot the past

week."

"Oh?" They turned into the driveway at the Burger Pit. "You sure ain't been saying much about it. Don't you think it would do you some good to talk about it with me, or whoever?"

"You know what I wan'na do, Ollie? Hey, watch this," Mark grinned as he turned into the Drive-thru, stopping at the speaker, trying to be cute. To his surprise a female voice asked, "welcome to Kelly's Burger Pit. How may I help you?"

"Double double burger, fries and a large coke." Mark thought he was being clever as he continued, "That's to go."

"That will be three seventy seven at the first window please."

All the money he had was stuffed into his pocket and he dug it out. "You got a quarter to spare, Ollie?"

"What did you do with the ten bucks? Spend it already?" "Naw, I put it away."

"Okay, I got a quarter. You already owe me two bucks from last Saturday."

"Get my allowance tomorrow."

"Hey Mark, ain't we gonna eat inside?" Moving up to the speaker he placed his order.

"You know what I want to do, Ollie?"

"Ain't got a clue."

"Let's eat while we ride. I dread thinking about this . . . gonna have to force myself to do it . . . but I want to go back out to that place to have a look around. Something I need to check out."

"What place you talking about?"
Mark could tell his friend already knew what place he referred to.

"You mean that place?"

"Exactly what I mean. When I was sitting out there waiting for you to come back from the phone I was pretty much in outerspace 'cause I didn't want to look at Laura. I saw what he did to her but I also saw something else but can't remember what. Something that I know was important."

"Marcus, I'm not following your line of thought. Why bother. Sheriff already has Walter in jail. Why not let it drop?"

Mark snorted. "Ollie, think about it. That jerk arrested Weird Walter of all things. Our so called sheriff has gone off the

106

deep end this time."

"Marcus, Marcus, Marcus! Give it up. Let's get back to enjoying life. Right? We got to split twenty bucks for riding our bikes for a hundred miles to get those reward posters all hung up and then the sheriff makes an arrest. What a bummer. Looks to me like it's all over, Dude. Weird Walter? Who would have thunk it? Hey! Let's ride over to the school and shoot some baskets. Maybe we can scratch up a game."

"I'm tellin' ya, Ollie, use your noodle. Weird Walter didn't do it."

"I don't know how you can argue with the fact they got a confession."

With a look of disgust Mark told him, "Think about it. Knowing how Frank operates, he probably talked Walter into thinking he did it, or beat him with a rubber hose. Sheriff is only trying to cover his own ass. I know that somehow the sheriff is involved. He's so eager to make an arrest he doesn't even question how Walter might of done it. Tell me this, Ollie. How would Walter manage to take Laura's body three miles out in the country? He can't drive. Doesn't even ride a bike. Walter liked Laura and she thought he was nice and that he was funny."

"Well. She was little. He could have carried her. If you don't think he did it, then what's your plan? Are you of a mind to find out who did it yourself?"

"Ollie, the way our sheriff is handling this thing, we gotta do something. If it's him or not, I'm going to do everything I can to find out who did it."

"Okay man, can't hurt to take a look, only today is my turn to be Superman. You can be Jimmy the Boy Reporter. I'll let you tag along for your big break in getting a scoop."

"Superman on a bike?"

"Why not? Watch me make this thing fly."

The two boys ate their lunch as they rode, at times pedaling without touching the handlebars. As a result it took nearly twenty minutes to ride out Lone Pine Trail to the location. At one point Mark called out, "You know what, Ollie? It's rather strange, but the horrible feeling I had all last week seems to have lightened up. What I'm feeling is a terrible hatred."

They continued to ride until Mark skidded to a halt about a

hundred feet short. Ollie nearly crashed into him, actually laying his bike down and sitting on it as he slid to a stop. "Hold up!" Mark whispered loudly.

"Whatcha trying to do kill me?"

"There's somebody there ahead of us. Looks like three guys."

Ollie looked. There were three ten speeds sitting in the exact spot they had parked theirs nearly a week ago. "What the heck?"

"Wonder who they are? Wonder what they're doing out here?"

Ollie studied the bikes then told him, "I know who two of them are. Recognize that old blue bomb. Belongs to Shannon and that new one is my sister's. Ain't never seen the old beat up maroon boys bike."

"I have."

All three had water bottles and small tote bags. The yellow police tape Frank had stretched between two trees was loose and flying like a kite tail from the juniper on the right. When they reached the bottom of the embankment they found Shannon, Jodi and the redhead nosing about the place. Mark looked the three girls over. Ollie's sister was standing on the same boulder where he had perched waiting for the sheriff. Red was wearing a green and white striped sun-suit. There were dirt and grass stains on the seat to indicate she'd followed the sheriff's example by sliding down the slope. A red baseball cap was perched on her head with her hair coming out through the opening in the back. On the front of the cap in white letters was the word 'BAMA'. He hadn't reached the stage where he'd notice how shapely a girls legs might be, he was only aware of what a stark white hers were compared to Shannon's.

Ollie spoke first. "Hi good lookin'," he grinned at Candy. "Hey sis, what's going down?"

Mark stood with his thumbs hooked in his front pockets, somberly eyeing the bush where Laura had been found. Moving away he acknowledged the threesome. "Hi Shannon." There was a small wave toward Jodi on the rock. "Well Red? What are you three birds doing out here? Trying to solve a crime?"

* * *

"Hey Frank, congratulations. Good job." John Frazier, Ollie's father, came barging into the sheriff's office followed by Kim Kamamoto, the local photographer. "I'd like to get an interview for Sunday's paper."

Glowing, the sheriff told him, "I caught the sucker."

"You sure did. Town's been tied up in knots for a week but we can relax. What led you to Walter Jordan?"

"There was a number of things I was already on to. Had my suspicions right from the start. Can't talk about specifics at this time. You know, 'till after the trial."

Marion, sitting at her desk was shaking her head. "Never in my wildest dreams did I believe it would be Walter. He's so mild mannered and seems to get along so well with all the kids."

"Well it's him alright. Got me a confession. Taped the whole thing."

"Oh that's right," agreed Mr. Frazier. "Walter doesn't know how to read or write."

"Sure don't. Amazing thing is how he is a genius in remembering all these statistics regarding every ball player in the Major Leagues."

"You got that right," Marion smiled, "but he has no concept about money. Would mow lawns all day for fifteen cents. Everybody in town liked him so something like this comes as a complete surprise."

"Will he be able to stand trial?" Kamamoto spoke for the first time.

Frazier was gesturing. "How 'bout standing over next to Marion's desk like you were revealing some fact to her. I'll have Kim get a couple of shots."

"Like this, huh? No reason why he can't stand trial. Walter is as sane as you or me when he isn't having one of his spells. In any case, he's gonna be put away for a long time."

* * *

"What is there," the redhead snapped, "about the word Candy you don't understand? You some sorta retard?"

"Hey, candy I understand. It's sweet and chewy, which no way fits you. Sticky maybe." Mark forced a laugh but it didn't show in his eyes. "So why are you guys out here?"

"I hate you," she snapped under her breath. "Your T-shirt

says it all." She read the words aloud. "'Bad to the bone'. Boy does that fit." She had been thinking about Mark ever since she learned about the murder. Never having known anyone who had been murdered or had a close family member killed, she couldn't begin to imagine what it would be like. How would she feel if someone kidnapped and killed Michael?

"Mostly morbid curiosity," Shannon told him. "Jodi's dad was talking to my dad about the Sheriff arresting Weird Walter and my dad was wondering how Walter would manage to haul your sister out here."

Mark shuddered but didn't answer for it was nearly an echo of what he had told Ollie.

"Yeah," Shannon continued. "Dad talked about this place so we decided to take a ride and when we saw the police tape we decided to take a peek. That's where they found her, isn't it?"

Candy glanced up at Jodi who called down from where she was standing on the rock. "Guess you must be pretty happy that they caught the killer, huh Mark?"

"Two of a kind. You think exactly like your brother. I happen to know they do not have the killer."

Mark's remark made Candy curious. "But this guy, Weird Walter, confessed."

"And ain't that a joke? Walter has a mind like a batch of Silly Putty. All he needs is somebody like our fantastic sheriff pumping enough crap in there; next thing you know Walter thinks it's his idea. Like I been tellin' you guys, I have countless reasons that convince me the killer could be the sheriff. Right this minute I got something I need to do."

Candy squinted as she watched him. His last few words made her inquisitive. "So, why are you and Ollie back out here?"

Ollie shrugged. "Personally Candy, I was out looking for you. Hey babe! When you gonna ask me out?"

She was beginning to like the big lad. He was cute.

"In your dreams. You're the kinda guy that would probably want to spend all evening at the Pit loading up on cheeseburgers and I'd have to pay."

"Ha ha! Aren't we funny? Mark thinks he remembered seeing something. Might be an important clue, only he doesn't remember what or where."

110

She noticed that Mark continued to avoid the bush where Laura was found.

"Yeah. Thought if I came back out here, maybe wandered around, might see it again. Maybe sit on the same rock where I waited for the sheriff and have it come back to me."

"Oh?" Shannon inquired. "You're saying you saw something that might help the sheriff find the real killer? Like they say on TV, 'A missing piece to the puzzle?'"

"Shannie! Our sheriff couldn't find the killer if he was sitting on the guy."

"Me and Mark," Ollie explained, "are gonna work on this mystery. We got some ideas."

"And I'll tell ya this for sure," Mark walked directly to the bush. Candy could see him clinch his fists. There were a couple smudges of dried blood in the parched soil. "If we find anything we sure aren't going to give it to the sheriff."

The whole idea intrigued Candy. Excitement was showing in her eyes as she asked, "Is it okay . . . I mean, do you mind if we help?" She was wondering what made Mark so sure Weird Walter wasn't the killer.

"Heck, knock yourself out. You guys can't do any worse than our local law men."

"This place isn't even roped off or anything," Ollie told him. "I'll bet that jug-head hasn't even been back out here."

Candy watched, when in spite of his size, Ollie made his way to the top of the huge boulder. Pushing his sister off he stood on top like he was king on the mountain.

"Jerk." Jodi glared up at him.

"Okay." Mark folded his arm and looked at the group. "You guys insist on helping . . . here's what I want you to do. Start right here, where Ollie and I found Laura. Go over the ground inch by inch. Anything you find . . . anything at all, I want it." From his rear pocket he produced a handful of Zip-loc, plastic, sandwich bags and passed them around. "This is the way they do on CSI on TV."

Candy studied Mark as he moved to the bush. He drew back, closing his eyes, trembling slightly. She also could see small stains of blood spotting the gravel and it made her shudder. At that moment Ollie jumped down off the boulder. She joined the other teenagers who fanned out in all directions in a sweeping motion. They went at it for a long time, deadly serious.

It was Mark who finally asked, "so what do we got?" Candy looked grim. She didn't know why but each of the kids had been handing the baggies to her. "So far, the total of all the clues sure ain't much. Let's see. Lots of scraps of paper, a cigarette wrapper, Winstons, couple of butts, some pieces of a magazine, older than dirt, and a small sticker that looks like a price tag. She handed these things to Mark. Each item was in a baggie. She watched him study each package, thinking about a problem she had similar to Mark's. Her mind told her she too had spotted something; when they first got here. What and where? Thinking that Walter was probably the killer had made it unimportant at the time. With Mark saying, 'No way,' and all of them looking for clues, whatever it was became a burning issue. Wonder if I saw it when I slid down the embankment. She glanced at the slope, trying to remember where she came down. Can't tell from here. She jerked when she heard Mark exclaim.

"I got it! I got it. It's coming back." He was again standing in front of Laura's bush. "I remember the two cops looking under this sage brush. Ralph grabbed a branch and it broke off and he shoved it into the bush. That's why I couldn't spot what I thought I'd seen."

It was easy for Candy to tell which branch since there was an eighteen inch round spot of dead leaves. Mark reached down, grasped a handful of twigs and pulled it out.

Ollie moved alongside. "What'cha got, Mark?" Both boys had dropped to their hands and knees. A dark cloud moved across the sun. Candy was thinking how ominous it made the area feel as the three of them crowded around the boys.

"Walla! Look at that. Must have seen this when they were looking at Laura."

Candy found herself pressed against Mark's back trying to see between the two men. Through the opening from where Mark had removed the broken branch she could see a patch of blow sand. Directly in the center of the six-inch wide by eighteen inch long drift was a clearly defined footprint.

"Dress shoe," he volunteered. "And it's pretty fresh. Hardly any sand has blown in it."

Candy wormed her way between Mark and Ollie, peering at the impression, her hair hiding her face. She could tell, even though the tall lad frowned at her intrusion, he was totally freaked out by his discovery.

Mark used a finger, not touching the sand, to point out details. "The sole is smooth, like leather, but look at the heel. See this? Got a ridge running all the way around 'bout half an inch in from the edge. Then look, right in the center is this imprint that looks like a bat."

"I'd say it is supposed to be an eagle," Shannon was holding the branches to one side.

"A Vampire bat?" Candy turned, moved away from the group, intently staring toward the slope. She needed to have a look. "My mouth is as dry as sandpaper. Going up to my bike to get my water bottle. Anybody want me to fetch theirs?"

"Bring mine," Shannon called after her. "Hey Mark, if you think the sheriff did it, somehow we need to get a look at his shoes."

Candy had no problem clambering up the slope. The difficulty was the return trip down. Looking it over carefully she picked the spot she was sure she'd used before. Again she sat on her rear, using her feet and the sides of her hands, while clutching the water bottles, to inchworm her way down. She could see Mark intently studying the footprint.

"I want to etch this thing in my memory," he screwed up his face as though deep in thought. "Wish we had some of whatever it is the police use to make an impression and Shannon is right. We need to see what kind of shoes the sheriff wears."

"Plaster of Paris," Ollie told him. "Got some at home. We could come back out." Reaching further under the bush he came out with an empty beer can, handling it by inserting his finger in the hole. "Don't want to smear the prints. Fairly fresh and there's a splash of liquid in it." He handed Mark the can.

"Looks as though the guy liked Budweiser. You're right. Could be prints. Wonder what it is they use to make them show up?"

"Probably could go on-line and find out. But then we'd have to snatch something with Frank's prints on it."

Shannon looked at Jodi who was perched on the rock again.

113

"Doesn't prove much," she told them. "Most likely stepped in the sand when he was looking at the crime scene."

"No way," snapped Mark. "That print was there long before he and Ralph showed up."

Candy was nearly to the bottom of the embankment when she squealed.

"What's up Red?"

She could see Mark squinting his eyes at the afternoon sun and she replied, "I've found something." Jodi leaped down from the rock. All four teenagers moved to crowd around her. She was digging dog fashion at the rocks and dirt.

"What is it?" The tension was obvious in Mark's voice.

"Don't know yet. Think I could have found another important clue; something metal and shiny." She pulled the object free.

"It's a watch," said Ollie. "A man's wristwatch. Like wow. First the footprint and then the watch, we got us some clues."

"Any idea whose it is?" Jodi reached out to touch it.

Candy handed it to Mark. "Does our sheriff wear a watch like this?"

"I've never seen one like it," said Mark. "It's running. Looks expensive. I'll bet those are real diamonds all the way around the face."

"Uh . . . " Shannon hesitated. "My Dad has one like that. It is expensive."

Mark turned to look at the black gal. "Pretty rich piece of jewelry for a man of God, don't you think?"

"Oh?" Candy was intrigued. "That's right, your father's a preacher.

"That he is," Mark grinned. "A Bible thumping, Hell and brimstone, leader of his flock, if you believe in that sort of crap."

"Don't you believe in Gawd?" Candy asked.

"I don't know what I believe anymore. I guess I do, but what kind of God would let such a thing happen to my sister?"

"Well, He . . . "

"What kind of God creates a monster that would find pleasure in doing something so vile?"

"I certainly don't have any answers," Candy told him, feeling more and more attached to this boy she was convinced she didn't care for. "But I know this. He has to answer to Gawd for what he's done."

"If I find him, he will have to answer to me, that my friends, I guarantee."

Candy turned toward Shannon whose face looked like it was covered with dark chalk. "What's wrong, Shannon." She was trembling.

"Oh my God. Oh my God. My dad's watch is missing. Told us he lost it. But that's not all."

Candy had moved next to her friend, slipping an arm about her. "Shannie? What are you trying to say?"

"My dad probably hates kids more than the sheriff does, especially little girls. 'Spawns of the Devil' he calls them.

* * *

Frank and Doc Snyder were having a cup of coffee before the sheriff went home for the evening. Officer Porter came ambling in, giving Doc a salute.

"Saw your car out front," he told Frank. "Thought I'd grab a bite for our prisoner to eat."

"Set yer ass down, Ralph. Buy you a cuppa coffee."

The three men chatted for a few minutes about the case, about Walter Jordon in particular. Frank looked up at a group of people who were leaving. "Hey Ralph, have you noticed lately how many fat women there are?"

"Trying to keep up with you, Frank," Doc told him.

Ralph was nodding in agreement. "What I've noticed is how many fat kids there are. I'm talkin' 'bout kids nine, ten, eleven years old."

"You're right, Ralph." Doc was waving his coffee cup at Peggy. "Most of the teenagers look pretty fit, but the youngsters don't get any exercise anymore. Sit in front of the TV and stuff their faces."

"Damn brats these days want to be driven everywhere they go. Even if it's only a couple of blocks to the store." Frank had his cup in the air too. Peggy spotted them and nodded. "I agree though, the teenagers in Dalton look pretty good."

"You know why?" asked Doc. "Because they are active. They walk and use their bikes the way we had to when we were kids."

"Yeah," Frank nodded. "Even seen some of 'em riding their bikes all the way out Lone Pine Trail. 'Bout noontime was out investigating a fender bender on Quarry Road. That dumb jerk Lloyd Parker was talkin' on his cell phone. Made a left turn into the quarry. Old lady Maxar hit the passenger side. Man was she mad. Thought she was gonna croak."

"These kids?' asked Ralph. "How many? What were they up to?"

"No idea. Was writing up the accident when I heard this gigglin'. Saw these three gals on their bikes turnin' off Quarry Road onto Lone Pine Trail. 'Bout the time I was finishing my report, here comes a couple of boys on their bikes. No idea what they were up to but to. Probably nosing around the crime scene I'd suspect."

"Typical kids. Most likely curious 'bout that place where we found the body," Ralph turned to look at the waitress. "Hi Peggy. How's it going?"

"Kinda quiet for a Saturday. Is coffee all you want, Ralph?"

"Make me a burger and fries to go, Sweetie. Weird Walter has to eat too, ya know.

Doc grinned up at Peggy as she filled their cups then left, calling out toward the kitchen, "Burger and fries to go."

Frank continued. "Well, same as you, Ralph, I would have thought they were kinda curious . . . 'til I noticed they were being led by that Goodwin kid."

"Probably looking for clues like you should have been doin'." Doc chckled. "Guess they haven't heard about Walter yet."

"Most likely not. Too late last night to make today's paper but it'll be all over town tomorrow. As for the murder site, me and Ralph looked it over real good. There weren't any clues out there. Hey Doc! We got this thing under control. Last thing we need is a bunch of teenyboppers nosing around. They start snooping in places where they ain't wanted. First chance I get I'll put the fear of God in 'em."

* * *

Mark's step-dad took him totally by surprise when he poked his head inside the room and told him, "By the way Mark, that blue trim on the garage looks great. You boys did a nice job."

Compliments from his dad were so rare, Mark felt himself

glow all over. "Yeah . . . well. Thought it would jazz it up."

"Makes the trim on the house look kinda shabby. We'll have to talk about that. Get back to your studies."

He was gone. Ollie was right. Knew that was coming. Having a hard time concentrating on this homework 'cause all evening I been mulling over the afternoon's events. The gang had rode their bikes back into town, gabbing all the way about how they ought to handle things. Then he and Ollie had picked up the bag of plaster of Paris along with a plastic milk jug full of water and rode back out to the site. Ollie would cup his hands where Mark mixed together the powder and water. Had to make about four batches to totally fill the impression but it was worth it. The resulting cast was perfect. So . . . what next?

The gang had found a number of possible clues if he knew how to use them. But the watch and the footprint were definite finds only where the heck do we start?

* * *

Damn, I sure wish I could have found that watch. Might find it somewhere in the house, but this isn't like me. I always have everything organized; planned out. That's why I know there is no way for Frank to ever find out that it's me. It's time, and I can hardly wait to punish another person on my list. Wednesday night and it's the Kraut family's turn. What was the name of their little brat? Gretchen? Yeah, Kraut name. Gretchen Heinz. Well Gretchen honey, Wednesday is your big day. And mine.

CHAPTER TEN

"**M**ark Goodwin!" Miss Radick, the history teacher, stood next to his desk with her hands on her hips looking down at him.

"Yes Ma'am?" He looked back at her, knowing what was coming. It had to do with the black Tee shirt with the sleeves torn off.

"Don't you think we could dress less like a gang member?"

How many gang members are we acquainted with, he wondered. "I ripped one of the sleeves on a nail in the garage. I figured the rest of the shirt was too good to throw away."

She shook her head in disbelief. "You always have an answer, don't you? You ought to be a writer, the kind of stories you can tell. I would think, considering the sheriff has apprehended your sister's killer; you'd be more subdued today.

"Yes ma'am. I'm sorry, but I guess I wasn't thinking." If she only knew what he was thinking.

"We're going to overlook this incident today, but I don't want to see this shirt in class again. I suggest you wear it fishing."

He spread his hands. "Does that mean I can have tomorrow off?" There were titters and chuckles throughout the room.

"It might be a good idea for you to concentrate more on your homework instead of watching TV movies that glamorize big city gangs."

Mark glanced about the room, satisfied at the reaction from the other students. At the same time he was thinking, why do I act like this? What the heck? She's the crank and I'm trying to make a point. "Yes ma'am. I won't be wearing it again."

* * *

During the morning break Candy found herself alone with

Shannon. Mark, Ollie and Buzz waved as they passed the pair but didn't stop. She had no idea where Jodi was. "Hey Shannon, you look positively glowing today. What's up?"

"I don't feel like glowing. Dad hasn't found his watch, which as far as Mark is concerned makes him a suspect."

"Mark's shinin' ya on. We don't suspect him."

"I don't really, but Mark knows he wasn't home that night."

"Mark is hung up on the sheriff. Worst thing is, he could be right and there isn't one dang thang we can do 'bout it."

"Something bothers me. Asked my dad about that last night in a roundabout way. Says he was busy making arrangements for a visit by the AME president. Guess the guy was going to speak at our church that Sunday. All I know is, Dad didn't come home until midnight. I specifically remember it was that night 'cause Jodi and I went to the movies. I didn't get home till after eleven. Supposed to be in by ten. Kinda worried he'd catch me. Was wide-awake at twelve fifteen when he came home. I help teach the kindergarten class at church and was getting things ready."

"Is church where you and Buzz got together?"

"Nah. Buzz doesn't go to church all that much. When he does he goes to the Baptist church. Dad doesn't know about Buzz"

"What's to know? He's only a friend."

"You don't know my dad. Has some down right strict rules about boys. I don't cross him 'cause he has a terrible temper. Even give us kids a whippin' once in a while."

"That's the awfullest thang. Sure lucky my folks aren't into that kinda crap. You and Buzz make such a neat couple," Candy sighed. "Sometimes I wish I had a boy friend."

"Well, Ollie's been putting the move on ya."

With an embarrassed grin she told her friend, "I know. I think he's cute, but somehow or the other not exactly my type."

"So who is your type, Missy? Mark?"

"Over my dead and bleeding body. How come Buzz never carries a lunch? Every day the rest of us meet out by the ball field with our brown bags."

Shannon frowned. "They say, 'Don't try to change people,' but in this case it's probably my responsibility. Lots of times Buzz wanders down to Steven's Store to pick up goodies. Sometimes he pays for this stuff. Other times, when Steven's back is turned, he cops several things. Stuffs them inside his jacket."

Candy tried to tell herself it was none of her business, but it was. She liked Buzz. "You talk to him about it?"

"Of course. I'm trying my darndest to break him of it. Doesn't seem to understand what the results could be if Stevens caught him. Might decide to make an issue out of it."

"Golly Shannon. I've never been involved in anything like this. This is just me talking but I'd tell him, 'Buzz, you gotta choice. You got me or got a life of crime but you can't have both.'" The bell sounded. "Whoops. Time for math."

"Yeah. Test today. You ready?" Shannon didn't say anything all the way down the long hall, but at the door she paused. "Thanks for listening, Candy. You know what? What you told me might work."

* * *

The Man was highly upset over the loss of his watch. The more he thought about it the more sure he was that he had worn it Saturday. And yet know damn well I didn't have it on when I was doin' the little brat. So where? If I left it laying somewhere or if I accidentally dropped it someplace then it's long gone. Five hundred dollars down the drain. What could he do if he saw somebody around town wearing it or one like it?

Probably better forget it. Keep my mind focused on what I have planned for Wednesday night. One more day.

It was about ten o'clock when he was filling his gas tank at Five Points. He heard a commotion and looked up to see two teachers with a group of about twenty kids making their way down Washington towards Riverview. Field trip, so I hear, all carrying their lunches. Understand Chief Tarmen is going to give them a guided tour of the fire department. They were marching in two columns like little soldiers. Pretty good considering most of them were seven or eight years old. Good teachers.

Several kids spotted him next to his sedan. There she is, my little blond sweetie; Little Miss Heinz herself. No way he could do anything about her in broad daylight. I gotta be patient. The tiny kid waved as did a couple of the others and he waved in return. Best that I move on. Don't want to spook the teachers.

120

$*$ $*$ $*$

Two hours later Candy and the other five teenagers congregated on the bleachers next to the baseball diamond to eat their lunches. Candy knew if it had been up to Mark, she wouldn't have been invited to join the group. But, as it happened, Shannon and Jodi had decided to adopt her.
She was right. Everyone except Buzz had a lunch. Buzz did have some candy and a bag of chips. She didn't dare say anything that would betray the confidence between her and Shannon.

"Wow Mark," Shannon teased, "Miss Radick sure likes to get on your case, doesn't she?"

"You mean, Miss Radish? Miss Turnip is more like it. She's on some kind of a trip. Bends my mind trying to figure out how come you and Red can wear blouses without sleeves and you guys are stylish. I wear something without sleeves and I'm a hooligan?"

"Maybe," Candy snipped, "it's a given that with or without sleeves you look like a cheesy crook." She wanted to retract the statement as soon as it left her lips. What happened to her deal of trying to say more complimentary things to people? Actually she thought he looked cool, but she couldn't bring herself to say so. There are muscles on his arms that make him look like a body builder.

"Well look who's talking. Miss Piggy herself."

She stuck her tongue out at him then looked at Shannon and Buzz who were facing each other, holding hands. Shannon was teasing him with a piece of Oreo cookie held in her teeth. Jodi was talking to two guys who were under the bleachers. Ollie was stuffing his face as usual.

Candy opened her lunch box right next to Mark's brown paper sack. Inside were a ham sandwich, Ding Dongs, a thermos, a peach and a banana. Like Mark, she packed her own, but his consisted of two baloney sandwiches and a plastic bag of cookies.

"Hey Red, I'll trade you my homemade chocolate chip cookies for that peach.

"Bite your tongue, she told herself. "No way! I'm a real glutton for peaches. I'll trade for the banana." She would darn near trade the peach for the cookies. Chocolate chips were one of her weaknesses and these did look homemade.

121

"That's not what I would consider a far out deal. I'll swap you half the cookies for the banana and a bite of the peach."

A vision went through her mind, which made her shudder. She could see herself holding a chunk of succulent peach in her lips waiting for him to take it with his. Oh yuck. He's gonna make me barf. "Works for me." Handing him the banana, she licked her lips and asked, "Are we going to continue with our investigation? According to this morning's paper, everybody is convinced Weird Walter did it. Sounds like it's all over."

"It is not all over." Mark was talking with his mouth full of banana.

"What about the confession? I saw in the paper that Walter knew things about the murder only the real killer would know."She watched as he counted out the cookies. There were seven. To keep his end of the bargain he started to break one in half, then changed his mind and gave her four.

"Red, that's bull pucky. Sheriff is barking up the wrong tree."

"You keep saying that, but you never tell us why. How can you be so sure?"

"You want to know," he asked. "I'll tell ya."

Shannon got up from where she had been laying on the bleachers with her head in Buzz's lap. Candy felt a sudden tension. She could see that he had everyone's attention.

"Last year," Mark began, "we went to the Fourth of July thing at the fairgrounds. Dad was driving up and down every aisle looking for a place to park. Saw a spot big enough between a police car and a fire engine. No more than pulled in and here comes Frank . . . totally ballistic. Screaming that we couldn't park there. Got into an argument with my dad. Words were flyin'until my dad told him, 'You're nothing but a fat pig.' Frank is all red in the face, yellin' at dad to move it right away or he'd have our car towed. I mean he was like a mad man."

"And that's why you suspect him?" Candy asked. "Come on Mark, so the sheriff is jest plain ignert, but get real."

"Hey. I ain't done. The sheriff has never liked me. He hated Laura. My folks wanted me to watch my sister while she went on the pony ride. After she was through she was jumping and dancing around like little kids do. Right next to the fence was a big pile of pony pucky. She accidentally kicked it. It was wet. Went spraying all over. Most of it landed on a pair of spit shined shoes."

"The Sheriff." Shannon grinned.

"Wouldn't you know? Was there watching his kids ride." Mark was shaking his head as though in disbelief. "Talk about ballistic. He called Laura a rotten little bitch and some other things I wouldn't even repeat. Told her she ought to be severely punished." Laura stuck her tongue out at him and told him, 'Your a fat pig.' And that's when it happened." Like a good public speaker, Mark paused. Watching the faces of the others.

"Whaaaaat?" Asked Ollie.

"Sheriff warned her, and I quote, 'Put that f'n tongue back into your mouth, you little witch, or I'll take out my knife and whack it off. This world would be better off without your kind.' I was so shook up I couldn't say a darned thing."

"I would have popped him," Ollie remarked. "Sheriff or not."

Mark snorted. "Not last year. I couldn't of tangled with him. I was only 'bout five foot tall and a hundred twenty pounds. And I was on crutches. Remember? Broken leg? Probably be a different story today. Sheriff tells me, 'if you don't want ten thousand little red ants kicked outta yer ass, you and your sister better get the hell outta here.'"

"Well damn," Ollie rested his chin in his hands. "I don't blame you for thinking it's him."

Candy was glad they weren't dropping the investigation. "That's pretty awesome, but suppose you explain why Walter couldn't be the one."

"Think about it. We have the footprint. A dress shoe. 'Bout a size eleven. Measured it with one of my shoes. Walter always wears tennies and his feet are small. We have the watch. Walter tells time by where the sun is or by when it's time to eat. And did you see what the paper had to say? That Walter had been to the movies then went walking out Lone Pine Trail. Carrying my sister's body for three miles. Not hardly. The show doesn't let out until nine or after. Dad and I were looking for Laura about seven."

Candy was fascinated. Mark was working this thing like a CFI investigator.

Ollie shrugged, "then why did he confess? And how did he know details about the murder."

"That fat sheriff has no suspects. Everybody in town has been on his case to make an arrest. Walter was available. Tell Walter some facts about the case in such a way he thinks he's saying them. I'm telling you, they don't have any clues. They don't have any proof. We probably got more clues than they do."

"I was thinking 'bout that." Candy knew everything Mark was saying made sense even though she didn't know Weird Walter. "Know what I'd like to see us do? I'd like to see us form a club with the sole purpose of solving this case."

"A club? Oh wow!" Shannon's eyes glowed with enthusiasm. "What a great idea. We can have meetings to discuss what we might have seen, what we might hear and even what each of us thinks. And what we should do next. With six heads together . . ."

Ollie was shuffling about. "Might stumble onto another important clue like the one Candy found. Pretty tough sledding all by yourself, Mark. What do you think, Marcus? Might work, huh?"

Marks eyes looked fierce as he told them, "If we do it, I'm going to be in charge."

"Right on," squealed Jodi. What are we going to call it?"

"Kryptonites," he answered without hesitation.

"Krypto what?" Buzz frowned. "You mean those guys who have to steal things? Know what I mean?"

Shannon giggled. "That's Kleptomaniacs."

"Krypton is the only thing that can stop Superman," Mark let them know. "So here is where we'll start. We have the watch and after school we'll drop by the Jewelry Store to see what Hoggie can tell us."

"Hoggie?" asked Candy.

"Yeah, Hoggie. I have no idea why but the kids around town call him Hoggie Quagmire. His name is Quathorne or something like that and I don't know where the Hoggie thing comes from, but everybody in town calls him that. Okay, let's review what we have so far. Need to hear what each one of you guys thinks. Let's start with you, Red."

"Oh, like wow, what a trip," exclaimed Candy. She'd been

included. The nickname, Red, didn't even register.

* * *

Hoggie's Jewelry was actually called Dalton Jewelry, TV & Appliances. He opened the business as a jewelry store but over the years added other lines as the store didn't make enough on jewelry alone. First it was house-wares, then small appliances. Later he added radios, TVs, large appliances, sewing machines and video rentals. When the five teenagers entered his store, Harold 'Hoggie' Quathmore was at once alert. Most of these kids he didn't trust any further than he could throw a frog by its eye-balls. One of the boys he trusted, the other he didn't.

Ollie he knew personally for he coached the Deiter Ford team in Pop Warner Football. Ollie's was probably the reason they had won the championship two years in a row. From what he knew about the Goodwin boy, he would bear watching for he was always up to some sort of devilment. The group didn't wander around in the usual fashion of potential shoplifters, instead charged right up to the counter.

"We found this watch," the Goodwin boy told him. "Was wondering if you had any idea who it belongs to, or if not, if they might have bought it here?"

"Looks fairly expensive." He took the timepiece and peered at it through his jeweler's eyeglass. "Le Couture. Not a brand I sell but I've heard of it." He turned toward Ollie. "What I'd do if I were you is put an ad in your father's newspaper. You know, Lost and Found. Expensive watch like this, somebody will probably claim it. Solve all your questions and put your mind at ease. Better let me hold onto it for a few days. I'll try to trace its ownership."

"Negative," snapped Mark. "I'll hold it for the rest of the week in case someone answers this ad you're talking about. Come on guys let's get going. Right after basketball practice, we'll stop by the Union and see how this ad thing goes down."

Hoggie frowned when the one called Mark stopped and began checking through the videos for rent. Fortunately these were empty sleeves or the kid would probably try slipping some inside his coat.

* * *

Ollie pushed open the door and held it like a gentleman for

the gals. "Come on Marcus, we'd better run. Coach is going to be biting his nails wondering where we are."

Mark was wondering why Ollie was acting so peculiar, fidgeting and looking over his shoulder. "What's with you man? You look scared to death. A week ago you didn't even think about playing."

"Hey Dude! That's not what's bugging me. We're on the team I'm looking forward to it, but it's this thing about placing an ad. Wonder if it's such a good idea?"

"What's the problem? We place an ad. The guy calls. We find out who he is."

"Yeah. Only thing is what do we do if it is Frank?"

"My Gawd Mark," Candy was actually touching his arm. It felt strange and yet he didn't shrug it off. "This could be dangerous. He'd know that you knew."

"Don't be silly, Red. Even if it is the sheriff, I'd give him the watch. Tell him we figured he'd lost it when he slid down the bank. Who knows, maybe he did?"

"Oh," she disagreed. "Wouldn't he be concerned as to why we went back out there?"

"Come on, Red. I don't think the guy will be suspicious just because we found his watch."

"Heck no," added Shannon. "I'd think he'd be happy to get it back. Problem is, these clues don't mean he's the killer, only that he was out there and we knew that."

The group paused where the sidewalk turned toward the gym. "You guys gonna watch us practice?" Mark asked.

Shannon shook her head. "Can't. Have to cut out. You know how it is? Supposed to go straight home from school tonight."

"Me too." Candy teased. "Unless you can't handle things by yourself."

Mark studied the redhead for a moment. Ann Margaret? Not hardly. "There isn't anything I can't handle, including you Red. See ya later."

"Not if I see you first."

* * *

Once practice was over Mark and Ollie came out the side door of the gymnasium. They headed for the corner of Main and

126

Palm, a block from the school, where they went into the Dalton Union to see about placing the ad.

"Hi Dad." Ollie waved at his father who looked curiously at the pair when he came in from the shop. "We found this watch Saturday and we want to put an ad in Lost and Found."

"Good idea son. You made it in the nick of time. We're putting this edition to bed as we speak. Get your ad ready and I'll make sure we get it in."

A pretty, older lady, probably in her forties, helped Mark with the wording. There was a small sign on her desk which stated: 'LOST AND FOUND: Up to three lines FREE. That was cool. The ad ended up simple enough. 'Found: man's watch. Vic. Lone Pine Trail. Call to identify,' followed by the Goodwin phone number.

"Hey Marcus. I don't think tellin' where we found it is such a good idea."

"I don't know of any other way of getting a line on who the killer might be."

"Yeah, you're probably right. That ought to do it if the guy reads the want ads. I can't shake off the willies because of the question of what do we do if this guy calls?"

Mark walked the two blocks as far as Locust Street with Ollie where they did their secret handshake. Then Ollie went right while he went left. To his surprise he discovered himself on the corner of Main and Locust looking in the window of Hoggie's Jewelry. Think I'll check somethin' out. Pushing through the glass door he made his way to the video rental section. There was a lady behind the counter on her knees rearranging movie boxes.

"Uh, ma'am."

She looked up and frowned. "Yes? I thought I'd locked the door. It's actually time for us to close up. What can I do for you?"

"I was wondering if you had any movies for rent with Ann Margaret in them?"

"Of course we do. Got Grumpy Old Men One and Two."

"Was thinking of something older," What was it the flick Ollie suggested? "Like maybe Bye Bye Birdie?"

She acted as though he was being a pain but told him, "I'll look in our catalog."

He waited. The lady was humming as she searched.

"By golly, I do have one. Viva Las Vegas, with Elvis Presely."

"I'll take that. How much is the rent?" This is stupid, he thought.

"These older ones are only a buck if you have it back by noon tomorrow."

"Cool."

"You take good care of it," she warned. "I don't think I've seen that one and I adore Elvis."

I'm sure you would at your age, he was thinking. "Yes ma'am, I surely mean to."

* * *

The Man was eating his evening meal at the bowling alley. He liked their huge, quarter pound hot dogs, smothered in chili, onions and cheese. Two of them and a beer was a meal fit for a king. The past couple of days there was only one thing on his mind, sixteen hours a day, like a teenage boy thinks about sex. Except his thoughts concerned the one he intended to do next? Not that he was on any sort of a timetable but he was getting antsy. What was the use of making a list if you didn't intend to carry the whole thing out.

CHAPTER ELEVEN

This is Tuesday, Mark was thinking, using his two index fingers to create a quiet drumbeat on his desktop. Two weeks from Thursday is Halloween. Wonder what sort of devilment I can come up with this year. He was beginning to recognize the fact it was easy for him to convince others to help him do things. What did they call it? Born to lead. He grinned. Born to be bad? Look how easy he took over the Kryptonites. Even the principal calls me a rebel. Lost count of how many times I been sent to his office. So what's the big deal? I like to have some fun, that's all. Every time all the kids look at me like Superman has done it again. I know what we can do. I'll round up . . .

"Mark Goodwin. Would you please step out into the hall for a moment."He started, turning to look as the classroom began to buzz. Sheriff Martinez stood in the doorway next alongside principal Hernandez, looking grim.

When Mark didn't immediately respond, Hernandez snapped, "That's not a request, young man, that's an order."

Twenty pair of eyes were staring at him, but he didn't show the least bit of concern. "Sure Bobby. I believe I can fit you guys into my schedule." He felt nowhere near as confident as he tried to appear, wondering if he was in trouble over placing the ad.

Both men stood glaring at him, so he pushed his papers aside and stood, then walked with his usual arrogance toward the back of the room. He was surprised that 'outside' didn't mean in the hall but all the way outdoors. In fact they continued across the campus to the athletic field where they stopped next to the broad-jump area. The principal was scowling the entire time and was carrying a brown grocery bag.

They stood in silence for several minutes. The sheriff stood looking at him like he was a piece of vermin. Mark thought enough was enough. "You got the gun, Frankie Boy, so why don't you start?"

The sheriff actually placed a hand on his gun before speaking. "You think you're a real big shot don'tcha? This time you are in deep shit." He hitched up his pants, that weren't about to stay in place around his ample belly. "Can you account for your where-a-bouts last night from seven o'clock on?"

"Of course I can," he smirked. Wish I could turn into Superman. Where is the Man of Steel when you need him? "I was at home eatin' pizza and ice-cream."

"Knock off the smart ass crap. You'd better come up with some straight answers, boy."

I tell this jerk the truth and he doesn't believe me. He considered making some clever remark about talking to his attorney, but the principal looked so distressed he thought better of it. "Check it out. I went straight home from basketball practice. And that's where I was . . . all night."

"I think you snuck out."
The sheriff was slapping his palm over and over with his two-foot long nightstick. Mark wondered if he thought doing so would put the fear in him. "What am I supposed to have done while I was out?"

The sheriff caught Mark by surprise when he handed him the nightstick and then indicated the smooth sand of the broad-jump landing area. "I want two things." Make an impression in the sand with your foot."

What the heck? Mark was startled. Had the fat man been back out to the site? Had he discovered the footprint? About time. Sure wasn't his. He always wore cowboy boots. Was he blind enough to think it was mine? Confidently he stepped into the sand and rocked on his right foot to make sure the print was visible.

The sheriff nodded. "Okay boy, I want you to take that stick and write your initials there in the sand."

Mark didn't question why, automatically doing as he was told. The 'M' and the 'G' appeared in bold script with a flourish on the tail of the 'G'. Looking at the sheriff's highly polished black dress shoes, he was wracking his brain, wondering how he could get the sheriff to step into the sand.

The sheriff glowered. "Can you print them so they look like printing?"

"Suppose I can, but I never do." He proceeded to print the two letters but out of habit added a curling tail to each. Before he straightened up, he laid the nightstick in the middle of the pit.

"Are those the boots you were wearing last night?" Frank's tone betrayed his growing dismay.

"The ones I wear everyday . . . even to bed. You mind letting me in on what's going down here?"

The sheriff conferred with the principal who had removed two plaster of Paris footprints from the bag and stood shaking his head. "Could have been somebody with him," Frank stated. "Crap! You were there, I'd bet money on it. Deiter Ford is building a new showroom, as if you didn't know. Yesterday afternoon they poured about three thousand square feet of red colored cement. Sometime after 6:45 last night, you and some of your buddies stopped by, scratched the initials 'M and G' into the newly finished concrete then took a sharp stick or a spade and messed up the whole floor. Gonna cost somebody ten/fifteen thousand bucks to jack hammer it out and replace it."

"Holy crap," Mark exclaimed. "Like wow!"

"Yeah, wow. And I'm sure you were involved."
"Before you blow your cool you'd better call my folks. They can vouch for where I was. How come you keep jerking me around?"

"I'll tell you why. This is the type of thing I've grown to expect from you and your gang of hoodlums. You and Ollie Frazier and that black boy have been trying to get a gang started here in Dalton. I'm not going to stand by and watch it happen. I think you are somehow involved."
Principal Hernandez looked like he'd seen a ghost.
Mark was so relieved he felt weak. "Well, you got the wrong guy."

"Listen to me, tough guy. You better learn to show some respect. Get me my nightstick, boy."
Mark glowered but did as he was told. "All I'm askin' is, check it out, Sheriff. It sure as hell wasn't me."
"I intend to, and we'll see. One of these days I'm going to nail you and your bunch of wannabe gang members."

Better than a cold-blooded killer, Mark was thinking.

* * *

After the last class on Wednesday Mark and Ollie were crossing The Quad when they ran into Buzz who called out, "Hi guys. Saw the ad in the paper."

Mark ran his hands through his hair. "Cool. Hope that jerk is dumb enough to call. Had to clue my folks in. Not about our suspicions, only that I had the watch." He chuckled. "My mom actually complimented me for placing the ad. Like she thought I would have kept the watch without saying anything."

"Well," said Ollie, "Let's head for the gym. We're only guessing that it belongs to the killer. Might be dumb luck that it was in that spot. Hey men, this is it. Coach wants to do a shoot around before Citrus shows up. Last practice before the real thing."

"Yeah," Buzz was carrying his gym bag. "What do you think, Mark? Any chance we can beat Citrus?"

"What do you mean, 'is there any chance? Our biggest edge is that they think we can't. Between you and me and Ollie, we are going to make them earn every point. Coach told me he got the school to spring for all new uniforms this year."

"You're jerkin' me, you seen 'em?" Ollie was walking on top of the stone retaining wall. After a half-dozen steps he jumped down from the three-foot height as easily as someone half his size. "Hey Mark. Tonight, after the game, me and Buzz and Shortie Carr are going to hit Old Man Fargas' watermelon patch. You in?"

"After the game? Naw, I don't think so. I uh . . . "

"What's with you? Got a date? You and Red gonna get it on?"

"When hell freezes over. Got some studying to do after the game."

"Hey Marcus, this ain't like you? Most of the time you're the one to come up with the far out ideas."

"Well . . . you know. It's only been a week since the thing with my sister. Like I been kinda out of it, know what I mean?" Going through his mind was his run in with the sheriff this morn- ing and since he'd told them all about it, they should be thinkin' the same way. Man didn't like him one little bit. Sooner or later if

132

he kept doing things that could get him into trouble, Frank would make good on his threat to 'nail him'. At the moment he wanted to keep concentrating on their investigation. Of course raiding Fargas' watermelon patch was probably safe enough. Use the railroad bridge to cross the river, then keep close to the water.

"That's a cop-out." Ollie told him. "You need to get out and do something. Take your mind off it."

"Well look who's turned into a wimp." Buzz leaped up to swing from the branch of a mulberry tree. "Have you seen the size of them boogers? Fargas' second crop of the year. These babies look like they're twice as big. Must go thirty/forty pounds. You hear what I'm sayin'?" The smaller boy always looked like he was grinning, his large teeth a pure white next to his ebony skin.

"Okay, okay. One thing you can bet your ass is, I'm not a wimp. I'll go ahead and study 'til everybody's sleeping. But this is the last of this kinda crap. After my run in with the Sheriff yesterday, I'm gonna kinda cool it."

"All right! We're gonna meet down at the cemetery dead on Midnight. The sheriff will be sound asleep."

"Okay then, got that settled. Hey, Ollie? How 'bout telling the coach I'll be a few minutes late. Told the drama teacher I'd drop by the auditorium to hear what he has to say about my being in his play."

"What?" Ollie placed a hand behind his right ear. "What makes him think you can act? Tell him you're a fighter not an actor."

"So was Sylvester Stallone, but without a doubt, that man can act. Thought I might give it a try. Be something different."

* * *

At five o'clock, Candy stopped by the Music Department as she had promised and to tell Mr. Kelly she couldn't stay. Mrs. Turner wanted to run the team through one more practice.
Actually she would have liked to be in the play, but was certain once the music teacher thought it over, she didn't qualify. Nervously she approached Mr. Kelly who nodded then turned to one of the students who was carrying a box full of scripts. "Thanks Norman. Sit the box on one of those chairs."

There were half-dozen additional students already there, including Heather and Carmelita Hoover. It made her feel peculiar for it was the first time she and the Mexican gal had crossed paths since the incident. "Hi Heather. Uh . . . lookin' good, Carmelita. Great outfit. Makes you look like you're eighteen."

The stocky girl frowned. Candy expected some sort of cutting reply.

Carmelita's expression softened as she looked down at her bright red, form fitting jumpsuit. "I like it. Got it down at Rice's Clothing last Saturday."

"Cool. Wish I could wear things like that." Candy turned toward Mr. Kelly. "Uh . . . I dropped in to let you know I can't stay. Got cheerleading practice." He grinned and she nearly melted. Was he handsome or what?

"All my fault. Didn't check the schedule. Senior moment." He tapped his skull,"

"Not hardly," her look could have been taken as flirty. "You're a long way from being a senior."

"I guess I'm not over the hill yet. Anyway, none of us are going to stay this evening. I'm merely going to hand out copies of the script to each of you. Take them home; read them through, paying particular attention to the part I want you to try out for. As for you Candy," he handed her a copy, "carefully study the part of Deirdre. I've already decided you're the one for that roll. You may as well start memorizing your lines. We will begin preliminary rehearsals Friday."

"Oh my Gawd. Are you sure? That's the lead." She turned in surprise as Mark sauntered in. "Are you lost? Basketball practice is in the gym. This is a meeting for people who have talent."

"Gee Red. How come you're here?"

He squinted and looked at her for a long uncomfortable moment. No way she could know he had watched an Ann Margaret movie the night before and was making a comparison. Jodi was right; darned near a spittin' image. Who knows? Maybe she can act too.

Brad reached out to place a hand on Mark's shoulder. "Miss Swanson is going to be Deirdre, our leading lady. I've got a feeling the two of you can make this the best eighth grade play we've ever had."

Mark looked at Candy in her green and white cheerleading outfit. "Hold on here. You mean Red is the one I'd have to kiss in the last scene? I . . . don't . . . think so."

Brad handed Mark a script. "It's not for real, you know. It's called acting. All of Dirk's lines have been highlighted. Dirk is a soldier of fortune and a very exciting role. We are going to discover a whole new side to Mark Goodwin. That's a promise."

Mark looked at the blue covered manuscript then over at Candy who was smirking. "Hey bimbo," he whispered. "I ain't never gonna kiss you and that's for sure. What the heck, they want me to be an actor, I'll fake it. Let's go. We gotta go kick some ass."

* * *

The group of cheerleaders completed their final practice session after which they all walked out into the Quad for a breath of air. Jodi saw Shannon and Candy heading for the drinking fountain. She was standing with Heather and Joyce Martinez near the parking lot fence. She watched as the white-haired girl fumbled in her bag for an atomizer from which she shot a quick burst of spray into her mouth.

"That work?"

"Sure does. Like right away."

"Darned if that ain't pretty cool," Joyce told her, "you know, with your asthma and all, that you can do things like cheer-leading."

Heather made a couple of quick cheerleading moves then grinned. "Most of the time the pill I take keeps it under control. Once in a while I gotta use the spray, like if I get overly excited."

Jodi loved Heather's devilish laugh. She waggled both hands at a pair of boys walking by. "I've got an uncle who had it to the extreme. Outgrew it when he got out of his teens."

"I sure hope I do. My folks are both coming, what about yours? Like we better get our butts in gear. Half hour till game time."

"My dad for sure." Jodi let them know. "Our local paper is so small that he is the editor, the advertising manager, helps run the presses and in the fall is the sports reporter. Shannon's mom is coming but Candy's mom told her they couldn't pay her to go to a basketball game

"If it wasn't for Peanut Head Brennen your dad would have to deliver the papers too." Heather was curious. "I was wondering.

Do you ever wish your twin was a sister? Like even identical?"

"Sometimes I wonder 'bout how much fun it would be, dressing alike, fooling people, but I kinda like being one of a kind. I like having a big brother."

"He's big alright. You guys remind me of Arnold Swartzenegger and Danny Divito."

Joyce was walking backwards in front of the two girls. "My dad's coming. Mom has to watch the rug rats. Man, wasn't Twins a cool movie? Only I'm sure you're a lot better looking than Danny Divito. But wouldn't it be totally extreme for the world to have two Jodies."

Jodi giggled. "Better than having two Ollies?"

She had Heather also giggling. "That would be extreme. Like one would make me happy."

"Why don't you let my brother know you're sweet on him?"

"I'm not sweet on him. Like it's really that I . . . "

"When I found out my brother was going to play on the team, I thought it was the most awesome thing I ever heard of. Football you'd expect, but basketball? Hold on. Here come the buses from Citrus. Let's check out the guys."

"I can hardly wait to see him play," Heather told Jodi. "I hear he's pretty good."

Jodi could read the excitement in Heather's eyes even though she tried to give the impression of shining it on.

A black and white police cruiser pulled into the parking lot. She watched Frank go through his usual squirming maneuvers to get from behind the wheel. "Hey Joyce, here comes your Dad." Wriggling into her mind was a horrible thought. The way Mark and Ollie feel about the sheriff, how will they play having him on the sidelines?

* * *

Coach Donnelley was heading for the locker room. This is a big, big night for these boys and for me. He was eager to see how they performed under the gun. As he left the Quad and made the turn toward the entrance he nearly ran into five of his boys. One of them was Goodwin.

"Mark! Hold up a minute."

He had been concerned about the Goodwin boy all week. During their frequent practice sessions the kid seemed to be play-

136

ing in a daze. Couldn't seem to shake off his sister's death, or at least I assume that's what's on his mind. Had thought that as the boy's coach he might be able to talk to him.

"Hi coach. What's hangin'?"

Donnelley acknowledged the rest of the boys but motioned for them to move on. "Mark? There is something I've been wanting to tell you."

Mark cocked his head, looked back toward his teammates who were horsing around as they went inside. His blue eyes were full of curiosity as looked at the coach.

"Mark? I know that you have been kinda down for nearly two weeks, and I understand. As I told you earlier, I actually do know how you feel. I lost my own little brother when I was sixteen. Was trying to teach Danny, who was eight at the time, how to ride a bicycle. Except I didn't teach him enough. My brother went down the drive then discovered he didn't know how to turn or use the brakes. Pedaled right out into the street. It was a hit and run. Never did catch the bastard."

"That ain't the same," Mark snapped.

"No it's not," he replied fiercely. "Living with the guilt is pure hell. But Laura wasn't your fault. And I want you to do what I did. Starting tonight, I want you to get on with your life. Live it in such a way that if tonight she were sitting out there in the audience, she'd be proud. That she'd tell her friends, 'That's my big brother!' Now . . . let's go get ready to play ball."

Mark straightened his shoulders and stood tall. "Okay, let's go out there and kick some ass!"

* * *

The ladies gym teacher saw about what she expected. The cheering section for Middle School games was never overflowing. There were about a dozen parents, perhaps twice that many students. Her six cheerleaders represented about a quarter of the female population of the eighth grade. At four foot eight each, Heather and Jodi were the tiniest. Patty and Joyce, the sheriff's daughter, were each barely over five feet so Candy and Shannon who were both five-foot six, truly stood out. In their Kelly green mini-skirts and white letterman's sweaters they also attracted the most attention. Those two could easily be mistaken for seventeen year olds.

Mrs. Turner sighed. Even though she's had so little practice, Candy remains the most awkward, but she's also the most vocal. They were leading some cheers as the teacher glanced about. Out on the court she could see the Goodwin boy warming up. Even though he was somewhat of a rebel, Mark was one of her favorite students. He was full of pranks and always kept his fellow classmates stirred up, but the kid was smart and he loved English. Her heart had gone out to the boy all week. She couldn't think of anything more devastating than losing a sibling, unless you were involved, as Mark was, in discovering the body. How horrible that had to have been. After the way he has been all last week, I'm glad to see him recovering.

She smiled. All the Dalton fans in the gym were watching the cheerleaders, as were those boys on the Citrus team who were beginning to notice girls. And look at Heather, bless her heart. In spite of her asthmatic problems she is jumping, leaping and screaming, trying to fire up our meager rooting section. Speaking of the Dalton spirit. Gotta love it.

How about the Citrus spirit? Boy does it show. Their team bus drove up jammed with players and school personnel. Following them were two booster busses and a parade of cars. Must be close to two hundred . . . boisterous fans. Our gym only seats three hundred. This is the eighth grade for crying out loud. The Panthers have only four cheerleaders. Two boys and two girls, but it's obvious they have talent.

She noticed her team in a huddle with their heads down and wondered if they were saying a prayer. Candy was talking, looking very serious and then they did something that took everyone in the gym by surprise. The girls walked across the floor, right on the centerline between the two teams that both stopped to watch the procession. The girls were shaking hands with the opposing cheerleaders before returning to the Indian side of the court.

"What's going on? She asked, looking directly into Candy's glowing green eyes. "Don't you realize that these are our opponents? Our enemy?"

Candy shrugged and then told her, "I figured it would addle their thinkin'. Make them think we are softies. Only we're here to show them something different."

138

I'm underestimating that little redhead. Mrs. Turner was grinning.

* * *

Donnelley had to take care of a couple of things before he went in to give his team a pep talk to get them fired up. As he walked into the dressing room the first thing he spotted was the condition of his three key players. He stopped short. "What the heck do you call this? You men get that crap off your faces."

"Hey coach, we're the Dalton Indians and proud of it." Mark had done the best job with the red, white and black war paint, appearing absolutely fierce. "You're looking at the meanest, toughest basketball machine in the Juniper Sierra League."

"Yeah," Ollie told him, "Like the Raiders, we don't back down from nobody."

The coach studied Mark's face. My Indians, he thought. A lot of schools are doing away with that name; trying to be politically correct, but no one around Dalton had been complaining. "What the heck? You got anymore of that makeup." He could scarcely contain his elation.

When all twelve of the boys were in full war paint, Donnelley repeated the words Mark had used a few minutes earlier. "Let's go out there and kick some ass."

He didn't make an issue over the war paint for the reason he was seeing a new Mark Goodwin. His talk must have done some good and thank God the sheriff had arrested the killer, for it also lifted the boy out of the doldrums that had possessed him all last week. This boy was ready to play.

Before he picked the three new team members, he expected to lose to the Panthers by twenty points or more. But tonight he had visions of keeping it to ten points or less. Winning was only a wild dream. When the Indians came out onto the floor everyone in the gym, including the opposing team, seemed to be stunned. Donnelley met the Citrus coach at the scorer's table when he went to turn in his lineup. Where Dalton had only two blacks on their team four of the Citrus starting five were black as were three of the seven on the bench.

"What are you trying to do Ed, intimidate my boys? Girls are girls. Dabbing on some war-paint ain't gonna change that."

In the huddle, before the tip-off, he let his men know. "The

Citrus coach called you a bunch of girls. Are we going to take that?"

Mark's laugh had a wicked tone to it. "We're cool coach. Panthers? Okay men, let's show these jerks how mean a bunch of girls can be when they playin' against a bunch of pussy cats."

Donnelley grinned.

* * *

"Where is everybody?" The Man asked, looking out over the sixteen vacant bowling lanes. The lights on the pinsetters were off. Jim Patterson, the deskman, was sitting on the counter drinking a beer.

"No league play tonight. No play of any kind."

The Man's heart seemed to drop into his stomach. "How come? Some kinda holiday?"

"Wanta beer?" Whistling in such a manner the waitress in the lounge heard him, he held up his empty showing her two fingers. "Got a bad short in the main electric panel. Blew out the transformer that controls the automatic equipment. Can't get a replacement' til tomorrow at the earliest. Had to call everybody with the bad news."

Crap, the Man thought. Crap, crap, crap. His plan had been to stop by the bowling alley for a bite to eat while he was waiting for Heinz to show up. The minute the Kraut walked in, he'd be on his way. When the waitress came with the two beers he told her, "Hey Kelly. How 'bout bringing me a chili size? Far as I'm concerned, you guys make the best chili size west of the Mississippi." Crap! Gonna have to wait' til next Wednesday. Maybe I'd best look at some of the others. I need some action. I need some action right away.

* * *

Mark stared straight into the eyes of the Panther center, his own like pinpoints of flame. Easily out-jumping the taller man he accidentally knocked him off balance with an elbow in the ribs as he tipped the ball to Ollie who drove the lane with three players sagging to stop him. Ollie made a blind pass behind his back to Mark. Glancing down to make sure his toes were outside the three-point line he put it up. Dalton was up three zip five seconds into the contest. Donnelley was jerking his fists in front of his chest saying, "yes, yes, yes."

It had been Shortie Carr's idea to use a full court press and there were immediate results. Mark deflected the inbound pass to Shortie who fed to Ollie coming baseline. With two defenders hanging all over him he took the ball all the way to the basket while the referee was calling a foul on number six. Ollie made the free throw. The Indians led six to nothing.

Mark knew they had the Panthers confused. They seemed to be struggling to fight their way through the press and once they did, found themselves facing a sticky, floating, man to man defense that forced the center to take a bad shot. Mark rebounded and while he was in the air, gunned it out to Buzz who was an excellent ball handler. With a stutter step dribble between the two guards, he sent a bullet to Shortie who handed off to Romero coming across and he made a hook pass to Mark coming down the lane. Mark felt like an NBA forward as he seemed to glide and hang and hang, forcing an underhanded shot that was good. He too was fouled. He missed the free throw but it hit the heel of the rim ricocheted right back into his out stretched hands and he pushed it back up. It swished and he could see the Panther coach frantically calling for a time out. The clock told him the game was only one minute and thirty-seven seconds old. The score was ten to nothing Indians.

* * *

Candy and the other five cheerleaders had three-dozen Dalton fans sounding like two hundred in the tiny gym. She leaped into the air waving her pom-poms. Looking left then right she was uncomfortable. There was Sheriff Frank, not ten feet away, staring straight at her. Not at his daughter, Joyce, but directly at her. *Why me? If he is, as Mark insists, the killer then I sure don't like him watching me.*

"What's wrong?" Shannon asked as Candy had stopped.

"Uh . . . nothin'" she responded hastily. "Nothin'."

* * *

The whole team surrounded Donnelley who was trying to keep them pumped up but Mark listened without hearing a word. The sheriff was sitting between the team bench and the cheering section watching the six cheerleaders do one of their routines.

Coach Donnelley had been wrong. The arrest of Weird Walter was not the reason he played so well. The formation of the Kryptonites had given him a purpose and five of his friends . . . yeah, he was including Red . . . had the same feelings regarding the sheriff.

It was strange how he had never noticed Frank in the past and that was usually when the guy got on his case over one of his pranks, or over somebody else's deeds for which he always got the blame. Lately Frank seemed to be the only man he ever saw. Every place he looked, there the jerk was, bigger than life.

Frank turned his way. He wanted to shrink down to hide behind the other players. Didn't want the guy to be able to read what had to be showing in his eyes. Strange. The sheriff's left wrist was bare. Doesn't he always wear a wristwatch? Realize that doesn't prove anything, but its . . . what do they call it? Circumstantial. The Kryptonites need to find something to put him away. The Kryptonites? He didn't know about Buzz and Jodi; seems like they are along for the ride. Shannon was a good head. So was Ollie except he wanted everything in black and white. However, much to his surprise, the little redhead was deadly serious.

The horn sounded and Mark moved to return to battle, looking at the cheerleaders as he passed. Those outfits make these gals look pretty darned good, including Red. Sure didn't plan on telling her so.

As the game progressed, Mark began playing with a grin. Every time the Panthers made a run he would can another three or Ollie would muscle up a shot from down under. Citrus couldn't seem to get on track as Dalton maintained their lead. The fact that he started at center and then moved to guard seemed to completely confuse them.

Buzz, with his quick hands, batted the ball away from a Citrus player. It skittered toward the sidelines with both Mark and his opponent diving for the loose ball. They slid along on their bellies all the way to the seats with both men hanging on for dear life. The Referee was calling jump ball. Mark had come to a stop directly in front of a man who had raised both his feet to avoid the sliding players. Mark rolled over, ready to sit up. Directly above his face were the bottoms of a pair of dress boots. There was an impression on each heel of an eagle. By the time the image registered in his brain, the guy spread his legs and dropped a foot on each side of his body. Frank's feet. "Oh man," he scrambled to his own feet. Once he was out of range he told himself, "It's him."

CHAPTER TWELVE

The full moon washed over the tombstones, casting eerie shadows, turning the area along the river into a gloomy, practically supernatural, hiding spot for the boys. The old and gnarled trees hung out over the water creating grotesque shapes, which seemed to be alive. Two figures moved furtively along the dark side of the stone mausoleum building, stealing glances back toward the populated area.

"Ollie, where the heck is Buzz?" Mark asked, for the first time in his life feeling uncomfortable about his actions. "First Shortie couldn't get out and then guess who's the no show? The guy who came up with this idea." He squinted, trying to make out his, so-called, 'Glow in the dark' watch. "Its ten after twelve so that guy gets another five minutes, then we go on without him." Less than fifty feet from where they stood was Laura's grave. Mark shuddered.

Buzz appeared out of the blackness as though by magic. With his dark skin, dressed entirely in black clothes from sock hat to shoes, he seemed to be part of the shadows. "Never fear. The Buzzard is here. Did you guys hear the news?"

Ollie was already heading for the fence. "Come on man, let's go get us some melons."

"No, wait. Tomorrow afternoon they are sending some doctors up from Clarksdale to see if Walter is sane enough to stand trial."

"What?" Mark stopped mid-stride as though someone had pushed the 'Pause' button on the VCR. "I thought murder suspects were always brought to trial."

"I guess sometimes they don't," Buzz told them. "Since they already have a confession. Know what I mean?"

Mark was shaking his head. "The sheriff has had Weird Walter in jail since Saturday. We all know this so called confession is a joke. This isn't fair. Even someone like Walter should have the chance to prove his innocence."

Ollie was clinging to a metal post, one leg on each side of the fence. "We already know the sheriff is the killer."

Mark easily scaled the fence and at once found himself with a number of feelings. Knowing his friends were itching to move on, he was remembering two things; the watch and a cast of a very clear footprint that matched a certain pair of boots. Boy is this dumb. Shouldn't be out here. None of us should. Tugging at his lower lip between his thumb and forefinger he informed them, "If Walter is shipped off to the nut farm, the sheriff is home free. We gotta do something."

"Like what," Ollie asked? "Sure nothing we can do tonight."

"I know that. But I probably know Walter better than any kid in town. Kinda looks at me like I'm some sort of a hero. Always calls me 'Mr. Mark.' Not only that, but Walter liked Laura. That fat bastard has been able to pull one off. I know why they call them pigs. Wonder who we could talk to about this? There must be somebody who would listen." He threaded his way through the headstones heading toward Fargas' field. "Let's go get some melons. We can use the railroad bridge goin' back. Nobody in the world will see us."

The threesome rapidly made their way over a second fence out into the middle of the patch. The moon was behind the clouds yet there was enough light that Mark was able to see the dark lumps and calculate their dimensions.

"Oh wow! Look at the size of them beggars!" Buzz was thumping his knuckles from melon to melon searching for the right sound.

"Yeah," Ollie was also checking the sizes, "I'm going to get me two of 'em."

The moon found a break in the clouds. It was about a quarter of the way up in the eastern sky. Mark looked at Buzz and Ollie. It made the dark figures look like two ghouls. "I got mine," Buzz was whispering.

"Got me a biggen." Mark told them. "Let's cut out." He was already heading toward a stand of trees.

A dark shape came out from behind the trunk of a huge sycamore. "Hey you boys! Drop them melons!"

The first blast was deafening. Mark could hear the swish-slap-slap as pellets whipped through the oak leaves over their heads. "Oh shit!" he yelled as all three boys ran like rabbits, leaping, darting, heading for cover. The second barrel of the twelve-gauge shotgun exploded and Mark cried out, "Oooh, oooh, oh God. I've been shot!"

* * *

Candy was completely absorbed with a computer program she had created regarding the murder. She had a habit of letting the tip of her tongue protrude from the corner of her lips when she was concentrating. So intent on what she was doing, she was out of touch with time. Glancing up at the clock she told herself, "Twenty after twelve. Already?" She clapped both sides of her head with her palms. "I better hit the sack. I'm usually out of it by ten. Good thing my folks are gone."

"Just a couple more minutes." She returned to the computer with the thought, let me finish what I was digging into and then I'll hit the sack. Wouldn't it be something to be a high flyin' criminal investigator. I could dig that. Letting her imagination drift she saw herself at a crime scene; the one where Mark's sister was murdered. She was explaining to a group of men, several had FBI on their coats, that she'd found many tiny clues, which as soon as she could get them to her lab, would provide absolute proof that Sheriff Martinez was the Perp.

* * *

The boys were safely over the fence and into the trees. "Marcus? Did you get hit?" Ollie was crashing through low growing brush while the others ducked under tree branches.

"Yeah. It was me," Mark choked, "Man does it hurt."

"How bad?" Buzz was black and yet he appeared ghostly pale in the moonlight.

"Don't know. Hit me in the ass."

"Man, we bettter get you to the doctor." Buzz had stopped and was looking up at the lights of town across the river.

"No way! Doc Snyder will blab it all over town. We'll all be in over our heads. Gotta take care of this ourselves. Come on, let's keep goin'. Hope my folks are sound asleep. Gonna have to doctor this on my own."

By the time they reached Riverview and Main it was nearly One a.m. Except for a couple dozen hanging streetlights and the sign at the Lucky Lady Bar, the town was totally dark. A hundred feet short of his house Mark came to a halt.

"What's up?" Ollie whispered.

Jerking his thumb toward the Swanson place he whispered, "look at that, Ollie. There's a light in Red's bedroom window. I was thinkin', since it feels like only a couple of pellets, maybe she has a first aid kit and something we can dig them out with."

"I don't know, Mark. We're liable to wake up her folks then we'd have some serious explaining to do."

"No, no. Her parents aren't home tonight. Heard Red tell Shannon when we were at the Pit after the game, that she had to cut out early. She had to baby-sit her brother 'cause her folks were going to a party up at the lake. Guess they're plannin' to stay over. Let's do it." Cutting across the lawn he rapped on her window, trying to mute his voice as he called out. "Hey Red, open up."

"Who's out there?" Came a cautious reply.

"It's me, Mark, and Buzz and Ollie."

She came to the window dressed in green and white striped pajamas. "Mark? What are you guys doing out this time of night?"

"Figured you'd be racked out by this time. Keep it quite. Don't want to wake up the neighbors. Uh . . . I got me some kinda hurt, from a shotgun. You got some tweezers. Maybe some Methyolate or something like that?"

"You're kidding. Gosh! Nobody's home but me and Michael who's in bed. Come 'round to the front. I'll let you in. Probably can find what you need. Who shot you, the sheriff?"

She opened the front door jumping back in surprise. "Where'd you get that watermelon?"

Mark was clutching a thirty-five pound monster. Rest of the guys had either pitched or dropped theirs when the shooting started. "Fargas' melon patch," he told her. "That rat-faced jerk took a shot at me. Got a couple of pellets in my thigh." He touched the spot on his hip. "I can even feel 'em."

"What can I say? Serves ya right."

"You gonna find me some medicine or what? Need to get

my fanny home."

"What you're going to have to do," Candy was already digging through an open first aid kit, "is dig them out then put some medication on them. In the thigh? Which side?"

"Right here." He showed her the two blood spots on the seat of his Levis.

"Well, you need to pull your pants down far enough for me to take a look."

"Drop my pants?" Mark's tone was incredulous. "In front of a girl?"

"What's your problem? Oh I get it. No underwear, huh? I'll go get a towel you can wrap up in. Do you think you can dig them out or jewant Ollie to do it?"

"I'm wearing underwear. It's simply that . . . oh what the heck?" He undid the zipper, unhooked the western belt buckle, letting the pants slide as far as his knees. On his white jockey shorts were two red spots, one about the size of a dime, the second the size of a half dollar.

Candy didn't hesitate, pulling the back of his shorts down far enough to expose the wounds as the two boys crowded around. She winced. "One of them has barely broken through the skin. Other one feels like it's in about a quarter inch."

He looked down, trying to see, but the pellets were far enough to his rear he had to push at the flesh with his fingers and crane his neck. One stood out darkly through the whiteness. The second was the problem. He grimaced as she felt the spot with her forefinger. "No way I can dig it out myself," he winced, "'cause I got all I can do to see 'em. Gonna need me some help."

"Looks like you'll have to let Candy cut them out," Ollie suggested.

"No way," Mark snapped. "I'm not having this wild redhead cutting on me."

"Suit yourself." She let the elastic waistband snap back into place. "Like I told you, let Ollie do it. I'm not all that keen on having to touch your slimy flesh."

"Not me," Ollie shrank away. "I get sick when I see blood."

"Looks like she's all we got," Buzz offered. "Or we can call Doc Snyder."

"All right! All right! Go ahead Red. Do whatever you have

to do."

"I don't like this," she groaned. "Try the easy one first."

He watched her cross the room to paw through some sewing notions, coming up with a large darning needle. "Lay down on your left side on the couch," she said. "Going to have dig for the other one. Might even have to make a cut."

He felt her soft hand on his bare hip guiding him into position. First she dipped the tip of the needle and the ends of a pair of tweezers into some alcohol then easily removed the obvious pellet, dropping it into a saucer.

"Makes me feel stupid," he told her.

"Um huh," she asked. "No call on the ad yet, huh?"

"Not even. Maybe the sheriff can't read."

"Hey Mark," Buzz always seemed to take the negative side. "It might not even be his. Know what I'm sayin'? Before he arrested Walter he was telling everybody that the killer could be somebody from out of town."

"Okay, let's get serious." Candy probed at the deeper wound with the needle. Mark sucked in his breath but was able to keep from crying out.

"Hold on a minute." She went to the refrigerator from which she produced an ice cube. "Hold this on the wound for a couple of minutes. Should numb the flesh some like it did when I had my ears pierced."

Mark held the cube to the sore as she suggested but shuddered when he saw her extract a single edged razor blade from a small packet. "I was wondering, Red. How come you're up at this hour of the morning on a school night?

"Wasn't watching the time 'cause I been working on our case."

"Working on the case, like how?"

"I'm putting everything into the computer. A chart more or less of everything we've heard, the clues we've found and their possible link, our suspicions and why. I think you'll find it fascinating. I made me a program that will search and compare. I used to think that after I got out of school I'd become a nurse. Lately I'm thinking law enforcement, perhaps a criminal investigator."

Mark's brows rose. "Do we get to see this chart?"

149

"I figured I could give a presentation at our next club meeting. In one column I've listed everything . . ." She looked his way before she continued. "From you and Ollie finding the body all the way up till today. In the next column is every possible reason, person or thing connected with the item. We are going to have a meeting, aren't we? So we can discuss things and you guys can add your ideas?"

"Damn," Ollie remarked. "She sounds like a professional."
"That's me," she was serious. "Okay, that's long enough." Sinking to her knees so her face was only inches from his thigh she poised with the blade above his skin. "Here goes nothing."

"Are you sure you know what you're doing there, Red?"

"You call me Red one more time and I'm liable to slip."
He could see the bright sparks in her eyes and then she closed them for an instant. Touching the razor blade to his flesh his skin parted when she made the tiny cut. Wincing, he buried his fingers as deeply as they would go into a small pillow, refusing to make a sound, feeling the peculiar push as the blade touched the lead pellet, surprised most of the pain was in his mind. Again she was using the long needle and the tweezers. Her pink tongue was sticking out the left corner of her mouth. She smelled so . . . clean and he was aware of the pajamas and that she would be naked underneath. What a crazy thing to think about!

Quickly he shifted his thoughts to the investigation. She'd made him curious. "You mentioned suspicions. Am I listed as a suspect?"

"Of course, but according to the computer, you're the last person in the world who had anything to do with it. We already know you were at home that night. You told us you and your dad went looking for her. Hey, that's not all. Found out that Frank was not home that night."

"You did what?" Mark was flabbergasted. "How in the world?"

Candy was chewing on her lower lip. "Ah, not as deep as I thought. Hardly bleeding at all. I'm gonna make a tiny cut into the fat. Ummm . . . maybe a tad more. I think it's moving. I'll have it out dreckly."

Mark joined the other boys in holding their breaths in fascination.

"Got it!" She held it out for all to see then dropped it into the glass saucer with an audible 'clink'. "Jewanta keep them for souvenirs?"

"Not a chance. Wow, what a gas. So how did you find out Frank was not at home?"

"Wait a minute. She was holding a bottle of medicine and a Q-tip. I need to put something on the wounds. Brace yourself, kiddo. This is going to smart some."

"I hope that's Kryptonite."

"All I can say is, you better be The Man Of Steel since this is Iodine." With the cotton swab she daubed the brown liquid directly into the deeper wound. He nearly came off the couch.

While she was covering the sores with gauze pads and taping them into place, she told him, "You're a pretty tough guy, you know that?"

"That's all right. You make a pretty good doctor. So what's the scoop on the sheriff?"

"Come on, bring that melon into the kitchen and let's dig in, then I'll tell ya what happened."

Ollie set the melon on the counter. There was a maple knife caddy next to the sink and Candy used a long bladed one to cut four huge wedges. "You guys want fawks?"

"Fox?" Mark teased. "Might as well." The others nodded.

Candy took a huge bite then talked with her mouth full. "It was kinda by accident. When we were down at the Pit after the game, Officer whatsisname . . . Porter?"

"Yeah," Mark answered. "Ralph Porter."

"Yeah, well, guess he was on duty. I dropped in for a cup of coffee. Made a couple of remarks to me, actually I'd say he was flirting with me. Can you imagine? An old guy like him? Must be in his thirties. He is good lookin'. Anyway, I made a remark to him about how great it was that he and the sheriff solved the crime so rapidly and you know what he said?"

Mark paused with his fork piercing the red fruit, leaning toward her. "I assume you are going to tell us."

"Was surprised he'd rattle on like this to me, but he said, 'Yessirree, we been on this thing right from the get go. Don't know where Frank was that night 'cause he wasn't at home and he wasn't at the Lucky Lady either, but I was out looking for a lost child. Frank showed up 'bout midnight. That's when I told him I had a premonition that this time she hadn't run away. What can I say? I was right.'"

"I'll be darned," Ollie agreed. "Then that proves the sheriff was out somewheres till midnight. I guess you also found out why they say police work is ninety percent footwork and ten percent luck. Was that all he had to say?"

"He was saying somethin' 'bout the sheriff suspecting . . . his words; 'Your friend Mark,' but that he, meanin' Ralph, insisted all the time that it probably was some weirdo."

I'll be darned, Mark was thinking. Whether he liked Red or not, with the ideas he had and this gal's ability, they were going to have to work together as a team. "I've got something to add to your program. Something I saw at the game tonight."

* * *

Mark was surprised to find his stepfather in the kitchen when he came in for breakfast the next morning. Didn't get home until two and had to set the alarm or he would have slept till noon. His dad was generally gone by the time he got up. Made him wonder if this wouldn't be an opportunity to talk to someone about his suspicions regarding the sheriff; if he'd listen. Mark was totally convinced that Weird Walter was not the one.

There had been this horrible dream during the four plus hours he was asleep. The killer was in the dream but he was wearing a gorilla outfit. Whether it was the sheriff or not there was no way to tell, but the man had one arm about a little girl . . . not a child he recognized . . . and in the other hand was a chain saw. Running. That was terrifying enough, but the real nightmare was Red Swanson being there too and she was ordering me around. Couldn't even recall the details, something involving a baseball bat and a policeman who looked like Ralph Porter. She had struck the gorilla over the head with the bat. Then Ralph was heaping piles of praise on Red for rescuing the captive.

"Why are you limping?" His stepfather asked as Mark walked over to reach into an upper cabinet for a box of cereal and a bowl.

"Uh . . . " He touched the spot where Candy had performed her surgery. "We had a tough ball game last night . . . but we won. Downed Citrus 73 to 57. I scored 26 points. Man oh man

152

we were hot. Wish you could have been there."

"Happens sometimes. Even a team like Citrus can hit a cold spot. Eighth grade sports isn't something high on my list of priorities."

"I figured maybe, you know, since I was playing . . . "My Dad doesn't care. Never a, 'Great job Mark,' or 'I'm proud of you son.' Never.

"Incidentally, you happen to be having breakfast with the new president of the Dalton Lion's Club." He was showing off a piece of wood with the Lion's club seal on it and a walnut gavel.

Mark was thinking about talking to someone about his suspicions, but his step-dad wasn't that person . . . for sure. Big deal, he thought dourly. Take that wooden hammer down to the Green Spot with a dollar it'll get you a cup of coffee. "Congratulations," he mumbled.

* * *

Peggy Watson, the waitress at the Green Spot, wondered about Officer Porter. The place was unusually quiet considering it was nearly noon. 'Course it was Thursday. She moved to where Ralph was sitting in his favorite booth having lunch. What bugged her was why he kept flirting but never asked her out? Lots of guys asked her out; generally full of hot air promises. Most always married with one thing on their minds. Even Sheriff Martinez flirts all the time. Slob keeps offering me money. Frank always called Ralph his deputy, but Ralph didn't like it 'cause Frank was elected as Chief of Police and he felt he should be addressed as Officer Porter. Don't know how this sheriff crap got started. God, he looks sharp today in his sport clothes. Couldn't remember ever seeing him out of his police uniform.

"How we doing, Ralph? Want a warm up?"

"Tell you what, Peggy. Think I'll have a beer."

"You're not supposed to be drinking and you know it. You know what AA says" 'Don't even take the first.' Anyhow, you're on duty."

"Not yet. Not due on till three. One beer isn't going to hurt me. Heckafire, I know you're wrong 'cause I been having; 'One beer' every so often for four or five months without falling off the wagon. It's the hard stuff that'll kill ya."

"Okay, this time." She brought him the beer then sat across

153

from him in the booth. "Frank came in this morning. Was say-ing something 'bout a couple of psycho doctors coming to talk to Walter today." Man is Ralph ever good looking. A widower and has a good job. It's been what? Eight months since he lost his wife? Maybe he didn't go for her type. She checked out the only other customers, two men in a booth at the far end.

Ralph was grinning. "Hadn't heard that. I suppose these, so called, doctors are going to decide if Walter is sane enough to stand trial. He probably is as long as he doesn't have one of his spells. Did Frank say what time these doctors were coming?"

"One o'clock, as far as he knew."

"Maybe I'll slip in there to hear what they have to say."
"Well, I'm glad they caught him. I'm tellin' ya, he had me scared to death. Laura was one of my daughter's playmates. I was remembering last month Shelly went to a birthday party at the Goodwin's. Ralph?"

"Yeah?"

"How come you don't date anybody? Or don't any of the local ladies appeal to you?" He seemed to consider the question for a long time. She felt him watching her as he took a long drink of the beer.

"Oh, you know. The hours I work; three to midnight make it tough to think about going out. The last two weeks we been buried by this murder investigation."

"So? Couldn't you and Frank swap shifts once in a while?"

"I don't know. I've been out of the dating scene for twelve or thirteen years and I work nights you know. Most of the avail-able women in Dalton don't much turn me on. They're either fat, rotten disposition, or have a house full of kids. You got some kids, don'tcha?"

She wanted to cry. She was a widow with three kids. But she wasn't fat and most people thought she had a wonderful per-sonality and she didn't look all that bad. "Yeah, I do. Three."

"If you want the truth, you turn me on."

"I . . . I do?" She choked. "Then why don't you ask me out?" He grinned all of a sudden and she liked it.

"So? You want to go out with me?"

Eyes shining, she nodded. "Yes I do. Any chance you can get Frank to cover for you on Saturday night. There's a dance in the community building during the fair. We could take in the fair and then do the dance at nine, or am I rushing you?"

"Lady Luck is looking down on us. Frank wants to take his family to the fair tomorrow night so he's already told me he'll do the duty Saturday. Uh, I better have another cup of coffee before I go on duty."

She hurried over to the counter, returning with a fresh pot, filling his personal cup. "Since you have the Laura Goodwin case solved you should have more time for yourself.

"Pretty much locked up. Once we got Walter's confession . . . heck, I look for these psychiatrists to suggest we ship him off to someplace like Shady Acres."

"What a shame. You know what Ralph? I have this big . . . 'What if?'"

"What if?" He frowned.

"What if Walter didn't do it?"

"The guy confessed. What the heck are you getting at?"

"I've had Walter over doing work around my house. The kids loved him. And this confession? I know how police interrogation can muddle the mind of a smart man. Walter has the mind of a kid."

"Uh hmmm. Then who do you think did it?"
She forced a laugh. "If I knew that I'd have your job. What concerns me is if it was somebody else, I was thinking how it could happen again. You know? Once they start . . . "

* * *

As they left school on Thursday, Shannon had to force herself to be patient and not run for home. "Hey Candy, I have to take the outfits I made over to the fairgrounds to get them entered in the competition. You wanna walk down there with me?"

"Heck, I surely will. Told you I had something awesome to tell you 'bout last night."

"Fair starts tonight. Too bad we can't stay, but what the hey? The whole gang is going tomorrow night. So what did I miss out on last night?"

Candy filled her in on all the details regarding the shotgun pellets and the melon.

"Holy cow! Those guys are gonna have to stop this wild crap or someone is going to get hurt . . . or end up in Juvi." She

155

stopped in front of a partly open gate. "This is where they told me to go in. Then we go to the side door of pavilion number two. They'll be judging tomorrow afternoon so I'll be on pins and needles all day."

"You got nothing to worry about. The clothes you make are outta sight. Better than anything I've ever seen in a store."

"I'm the worrying type. Come on, let's hurry."

"The big thing is, I told Mark about us running into Officer Porter at the Pit. He insisted Frank was nowhere around the night Mark's sister was killed."

"You're right, he did say that didn't he? The way you go about things, you need to get a job with the FBI."

* * *

The Man had remembered that if you type a phone number into the Google subject box and hit Search it would spit out the name and address. It was as simple as that. He squinted as he checked out the Goodwin house. Mostly it was a question of what course of action to follow. It was a one story with no dogs, no fence. He could take a chance, answer the ad and pick up the watch, or he could wait until no one was home and break in. Should be easy. Hardly anyone in Dalton locks their doors. Checking the surrounding houses he was satisfied that there were enough trees and shrubs around the Goodwin place for cover. Neighbors wouldn't be able to see any activity. Property goes all the way through to Riverview Drive, and that's good.

What bothered him the most was, how did the Goodwin's come by the watch? The kid? I'll bet that's how. He and his gang must have rode out to the crime scene last Saturday. Could be a problem. Take a drive out that way and check the place later. Maybe they'll all go to the fair tomorrow night. Leave my car over in the theater parking lot; hoof it for a block down Locust. Get in the back way, ransack every room to make it look like a burglary, find the watch and cut out. Won't even have to leave any dead bodies behind. Now ain't that a shame?

CHAPTER THIRTEEN

Don Yugolaski and Lester Judd, the two psychiatrists from Clarksdale, had driven up early enough to have lunch in town. The doctors were the two men Peggy served prior to talking to Ralph. At precisely one 'o clock Friday afternoon they walked into the Dalton police department asking to see Walter Jordan.

Frank took them to a room where Walter already waited. It was obvious he wanted to hang around but Don waved him away. They spent a long time with Walter making small talk before getting around to discussing the murder. Ordinarily the county wouldn't send two doctors, but the county prosecutor, the Dalton police department and Walter's mother agreed to this process rather than a drawn out court hearing. Even though he'd been charged in Dalton, the location of the body placed the crime in the county's jurisdiction.

At first Don did most of the talking while Lester took notes. He could tell Walter enjoyed their company and the many questions about his childhood. He obviously liked to talk about himself. Don noticed the fact Dalton jail didn't have prison type clothes for their guests and Walter was wearing his street clothes and the Los Angeles Dodgers sweatshirt caught Don's attention. From several phone conversations he'd had with Dr. Snyder he learned Walter had the I.Q. of a ten year old and yet possessed a photographic memory concerning baseball statistics. The boy could tell you at any given moment, who was playing, where they were playing, what the batting averages and RBI's of dozens of major league-players were. Armed with this information and wanting to put Walter at ease and instill a feeling of friendship, Don reached out to touch the sweatshirt then questioned, "hmmm, Dodgers huh? You like baseball, Walter?"

"Oh man. You bet. Watch every game on TV."

"Do you think Ryker will win twenty games this year?"

"Oh you know, he's won eighteen and lost only three. Got a 1.88 e.r.a. Struck out fifteen Phillies last week. Dodgers gonna go all the way."

"Could be, only a few games left. They have some awfully good players."

"Lefty Garcia got thirty-nine homers. Batting 335. Pitchers scared of him, you know. Walk him half the time."

"Tell me Walter, do you like to walk?"

"Oh sure, I walk all the time."

"The sheriff told me you were walking out where the Goodwin child was killed last week. Is that right?" Don was thinking, the time is right. With his baldhead on a level with Walter's, he leaned forward, his quarter inch thick glasses three inches from the man's face. "Walter, did you kill Laura Goodwin?"

Walter didn't answer, sitting with his mouth open, hands widespread.

Lester spoke for the first time. "Did you Walter? Did you kill the little girl?"

"I don't 'member. Mr. Frank . . . he say I did."

"What do you say?" Don continued while Lester was making notes on a tablet. Don knew it wasn't their purpose to interrogate the man but to merely compare what he told them to the confession, which seemed very lucid, perhaps too lucid.

"Don't know." Walter was in distress. "I would never hurt Laura. Laura liked me. Laura thought Walter was fun."

"Hmm. That's different," Lester spoke to Don and then asked another question. "You get sick some times and don't remember what you did, right?"

Walter reached up to touch the lump on his forehead. "I fall down sometimes. Doc Snyder say I got a sickness."

"Where were you the night Laura was killed and what were you doing?"

"After I seen the movie I went walking. I like to walk, you know."

Lester scanned his copy of the report, frowning. "I see. What time did you leave the movies?" Something in the report didn't sit right with him. Something about the timing.

"I don't do time very good. Lotta people already in bed. I went walking, you know."

Don was silent as their method of questioning was planned. He made a note on his pad, "Check show times." He watched Walter's eyes as his partner, a short, dark complexioned man continued.

"Yes, so you told us. Tell me Walter, do you own a knife?"

"Own? You mean like buy one?"

"Do you have a knife?"

"No. You see Mr. Frank take my knife. Tell me I couldn't use it in jail."

"Was it a big knife?"

Lester folded his arms and waited while Walter thought about that.

"It was . . . " He showed them with his fingers held about four inches apart. "I keep it sharp though. Mr. Stevens down at the store lets me help open boxes. I keep his backroom clean. Mr. Stevens likes me. He's a nice man you know."

"I believe you told Sheriff Martinez you used this knife on the girl. Is that how you killed her?" Don felt they were getting close and watched as Walter pondered this question.

"I don't never cut nobody with my knife. Not . . . I not ever!"

"Whoa," Don glanced at his partner. "Walter, you told the sheriff that you did. Don't you remember?"

"Mr. Frank said he would make me 'member.'"

Don's baldhead came straight up, glistening in the light. Walter's remark was innocent enough and yet a red flag was there. He motioned for Lester to come off to the far side of the room where they spoke quietly.

"Did what the boy just say strike you the same way as it did me?"

"You mean, 'Mr. Frank made me?' Could be a new twist."

"What's bothering me, Lester, is that some of his answers are not jibing with the report. He claims it was quite late when he left the movie. The child disappeared around seven or so. Did the boy do it or didn't he?"

"It's not our job to find out. Leave that to the courts. Kid seems kind of slow but pretty competent. I'd say he deserves a trial."

"Okay. But before we turn in our report there is something we'd better find out."

Walter didn't seem to be having any problem with the questioning. He sat wiggling his feet like most men do, busy checking out something on the ceiling.

Don asked. "Walter? Did Mr. uh . . . Sheriff Frank? Did he hit you at anytime?"

"I . . . I don't think so. Mr. Frank don't like me, you know. He push me."

"How many times did he hit you?"

Walter grinned. "I can't do numbers, you know. Mr. Frank say he wanted for me to tell him I kill Laura and that I cut her with my knife. He say I got sick that night so I don't 'member."

Lester had his fingers to his lips, talking through them. "Do you have any bruises?'

"Oh! Yeah." Walter seemed delighted at the prospect. "You wanna see my back?"

"Yes Walter, I believe we had better see your back."

Walter unbuttoned his shirt and let it slip to his waist. His smooth shoulders had several red and purple welts.

"Holy shit!" exclaimed Don, not realizing his mistake at not asking where the bruises had come from.

Lester stood with his arms crossed. "Thank you Walter. You can put your shirt back on. That will be all for today. You have been of considerable help." He turned to his companion. "We better have a chat with the sheriff."

"When can I go home? I don't like it here. There is no place to walk to."

Neither man answered him. Sooner than you might expect, Don was thinking. At this time we have other problems on our minds.

* * *

"That's the wildest thing I ever heard," Frank told the two doctors. "That clever S.O.B. has made all this crap up. Had those marks on his back when we brought him in. Told me he got those bruises a week from last Wednesday. I never laid a hand on him." Frank glanced at Ralph who was nodding in agreement. His deputy had come in early out of curiosity. It was unusual to see

160

his partner in street clothes, but Ralph had driven over to Cotton to look at a classic 68 Mustang someone wanted to sell. The sheriff was aware that he looked the part of a southern redneck. He could tell by the doctors' stares the men didn't believe him. "Look, I'm telling you, that is one dangerous man."

"I wonder," Don was frowning. "Do you have any proof that Walter did not receive those marks while in your custody?"

Frank squirmed. "Not actual physical evidence. Walter told me some hobos jumped him down by the railroad. Beat him up. Took what little money he had."

"That's a fact," Ralph put in. "One of 'em hit him with a cane or something. It sure as hell wasn't Frank."

"I mighta been somewhat harsh with the boy, but I was trying to find out if he had seen or heard anything. The confession came as a complete surprise. Once I got that, I figured I didn't need any other evidence."

"What you are telling us is, he is clever enough to concoct a story that plausible?"

"You bet he is. When he's not having one of his spells, he's as sane as you or me, retarded but sane. We do not mistreat any of our . . . frequent guests here. What he is telling you is a total fabrication. You can have Doc Snyder check him out. He can determine how old those bruises are."

Don picked up his briefcase. "We have to report this, you know. As for checking the bruises, once he's in Clarksdale, we most certainly will do so. A sheriff's department van is on its way from the county jail as we speak to transfer Mr. Jordon into county custody. In the meantime I'd say we all three have a problem. We have discovered that Walter is highly susceptible to suggestion. Also, Lester and I agree that on what we learned from the boy, from his doctor and from what you have told us, we will have to certify him competent to stand trial."

Oh crap, Frank thought. What did I say?

"I am sure you are aware that Walter has a right to a trial and a public defender. If he should go before a judge and plead guilty, then it's over. But if he even so much as suggests to an attorney that police brutality might have been used to elicit a confession, and that attorney convinces Walter the damage was inflicted while he was in your custody . . . whether it was or not, then you and Officer Porter would find it in your best interests to come up with some concrete evidence before you go before a jury."

The sheriff slapped his right palm on the desktop. "This is bull shit."

"We'll be in touch," Don let them know as the two men walked out the door.

* * *

"What a load of crap, Ralph. I never touched him."

"I know you didn't, Frank. So what do you think we ought to do?"

"Man, ya got me. We've got our work cut out for us, that's for sure. Any ideas? Think it would help if we try to find some witnesses to the mugging?"

"You gotta be jokin', Frank. If it was hoboes as he said, then they are long gone. We play Hell locating anybody who was out that time of night. I'm thinkin' the Jordan home would be the best place for us to start. Especially Walter's room."

"By God Ralph, now you're cookin'. I'll call Judge Elliot and get us a warrant."

"Great." Ralph was already heading for the door. "Got to run home and get into my uniform. Meetcha at the court house."

* * *

Frank sniffed at the aroma of something baking. "Mrs. Jordan. We have a warrant here to take a look through Walter's room." The sheriff didn't like doing this sort of thing. Worse, it bothered him that the plump woman's eyes were dark and hostile.

"I can't believe this, Frank. Why aren't you out looking for the real killer instead of tormenting poor Walter."

"Mrs. Jordan. I have a search warrant."

"You're not going to find anything, so help yourself."

"Thank you ma'am. We'll try not to disturb anything more than we have to." The woman, wearing an apron spotted with flour, followed them down the hall then stood in the doorway glaring. Frank looked about, wondering where to start. The room was about ten by twelve with a closet at one end.

"This looks like Walter," Ralph told him. "Baseball crap everywhere."

Frank grunted looking about. Dodger pennants on the

walls, pictures of players and a baseball covered with autographs. Next to a fair sized TV on a desk was an assortment of baseball cards. Even the quilt on the single bed, probably a creation of Mrs. Jordan's, was covered with figures of catchers, batters and runners. He wished she'd get back to her baking. Made him feel uncomfortable having her watch.

"Okay Ralph, you go through the closet. I'll look through the desk and the dresser." He heard Mrs. Jordan breath a deep sigh as they began. The fact she was there made him great deal more careful than he would have been otherwise. Imitating some of his favorite TV cops, he went through every drawer, looked under the bed, under the mattress. He could see Ralph moving all the clothes, pawing through all the items stored on the upper shelf.

"May I ask what is it you are looking for?" Mrs. Jordan snapped.

"Anything that might connect your son to this crime." He wasn't sure himself what he was searching for. It would help if they could find some pornography or something like that but they were drawing a complete blank.

"Oh oh! Frank, you better take a look at this." Ralph had lifted the side of the mattress next to the wall where he reached under to pick up a soft pile of wadded up, silky material.

The sheriff snatched the garment from his grasp and shook it out. "I'll be damned, a pair of little girl's underpants. This about cinches it." He turned to Mrs. Jordan. Her expression told him he had a winner. "We'd better go and see Mrs. Goodwin."

* * *

Mrs. Goodwin nearly collapsed, leaning her head against the sheriff's chest, clutching the coral colored pair of rayon briefs against her cheek.

"Did these belong to you daughter?" The sheriff asked gruffly.

She began to wail. "I don't know. They are like some of the ones she wears." Then she began to shake all over with wracking sobs, crying out, "Oh dear God. They could be Laura's." The sheriff looked helplessly at his deputy.

When the two officers left the Goodwin home Frank paused next to his cruiser staring at his deputy, a peculiar notion flitting about in his mind. "Ralph, tell me something." He'd placed the

163

silky garment back into the plastic baggie, which he waved at Ralph. "I looked under that mattress right after we got there. I didn't see any panties. Then you lift the mattress and there they are. Where the hell did you find the little Goodwin girl's panties?"

"Didn't find them anywhere, boss. They ain't the Goodwin girl's. I was anticipating you might need some cover due to what those two docs think about Walter's bruises, so I ran into the Thrift Store and picked up a pair. Actually I swiped them since I didn't want the clerk to be suspicious. We got what we wanted. Mrs. Goodwin says they are her daughters. Hell, they'll haul Walter off to the nut farm and your troubles are over."

"Damn it Ralph, you are a lot smarter than you look."

"You damn betcha. So why don't you go head on and join your family at the fair? I'll take these panties down, put them in the evidence locker, then I'll come do my duty."

* * *

Right after school each of the Kryptonites dashed home for the mandatory quick meal, a few chores, then along with a whole gang of kids, were off to the fair. On the way to the fairgrounds Candy could see Buzz and Shannon holding hands while Jodi was busy carrying on, flirting and teasing with three high school boys. Candy made a face when one of these guys, a pretty boy not much taller than her friend, eventually decided to hang out with Jodi. He was a junior in high school whose name was Clinton something or the other.

As they passed the Lions Club Chicken house, Mark gave a half-wave to his stepfather who was working in the booth. "My dad wouldn't go to the game Wednesday 'cause that's his night at the Lion's Club, but he has time to take in the fair. I got to have the worst father in the whole world."

"Second worst," Candy snorted. "Mine doesn't even know I exist."

As though by magic, Heather Deiter appeared from behind the Chicken House.

"Hi you guys. Hi Ollie."

Candy thought the blonde looked fantastic. She was wearing black, skin tight, stretch slacks and a Kelly green pullover which made her white hair all the more noticeable. It was obvious where this was leading as Ollie looked curiously at the tiny

164

girl. Candy shook her head feeling a small stab of jealousy. Ollie had always been flirting and saying complimentary things to her, but since she pretended to ignore his attention, it came as no surprise when he turned his charm on Heather.

"Man do you ever look bitchin'. Are those new threads?" Candy sighed, simple as that they were hooked up. She looked at Mark, who was wearing his prized blue T-shirt with the big red and yellow Superman logo on the front. He had his arms outstretched like he was flying as he made a swooping circle around the group. "Here I am, the Caped Crusader. Look! Up in the sky! It's a bird. It's a plane . . . " With a disgusted grimace he wiped his face. "Crap, it's a bird. Hey you guys, let's head for the Midway."

Candy extended both arms straight out, stopping the rest of the group. "Hole up. There's that good-ol'-boy, Sheriff Frank. He's watching us."

Frank and his family were walking directly to where they stood. "Hi Joyce," Candy and Shannon spoke in unison.

The Sheriff's short, dark-haired, dark eyed daughter moved away from her family and told them, "looks like every kid in school turned out tonight."

"Jewanta hang with us?" Candy asked. "We have to go check on Shannon's entries in the sewing competition then we're heading for the Midway."

Joyce made a face. "Ever since Mark's sister was murdered Dad won't let us kids out of his sight. Since he's caught the killer you'd think he'd lighten up. I'd sure rather hang out with you guys."

Mark was staring directly at the sheriff. Candy had to smile when he asked, "Whatcha say, Frankie Boy? You enjoying the fair?"

"As a matter of fact . . . Mr. Superman, we are." When his daughter rejoined him he his voice held a warning tone, "you guys behave yourselves." Turning to usher his family toward the Midway, he looked back, eyes narrowed, then added, "That goes double for you, Superboy."

Candy smirked. "She wasn't much impressed with the Superman crap. As soon as the sheriff was out of earshot Candy told them, "My God, Joyce could be living with the killer. "I wonder if he's seen the ad?"

"If he has," Mark replied, "he could be thinking we are the ones who put it in the paper. Come on, let's head for the Midway."

"In a couple of minutes," Candy paused. "Shannon wants us to go with her to check on her entries. If you guys want to go on, we'll meet you over by the Ferris wheel."

"Okay," Mark answered, "only make it quick."

"Come on Buzz," Shannon was tugging at his hand. "I gotta know how I made out."

"Aw, you go ahead. I don't care about looking at a bunch of sewing. You know what I mean? I'll go with the guys." Candy could see the disappointment on her face but it disappeared when Buzz told her, "I kinda dig the outfit you have on. Did you make that one?"

She nodded. "I made the skirt." Above the flouncy blue skirt she was wearing a knitted tube top. It showed a couple of inches of skin at the midriff and she was bra-less. The garment left her arms and shoulders bare. It was tight, showing everyone she was developing a figure.

"Y'all are some sorta friends," Candy snapped. "This is important to someone like Shannon. We're supposed to be a club. You know, all fer one and one fer all. Be nice if we'd all back her up. You jerks can stick it. Come on Shannon. I'll go with you."

Jodi looked at her 'Date' and told him, "Clinton? I had better go too. Will you wait for me?"

"Hey," the boy named Clinton made a face and shrugged his shoulders. "I don't mind looking at sewing stuff. I'll go with you."

"Count me in," Heather took a playful punch at Ollie's upper arm. "Like I'll meetcha at the wheel."

"Oh what the hell," Mark told the rest of the group. "Let's all go have a look see before Shannon wets her pants."

Shannon was in such a hurry Candy found herself rushing to keep up. At the entrance Shannon slipped inside but the rest of the Kryptonites paused to let another couple come out. A stocky girl with her arm linked through that of a tall, handsome boy looked directly at Candy and paused.

"Oh, hi Carmelita. Aren't you gonna innerduce us to your friend?" She could tell the girl didn't know what to make of the

166

apparent friendliness.

"Uh . . . this is Toby Martin," she exclaimed proudly. "He's a Junior." The boy gave a half-wave to the group but Mark seemed to know him and the two guys hi-fived.

Candy leaned close to the stocky girl's ear and whispered, "Is he good lookin' or what?"

Carmelita beamed.

Once they were inside Jodi snidely told her, "She's been running with the high-school football players. From what I hear they only go with her seeing as she puts out."

"Come on, get real. She's only thirteen."

"Yeah? Only like you, she looks a lot older. What the heck is the matter with Shannon?"

Candy looked toward her friend who stood in a state of dismay. What the heck was wrong?

"It's gone." She stood with a look of shock on her face, dejectedly wringing her hands.

Jodi squealed, "Hey Shannon, what a trip. You got two blues and a red and a white."

"Someone has stolen it. My western jacket is gone."

"Oh my Gawd," squealed Candy. "Look at this." She nearly had to drag Shannon to the glass case. Inside, under a spotlight, decked with a huge white satin ribbon was the blue jacket. The neatly embossed card at the bottom stated in gold; BEST OF SHOW.

Shannon was bawling as Buzz, in a state of confusion, tried to comfort her. Then Candy witnessed something incredibly moving. Mark was wiping at his cheeks. "Got a bug in my eye," he told her.

The group moved out to the Midway. "So enough about the sewing already," Mark growled. "Thought we were going to stay there all night,"

"Told you we'd meet you guys later," Candy reminded him.

"Aw, the rides aren't much fun without a bunch of squealing gals. Man, look at all the rug rats tonight."

"Want to hear something gross?" Candy asked. "Mom wanted me to bring Michael. Wouldn't that have been a bummer? Lucky for me they had to drive down to Los Angeles for some sort of meeting. They left Michael with Mrs. Baxter 'til I get home."

Shannon agreed. "Good thing mom didn't make me bring mine. Those three brats are uncontrollable. I'd have killed me a couple of kids before the evening was over. One for sure."

"I'll tell you one thing," Mark was speaking directly to Candy. "You have no idea how much I wish I could have brought Laura." There was a moment of total silence until he snapped, "What the heck is with this guy? It's the sheriff again eyeballin' us. This is getting spooky."

"Come on, Mark," Buzz admonished. "Get a life. The man is not this murderous fiend you keep making him out to be. All you got is a bunch of circumstantial evidence. Frank has the killer and a confession. It's all over. You know what I'm sayin'?"

"I know whatcher sayin'," Mark told him. "We shall see. Let's go on the Hammer."

Candy frowned, feeling slightly depressed. Buzz and Shannon were obviously a couple. Jodi and Clinton were walking together, holding hands. At one point Jodie did the, "Ollie's got a girlfriend, Ollie's got a girlfriend," routine. Ollie glowered at his sister but Ollie and Heather had paired off for the rest of the evening. Sitting together on the rides, sometimes holding hands. At other times, like on the Hammer, he kept his arm about her.

This left her and Mark as the only singles and she was thinking, I'm going to have to get me a boyfriend. Missed my chance with Ollie so . . . maybe a high-school guy. All the eighth graders are so immature. At least I wouldn't be saddled with Macho Man Mark all the time. With Mark scowling on the next several rides she was seated in the seat next to him, and by scrunching against the sides was able to stay as far away as she could. She showed him though. On the Tilt-a-whirl, the Hammer and the roller coaster, she matched his bravado move for move.

* * *

When Eric arrived home he was shocked at his wife's appearance. Her eyes were red-rimmed, he face drawn and ashen. "Julie? What's wrong? I thought you . . . "

"Oh dear God, Eric. The sheriff and Officer Porter were here about an hour ago."

"They were here? What did they want?" Took an hour last night to convince Julie to go to the Judge's house for a party tonight. Her first time out since . . . and this happens.

168

"They searched Walter's room looking for more evidence."

He cocked his head. She seemed to be under control. "But why? They already had a confession. Why do they need evidence? What evidence?"

"I don't know why, but they had a pair of rayon underpants. Pink."

"Oh my God. Laura's?" He was holding her, patting her back like a child's.

She was shaking her head. "Not Laura's. At first I thought they were. Told Sheriff Frank they could be. Then I cried for an hour."

"They weren't Laura's? How do you know?"

"After I got over the initial shock, it occurred to me they were rayon or nylon. My baby was allergic to either of those. Made her break out. She always wore cotton. Those belonged to some other little girl."

He didn't understand why but he was tremendously relieved. "I guess we had better let the sheriff know. Uh . . . Julie . . . honey? Are you going to be alright?"

"Don't worry. I'm going to be alright. I already left a message on his machine. I'm going to take a hot shower." She slipped out of his arms, heading toward the bedroom. "There is a party waiting for us."

"Julie?"

She stopped, looking back.

"Where's Mark?"

"Oh, he's gone to the fair."

He was grinning. "Uh . . . Julie?"

She knew where this was going. It had been a bad two weeks, but it was time for them to move on.

"Would you like to uh . . . ummmh . . . What I'm trying to say is; would you like to have another child?"

She was in his arms again. "Oh Eric, could we?"

"It might not be a girl."

"So? Then you'd have the son you wanted. Your own son."

* * *

Some of the group wandered off to look at the prize animals. "Of all things, I have to be home by ten o'clock," Shannon told Buzz as they stopped under an arbor in an isolated area of the garden displays. He was standing behind her with his arms about her waist. She turned her face to look back at him. It seemed like the most natural thing in the world for them to kiss.

The first one was a bare touching of the lips, like a butterfly to a flower. Then they kissed again, lips parting slightly, both imitating what they had seen in movies. She had crashed and gone to heaven. Oh no! Why does he have to go and spoil it? Buzz moved both his hands up inside the top onto her bare breasts where they remained for a heart stopping moment before she jerked them away.

"Don't you ever touch me like that!"

"Well gee, I wasn't going to do nothing." He drew away, looking totally dejected, walking several paces down the gravel walkway.

"Buzz Tarmen, you come right back here."

The boy stopped for a moment and then turned to shuffle toward where she waited. She grabbed his hand and shook her head, looking deeply into his eyes. "You can walk me home."

Neither of the teenagers was aware of a person standing in the shadows, a pair of glittering, beady eyes watching them from a bird beaked face.

Only a shadow.

* * *

The Man, by carefully planning his time, made it to the fair then was frustrated when he had to wing it. He'd been so certain the activities would provide uncountable opportunities. Everybody was there including the Morris' and their little kid, Eugenia. Even the Parker's and their daughter, can't remember what her name is. Best of all, the Heinz's were there, but as parents were much more protective than most, hovering over little Gretchen like a pair of mother geese. Maybe I'd best concentrate on the Morris kid. Even if he could make the snatch, there was the problem of how to get her out undetected. Can do the thing on Wednesday as I planned. And then, as if in answer to some devilish prayer, things turned.

Lurking constantly in the shadows, behind concession stands, into the tall shrubbery that acted as a fence between the fairgrounds and the Riverside Park next door he kept the trio in sight. They were completely unaware he was stalking them.

They did the normal fair things; ate hot dogs and cotton candy, walked through the exhibits and giving in to their daughter's whining went to the Midway.

A couple of times the Man could see the Goodwin kid . . . Mark, and his girl friend; little red headed tart. They both watched him from time to time making him wonder, thinking about the watch. How in the hell did the Goodwin kid get it? Had to have gone back out there. Was he suspicious? He couldn't know . . . could be? Be digging his own grave. I don't like being watched. The two kids disappeared in the crowd as he waited for the group to finish riding the merry-go-round. Actually the parents stood alongside the painted pony while the girl rode, shouting, "giddy up horse." Next they let her go by herself on the Tea Cup ride. Then her father, damned Kraut, won a soccer ball by throwing at the milk bottles and the little tike's eyes were shining as she possessively clutched the red, white and blue ball.

What is she doing over there? He watched the group of children standing in line at a small booth to have body paints applied in decorative fashion to their faces. The spoiled brat was pleading for permission to have it done. Come on, come on, he thought, even though he too watched in fascination as the artist skillfully used his brushes. The parents probably were considering if they should spring for the five dollars to make little Gretchen happy.

Someone jostled the girl's arm. The ball popped free, bouncing through the legs of a dozen revelers. The tiny blond darted after the red and white sphere but someone accidentally kicked it. The ball skittered into the bushes behind which he squatted, directly into his hands. She appeared at the opening between two shrubs, peering under the branches. He held the decorative ball out for her to see. She was smiling as she came directly to him. So was he.

CHAPTER FOURTEEN

Buzz and Shannon stopped at the corner by the Greyhound Station a block and a half from her house.

"Nelson?"

Buzz took her hand. It had been a long time since anyone other than his mother had called him Nelson. Coming from her it pleased him. "Uh huh?"

"You're my man, okay?"

"Well I . . . I sure want'ta be. You know what I mean?" His heart felt like lump of putty.

"Okay then, we need to keep it cool."

"Hey, I'm sorry 'bout . . . "

"Don't worry about it. I understand. You're a guy. But neither of us is ready to handle that kind of a relationship."

"It won't happen again."

"You're absolutely right, it won't. But you, buddy boy, keep this in mind. Don't go bragging to your buddies about what happened or you can kiss our friendship good-bye."

"Gee Shannon, I wasn't . . . "

"If you want to brag that you kissed me, that's okay since it won't be the last time. In fact, I have about five minutes before my curfew, so if you plan to kiss me goodnight, you better get with it."

Oh man oh man, he thought as he moved to face her. She was four inches taller than he was, but it didn't matter. He was ten feet tall.

* * *

Shannon turned to walk toward the house filled with strange, wonderful emotions of her own. However, she'd have to be careful that her dad didn't find out Buzz was no longer nothing but one of a group of friends. She had learned over the years to be very cautious about doing anything to rile him.

But what a day! Best Of Show. Wow! She could hardly wait to tell them. Anxiously she moved inside since she knew they were waiting to hear how she did with her exhibits. What she found instead was a confrontation with an irate father.

"We had an agreement," he yelled at her. "No dates until you are sixteen. You were seen at the fairgrounds with a boy. And look at you! Dressed like a harlot!"

"It wasn't a date. We just hung out together. It was totally innocent. We were with half-a-dozen other kids. That's all."

"'That's all' you say? The way Mrs. Cripe tells it, you were making out. The two of you were kissing. She told me he was fondling you . . . intimately."

"Well . . . well, he bought me a coke and some popcorn and . . . I was thanking him for being so nice. I don't know why this is such a big deal."

"Psalms 120:2 says, 'Deliver my soul, O Lord, from lying lips, and from a deceitful tongue,' because that is where it starts. Next thing I know he will be asking you to spread your legs to thank him for a good time. Romans 12:9 says, 'Abhor that which is evil'. I do not intend to put up with this. No dating until you are sixteen means exactly that. The worst part of your offense is the lying to cover it up. There are two things I will not tolerate, lying and disobedience."

She could tell by the fierceness of his eyes his anger was escalating by the minute. She looked frantically for her mother but she wasn't in the room.

"I want you to come over here and lay yourself across my knees. In Luke 12:47 Jesus spake, 'If you do things against his will, thou shalt be beaten with many stripes. He that spareth the rod spoileth the child.'"

"Daddy! I'm darned near fourteen!" She had never seen him like this with his eyes so wild. Oh sure, she'd had her share of spankings as a child, but most of those she deserved and didn't feel any resentment over. He couldn't be serious. She hadn't had a spanking in over three years

"Shannon! I mean this minute! You need to follow the

teachings of First Peter 2:11: 'Abstain from all fleshly lusts'. I will not permit my daughter to turn into a harlot. You know what the Good Book says? 'Let the punishment fit the crime.'"

She was sure the Bible said no such thing. He was shaking a finger, pointing at his lap. Looking frantically about she called out, "Mom?"

"I mean now!"

She began to sob as she was forced to squat in order to place her slim mid-section across his lap. She hadn't even noticed when he removed his belt. Before she was aware as to what he intended, he grabbed the waist of her short skirt and all in one motion dragged the garment and her underwear down to her knees. The stinging leather struck her fiercely and she cried out. This was nothing like her childhood punishments; a few swats with a switch, the yardstick or a bare hand. This was a beating. Over and over the broad whistling strap hit her. She had never seen him like this. At the time she couldn't see that the leather strap was raising welts and drawing blood where they criss-crossed.

All of a sudden she was aware of something. What was he doing? Her father was restraining her with his left hand grasping her upper torso, fingers buried in the softness of her already ample breast, moving, squeezing, probing as he beat her. She tried to twist and squirm but his fingers clamped like a vise into the flesh. Worse, she felt his hardness against her belly. She closed her eyes and gritted her teeth but it had nothing to do with the beating. Her revulsion was so intense she hardly felt the belt.

When he at last stopped he told her, "Alright young lady, go to your room. Fall down on your knees and say your prayers. Ask the Lord to forgive you for lying to your parents and for being disobedient. As it says in Acts 8:22, 'Repent therefore of this thy wickedness, and pray God, if perhaps the thoughts of thine heart may be forgiven thee.' I want you to thank him for giving you a father who loves you enough to watch out for your wellbeing. Now go!"

As she stood her clothes fell about her ankles causing her to trip and stagger, so she stepped out of them to run sobbing beyond control to her room. Not with tears from the physical pain, but for another pain, one that would never heal.

* * *

Marie Heinz looked at her watch, deciding it would be okay, perhaps even fun, to let Gretchen have her face painted. Then it would be time to go. She turned to tell her daughter. "Karl! Where's Gretchen? Gretchen," she called, then screamed, "Gretchen!" She was frantically trying to look through, over and behind the crowd.

She trembled as Karl looked to the left then to the right, around both sides and behind the painter's booth. She desperately grasped his arm as he began to question bystanders. "Did you see a little girl . . . blond, this tall, with a red, white and blue ball?"

There was nothing to see but frightened eyes, blank stares or shaking heads. She found herself darting about, jumping into the air to look over the heads of other fair goers. Slowly seeping into her mind were three horrifying words. Laura Goodman. Murdered.

Her husband asked the boy tending the fried zucchini stand next to them the same question.

"Blond? 'Bout so high?" The boy held his hand three feet above the ground.

Karl nodded frantically.

"Yeah, I saw her. Couple minutes ago. Kid was chasing a loose ball." Rolled under those bushes right over there." The boy bent forward like he was trying to see under them.

Marie fought her way through the crowd, clawing at the branches, going to her knees to crawl under. "Gretchen?" She called out. "Dear God. Where are you?" There was a flash of red, white and blue. Then she had it, the soccer ball.

* * *

When Shannon's mother came home from the store, her husband told her, "I had to punish your daughter for her transgressions."

"Shannon? I don't understand. Whatever for?"

"She was seen consorting intimately with a boy at the fair. I have no intention of permitting her to openly lie to me about it. You are her mother so you need to back me up."

"I'll go up and have a mother/daughter chat with her.

"Don't coddle her, Ruby. She has to understand that I will

not tolerate this sort of behavior."

"I don't intend to coddle her, Clarence. But I do intend to explain to her how important it is she follows the guidelines we set for her, guidelines that show how much we love her. What's wrong with that?"

"Do whatever you want. I'm going out for a while. Need some time by myself."

"At this time of night?"

* * *

The Man was washing his hands, smiling as he saw the pink water flushing down the drain. His planning, waiting and watching for such a moment had paid off. Snatched her right out from under their noses. Couldn't have been a better location. All those bushes. Right next to the City Park.

He had followed the family for nearly an hour but it had been hard to make plans for his mind was focused on how he was going to get the watch back. Red, white and blue ball; then there she was.

Picking up the blue plastic bag he easily swung it up onto his shoulder then headed for the door, locking it behind him. The last thing he'd seen was old lady Heinz jumping up and down like a kangaroo trying to see over the crowd. Sorry lady. You ain't never gonna see your little Gretchen again. No sir. Little rugrat is goin' on a trip.

* * *

Shannon was lying on her stomach crying softly, not aware her mother was there until she sat on the bed next to her. She had pulled a blanket up and over her bruised and bleeding body and she winced when her mother sat on the edge of the cover, pulling it tight across her rear..

"I hope," her mother told her as she brushed the hair out of her daughter's eyes. "You have learned your lesson. Your father was right, for you deliberately disobeyed. You know what the Bible says. 'Children obey your parents in all things.'"

"Oh mama, not you too. I even know where it says that. Someplace in Ephesians, but if you read the whole verse it says, 'Fathers provoke your children not to wrath.' Or doesn't he read the part that fits him?"

"Perhaps the punishment was somewhat harsh, but I'm

sure he wanted to make certain you understood his position."

Shannon couldn't believe her ears as she stared at her mother. She was close to being a carbon copy of the older woman, tall, slender, with lovely black hair and dark almond eyes. "Oh, I understand his position all right. Nothing but a Bible spouting hypocrite. I can quote Bible too. How about 'A wolf in sheep's clothing? That's what my dad is. And he scares me."

Shannon, honey. You are making too much of this. You should expect to be punished . . . "

"Mama. You weren't there. This was not a matter of punishment. He made me lie across his lap. Pulled down my skirt and my panties and beat me with his belt. But all the while he was doing it, my dad was squeezing . . . he was fondling my breasts."

"Don't you dare say things like that! It's not true and you know it. I don't understand why teenagers always make up this kind of crap when they are angry at their fathers. You know he only wants what's best for you."

"Am I making this up, mother?" She pulled the blanket away to expose the mass of cuts and bruises. Her mother's gasp was more nearly a screech.

"Oh dear God. I'll get some salve." She was hurrying down the hall. When she returned she told Shannon, "I know you are angry at you father, but that will pass. He has been under a great deal of pressure lately. You know he loves you very much."

Whatever the brown salve was, it was amazing for she felt immediate relief. "You can make excuses all you want, Mama, but are you blind? Haven't you seen how he touches and pats Janice and Rochelle when he is holding them?"

"Shannon! You are letting your imagination . . . "

"Then she turned on her side and pulled the tube top down to expose her left breast. "Is this my imagination?" There were ugly purple bruises on both sides of the softness. "And even you let me down. I'll tell you, Mama. If I live to be a hundred, I will never forgive him. If I thought there was any way I could make it on my own, I'd run away, only I happen to have enough sense to know I can't. However, the day I turn eighteen, I'm out of here."

"Oh, honey, honey, time will . . . "

"Mom. You can believe whatever you want. I will never

forget, and I promise you, he will never touch me that way again. If he tries I will call Child Protective Services."

* * *

The sheriff and his family were watching the ostrich races unaware as the terror and panic for Mr. and Mrs. Heinz increased when they were unable to raise the deputy on his pager or on the phone. The loud speaker boomed out: "Sheriff Martinez, would you report to the Administration Office immediately."

"I better find out what they want," he told his wife. "Why don't you take the boys over to the Chicken House. Go ahead and order for me. I'll take a three piece dinner box."

In less than two minutes he was answering the call. "Hey Paul, what have we got?"

The fair's assistant manager, who seemed to be in charge, looked grim. Young fellow had a rugged outdoorsy look that made Frank think he ought to be in the north woods somewhere.

"We tried paging Ralph but didn't get any response. Some-one spotted you on the grounds so I figured you and Ralph switched."

"We switched alright. Only he is supposed to have the duty tonight. Tomorrow night we're trading off. That damn Ralph has probably snuck off to the Green Spot. He has the hot for Sally; that cute little waitress."

Paul rubbed both his palms on his plaid shirt as though they were damp. "Frank, we have a missing child. The Heinz's daughter. Probably got lost, but with thoughts of the Goodwin murder in their minds, the parents are about ready to explode."

"For how long? Where was she last seen? Where are her parents?"

"They're both out searching for her. She was standing with her parents watching the guy who paints faces. When they looked up she was gone. Something about her chasing a ball. I'll tell ya, buddy, they're running scared."

"I don't know why Ralph doesn't answer his pager. Bet he's got the danged thing turned off. You guys are lucky I happen to be here. I'll find the little tyke."

* * *

It was nearly midnight when Mark arrived home from the fair. The first place he headed for was the refrigerator. Opening lids on micro-waveable dishes he selected one with two pieces of leftover chicken. Grabbing a coke, he pushed the door closed with his knee then noticed, at eye level, a Post-it note. On it was printed the phone number for the Banker's house and the words, "Be home about two."

Great, he thought. Give me chance to complete my history homework before I hit the sack. Get that thing out of the way. Wouldn't have to worry about them bugging him for being up after hours. Since we're goin' to grandmas on Sunday I want to have my entire Saturday open. Man was he showing them this year, he thought with a grin. In spite of what everybody considered his devilish actions, his overall tough guy attitude, my grades were better than last year by far. Maybe he was starting to like school.

Sitting in front of his computer he had several open books on his desk. "Okay," he placed his hands on the keyboard. "Back to my report on the Grecian Empire of 1200 BC." Extracting excerpts from various reference books and Homer's The Odyssey and The Iliad he typed information into his computer. An hour later he sat back, scratching his head. What, he wondered, would his teacher say if he put in his report that he felt the Trojan War was a fantasy rather than historical. The story of Paris and Aphrodite as well as Helen of Troy was fascinating to him . . . but he wondered, true or false? How 'bout the Trojan-Horse? Wonder what I can discover on the Internet?

On a shelf, directly at eye-level was the copy he'd made of the Viva Las Vegas tape. Ann Margaret, he thought. Turning to the computer he typed in the name and pressed search. Holy cow. Gal has a jillion sites. The one he selected was 'Official Ann Margaret Web Site'. Wow. I've hardly even heard of her and yet this gal has made over fifty pictures . . . going back thirty years before I was even born.

After a couple of minutes he located a number of photos from her films. Then one of them hit him. It was a full-face view from Bye Bye Birdie. The film that either Shannon or Jodi had mentioned. It was like looking at a photograph of Red. Well . . . maybe. Same green eyes, same perfect teeth, same red eyebrows, same hair swirling about her shoulders and the same killer smile. Of course Ann was a lot more glamorous than Red. Not exactly that but a lot more mature. Red always looks grouchy. A total nothing compared to the movie star.

He pressed the Print Screen key, went into Paint Brush, selected Edit then Paste. And there it was. Using the erasure he removed all the writing, the icons and other crap from the page until only the picture remained. Then he saved it as a jpg file. Two minutes later he brought it up in his imaging program, enlarged it to fill the screen then printed it out. For a long time he sat staring at it. God she's pretty. So why is Red such a bitch? Nothing but a freak. Too bad she's not halfway human.

Amazed at the wealth of information available, he let the addictive nature of the Web suck him in until he became aware of the incessant barking of Judge Elliot's dog next door. The big German shepherd sounded frantic. It was probably a couple of high schoolers having a party or making out on the stretch of beach behind the Deiter place.

His eyes strayed to the tiny numbers at the lower right-hand corner of the screen. "1:38 AM," he groaned. "Man o' man. Hot shower and hit the rack." He liked to, whenever he could, turn the water up near to scalding and then steam himself clean. Dad always rags on me 'bout this 'cause I run it 'till it turns cold.

When he was through he pushed open the glass door, stepping out into the coolness. There was a sudden empty feeling in his stomach as though the heart which was in his throat had come from down there. Something heavy struck and hit him directly above the left eye and he staggered. The weapon was a large gun in the hand of a person dressed entirely in black from his shoes to the ski mask. He shoved Mark in the middle of the back toward his desk. His nakedness made him feel completely vulnerable. "Golly, let me put on some clothes."

Without saying a word, the intruder struck him again. Mark nearly went to his knees. Gesturing toward the chair, the cold nose of the gun prodded his ribs. Pain tears welled in his eyes and he was feeling woozy. What the heck was going on?

The robber grabbed him by his hair and jerked, forcing him to sit in the chair next to the computer. Mark was frantic. A roll of gray duct tape appeared from under the black shirt. The burglar was taping his wrists to the arms of the chair. Next he tore off a strip and slapped it onto his mouth, placing it so high it temporarily covered his nose. For a moment he was close to hysteria as his air supply stopped, but by working his upper lip and wriggling his nose he was able to open a tiny breathing hole. His guts seemed to be churning. He desperately wanted to go to the bathroom.

Then he was alone. His mind was in a haze from the two blows but he could follow the robber's progress through the house, hearing drawers slide open in his parent's room and things crashing to the floor. Next he was in Laura's room, which had remained basically untouched since the day she came up missing. Didn't spend much time in there, moving on to the family room. Mark couldn't believe this was happening. Why did the guy hit him? Minutes passed agonizingly slow. He tried contorting his face to pull at the tape, make it stretch.

Dragging a blue garbage bag filled with items, the robber returned and began going through Mark's room. He pulled things out of the closet, spending a long time pawing through the dresser drawers, dumping some on the floor, looking under things, even between the mattresses, muttering constantly to himself. Then he moved to stand with his butt against Mark's shoulder as he began searching through the desk drawers, scattering school work all over the place, discarding floppy disks and personal items onto the carpet. Then he found the watch. Pausing for a moment to look it over, he stuffed it into his pocket then continued to explore.

Mark's mind was in turmoil. If the guy took the watch then what? It was the major key in their attempt to identify the killer. Why was he thinking about this? Was the guy done?

The intruder moved directly behind Mark who felt a new terror as the cold metal barrel of the gun pressed against the back of his head. Shutting his eyes he tried to force his mind to go blank but was filled with more panic than he could stand. Was it possible this guy actually was going to pull the trigger? Wasn't there anything he could do? How much would it hurt?

There was a distinct click as the hammer cocked. Mark tensed, his whole face was being squeezed by giant fingers, his eyes pressed so tightly closed they ached. The sudden scream of a siren could be heard coming up Riverview Drive and the gun was jerked away. There was total silence behind him. Holding his breath, very slowly he turned to look. The burglar was gone. So was the bag of loot. The siren went on by with a diminishing wail. He could tell by the sound, fire engine. It was cool in the room but his naked body was covered with perspiration.

* * *

The Man was both elated and disgusted. He had the watch. His tracks were totally covered. But why had he let the sound of a damned siren spook him into not pulling the trigger? Should have forced the kid out of the house and into the SUV. Too dangerous though, left the SUV around the corner on Taylor. Somebody could have spotted them. Especially with that party going on across the street. Too bad. Could have done a number on him. Left my signature, so to speak. Two in one night. Don't like the idea of leaving a witness but it was too late to go back. His folks were due home. Saw that note on the refrigerator.

However, if later on I get any inkling that the kid suspects anything he's dead meat.

CHAPTER FIFTEEN

Mark sat for a long time trying to get his breathing back to normal, listening to assure himself the housebreaker was actually gone. Not a sound. No car doors slammed. No engines started. What did that mean? A transient? What could he do? There was a pair of scissors in the pile of papers on the floor. Could he upset the chair and get to them? He shivered, having a hard time catching his breath. Since the siren was past, would the guy come back?

Had to get loose. The strange thing going through his mind was not wanting to be discovered stark naked by his folks. If only he had a knife. The first thing he had to do was determine if he could get the tape away from his nose. Using the corner of the desk he worked and worked, scraping his cheek over and over as he felt the tape lift then begin to roll. He not only had it off his nose but also off most of his mouth. Should he yell? Who would hear him?

Ain't gonna work. What next? Could he dial the phone with his nose? Worth a try. What the heck was the number on the Post It note? How about 911? No way. It would reach the sheriff. Sure don't want him here. The instrument sat mutely toward the back of his desk. From where he sat there was no way to reach it. By bending as far as the restraints would permit, he was able to get his mouth close to the cord. Stretching his neck and upper body with all his strength he caught the coiled cord with his teeth then dragged it closer. Using his chin he knocked the receiver off its base. The only way he could punch the numbers was by using his nose. It was necessary to pull back after each number to look at the keypad prior to pushing each button but he did all seven digits for Ollie's house. There was no way for him to know he'd missed by one as he listened to it ring and ring. Come on Mr. Frazier; pick it up.

In front of his eyes was a scrap of paper on which was printed a phone number, and the one simple word: 'Swanson'. That's it. Mr. Swanson, right across the street. Using his nose he pushed down the hang-up button then went through the agonizingly slow motions again. It also rang and rang until he was ready to scream, then a muffled female voice answered, "Hello."

"Mrs. Swanson? Is your husband home? This is Mark across the street."

"Mark? This is Candy. Nobody here but me and Michael. My folks are at some sort of DGF meeting in Los Angeles. Won't be back till Monday. Why are you calling this time of night? It's two in the morning."

Oh God, his mind was in a whirl. "Look Red, we've had a break-in. Burglar tied me up and ransacked the house and I can't get loose. Can you go next door and get Mr. Deiter?"

"Where are your folks? How'd this guy get in?"

I probably left our side door unlocked when I got home. Dad and mom are at a party at the banker's place."

"I'm on my way."

"Great," he muttered to a dead phone. "Mr. Deiter will know what to do."

He waited, feeling a moment of panic when he heard the door open. What if the robber came back? "Mr. Deiter?" He called out. "I'm in here."

She came charging right in, then stood forever looking at his naked body. The fact he was sitting concealed anything important. "Oh my Gawd! There's blood on your face."

"Would you stop jabbering and find something to cut me loose?

She spotted the pair of scissors in the jumble of papers and books on the floor. "Man, if you ain't a sight. Better'n the side-show freak at the fair."

"Boy Red, you're hilarious. Come on. Use those things."

She half cut, half sawed at the sticky tape, managing to free his right arm. Then he seized the scissors to complete the chore himself.

Without thinking he came out of the chair to stand in front of her, displaying everything he owned. It was the most embarrassing moment in his life. He snatched his jockey shorts from where he'd dropped them on the floor then caught his foot in the elastic, dancing about, nearly falling in his haste to put them on. She never once looked away.

Managing to get his racing heart back to normal he glanced at the mess on the floor where he saw the picture he'd printed earlier. Couldn't let her see that. He put his foot on it.

There was the sound of a car in the drive then doors slammed. The front opened and his dad laughed out loud about something then made some remark about all the lights being on.

"Finally my folks show up. Where the heck are my pants?"

* * *

Had to spend all night sleeping on my stomach, Shannon thought as she walked toward the shower. Pretty darned uncomfortable but no way could she sleep on her back. Adjusting the water until it was as hot as she could stand she stayed under the stinging spray for nearly twenty minutes. At least she didn't have to face him this morning.

Couldn't remember anything in her entire life that hurt as much as his actions. Her anger was so powerful she could taste the bitterness in her mouth. Then he had the nerve to come up this morning before he and mom left for Clarksdale; to apologize? I don't think so.!

"Your mom and I are going to that AME pastors conference as we planned. You are to stay in the house. I'm leaving you in charge of the kids. Sunday morning I want all four of you go to church. Do I make myself clear?"

"Yes," she murmured.

"Yes what?"

"Yes sir!" she snapped.

"That's better. We'll be home late Sunday night.

In the bathroom she found the tin of salve her mother had used last night. She stopped short when she looked at the label for directions. 'Petro Carbo Salve' the label read. 'Thoroughly wash cow's udders before applying.' "I don't believe this," she dipped her fingers into the brown salve. "But what the heck? It works." She coated her entire backside with the soothing ointment, wondering what she could wear. No underwear for sure. Maybe some sweats.

The phone rang.

"Whoops." As she snatched the instrument from the desk, out of habit she flung herself backwards onto the bed. Twisting sideways she landed on her chest, the phone at her ear. "Hello," she groaned.

"Hey, Shannon. It's me. Have you heard?"

Jodi sounded breathless. "Heard what?"

"Mark's house got robbed last night in the wee hours and Mark was home alone."

"Oh come on. Get real."

"Hey Shannie, this is real. Guy had a gun. Tied Mark up and went through the house. Took a bunch of things. You know. DVD player, silver and jewelry and stuff like that."

"Have you talked to Mark?"

"Mom and Dad are over at Mark's place. Hey, can you come over. Everybody's gonna meet here directly so we can get the whole story. Ollie's gonna make pancakes and eggs. Mom says it's okay as long as we clean up the mess. Even Mark's gonna come soon as he's done with the sheriff and all that good stuff. This is so extreme."

"Jodi, I can't. My folks left early this morning for some sort of seminar down in Clarksdale. I'm going to have to beg off. Have to baby-sit and uh . . . I'm not feeling too hot. You know . . . that time of the month."

"Bummer. Dad called after they got there and talked to my brother. Told Ollie that Candy was there and she cut Mark loose."

"Candy? Why would she be at Mark's house in the wee hours?"

"Ain't got a clue, have to ask her. Only get this. The robber caught Mark coming out of the shower. Tied him to a chair but wouldn't let him put any clothes on."

"Oh wow, Jodi. That's outta sight. Candy musta got an eyeful, huh?"

"Probably did. Ain't that a trip? Dad told Ollie they called the sheriff and he and Ralph are over there. Mark's folks didn't get home until after two. Were both so crocked they didn't even see the mess. What they saw was Mark in his skivies and Candy

186

in her pjs coming out of his bedroom. You can believe that so-bered them up. I can hardly wait to hear the whole story."

"Skivies and pjs? Man is that off the wall. Call me back when you get all the details."

"Come on, Shannie. No reason why you can't make it. Bring the rug rats with you. Candy's bringing her little brother 'cause her folks are gone to some meeting with some big shots from Blue Ribbon Foods."

Shannon truly wanted to go, but . . . nuts to him. Dad isn't going to keep me from seeing my friends. I'll talk to the kids. Let 'em know they can go along if they promise not to tell. Even if they should, he'd better not touch me. He tries and I'll be out the door. The phone cord was long enough she was able to reach the closet where she searched for something she might be able to wear. "Give me a few minutes. What did you say Ollie was mak-ing?"

"Pancakes, eggs and bacon."

"Okay. Tell him to make plenty. I'm going to call Buzz then we're on our way."

* * *

Mark, Candy and Michael were the last to arrive. Mark was carrying the morning paper. "Would you look at this crap?" He spread it out on the countertop.

"Hi Marcus." Ollie was busy at the stove. "We're waiting to hear all about it."

"You kids follow me," Jodi glanced at the headline as she passed, herding the little ones into the breakfast nook, while the teens gathered around the kitchen counter where there were only four stools. In bold letters it proclaimed; 'DALTON MURDER SUS-PECT MOVED'

"So?" Shannon let him know. "Your robbery was too late to make the paper. What the heck happened to your head?"

Buzz moved up behind her and slipped his arms about her waist from behind but she scowled, jerked and moved away.

Mark noticed but was too wound up for it to register. He touched the white bandage with his fingertips. "Doc Snyder checked it out and said I didn't have a concussion and I'd live."

"You mean the guy hitcha?" asked Ollie.

"Yeah, he popped me a couple of times with the butt of his

gun, but I'm not concerned about that at the moment. Get what this says. He read aloud:

"'While conducting a search at the home of murder suspect, Walter Jordan, Dalton police officers Frank Martinez and Ralph Porter discovered a pair of underclothes that were identified by the murdered girl's mother as belonging to the slain child. In an exclusive statement to Dalton Union, officer Martinez told us, "this is an important development since the suspect has been certified as competent to stand trial."'"

"So it turned out to be Walter after all," Buzz reminded him. "Told ya all along it wasn't the sheriff."

"Look man. Listen to what I'm saying. This don't prove nothin'. They showed these panties to my mom before she and dad headed out. Mom told me she never told the sheriff the panties were Laura's, only that they might be. She called him later to tell him they couldn't be hers because my sister always wore cotton 'cause nylon or rayon panties gave her a rash."

"Then they have no evidence," Shannon suggested.

"They got nothing." Mark looked at Ollie. Sheriff probably planted the panties. They do that kind of stuff, like slipping a bag of dope into someone's car or planting it on a suspect."

"You ready for some hot-cakes, Mark." Ollie had worked from a griddle on the counter. "So come on, tell us about last night. Pretty hairy, from what Dad told me. How'd he get in?"

"I'm tellin' you it was scary."

"Guy even had a gun." Candy informed them.

Mark held out his plate on which Ollie placed a pair of steaming pancakes, then grinned as his friend motioned for more and he obliged. "Scrambled eggs and bacon are on the stove. Help yourself. So did you get a good look at this robber?"

"Wearing a ski mask so all I did was bust my butt trying to get loose. Used duct tape and wrapped it around my wrists and the arms of the chair. Never dreamed anything like this could happen in Dalton?" He turned to look at Red who had already eaten one hotcake. She was extending her plate for seconds and he guiltily looked away. Her eyes made him feel like he was still naked. He didn't feel embarrassed, he felt funny.

Ollie plopped two more hotcakes onto her plate. "How come the guy hitcha?"

"Didn't move fast enough to suit him. Whacked me with his gun. No big thing."

"No big thang huh?" Candy was glaring at him. "You're not using your half of a brain. Can't you see what has happened here?"

"Yeah I do, we were robbed."

"You were robbed by someone who knew you had the watch."

"Come on Red, that's a real stretch. If all he wanted was the watch, why didn't he take that and light out? Or why didn't he poke the gun against my temple and ask me where it was? He tore up the whole house."

Shannon spread both hands wide in question. "He took the watch?"

Mark sighed. "Yeah, he got our major clue."

"Hey guys."

Mark, along with all the others turned to look at Buzz.

"I gotta cut out. Promised Sadie Martin I'd clean out her garage today. I'm running late. By the way Ollie, you got any extra garbage bags?"

"Take a look in the garage, Buzz. Think there's a new box on the shelf above the washer."

"Cool. Won't have to run past the store, and don't forget, Ollie, you're supposed to help me today."

"Yeah, yeah, soon as we wind things up here."

Mark watched Buzz go out into the garage. "Garbage bag," he muttered to no one in particular.

"Yeah," said Ollie. "Takes a bunch of 'em to clean out a garage."

"The guy who robbed our house used one to haul off his loot."

"So why is that a big deal?" asked Candy.

"It was a blue garbage bag. You ever seen a blue one?"

She shrugged. "Black. Gray sometimes. Highway workers use white or orange ones. You think it's a clue?"

"I don't know. Sheriff says it was probably some dope-head from out of town looking for an easy score. Didn't mention the watch to the Fuzz. Guess they'd been up all night. Some-one's little girl got lost at the fair. They spent most the night look-

189

ing for her."

Candy was adamant. "You know what, Mark? You're full of it. If that man had taken the watch and nothing else, then you would know he was the killer. This way, the robbery was his cover."

"My God Mark," Shannon added. "Candy could be right. You could have had the killer right there in the house with you."

He could remember the click of the gun's hammer but didn't tell them how close it had been. "But it sure wasn't the killer. That guy cuts people. This guy uses a gun. Kinda throws a kink in my theory about the sheriff though. If he was at the fair part of the night and then at my house ten minutes after the robber left . . ."

"If you were tied up," Jodi asked. "How did you manage to get Candy over there to cut you loose?"

"I hear you were bare assed naked." Jodi teased, nudging Ollie, watching Candy's face.

"What can I say?" Mark shrugged. "I walked out of the shower when the man walked in. Wouldn't let me put anything on. Tied me up. Had to dial the phone with my nose."

"So, Candy?" Ollie was grinning. "What did you think of Big Boy Marcus?"

Mark's discomfort grew as he watched Red lift a strip of bacon to her lips then pause as she looked directly into his eyes.

"I thought . . . truth?"

He shrugged.

"I thought you were a hunk." She smirked.

He felt himself turn three shades of red but also felt a peculiar glow.

"Awesome. Wish I'da been there." Jodi was also grinning.

"Wait, wait," Candy continued. "You haven't lived 'til you've seen a neked guy dancing 'round the room with one foot caught in the elastic of his underpants." Everyone but Mark was laughing.

"Stick it in your ear, Red. I'll have one more," he told Ollie who was eating while standing next to the stove, doing a bang up job cooking breakfast for the whole group.

"So what are we going to do?" Candy asked.

"We aren't going to do anything, Red."

"Do you have Anheimers Disease or is your peanut brain so small you can't remember my name is Candy?"

"That's Alzheimer's."

"Whatever. I'm telling you, Mark, it was him all the way. You need to concentrate on everything you can about this guy. You know. So we'll have something to go on. Was he big like the sheriff? Maybe his shoes or something like that. Maybe something he said?"

This remark touched a memory bank somewhere. "I hate to admit it, but you could be right. Makes me think about something strange. As much time as he took, he had to know my parents were gone. Pretty much rules out a drifter. Could have been as big as the sheriff. Heck, I don't know."

"What was his voice like?" Candy, using a pen and a piece of paper, was making notes.

"What are you doin', Red, gonna put all this in your computer?"

She nodded.

"Man never said a word. And if he was the killer, as Red seems to think, then you guys need to back off or somebody is going to get hurt. As of today I'm the only one he knows."

"We are not backing off." Candy said fiercely, "I'm the one who found the watch so I'm in this as deep as you are. If it wasn't for me, you'd be tied up waiting for your folks to wake up."

"You're not in this as deep as I am. This guy knows who I am. He knows where I live. I'm the one he will come after if anything happens."

"What are you saying," Shannon was pacing back and forth. "You think we should drop the investigation?"

"No, that's not what I'm saying. I'm sayin' from here on anything you guys do or anything you find out, has to be kept as secret as possible. Gotta keep you guys outta danger. As for me, I'm going to have to be as sneaky as that slime bag is. Shannon. I wish you would quit pacing and sit down. You're making me nervous."

"This thing makes me nervous," was her answer. "You know what this proves?"

"Everybody got their fill of hotcakes?" Ollie asked. "So Shannon, what does it prove?"

191

"What it proves is that Mark was right. Sheriff Frank has arrested the wrong man."

* * *

The Man parked his car and walked slowly across the grass toward the gazebo next to the water in Riverside Park. He could hear the clanking and muffled roar of generators next door. The fair was preparing to open for the new day. Sitting on a stone bench he watched a broken branch, its leaves green, bob and rotate as it passed in the murky stream. Directly across the Sandstone River was Fargas' melon patch. To the north of that was the cemetery. Looking at the tombstones and remembering the last time he was there made him feel more cheerful. He'd gone from a state of euphoria when the little sweetie had come for her ball to an absolute gloom hours later when he had to leave the Goodwin house without disposing of the teenager.

That was a bummer, but there was a good side to it all. Everyone thought the burglar was some outsider passing through town and yet there was the nagging sensation of unfinished business. The whole thing about the watch bothered him. And what bothers me is that the Goodwin kid was the one who happened to find it. The newspaper ad bothers me. If I found a watch out by a crime scene and wanted to know who's it was . . .

The Man stood, again looking across at the cemetery. He nodded, wondering, then spoke aloud, "Know exactly what I gotta do."

* * *

"Hey guys, I need to head for home," Mark yawned as he told the group. "Gotta go rack out. My all-nighter is catching up on me."

"Ollie, don't do that," Candy ordered. Ollie was gathering up pans and utensils, stacking them in the sink. "You did a real cool job with breakfast. Us gals uh do the clean-up."

"Well . . . okay, if you don't mind. I'll walk down that way with ya, Mark. "I promised Heather I'd stop by. She has some CD's I want to borrow. Then I got to go give Buzz a hand. He took two jobs and turns out they both want them done today."

"And," Jodi teased, "Ollie and Heather want to make goo goo eyes again."

"What an airhead. You don't know zip. Come on Mark.

192

Let's split."

"What the heck is this?" Mark asked as they were heading down Riverview. A black and white police cruiser headed them off as they started to cross Main.

Ralph was leaning his head out the window. "Hey Goodwin, hold it up."

The two boys stopped and waited as the officer stepped out of his patrol car.

"I thought of a couple of things we forgot to ask you about concerning last night's break-in. Me and Frank were curious as to whether there was anything about this man you might have recognized, something that would give us a place to start?"

Mark shifted uneasily. "Tell ya what, Officer. Way my juices were flowing my mind didn't focus on anything about the guy. Ollie and me do have some suspicions about this dude."

"Is that right?" Ralph was curious. "Are these ideas you can share?"

Ollie was the one to speak up. "We're kinda thinkin' the man last night and the man who killed Mark's sister are one and the same."

Ralph seemed to be considering this possibility and then he asked, "Based on what? You mentioned there was nothing about him you recognized."

"Kind of a gut feeling," Mark gave Ollie a warning look that was meant to say, 'Don't tell him about the watch.'

"You're barkin' up the wrong tree there, buddy. We already have your sister's killer behind bars and a confession."

Mark wanted this conversation over with. "It's hard to believe because we've known Weird Walter for a long time. He's always been totally harmless so it makes a guy wonder 'bout this confession. Anyway, if I come across anything that might help I'll give you guys a call."

"'Preciate that and you boys take care." Ralph was back in his unit, making the tires squeal as he pulled away.

"Man," Ollie was shaking his head. "We have to depend on those two clowns to guard and protect us. This is where I leave you, Marcus. See ya later today."

"Yeah," Mark chuckled as he started up the walk toward the side entrance that led to the laundry room. "Reminds me of that fat cop Jackie Gleason played in those Burt Reynolds flicks." Something caught his eye. He drew up short, then yelled, "hey, Ollie, hold up a minute." Dropping to his knees he peered at something in the bushes. "C'mere Ollie and take a look at this."

"Whatzup?"

Ollie was already crossing the street heading for Heathers but apparently the tone of Mark's voice brought him to a halt. There was a frown on his face as he slowly turned. Mark watched him amble back, as though he was afraid of what he might see.

On each side of the entrance to Mark's room were flower-beds. "Look at that," Mark insisted. "Red was right all the way." In the soft earth, under the window, was a clearly defined foot-print.

"I'll be damned! Got that smooth sole, ridge on the heel and an impression of an eagle."

"Man o' man. It's identical." Mark had a feeling, a sense of danger, as though the ground had shuddered.

* * *

In an effort to keep Michael under control Candy had hauled him over to Ollie's in his wagon. Shannon was walking with her while trying to keep rein on her siblings. Michael refused to ride on the return trip. The four kids were darting into yards, up people's driveways, playing hide and seek with the gas pumps at Five Points Mini Mart. They took a shortcut through the theater parking lot. Even when the place was not open, a number of folks parked their cars there. The boys were chasing the two girls among the vehicles.

Something strange about Shannon, Candy was thinking. "Hey Shannie, what's with you? You're walking like a crippled old lady. Your period can't be that bad."

"Hey, look. I gotta get home. Last thing my dad told me before they left was to stay in the house with the kids. I'm not even supposed to be out here."

"Why would he do that? Is he mad at you or something?"

"I don't want to talk about it," she snapped.

"Well pardon me. I'm supposed to be your friend, remem-ber? If you have a problem I want to help."

"This isn't something you can help with."

"Why are you so bent? Have I done something or said

194

something?"

"Oh Candy, it's not you. It's my dad. He . . . " She glanced about. They were between a van and a large truck. There were no moving vehicles or pedestrians in sight so she pulled down the soft cloth exposing her striped, naked rear then as rapidly covered it up.

Candy's gasp was more nearly a shriek. "My Gawd! He did that? But . . . why?"

Michael had at that moment stepped out from behind a parked car. "Ooooooh, I'm gonna tell everybody I saw your bare butt."

"Knock yourself out peanut brain. Last night, you know, me and Buzz wandered off in the garden area. One of Dad's stoolies saw us."

"So, what's so bad about that?"

"This old witch saw me and Buzz kissing."

"So?"

"Buzz put his hands on my boobs."

"So?"

"I've been under strict orders; absolutely no dates 'til I'm sixteen. What ticked my dad off was that he says I lied when I told him I was going with you and Jodi."

"And you did, even though there was a group of us. Why is he so flipped out about it? Sumpin' like that don't earn ya a whuppin'. Criminy! Not a beatin' bad as that." She watched Shannon's eyes, instinctively knowing there was something more. "You ainta telling me everythang."

Shannon fidgeted and chewed on her lower lip. "You're right, Candy, that's not all."

The redhead waited patiently, for some unknown reason suspecting what was coming.

"All the while he was beating on me, he was groping me." She noticed where Candy was looking and shook her head. "No, no. Not there. Had his hands on my boobs. Kept squeezing and . . . and groping, and . . . Oh God, Candy. I don't know what to do. I hate him."

"Didja tell your mother?"

"I did. She thinks I'm making it up to get even with him. This scares the crap out'ta me, and it could get worse. We've been studying this sort of thing in Psychology."

"Gawd Shannon, I don't know what to say. Here I thought I had problems with my parents. Not even close."

"Psychology books could be wrong in this case. Could be just a one-time thing. In any case, I'm going to go out of my way to never do anything to make him mad at me again. I've never been so angry or so hurt in my life."

"Shannon," she hugged her friend. "Thanks for clueing me in. I don't know if I can help, but . . . "

"You've already helped by letting me dump on you. Hey! Talk about problems. What do you think about this thing with Mark? Come on you kids. Rochelle, get out of the street."

"Maybe Mark is right. All of us should leave detective work to the police."

"I don't agree and neither do you, Candy. Here's my place. I'm hoping I'll be able to sit down by Monday."

"Yeah." She stopped and stared down the street in the direction of the fairgrounds.

"Whaaaaat?"

"We were so concerned about Mark I only half heard something he said while we were eating breakfast."

"Yeah. What was that?"

"He said Frank and Ralph were up most all night looking for somebody's little lost child. I didn't hear him say if they had found her."

"Oh my God."

* * *

Officer Ralph Porter pulled his patrol car to a stop in the Jefferson High School parking lot. Stepping out he walked toward a couple of dozen men assembled there. He'd left Daryl Cline temporarily in charge.

"Hey Porter? What's going on out on the highway? You didn't say anything when you got the call. You went ripping out that way with your lights and siren goin'."

"False alarm. Got a call from some old lady 'bout a man's body laying 'long side the road. Turned out to be a dead deer. With this other killing on my mind it sure turned my juices up. How's it going here?"

"I was thinkin' 'bout what a bang up job Frank's done organizing the search parties." Daryl told him. We've already covered the twenty or so blocks from Main to here."

"Yeah, sometimes Frank's okay. Got a team working north and another the west side. But damn it Cline, he's turning this into one mean day for me. Didn't any more than hit the sack last night and Sheriff jerks me out to check out this B and E at the Goodwin place. Read me the riot act 'cause he couldn't reach me from the fair. Wanted my help lookin' for this missing child. So I says to him, 'how could I know the battery in my cell phone had conked out?'"

"Isn't that always the way?"

"Yeah, and this morning he says to me, 'gonna be up to you to take charge of the search. Been awake twenty-six hours straight and I gotta get me some shuteye.'"

There were muttered greetings all around as Ralph again took charge. "Okay," he told them. "Same as we been doing. Going to be working in pairs with two men to each side of the street. You guys form up into groups of four and let's get going."

There were few words among the grim faced men as they obeyed his request. They'd already been at it most of the day.

"All right," Ralph liked being in command. "I'll need men going door to door starting here at the high school." He began pointing to groups. "You four take Forest Drive. Next group will work Palm. You men, take Cedar. You guys, Locust and my team will cover Park out toward DGF. Then coming back we'll work the cross streets. We gonna be doing nothing but walking. Mostly apartments and low end housing in this area and since its Saturday most of people are going to be home.

"Like I told you this morning, this ain't no social visit. Ask the questions. 'Were you at the fair? If so, did you see anything that might help us locate the child? If not, have you seen, heard, or do you know anything that would help us.' Keep in mind that most of the kids this age have fights with their parents then run away. Tell folks some pretty wild tales. Worst thing is there are even some do-gooders who might try to hide the kid. Watch their eyes and how they react. If you see any red flags, let me know and I'll follow up. Okay Cline, you and Buster hit the west side of Park Street. Marty and I will do the east side. Let's move it out."

At the first house Ralph heard something that had been

echoing in his mind throughout the day. "The Heinz child? Mrs. Hidalgo asked. Oh my God. It's only been two weeks since you guys found the Goodwin girl's body. Do you think it's happened again?"

* * *

Henry McKane and Owen Shoemaker were about three and a half miles downstream from where the Main Street Bridge crossed the Sandstone River. The two men had reached a point where fishing was the single most important pursuit in their daily existence. There were days when they made the trip up to Sandstone Lake, taking along an ice chest containing a lunch consisting of soda crackers, salami, sharp cheddar cheese and plenty of beer. Sometimes, like today, a few pieces of fresh fruit.

Yesterday they fished from the railroad bridge, now standing black and foreboding a half mile further upstream. Other times they fished from the banks, but today Owen had put his twenty-year-old, 12-foot, aluminum, Sears and Roebuck, Homart Special, in the water. The ten-horse Johnson, barely making a sound, was idling fast enough to maintain a good trolling speed. Owen was doing the trolling, but Henry was casting with his new 'Dancing Jig' off the bow.

"Shoot another cold one up this way, will you Owen?"

"What the heck ya doin', Henry? Inhaling that stuff? You're 'bout three up on me already and we're dang near out."

"If this ole pole don't start bobbing pretty soon, we may as well put in at Miller's Landing. Can walk 'crost the street to the bowling alley. Dig into some real grub for a change. Getting pretty close to eatin' time."

"Sounds fair to me, Henry ole buddy. Since you started getting your Social Security you can buy."

"Got us some clouds off toward the mountains. Fish always bite better when the sun . . . holy catfish Owen, look at that pole bend. I done hooked me a biggun."

"Ain't putting up much of a fight. Most likely a catfish."

Henry was reeling, pulling, reeling like a deep-sea fisherman gleefully telling his buddy, "Looks like I win the pot for today. Don't seem to be running very deep. Can you make it out? Man, this is a monster."

"Keep that line tight, ya stupid jerk. Don't wan'ta lose

braggin' rights to this one." Owen was waving the net, leaning out over the murky water. "Ah, here it comes. Couple more feet and I got the begger."

Abruptly mute, both men stared at the gray blob a few inches below the surface. Henry didn't want to be the first to speak his horrified thoughts.

"It's a body, ain't it?" Owen croaked.

"Sure is. It's a little kid. Musta wondered off and fell in up by the fairgrounds last night. Should we uh . . . you know, pull it into the boat?"

"Reckon we better." Owen slipped his hand into the water and grasped a handful of once golden hair. As the body came part way out of the river he took one of the tiny arms.

"Dang," rasped Henry. "Buck neked. She's a little girl. Sumbitch, Owen, look at that. Somebody done cut off both her legs."

"What sort of sick S.O.B.? Let's get her in the boat, Henry. 'Bout all we can do is haul her up to the house and call the sheriff. All of a sudden I ain't the least bit hungry.

CHAPTER SIXTEEN

Ollie had jumped on Mark's bike and dashed home to pick up the remainder of the bag of plaster of Paris. While Mark's parents were catching up on missed sleep, there was something they needed to do. There wasn't enough left in the bag to fill the entire depression so Mark mixed the powder with some patching plaster. Took longer to dry but it did the job. When the two boys finished with the footprint, Ollie went off to see Heather. Mark did as he promised and hit the sack. Sleeping soundly for about three hours he jerked awake, discovering he'd been dreaming. In his nightmare he was in his room, his hands tied by ropes to an overhead beam. The sheriff was there, striking him over and over with his nightstick, which looked more like a baseball bat. He looked around. There was no overhead beam and there was no further sleep.

Rolling out of bed he began the task of straightening up the mess the burglar had left in his room. There were a number of things going on making him to wonder if it actually was the sheriff. Maybe he desperately wanted it to be him. Red is right about one thing though. This guy is the killer. The two plaster casts were identical. Same man, same shoe. If it is the sheriff then I'm not out of the woods for the guy intended to kill him. Would he be waiting for another opportunity? Of course he would. This thing has my gut a churning. Don't know what to do.

Hearing noises in the living room, he made his way down the hall where he paused; watching his step-dad sorting out the jumble the robber had left. He sighed, "Hi Dad."

"You couldn't sleep either, huh? Guy took our DVD recorder, a video camera, my laptop, some of your mom's jewelry among other things. You doing okay, Son?"

200

Son? What's going on here? Guy has never cared enough 'bout me to call me Son. "Are we insured?"

"You're lucky all the robber did was tie you up. Adjuster should be here within the hour. Did you lose anything from your room?"

All he did was tie me up? Bastard hit me a couple of times. Should I tell him about the watch? "Not that I can tell. Went through my closet and all my drawers. Didn't touch my computer stuff, thank God. Mom doing okay?"

"Sound asleep. Sheriff says they are pretty sure it was someone from out of town. You know, looking for stuff he could sell quick. Says Dalton hasn't had a break-in for several years."

"Well, tonight we've had one. Want me to help you straighten up?"

"I'm not straightening up. Mostly checking through things to see what all is missing. We'll sort this all out after the insurance adjuster leaves."

"I'm going to take a walk then, if that's okay."

Looking at his watch his dad suggested, "okay Son. I've finally got your mother to where she'll leave the house so we'll eat out. Why don't you meet us at the restaurant about six?"

Son? There it was again. Something new and he liked the feel of it. "You buying?"

"Of course I'm buying. Don't I always?"

"Works for me. All you can eat buffet on Saturday."

Planning to walk over to the bowling alley, he remembered they were holding a senior's tournament. No way. What a bummer. Better avoid main streets. As he was threading his way among the cars in the theater parking lot, he was filled with panic. A police unit was turning off Locust onto Main. Whirling, his heart thumping, he crouched behind a van as the flashing lights came on and the patrol car was past, heading for Park Street where it turned right and was gone.

"Come on Marcus, get a grip on it. The sheriff isn't going to shoot you in broad daylight." He was breathing deeply and yet he reversed his course, finding himself back in front of his house, looking at the dwelling across the street. Other than the incident with the shotgun pellets, Mark had never been inside Red's house to visit. He didn't want his dad to know that he had returned so he quietly used the side door. Off the shelf in the laundry room he grabbed a plastic, kitchen, garbage bag then slipped down the hall and into his room. Take all our clues including the two casts over to Red. See if she was doing anything with the criminal investigation program on her computer.

"Oh hi," she opened the door to a slit.

He sat the bag down next to the door. Her smirk, the way her eyes were checking him out, made him feel ill at ease. Like she was looking at him and he was naked. She swung the huge, ornately carved door wide, inviting him in.
"Brand new door, huh?"

"Heck no. Dad spent a million hours stripping off a hundred layers of paint and varnish 'til he reached bare wood. Then stained it and put on several coats of poly something or the other."

"Polyurethane. Gonna replace the hardware? It's all covered with green gunk and paint."

A tiny dog of undetermined breed, barking furiously, half its face black, half white with an orange spot between its eyes, came rushing at him. The animal took him by surprise when it leaped into his arms. "What in the world is this thing?"

"Anybody can see she's a dog. We're gonna keep this hardware. Dad says it can be cleaned and re-bronzed."

"Dog huh? Could have fooled me." The animal was happily licking his face. "Heinz 57, right? Weirdest looking dog I ever saw. Dog and a half long, half a dog high."

She giggled. "That's why I call her Funny Face. I'm doing some chores in the kitchen."

"Funny face? Just like you, huh Red."

"Well, it's too bad you weren't born good lookin' 'stead of so danged rich."

"Hey Red, my winning personality wires everybody. You're folks ain't home, huh?"

"Nope; they're in Los Angeles. I'm saddled with my brother all day today and personally, I'm getting fed up with this 'Red' crap. How would you like it if I started calling you Brownie?"

"Whatever makes your motor run, honey."

"I'm not your honey."

"Baby, you got that right, and you never will be. However, some of my best friends are Brownies." He liked it when she got riled.

"You make me sick. Whatcha doin' here anyway, you come over to rag on me?"

Stroking the dog's ears and rubbing his nose against the soft fur of her neck, his eyes followed Candy as she moved across the huge foyer toward the kitchen. Obviously Mr. Swanson was remodeling for the hardwood floor in the entry looked like it was new. It gleamed. Power floor sander, he told himself. The kitchen cabinets were a shambles. "What a mess," he muttered.

"Yeah," she giggled and he made a face. "Dad took off all the doors. Gonna reface everything with oak and make new raised panel doors."

"Actually I dropped by to see how you were coming with the stuff you been putting in the computer. Thought you guys were going to build a house."

"We're buying this one. Dad says the sub something or the other is actually very sound so he wants to restore it. The gross part is I'm stuck with having you for a neighbor . . . forever."

"That's sub-structure. Neighbor? Man that's a bring-down. Tell your dad he better start on the front porch. It's rotting out on the north end. We always heard this place was haunted and full of monsters but it looks like you're the only spook here. It sure doesn't look the same as it did when the gang went through it couple months ago. It looks . . . polished. Feels cozy."

"I'll show you what I have in the computer after I get Michael some supper. Put more stuff in this afternoon regarding your robbery. Kinda sketchy but you can help me fill it in."

Fill it in? "Tell ya what, Red, ever since last night I been thinking 'bout this. It's getting out of hand and for our own safety we'd be better off dropping the whole thing." They both turned their head at the sound of a siren a block away. He shuddered. "It's getting downright scary."

* * *

With house after house they struck out. The group of searchers Ralph was leading was slowly losing their fire. Many families had been to the fair. Some even remembered seeing the Heinz family. None could offer a hint as to the missing child's where a bouts. It was about time for Frank to come on duty so he told the men to continue on their own and headed for the office.

As he pushed through the glass door he was curious why Frank's unit wasn't there yet. "Any messages, Marion?"

"No luck, huh?"

He sighed. "None at all. Getting a bad feeling 'bout this." She didn't say anything and he knew why. She felt the same way he did. They weren't going to find her.

"Nothing goin' on here," she told him. "Actually that's not true. Been nearly snowed under with calls inquiring about the Heinz girl, but no one's been in."

"Let's don't give up hope. Little girl probably got mad at her parents over something and went home with a friend. Happens all the time. Wonder where the hell Frank is? My shift is over at three, but I'll hang around till he comes in."

She shrugged. "The sheriff had a pretty rough night. He's under a great deal of pressure. Maybe you ought to give him another hour and then I'll call him."

"Hell Marion, I'm pretty well beat myself. All I got was a couple of hours sleep. Here I got me a date and I'm gonna be walkin' round like a zombie tonight. I'm gonna go into the break room and try and get me a nap. Wake me up at five whether the sheriff is here or not."

"I leave at five whether the sheriff is here or not," she told him. "I hope you're right, Ralph . . . I mean about the girl. This is pretty scary after what happened to the Goodwin child."

"Don't know what to tell ya, Marion. We got all we can handle. This murder, all that vandalism down at Deiters, then last night the break in at the Goodwin's. We got a regular crime wave goin' on. Don't forget, wake me when you leave."

Ralph came out of a deep sleep when he felt the clerk shaking his shoulder. For a minute he was disoriented, but then there was the piercing jangle of the phone and they both jumped. "Is it five already? That better not be Frank saying he's too bushed to come in 'cause I got a date and I ain't staying past six for no reason in the world."

"Dalton Police Department," she used her syrupy phone voice. "How may we help you?"

* * *

"I don't ever want to go through another night like that," Mark told Candy who was continuing with her chores like she

204

hadn't even heard him.

"What I'd like to hear," she was at the kitchen sink filling a pan with water, "is everything you can remember 'bout last night."

Why is she so bent on continuing? Is she gonna say something dumb 'bout me being naked?

Her eyes looked past him and the happy dog and he turned to follow her glance. "Speaking of monsters," she grinned. "Here comes Jodi with Shannon and her rug rats. Wonder where they've been? Shannon's folks went down to Clarksdale for some kind of church thing."

"Hey! Anybody home?" Jodi yelled through the open door. "It's us, the Kryptonettes."

"Y'all come on in," Candy called in return. "Me and Mark are in the kitchen."

Shannon was grinning like a cat with a gold fish bowl, then frowned when she saw Mark.

"Well, isn't this cozy? You two goin' steady?"

"I hope you are referring to me and the dog."

Candy was stirring macaroni into the pan of water. "A dog is about all he could get." To Shannon's siblings she explained, "Michael is in the . . . as my mom would say, 'the parlor' playing with his Gameboy."

"Hooray," Randy, the eleven year old, yelled and the two younger girls followed him into the other room.

"How you holding up, Mark," Shannon asked.

"Guess I'll live. Did you guys see where that police car was goin'?"

"Probably a wreck out on 61. Went across the bridge and turned left." Jodi brushed against Mark heading for the window.

He made a face. "Phew, Jodi! You been smoking again."

"So?" Jodi was staring out the window.

"So," Mark wrapped both arms about the dog and cuddled it against his chest. "Personally I think it's gross. 'Specially when it's someone so tiny and . . . " Noticing the way she looked in her blue shorts, the pink and white striped top, he started to say immature but choked it off, glancing at Candy who was studying him. "cute," he finished.

"It surprises me that you don't smoke . . . or do you?"

205

Candy was busy at the counter chopping a slice of ham into cubes.

"Nope. Not one of my vices. What are you making?"

"Macaroni and cheese and chopped ham. Michael's favorite. You guys want some? It's kinda weird that you don't smoke like the sorta guys you hang out with. You being the toughest of them all, seems like you'd be the one most likely."

He shrugged. "Tried it a couple of times, didn't do anything for me. Didn't do anything to me. Hey, most kids look stupid sucking on a fag. I mean have you watched Jodi? She doesn't even know how to hold the thing in her hand or her lips. Bet she doesn't even inhale."

"Hey, Mr. High and Mighty,' Jodi snapped, "Ollie does sometimes and that's why I tried it."

"Think I've about got Ollie talked out of it. Wants to play football next year and has already found out from playing basketball how much smoking cuts down on his wind. Hey Red? Me and your brother have something in common. Macaroni and cheese is one of my favorites too."

"Okay, I can take a hint. I'll open another box. That'll feed y'all. Got plenty of ham. How did we get on the subject of who does and doesn't smoke?"

"Well I certainly don't," Shannon declared. "I have too much respect for my body and my health to use that dirty stuff."

"How bout you Red?" Her pure green eyes were staring directly into his and it made him uncomfortable. Usually it was the other way around but this time he looked away.

"I have . . . couple of times. Don't see where it hurts you if you don't become addicted. I don't feel like it's something I need."

"Hey Red, then don't do it."

"Hey dork, don't call me Red, and don't try to tell me what to do? You know how to make a salad? There's lettuce and stuff in the fridge."

"Doesn't make a whiz to me one way or the other. Whatever blows your skirt up." Opening the door to the refrigerator he began rummaging about.

"Let's change the subject," Jodi snapped looking out the window. Look at those guys down on the beach tossing a Frisbee. She made a face. "Me and Shannon and her rug rats were down there for a spell. Wonder where those dudes were then?"

"What were you guys doing on the beach? Mark asked. "Kids wanted to see if they could spot any fish." Jodi explained. "Lotsa times you do when the sun is shining. Saw those two old guys who live across the river fishing. Guys were clear down past the railroad bridge. Couldn't see what they'd caught, but it looked like a big one."

"I keep thinking about last night," Candy was looking at Mark. "I don't know what I'd do if someone broke into our house and I was home."

"He'd take one look at your face and run away screaming. I'll tell ya what though," Mark was serious as he turned to Shannon and Jodi. "You don't want to find out. Before you guys came I was tellin' Red how dangerous it was getting for us to continue with our investigation."

Candy made a face. "Mark thinks we ought to drop it. Hey Mark, there is some grated chedder cheese in the fridge, wanna hand me some? I like to add extra cheese to the package stuff. Oh! And Jodi? Would you mind settin' the table? This stuff is just about ready."

"Somebody has to do something," Shannon told them. "It's obvious Frank and his sidekick aren't getting anywhere."
"They sure aren't," Mark was using the cutting board to chop ingredients for the salad. "He and Ralph make a dandy pair. Couldn't find a clue if it was floating in their beer. The Kryptonites have found more things than they have. You should have heard those two jerks last night. Stumbled around our house making these intelligent remarks." He was imitating Frank's voice nearly to perfection, "Yep. Looks like we got us a burglar this time, right Ralph?"

Mark noticed Shannon was pacing without making an attempt to sit but didn't know she had a problem.
"How did you feel when that guy was pointing his gun at'cha?" She asked. "That's gotta be awesome."

"Something I didn't even tell my folks or the sheriff. The robber . . . Frank or whoever it was, intended to blow my head off. Had the barrel right against my temple and at one point actually cocked the hammer."

"Oh my God," cried Shannon. "And no way you could

move."

"I'll tell you what, it's a sound that makes ya wanna crap your drawers."

Candy swallowed like there was a sudden lump in her throat. "Gawd, are you lucky he changed his mind? Bowls are right above your head. Use one of those plastic ones. Salad tongs are in the drawer behind you. Are y'all ready?"

"Don't think he changed his mind. Heard a siren coming down Riverview and he cut out. Was so bent I didn't even realize how freaked I was 'til after. Adrenaline was pumping a hundred miles an hour. You have no idea what sort of fog you go into when someone is pointing a gun at'cha. I do remember a smell, like aftershave."

"So what are you going to do," Candy joshed, but her eyes told him she was uneasy. "Go around sniffing every man you meet?"

"Something you might do but not me."

"Was he big . . . I mean, like the sheriff?"

"I don't know. My mind is totally warped."

Shannon was helping Jodi set the table. "How the heck could he find you? You don't suppose, Hoggie, the jeweler?"

"Hoggie? Heck no. Remember? We ran that ad in the lost and found. Anyone with half a brain could go through the phone book and find an address. Even a dodo with one the size of a pea-nut, like Red." He stuck his tongue out at her and set the salad in the middle of the table."

Shannon pulled up a chair at the end and perched on her knees. "How come Buzz and Ollie aren't here? Figured they'd be all done with their job."

"They're both working," Candy shrugged. "Something Mark ought to try sometime." She placed three bottles of various types of dressing on the table.

"Kinda blows the meeting I wanted to have with the Kryptonites and the Kryptonettes," he added for Jodi's benefit.

"Supper's ready. I'll go get the rug-rats." Removing the pot from the stove, Candy placed it on a hot-pad next to the salad.

"Yippee!" Michael yelled. "Rockaroni and cheese."

The four children crowded in on one side of the vinyl break-fast nook. Jodi slid in first followed by Mark and then Candy.

Shannon remained on her chair at the end.

Candy dipped into the aluminum pot and served each of the kids then reached for the salad.

"Don't want no salad," Michael griped. "It's yucky."

"Hey buddy," Mark was grinning. "You should try some of this salad. Superman made it. It'll make you super strong." He flexed his arm. "See that muscle?

"Really?" asked eleven-year old Randy, "You really know Superman? Oh man! Give me a whole bunch."

"What the heck is this?" Candy probed at the salad with the tongs. In addition to lettuce and tomatoes she discovered sliced apple, corn, chopped green peppers, chopped boiled egg and shredded, cheddar cheese.

"Looks great to me," Jodi was holding out her bowl. "Fill her up."

"It's a man thing," Mark shrugged then smiled as Michael extended his bowl.

* * *

While they were waiting for the sheriff to show up, Owen Shoemaker paced the floor. "You know what, Henry? You and me been living in this little cottage going on five years." The two-bedroom house was situated above the high water line adjacent to Shoemaker Park, named after Owen's father and which he affectionately called, "My side yard." Directly north of the park were six estate-sized dwellings in a row belonging to some of the wealthy ranchers. Then there was 'Dalton Mountain', on which the Heinz dwelling was perched.

"My daddy built this house back in 19 and 17, the year I was born. Raised five of us kids here, four of 'em boys."

"How did you end up with the house? You were the youngest, weren't you?"

"That poor little girl," he said. "Never had a chance to know all the wonderful things about growin' up. Never going to have a family of her own. Even I managed to do that. All the rest of the kids left home and moved out of state. After Ma died, was up to me to take care of Pa 'cause he was ailin'. Bad heart. Lasted four years. Left me the house."

"Never had any family myself," Henry told him. "But if I had girl like that and someone . . .. " He blew his nose into a red bandana handkerchief.

"Raised me a family here. Married Kelly Morse. High-school sweetheart. She had some kind of medical problem and wasn't supposed to have any children. Even so, when she was thirty-seven she got pregnant. Thought she ought to abort. She wouldn't hear of it. Catholic you know. Kelly didn't make it. Had to bring up my son all alone."

"How come you tellin' me this?" Henry looked at the body, which Owen had covered with a terry cloth towel.

"Hell Henry. Trying to keep my mind offa things. Anyway, Jason's a stockbroker in San Diego. Got a lovely wife and three kids, all girls. It was hairy enough you and me finding this little girl's body, but the youngest of my grandchildren is about the same age, same size, same hair color as this little girl. When we first pulled her out of the water, I thought, my God it's my little Andrea. Soon as the sheriff is done here, I'm going to call Jason. Tell him not to come for a visit 'til this killer is behind bars. I better not find this freak or I'll do to him what he done to her."

* * *

Shannon was grinning. "This is pretty darned good."
Candy was at the refrigerator. "You guys want anything to drink? Got sodas or lemonade. Maaarrrk. Don't feed Funny Face. You won't be able to get rid of her."

"I'm the one who shouldn't be feeding my face. Supposed to meet the folks at the Green Spot in about fifteen minutes."

"You're what?" asked Candy. You sit here stuffing your face and then you're going out to dinner? I don't believe you."

"These are only appetizers." He wondered why Shannon's eyes were so filled with concern.
As if reading his mind she asked, "earlier you mentioned that little kid who was lost. Buzz told me his dad was out most of the night. Everybody in town is looking for her."
Lost girl? The memory of his sister remained in his mind and Mark asked, "Any idea whose little girl it was?" Why, he wondered, did I say was?

"Buzz tells me she belonged to the head butcher out at DGF. Think their name is Heinz."

"I remember seeing them at the fair." Mark was polishing off his plate of food and sneaking tidbits to the dog.

210

"Mark!" Shannon snapped. "Did you hear what I'm saying? Her folks have to be wired because of what happened to your sister."

Her remark made him feel sick to his stomach. He'd tried to put up a wall and she'd penetrated it. "I'll bet she's simply lost," he countered.

Candy was stabbing at a grape, obviously enjoying Mark's special salad. "What was the new information you spoke about having earlier about?"

He grunted. "Do have a couple of things. But like I was sayin', we're gonna drop this thing on our end."

"I wanta see what you got."

In spite of the tenseness of their conversation Shannon couldn't resist. "Thought you saw everything Mark had at his house the other night." She was smirking, eyes sparkling.

"You're a riot, Shannon." Mark didn't feel as embarrassed as he had earlier.

"I got to see plenty," she admitted, "and I still do in my dreams, but nothing that's gonna solve this case."

In her dreams? Mark sighed. How long am I gonna have to put up with this crap? "Oh well, since Ollie and me went to all the trouble, scootch out a minute, Red. Left something out on your porch." Rushing outside he returned with the plastic bag, the contents of which he dumped onto the table.

"Hey," Candy grimaced at the pile of trash even though each item, except for the two plaster casts, was in its own plastic baggie. "We're trying to eat here."

"Our bag of clues, huh," asked Shannon? "Doesn't look like much. Pieces of paper, Budweiser can. Everybody drinks Bud. What are those white things? Look like cement."

Mark picked them up holding them face down. "Not cement, plaster of Paris. Ollie remembered having some left over from a school project. Didn't have enough so we mixed it with some patching plaster." He turned them over.

"Oh my God, that's the guy's footprints. Same one we saw out on Lone Pine. Clear as mud." Shannon traced the imprint of the eagle on one heel.

"Pretty good, huh?" Mark placed the two casts in the center of the table and pointed. "This one we made out at the crime scene.

"You guys went back out there," Candy accused. "Without telling us."

"Well, what can I say? Thought it was a good idea. After we got back yesterday, me and Ollie rode out and did the one on Lone Pine Trail. Then this morning, after breakfast, made this other cast of a print we found in the flower bed next to my bedroom window."

"They're a perfect match," said Candy. "Same foot."

"It's him," said Jodi. "The same one who killed . . . "

"So what do we do with them?" Shannon asked.

"Can't turn 'em over to the sheriff," Mark explained, "'cause it might be his. It only proves that the same man was at both places."

Candy picked up the cast and studied it. "We know the sheriff was out there. He probably made this one when he went outside to check on how the robber got in."

"That joker? Never make it with CSI. Neither him nor Ralph left the house. Said it was obvious he came in my outside door. Lots of times I don't lock it."

"There's a possibility it's not the same man," Candy told him. "I'm sure there is more than one person who wears this type of shoe."

Shannon groaned. "Yeah, like my dad."

Mark was watching Candy run her fingers around the impression with her eyes shut, like a blind person trying to commit the shape to memory.

"Can I have some more Superman salad?" Michael interrupted, holding out his dish.

"Sure thing." Mark filled the dish again then reached down and squeezed the boy's upper arm. "Wow. Feel that. It's working already."

"How 'bout mine." Randy offered his arm and Mark felt the flabby flesh and made an appropriate sound.

"Other than knowing the guy wanted the watch, what do we have?" Jodi asked. "Cigarette wrapper. . . Winstons. Some pieces of a magazine."

Candy's hand went directly to a baggie holding a tiny round cornered piece of paper and she took it out of the container to examine it. "Price tag?"

Mark shrugged. "Could be. I figure all this stuff blew down from the trail. That thing you're holding has been walked on so much you can hardly make it out."

"Let's see it." Jodi reached out to take the small item, bending until her face was three inches away. "I can make out some figures. $1.95 per lb. Then what I suppose is a weight . . . ummmmm . . . and $4.75."

"Where do you think it came from?" Shannon's eyes seemed intense.

"And the question is," Candy prompted. "What does a price tag have to do with the sheriff?"

Mark spread his palms. "Someplace like Steven's Store, most likely, where they sell stuff by the pound. Like I say, the way it's worn, probably doesn't mean a thing. Hmm. Only a couple of tablespoons of macaroni left. I'll finish it off if no one wants it."

"Knock yourself out. I'll tell ya what. In this case I don't think so." Candy was looking at the backside of the tag.

"What do you see that we don't?" Mark leaned close, trying to see what held Candy's attention. He frowned at the faint aroma of perfume. Couldn't remember her ever wearing any. He'd never tell her, but he liked it.

"See that dark smudge on the back?"

"So?" He was examining the remainder of the papers and the cigarette wrapper.

"That's where it was stuck to somebody's shoe. Look real close. See the line? Like maybe it was stuck to somebody's heel that had a ridge around it. To be sticky, and it is, it can't be very old. Somebody walked down there and it was scraped off."

Four heads bumped each other, as each was instantly intent, straining for a closer look. She was holding the price tag close to the footprint in the cast. "You could be right, Red. Looks like it matches the raised edge around the heel"

"Which could mean the killer had it on his shoe. So what do we do next?" Candy asked, holding the tag down to compare the shape of the mark on the back to the ridge on one of the plaster casts.

Mark looked at the girls as sternly as he could. "I don't

know why we're even lookin' at this stuff. How long is it going to take to get inside your thick skull? You don't do nothing. This is getting too risky for us guys to stick our necks out." How could they know how dangerous this was, he thought. They weren't there.

"So?" Shannon asked. "What are you saying? You want us to drop it?"

"I believe we should." Mark's tone was sullen.

"What do you mean, drop it?" Candy was excited. "This is a perfect match. This came off the guy's shoe."

Mark sighed. "Doesn't matter, Red, we're done."

"Well who died and made you Gawd?" she admonished. "You're gonna turn chicken and run, huh? Let me tell y'all somethin', buddy boy. We formed the Kryptonites for one thang, so that as a club we could work together in solving the murder of your sister."

"Hold on a minute, Red, don't you go calling me chicken. I told you guys right from the start I was going to be in charge. Not much of anything scares me, but last night, when I had that gun pointed at my head and I heard it cock, with what's been going on, it's getting too dangerous to . . . the only thing I'm scared of is that something could happen to one of you guys."

"That's very nice of you," Candy was being sarcastic. "Let us worry about our hides. What we should do is have a meeting of all the Kryptonites. We'll take a vote. Maybe it's time for us to choose a new person to take charge."

Mark had a dreadful feeling of something slipping away. "Listen, Red. I'll admit I'm running scared . . . outta my gourd. So okay, let's get all the Kryptonites together and vote on whether or not we continue our investigation. If the vote is go then we keep going. With me in charge."

"Then take charge," Candy cut him off. "Or I will. I'm not dropping this thing. We're gonna have to be more careful that's all. You needta give each one of us somethin' to do."

He sucked his lower lip back across his teeth and bit down on it. Sometimes she could piss him off. "I don't see where you guys can do anything other than maybe enter things about our robbery into your computer."

Candy looked grim. "I'm gonna take this price tag and hit all the stores."

"What about me and Jodi?" Shannon asked.

Mark studied the two girls and thought, I'd better come up with something before I lose control of this group. "I don't like this one a little bit but since you guys insist on being part of this investigation, get me a pencil and a piece of paper and I'll show ya."

Candy located the items. "Since you can't read or write I assume you want to draw some cartoons."

"I don't think I can draw your ugly face." Laying the sheet of paper on one of the casts he used the side of the pencil lead to create an impression, an exact replica of the shoe-print, complete with a ridge on the heel and an eagle in the center. "You guys take this to the shoe store. Look at the men's shoes. See if they sell one like this and who buys 'em."

"Gotcha," Shannon was nodding.

"And," he grinned, "since we don't have much to go on yet, I'd say keep your eyes peeled for some guy with big feet, dress shoes, drinking a Bud and smoking Winston cigarettes."

"And wearing Mark's aftershave," Candy snickered.

"But be careful," Mark warned, "that no one realizes we are working on a case. Everything we see, hear, and do must be kept secret. If someone asks what we're up to, we're just playing a game. We are pretending to be crime scene investigators."

"Yeah," Shannon was serious. "If the killer discovers we're on his trail . . . or say he'd finds out Candy discovered his watch . . ."

"Oh my Gawd," Candy blurted, her green eyes filled with concern. "Then the killer would come after me."

* * *

The Man was gloating. Whole town is in an uproar. Now they knew. Everything was going according to his plan. Of course he needed to alter things from time to time to fit the circumstances. Take for example the Goodwin kid. It wasn't a matter of needing to exterminate him. I have an overwhelming desire to do so. The robbery had been a great success. If the kid had any idea who he was he'd have already blown the whistle. Punishing the others was the whole point of his plan. Getting the watch back was merely covering all bases.

That's right. Punishment. He smiled, remembering the

little tyke coming under the bushes after her ball. Those Krauts have to be suffering as much pain as he had. Yeah, at last they knew what sort of anguish he'd been through. But I'll tell ya this if that Goodwin kid so much as looks at me cross-eyed . . . he's history, and no big loss.

CHAPTER SEVENTEEN

Mark left first, heading for the Green Spot. A few minutes later the group began walking downtown dragging the tiny tots with them. "We better move it," Candy told them. "Clinton's Shoes closes at six and it's five thirty a'ready." Shannon was grinning so broadly Candy wondered what she was up to. "So what's so funny?"

"You are a wire. You try so hard to hide it, but I can tell you have a crush on Mark. You two are at each other all the time and you know what that means? It means you like him."

Jodi also teased. "At breakfast she told us that after seeing him in the buff, he was a hunk. And you said somethin' 'bout dreamin' 'bout him."

"Y'all so fulla grits your brains are addled. Not exactly a dream, more like a nightmare and I most definitely do not have a crush on him. He's a smuck and I detest him. Take one look at him and you see nothin' but trouble. Let's cut 'crost the movie parking lot." Going through her mind was a vision of Mark's room and a naked hunk standing in front of her. She'd never seen a guy without his clothes. It was something she didn't intend to mention to her friends, but it gave her the weirdest chills.

Michael and Randy were busy playing two-man tag among the parked cars. Rochelle and Janice were sticking close to Shannon, one on each side holding her hands.

"We can go through the back of the Greyhound Bus Station and out the front. Put us right at the shoe store." Candy told them. "And I wouldn't give Mark a second look if he was the last man on earth."

Jodi continued to snicker. "Candy, you are so full of it. I've never seen anything so extreme. Your eyes are like yo-yos every time he comes around."

"Are you jerks out of your mind? He's a degenerate. Anyhow, he sure doesn't like me."

"Wrong!" Shannon seemed very serious. "He isn't even aware of it yet, but that's what this taunting and teasing and picking on you is all about."

"How come you know so much?"

"Gonna to be a psychiatrist when I finish school. I've read all about this sort of stuff."

"This time you are so totally warped that you can stick it. This is where Michael and I leave you clowns. You guys hit the shoe store while I go snoop around a couple of other places."

"I want to go with Randy to the shoe store," her brother whined.

"You have to stay with me, Michael."

He stood, stomping his feet.

"Look, we're going down to Steven's store. If you behave I'll buy you an ice-cream bar."

"Chocolate chocolate?"

"Whatever.

"Okay Candy," Shannon told her. "We could be on to something here. Jodi and I will go in and look around."

* * *

Ralph pulled into the drive, figuring Owen must have been watching for them as he came down off the porch and walked up to the patrol car. Rolling down the window, Ralph called out, "What do you say, Owen? Sheriff ain't here yet, huh?"

"Come on in Ralph. Got the body in the house."

"Okay, Frank's on his way. Where's Henry?"

"Inside. Taking it pretty hard. He's the one who snagged her with his fishing line."

"Oh boy. I can't even imagine. Gotta be pretty gruesome."

"Talked to the dispatcher in your office but she ain't heard from Frank."

Dispatcher, he thought. That's a good one. "A minute ago he called me on the radio. Says he's on his way. Ralph was thinking about the fact many town folks believed Owen and Henry were gay. Hard to tell the way they snapped at each other and called each other names. They were also affectionately known as

Dalton's own 'Grumpy Old Men'. Turning to look down Highway 61, he nodded. "Here comes the sheriff, Owen. Sure ain't looking forward to being involved in this sort of thing. Frank's gonna be one unhappy mother since he knows Weird Walter ain't the one."

* * *

The shoe-store-clerk, a senior high student, glanced up and then returned to her phone conversation.

"Boyfriend," Shannon whispered, nodding toward the left side of the store. "There's the men's department." Her friend seemed to be more interested in a pair of red pumps than the purpose of their visit.

"Jodi, would you quit snapping your gum? You're flipping me right up the wall." Shannon plucked a black dress shoe off the aisle display, looked at the heel and made a face.

"That's half the fun of chewing gum, making it snap," she made a face. "especially in school. Let's ask the scarecrow over there." She had the drawing Mark had produced and stopped in front of the counter.

The clerk looked up and frowned, then spoke into the phone, "Hey, Corky, got a customer. Gonna lock up in about ten minutes so why don'tcha meet me at the Pit?"

"Do you carry dress shoes that make this kind of print?" Jodi laid the paper on the counter.

"Nope."

"Rats," Shannon was discouraged. "Are you sure?"

"Hey, I don't look at every pair of shoes that comes through here. All I'm sayin' is, we don't carry dress shoes in that brand."

Shannon was curious. "This is a brand?"

"Yeah, that's what it is, but not in dress shoes. We got some boots with that kind of heel. They're called Eagle Gold. They for your dad? I can show you a pair."

Shannon and her friend both nodded.

The clerk needed a small stepladder to reach a pair off the top shelf. "What size?"

"Doesn't matter," Shannon told her. "We want to see what they are like and . . . you know, like how much they cost."

The clerk handed a boot to Shannon who examined it closely while Jodi looked at it over her shoulder, even taking a

219

sniff of the new leather.

"They ain't cheap. Start in at eighty-five bucks. Take a feel of that leather. They go as high as a couple of hundred."

"Wow! That much? Who would buy this kind of boot?" Shannon was holding it out at arm's length studying the rubber heel.

"Oh, guys that like to wear boots but want to look dressy on Sunday . . . or for their jobs. Ranchers, lawyers, highway patrol guys, or even a preacher."

'Even a preacher,' Shannon thought. Had she been right about the timing that night . . . and her dad? After what he did to her last night she was beginning to have doubts again. "You sell any lately?"

"Not me. Those kinda guys always want to deal with old man Clinton." She shrugged. "You know. Want to try to chisel him down."

Shannon found the clerk studying her and wondered why.

"You're Reverend White's daughter, ain'tcha?"

"One of three. The oldest."

"Your dad buys 'em."

Shannon choked, "yeah, I know."

Jodi didn't pick up on what the statement could mean. "Anybody else you can think of?"

"What's this all about?" the clerk asked.

"Nothing important," Jodi told her. "We're doing a pretend crime scene investigation. You know? Like a school project."

"Cool. Sounds like fun." She stood scratching the back of her head like she had a dose of the fleas.

Shannon leaned toward her. "Any others?"

"Trying to remember. That guy who runs the lumberyard . . . Turner. He does. There's a couple of others. Judge Elliot buys the expensive ones. So does the sheriff."

"Bingo," Shannon spread her hands.

"Hey guys," the clerk was looking at a wall clock. "I gotta lock up."

"That's okay," Jodi was already heading for the door. "Thanks for your help."

"Man-oh-man," Shannon whispered. "We're getting close."

* * *

220

Frank pushed his large frame out of his patrol car and looked back the way he'd come. "Here comes Doc Snyder. Old fart was kinda pissed 'cause I didn't call him 'bout the body out on Lone Pine Trail so this time I gave him a buzz."

"She's in the house," Ralph told them, watching the doctor get out of his Chevy van, turning to retrieve his medical bag.

"Anybody call the M.E.?" Doc asked.

"On his way," Frank was stalling, wanting Doc to go in first. "Should be here directly. Was on a call over in Cotton. Couple of them wetback field workers got into it and one of them used his switchblade."

"They're not wetbacks, Frank. These people are Mexican American or they are working with a green card."

"Yeah, Doc. Taking jobs away from people in this country who desperately need 'em."

Owen was holding the door for them. "Taking stoop labor jobs that no one here wants. Looks to me like you guys have a big problem of your own. I'd say you fellows got yourself a serial killer right here in Dalton."

"That's the theory me and Ralph are working on." He and Ralph hadn't even discussed the second one.

Doc went in first and the three men entered the small house as Owen stood inside the door to watch.

"This place sure is a lot neater than I expected, Owen." Frank could see Henry sitting on a kitchen chair looking drained. Nodding toward the couch he asked. "That the body?" Someone had covered the tiny body with a blue bath towel.

Dock walked over and slowly pulled the cover off. "Oh dear God," he cried and then shuddered. "I believe I'm going to be sick."

"Hey, you're a doctor. You see this sort of thing all the time."

The doctor was shaking his head. "I see cuts and bruises and an accident victim once in a while. What kind of psycho does it take to do something like this?"

"That's what me and Ralph are trying to figure out."

"Is it the kid from the fair?" Ralph asked. "Been in the water so long the blood's been washed away and her skin's all puffed up."

221

"Yeah." The sheriff had moved over and was using an arm to turn the torso over. "Because of that she's nowhere near as gruesome as I expected."

"Best not mess with her, Frank," Doc warned. "Medical examiner is supposed to do his stuff first?"

"Here he comes," Owen called and they could see the flashing red lights through the front window.

Owen let the rather plump, ruddy-faced man in. He was carrying what appeared to be two aluminum suitcases, one of which he sat down in order to shake Owen's hand like he'd stopped in for a visit. "I'm Bill Rogers from the Coroner's office. Well hi Doc and you too Sheriff." He nodded at Ralph. "What we got?"

"Busy day, huh Bill? Take a look at this. The perp cut off her legs the same as he did with the Goodwin kid. Frank was holding the corpse by an arm like it was a stuffed toy.

It was obvious the medical examiner couldn't believe his eyes. "Frank, you have to be the most insensitive slob on earth."

"I ain't insensitive," Frank gestured with his open palms. "What the hell, she's dead and it looks to me," he was checking a couple of the deeper cuts, "like someone used a razor blade to chop her all up and a hacksaw to whack off her legs."

"Or a fishing knife," suggested Owen.

The M.E. clutched his forehead with both hands. "I don't believe this. No one . . . and that means you too Frank, is supposed to touch the victim until the medical examiner is through." He bent over the body then drew a deep breath. "Son-of-a- bitch."

* * *

Ruby White studied her face in the mirror. She had to say something to Clarence. She had to. A remark Shannon made last night touched a nerve. She was not totally blind, as her daughter had accused, she simply had no idea how to handle it. He has such a terrible temper. Be best if I get dressed. Wait until after the dinner and the seminar.

Clarence was looking into another mirror, making sure every hair was perfectly in place. "You never did tell me what your daughter had to say when you went in to see her last night."

"My daughter? All of a sudden she is my daughter."

"He raised both his palms to face her. "All right, our daughter. Has she learned anything from all this?"

"Clarence, I'm starting to get scared."

He seemed to ponder on her remark until at last he asked, "What do you mean, scared? Of what? Of me?"

"Quite frankly, yes, of you. Not only this handling of Shannon last night, it's some things . . . with the other two girls."

"What are you suggesting, that I shouldn't do my duty as a father and discipline our children?" Proverbs 13:24 says, 'He that spareth the rod hateth his child, but he that loveth him chastises him.'"

"Clarence, don't you see what's happening to you? You're not the same. It's getting to where it isn't entirely discipline. You need to see someone, talk to someone."

"What kind of crap is that brat putting in your head?" He roared. "The Lord is my consul. I don't need some outsider . . . "

"But you do. That incident with the Hubbell girl last January followed by this thing with Shannon. If she were to tell the authorities at Child Protective Services you pulled down her underwear to . . . "

"As for your daughter, according to the gospel of 2nd Peter, it is the father's duty and right to decide what type of punishment a child deserves. And that wicked little Hubbell monster was lying when she didn't get her way. I never touched her and if it were up to me, that evil spawn of the Devil the Hubbell's conceived would be severely dealt with."

She remembered something. He had also called the Goodwin children 'spawns of the Devil', particularly Laura. A horrible possibility entered her mind. "What do you mean by 'severely dealt with'?" Oh dear God, the Goodwin child? Sucking in her breath her eyes betrayed her fright. She had to ask. "Did you . . . Did you also punish Laura Goodwin?"

"Woman, are you out of your mind? What are you implying? I am an ordained minister of the Gospel. A servant of the Lord, and you are supposed to be my helpmate, to believe in me. Titus 2:5 is God's word. 'Women are to be keepers of the home, obedient to their husbands.' It is your duty to obey me."

"Obey you? Obey you?" There was fire in her eyes, her black cheeks glistening. She could feel the anger and fear turning her subservience into action. "You think you can justify everything you do by quoting scripture . . . " She repeated the words Shannon had used last night, not aware he was moving nearer, one step at a time. "You are nothing but a Bible spouting hypocrite. I have been trying to turn a blind eye to the way you fondle and touch my little babies in the guise of affection or during times of punishment, but from what Shannon told me you did to her, it is nothing less than child molestation."

He struck her. The fist connected directly with her nose and there was a black spot filled with bright lights. She was on her knees.

"Don't you ever accuse me of that!"

She cowered waiting for the next blow.

"Don't you ever question my rights as a father."

Shaking her head she was trying to make him out. He was removing his belt.

"You are the one who needs to be punished. 'The husband is head of the wife, even as Christ is head of the church.'"

As he raised his arm she screamed, then screamed again.

* * *

"You would think killing her would be enough," the medical examiner told them. "Exactly like the Goodwin case, it appears he was doing it as some sort of warped kind of punishment. Going to be harder to determine if she was alive during the ordeal as was the Goodwin kid. The river water has totally dissipated all the blood from the wounds and distorted her flesh considerably. It also causes a significant rapidness in body cooling. And yet I should be able to pin point the time of death."

"I don't know how you guys can tell about that sort of thing," Ralph shrugged. "I guess that's why they pay you the big bucks.

"Who's little gal is it, Ralph?" Henry was stroking his Willie Nelson beard.

"It's the Heinz kid. You know, the head butcher out at DGF. Disappeared last night at the fair. Any idea how she died, Bill?"

"Won't be sure until after the autopsy, but I have some suspicions." He pointed at the girl's face with a medical tool he was using. "See these gray traces on her chin and on the right cheek? Appears to be residue from masking tape, again like the other case. Probably asphyxiation."

224

The medical examiner was using his gloved fingers and some forceps to check some of the deeper wounds. "I hate to say this, but from the cuts and punctures, the fact her legs have been severed with a bone saw, clearly identical to the injuries we found on the Goodwin corpse, suggests this child was killed by the same perpetrator."

"You know what that means don'tcha?" Frank asked Ralph who was nervously pacing the worn carpet.

"Yeah I do. Confession or not, Weird Walter Turner ain't your man."

"Well, that too. It means we got us a maniac on the loose."

Ralph sounded exhausted. "Yeah, and one who lives right here in Dalton." He had one hand across his face looking at the scene through his fingers. "One sick bastard," he muttered.

"What I'm wondering," asked Frank, "is where the hell do we look for clues on something like this?"

Even though it had been doing so every fifteen minutes since the men arrived, no one had noticed until a six foot tall grandfather clock began striking the hour and Ralph turned to look. "Hey, Frank, any chance of me cutting out? Told Peggy I'd pick her up at seven thirty. Looks to me like you got everything under control here."

"Go head on, Ralph . . . and uh . . . don't talk about this to anybody." Frank snorted, looking at Doc, then explained, "Ralph has got hisself a date."

"Peggy?" Doc asked, reaching into his bag to take out a form. "Don't see any reason for you to hang around, Ralph. You and Peggy make a good looking couple." He chuckled. "Should be able to make some pretty babies."

Doc Snyder placed the form on the kitchen table and took out his pen. If it's all right with you, Bill, I'll go ahead and make out a death certificate. Probably 'Causes unknown', wouldn't you say?"

Ralph was already heading for the door. "I'm outta here. See ya."

"I can leave that line blank and fill it in after the autopsy. How 'bout you Frank? Have you notified the parents?"

"Not yet." Frank seemed to shrink in size. "Uh . . . could you do it?"

"Not my job, sheriff. This is highly unusual. Generally we ask folks to come in to the morgue to make an I.D., but there is no reason to make them drive all the way to Clarksdale. See if you can reach them. We're ready to transport. Ambulance with the other body is waiting outside but we can hold her here till they come."

Frank was thinking, why didn't I have Ralph do it? "Sometimes I hate this job."

* * *

Mark wasn't concerned that he'd already eaten at Red's place. That was merely a warm up. Mom always told everybody he had a hollow leg. He looked about inside the Green Spot and it seemed to him like everyone in town turned out for the Saturday night 'All you can eat Buffet'. What was worse, there was a constant parade of people stopping by their table to offer words of pity about Laura or to comment on last night's break in. Mom for sure doesn't need this.

He was aware that it had been hard enough on her last night, going to a party. His father had called everyone he knew, who was going to be there, to tell them to mellow out around her. Then to come home and find her house ransacked . . . what next? Other than the party, the trip to the Green Spot was actually her first night out in public and he noticed her eyes dampen with tears from time to time but she fought them off. He was grateful when the waitress came.

"Hello folks. Have you decided?"

"We're all here for the buffet," his stepfather smiled. "You're new, huh. Where's the regular waitress tonight? Peggy?"

"I'm covering for her. She's in the restroom changing clothes. Got a date. Going to the fair I guess, with Officer Porter. Isn't that awful, another little girl disappearing at the fair last night?"

"What?" Mark's mom nearly wailed. "I didn't know that. Whose child was it?"

"The Heinz's daughter," his dad told her.

Mark wanted to kick the cute little twerp for bringing this subject up. "I think she only got lost Mom." He could see by her eyes she didn't believe him, suspecting the awful truth. Wasn't about to ask his dad if the child had been found. Already knew, in her heart, another family was facing their own horror.

"Let's get something to eat," he snapped, much too swiftly, pushing out of his seat and heading for the buffet. Turning back, his mother was right behind him looking pale and he wondered if she would be able to hold down whatever she consumed. What he did next surprised even him. Dropping back alongside her he let his arm go about her waist and he gave her a big hug. "You okay, Mom?"

"Oh Mark. You have been so strong through all this." She hugged him in return. "I'll be okay, only I'm starving," she squeezed his hand. "Have hardly eaten since . . . you know."

All three of the Goodwin's filled their plates with items from the extravagant buffet. Mrs. Mc Combs stopped by their table and was looking directly at Mark. "That must have been a terrible ordeal for you last night."

"Yes ma'am, it was. You can never tell now days, you know, what someone stoned out of their head is going to do."

She laughed dryly. "I probably would have panicked and gotten myself killed."

Fred Bateman, in his usual pushy manner, actually pulled out the fourth chair and sat down. "Have you folks considered installing a burglar alarm hooked up directly to the sheriff's office?"

"What good would that do?" Mark's father snorted. "Nobody is in the department at night."

"That's correct, but we can program it to forward an emergency to his beeper. I'd like to drop by your house tomorrow evening and show you our program."

Mark didn't care for Fred. He was one of those guys who'd tried it all. Used cars, vacuum cleaners, encyclopedias, pots and pans, insurance and lately, alarm systems. Burglar alarms? He'd soon go broke in a town as quiet as Dalton.

Mark was highly alert. Fred wore shiny, black dress shoes. Boots? It was hard to tell. Surprising at how few people wore dress shoes. It seemed everyone was into the Reebok craze. As if to refute his observation, Mark could see at least six other pairs of black dress shoes, or boots, Fred, his father and the guy by the window in the pimp suit. He's looking out the window so I can't make out who it is. The banker has black shoes . . . actually boots and so did the two strangers sitting in one of the booths.

227

They look like army guys on leave or cops.

As the dude rambled on and on, Mark continued to eat while watching the traffic pass on Main Street, his mind trying to focus on what to do next. If it was the sheriff, or as Red suggested, somebody else living right here in town, then that was more than spooky. Another scary thought crossed his mind. Laura's mouth and nose had been taped shut with gray duct tape. The man who robbed their house had produced a large roll of the same tape to use on him, one of those big fat rolls like contractors use. Was it something he'd recently bought? Would Mr. Stevens at the General Store remember such a purchase? Stevens probably didn't carry that big of a roll. Most likely it came from the lumberyard.

Other than Frank he could think of no other suspects. More and more he was having his doubts about the sheriff. He was pretty sure it couldn't be Shannon's father. Even had considered Hoggie the jeweler when he wanted to keep the watch, but Hoggie was smaller than the burglar and was a happily married man with four small children. And if I remember rightly, he wore rubber soled, running shoes.

For a short time he thought perhaps it could be Mr. Newton, a Math teacher from the grammar school who was filling in at the Middle school while Mrs. Jacobs was on maternity leave. Mark felt the jerk was awfully familiar with the females in the classes. He was a toucher and a hugger and he wore black dress shoes. However, by some careful sneaking around, Mark discovered Newton was with his family at an elementary school musical the night of Laura's murder. His own daughter was in the play. What the heck, little girls seemed to take to Mark as well, always wanting to be teased or hugged, and he sure as heck wasn't a killer . . . or a child molester.

* * *

The Man came in and found a seat directly in front of the window. He was very much aware of the Goodwin's and he had a side view of both of the men. Eric was wearing a disgusted expression, listening to that damned weasel, Bateman, making some sort of pitch to the family. I never get tired of looking at Goodwin's wife, good lookin' broad. What was her name? Julie? Yeah. Too bad she has her back to me. That gal's stacked like a brick safety deposit box.

What concerned the Man more than anything else was the Goodwin boy, who was staring past his mother and directly at him. His eyes are too damned piercing, as if he suspects something. It was enough to make his stomach churn. But what? He relived the entire scenario at the Goodwin home. There couldn't be anything because he didn't make mistakes. Not even when he discovered the place wasn't unoccupied as he had supposed. There was nothing he'd left behind. Not even the sound of his voice. Wore gloves and a ski mask every minute. Had he been too obvious about the watch? Probably could have been more thorough in making it look like a normal burglary.

If it hadn't been for that damned siren, kid wouldn't even be here to worry about. Had been that close to pulling the trigger. Should have recognized the siren as being a fire truck. Why doesn't the bastard look away? Punk has to be aware I know he's staring. Oh oh! He's looking at Bateman and the kid has thought of something. Obvious he doesn't know for sure or I'd already be dead meat. I don't need this crap. Have other things to take care of. From inside his shirt pocket he extracted a small spiral notebook and a black, ballpoint pen. On the second page was a list of names. Two had lines drawn through them. The Man added five words: Mark Goodwin - - -Knows too much. Then he added two more words; he's next.

CHAPTER EIGHTEEN

"**W**ould you mind walking home," Mark's stepfather asked. "Your mother and I have been invited over to the Albertson's. Gonna play cards for a while."

Great, Mark was thinking. "No problem . . . Dad. "I'll try to not let anybody in the house."

"Not funny, Mark."

It was and it wasn't. He intended to run all the way. Crap my pants if I see a cop car.

Leaving the Green Spot he avoided Main Street. Dashed down Palm and then cut across the City Parking Lot. Staying in the bright lights of the power company on Washington, he next slipped in behind Shannon's house, across Locust and home. Panting as he opened the door, he could hear the phone ringing so he snatched it up, sure it would be for him, and it was. Ollie always had a tendency, when he was excited, to have a difficult time making any sense. This time he was so wired Mark couldn't understand one word. "For crying out loud Ollie, will you cool it? Put a saddle on your tongue and I could ride it downtown. Slow . . . down . . . so I can get a handle on what you are yaking about."

"Yeah. Okay. Got it under control. Marcus, where the heck have you been? Called your place at least twenty times since five."

"Went down to the Green Spot with my folks. All you can eat buffet tonight. The . . . "

"You know how Buzz had me help him out today with one of his cleanup jobs?"

"Yeah? So?"

"Well, I did Mrs. Osborn's garage this afternoon, and you'll never believe what happened. Boy what a mess."

"What do you guys do with all that trash anyway? Haul it home?"

"Some of this stuff is good, you know, usable. We set it out front and The Thrift Store picks it up. Small trash we put in boxes and trash bags for the garbage men. Buzz has a deal with Johnny Hoover to haul off the bigger stuff. But that's not why I'm calling."

"Her garage has looked like Sam's junk yard ever since her old man died. House isn't much better, so why this sudden cleanliness kick?"

"Would you believe it? She's older than dirt, seventy something or the other. She's buying a new car. Was pushing me to hurry and there wasn't one dang thing she wanted to keep.

"Gee Ollie, freaks me out you sharing all this good stuff with me. Gotta go do me some studying. See ya when we get back from Clarksdale tomorrow."

"Wait wait wait! You gotta see this. She had something out there she wanted me to have Hoover haul off, you know, to the dump. I told her I wanted to take it home and her words were, 'knock yourself out."

"So? Don't keep me in suspenders. Whatcha got?"

"You better come on over and take a look."

"Hey man. It's after seven. Like I told you, I have to study for that History test for Monday. Won't have time tomorrow. Right after church we're going down to Clarksdale for Grandpa and Grandma Goodwin's anniversary. Gonna take them to dinner and all that good stuff. Look Ollie, I've been having a hard time concentrating with all the other things on my mind. Wish we could find some big time thing to pin this thing on the sheriff. I'm going around looking over my shoulder all the time."

"I feel for ya, buddy, but you need to come see this. You're missing something worth a million bucks."

"You're a real butthead, you know that Ollie? I'll change into my Superman outfit and fly over there but I can only stay a minute. This better be something far out."

* * *

Frank and Doc Snyder met at the Green Spot as agreed and the first thing the sheriff did was complain, "Doc, why in the hell don't you sit at one of the tables like a normal person. Full growed man like me can hardly squeeze into one of these damn booths."

"Been telling you to lose some weight. Carrying around all that extra blubber is going to take its toll one of these days. Man's heart can't keep up trying to supply all that fat with blood."

"Ain't nothing wrong with my heart. What's going to get me down is all this extra work. I'm returning from the Shoe-maker place. Had to stay there 'till Mr. and Mrs. Heinz came to I.D. the body. I'll letcha know that was a bad scene. I consider myself a pretty tough cookie, but Mrs. Heinz even had me bawling all over the place. I don't handle that kind of crap very well."

"I don't either. I always hate to have to notify someone of a death in the family. But glory be, Frank; does my ole heart good to find out your human."

The waitress stopped next to their booth. "Who's human? You're not talking 'bout the sheriff? Can I get you gentlemen something to drink?"

Frank looked the tall, slim teenager up and down. "Well if you ain't cute as a newborn puppy. Your daddy makin' ya go to work today huh? Which one of the twins are you?"

"I'm Shelby." Her eyes sparkled. "Shelly is practicing her tennis. Dad's having me work in Peggy's place."

"Me and Doc will do the buffet, honey. Take a cup of coffee though. Gotta eat and run. Got the duty at the fair tonight."

"Iced tea," Doc told her.

The two men made their way to the food and Frank didn't waste any time, using two plates.

Doc was shaking his head. "Guess we better move to a table, Frank. You eat all that grub, have to use a block and tackle to get you out of a booth."

"Heck Doc, these are only appetizers."

Doc Snyder sighed, running the tips of his fingers through the two gray bushes on each side of his head. "So, do we agree with the medical examiner? Same man, right?"

The sheriff talked with his mouth full of salad. "Looks that way. I can't tell ya why but this guy's got a thorn in his butt for little girls."

"Strange thing is, there's been no warning, seemed to start right out of the blue."

232

"Quite often the case." Frank had recently read an article by a prominent psychologist on this subject and began reciting the words as though he were the expert. "Killers of this type generally do, Doc. They generally do. Quite often start out as a peeping Tom. Problem is, once he gets past the first one he can't friggen stop. Guy becomes addicted like a doper."

The waitress brought their coffee and iced tea, glancing at the empty booth.

Doc was listening so intently Frank was warming to the subject. "Serial killers have a specific profile. Man is generally a white male between the ages of 18 and 35. Probably was abused as a child. A local boy since he is familiar with the territory.

"Well, that narrows it down some. Have you notified the FBI? Thought I read somewhere that after a second killing where they suspect it is the same man, they move in."

Frank wiped salad dressing from his mouth on the back of his hand. "Probably due to the fact we didn't report the first one."

"Why the hell not? I'd think you'd want their help."

"Didn't think we needed it and they only come in under certain circumstances."

"I hope you reported this one."

"The M.E. is gonna take care of it, but as far as the FBI is concerned, the Heinz kid is number one. Unless we get another body that's as far as it goes. Technically this victim is number two, but as far as I'm concerned the FBI has a tendency to get everything mucked up."

"So where do you stand, Sheriff? Got any suspects?

"Actually Doc, we do, only that isn't something I can discuss with you right now. Might jeopardize our case later. I'll merely say it involves a prominent local citizen. Got to get some more evidence before we make a move."

"Are you referring to Reverend White?"

Frank was surprised. "What makes you ask about him?"

He shrugged. "Thinking about that thing, some months back, with the Hubbell child. I've never been entirely convinced the preacher was innocent. Ever since that incident the preacher has had this thorn in his rump about small girls."

"Let me rephrase that, Doc. Way I hear it the reverend has always liked small girls. I haven't confronted him but by asking around I can find out if he has an alibi for the night when the Goodwin murder took place. Shouldn't be yakkin' 'bout this, Doc. Last night, when we were out looking for the missing child, I guess it was some-time around midnight, I saw him sitting in his car down in Riverside Park. Went up to his window and rapped on it. Was sitting there staring straight ahead. Asked if he was okay and he said there'd been a misunderstanding at home. Had driven down to the park to meditate and pray, so he says. That's pretty spooky if you ask me. I'll keep my eye on him and I'll be taking another look at the Goodwin boy."

"Neither one of these guys fit your serial killer profile."
"There are always exceptions."
"I'd think you'd have some way to put the fear of God into this joker before he kills again."

"Me and Ralph thought we had a handle on it once we made an arrest. Especially after we found the panties in Weird Walter's room. Turned out, after Mrs. Goodwin thought about it she called to tell me they didn't belong to her kid. Something about rayon and cotton."

"So whose were they?"

"Don't have a clue. Probably ripped them off somewhere to use for his personal pleasure. Anyway, the M.E. tells me the guy cut the legs from the Heinz victim with a fine-toothed saw. Thinks it's the same tool used on the first girl. Says he'll know after they do some tests."

"I guess that makes me a suspect. I have an assortment of scalpels and a doctor's bone saw or two and the know-how."

"Hey Doc, that's a good one, only you sure don't fit the profile."

* * *

"Oh man! Like wow! Totally awesome! Can't believe she'd give you that!"

Ollie was grinning like a baboon. It's Harry's old bike. A 1946 Harley 74. Like I was saying, she wanted me to haul it to the dump. Look at this. Springs on the front forks, hand shift, suicide clutch. It's cherry man."

"Think it'll run?"
"It will. The carburetor and the transmission are all in pieces in that old wooden box. She doesn't have the book on it so I

thought tomorrow I'd run down to Deiters. In addition to Fords, he's the local Harley Davidson dealer. They might be able to get me some info about it."

"Oh crap. Gotta go to church and then to Clarksdale. We probably won't get home early enough for me to come by tomorrow, but Monday after school I'll be camped out at your pad. I wanna help you put it back together. What does your Dad say about all this?"

"Dad says, if we get it running, we can ride it around the back forty on Grandpa Frazier's ranch, but not out on the street till I'm sixteen. What I want to do first is strip it totally down. Sand everything, you know, like to bare metal, then spray it a candy apple red. The chrome on the wheels, the springs and the handlebars all need to be polished."

Mark was sitting on the seat, which was in surprisingly good condition.

"Rrrrrrmmmm, rrrrruuummm." Giving it the gas he was leaning forward into an imaginary wind. "Spray the engine with a can of that liquid chrome and this thing will look brand new. Darn it Ollie, I'd like to start right in taking it apart, but like I told you, gotta study. Gotta keep my History grade up in order to keep playing basketball. Like man, I can hardly wait to see this baby in action. If we get home early enough tomorrow, I'm comin' by. You lucky dog."

* * *

The Man was cruising. Not looking for anybody in particular. That's when he saw this figure jogging . . . jogging hell, running. Full bore. As the boy cut through the Texaco Station the bright lights showed who it was. I'll be damned, it's the Goodwin kid. The boy crossed Main and went in the side door of the Greyhound Bus Depot. Means he'll come out the alley by the theater. Should I try to cut him off? Better hadn't.

Through the glass windows facing Locust he could see the lad taking a breather. Too many people around tonight. Got a bus due at 7:30. Fact is here it comes. Kid's only a couple of blocks from home. Let it go. Get the bastard later. For the time being I'll take a cruise out Lone Pine Trail and back, for old time's sake.

* * *

Mark felt so uneasy he took the long way, avoiding busy Park Street, running down Locust instead. He cut through the Texaco Station at Main and Locust Street, walked through the bus depot, through the theater parking lot and ended up in front of the White residence. He remained highly alert as he walked, each time a car approached he'd slip behind anything convenient. When he reached the White residence, Shannon and Candy were sitting on the front porch swing shooting the breeze. As he passed under the streetlight Shannon spotted him and called out, "Hey Mark, c'mere a minute. Tell you what we found out at the shoe store."

He stopped in their driveway. "Gotta go study so make it quick. What are you guys up to?"

"Baby sitting. Like I told ya, my folks are gone for two days to a seminar at the AME Church in Clarksdale."

"Baby sitting?" Mark teased. "I would think Randy would be old enough to baby sit himself. Or are you babysitting the redhead?"

"Bite me, dork." Candy was wearing black, hip hugger jeans topped off with a belt made of short strips of black leather held together by chrome rings. A black denim vest over an orange T-shirt exposed about three inches of her white stomach and her naval. Something about the narrow strip of naked skin seemed to draw Mark's eyes. The only thing he could think to say was, in a sarcastic manner, "Well ain't that the cutest belly button you ever saw?"

"If it bothers you, don't look," Candy snipped.

Shannon grinned. "Randy and Michael are up in his room doing whatever it is ten and eleven year olds do so I have to keep my eyes on the monsters. Rochelle and Janice are glued to the TV. The Simpson's, you know."

"So what's the poop on the shoes?"

"They aren't dress shoes at all."

"They aren't dress shoes?"

"Is there an echo in here?" Candy asked. "They're boots."

"Clinton's has the exact pattern," Shannon continued. "Clerk told us, guys buy them so they can wear boots but look dressy. Expensive boots. They're called Eagle Gold. We looked in my dad's closet. Even he has a couple of pair"

236

"Boots? No idea who, but I saw someone down at the Green Spot wearing black boots."

Candy leaned toward him. "Who was it? Maybe the killer was eating there."

"I can't remember; it was some guy. Practically all of the men are wearing boots. Seems to be the style these days."

"The clerk gave us a list of some of the people that bought them. And guess what? The sheriff was one of them."

"Tell me something I didn't know. There are too many things that point . . . " A phone inside the house rang.

"Whoops! Gotta catch the phone. Be right back." Shannon dashed inside, the screen door banging heavily behind her.

Mark shuffled around feeling ill at ease. He sat on the porch railing glaring at the redhead. There was a fluffy white pillow next to Candy on which Shannon had been sitting but it didn't register as unusual to Mark. Something about Candy made him uncomfortable, most likely her eyes. The way she could look right through you without blinking. What the heck? I'm over the deal of her seeing me bare-assed. Fact is . . . I'm kinda proud of my build. She's weird, that's all. "Yo Red, you and Shannon are getting to be pretty chummy like a couple of lovers."

Candy made a face. Wonder if this guy will ever turn into a human being? "Best friends," she let him know.
He shrugged. "Okay if you like 'em lean and mean."

"She's not mean."

"I was referring to you, bimbo. I like Shannon. She's smart and she's witty."

Candy felt the anger well inside her chest. Ought to haul off and . . .. This is one of those times when Grandma insisted she should try to say something nice. Force yourself, Grandma said. What? His face was highlighted by the glow from the porch light. "You know what? You have the prettiest blue eyes."

He opened his mouth to make some clever retort but nothing came out.

Candy discovered he was again eyeing her exposed belly button. She tugged at the front of her pullover. Her thoughts were interrupted with Shannon's return. Her friend was sobbing, tears shining on her cheeks.

"Shannon? What's wrong?" Candy stood to reach out to

237

her.

"That was the police. From Clarksdale," she choked and spluttered. "My mom . . . my mom is in the hospital and my dad is in jail."

"What?" Mark looked puzzled. "Whatever for?"

"He . . . he . . . he beat her up . . . bad. Oh God! I need to find some way to get to Clarksdale."

Mark stood his mind racing. "Uh, I gotta idea. I'll give my step-dad a call and see if he'll drive you down there. I know he'll help 'cause he never has liked your dad. Calls him all sort of names. 'A reverse racist, rabble-rouser, trouble maker', and even occasionally he uses that word, you know . . . 'Nigger'." Running both his hands through his hair he told her. "I'll see if my mom can stay with the kids or if she can't, I could."

"Oh Mark, would you?"

"Show me to the phone and I also need a phone book. They're at the Anderson's playing cards. Need to get their number."

"Mark, you're gonna have to watch Michael too," Candy followed them into the den. "I'm going with her."

* * *

Mark's parents arrived within minutes. "We'll both be glad to help," his mother slipped an arm about Shannon's shoulders. "I don't know what to say, dear. You go to your mother and we'll talk when you get back."

"I'm going along," Candy told them.

"Well then, I guess I'll tag along," said Mark. "Got somewhat of a problem here," his stepfather held up a hand. "I was thinking it would be Shannon going so I'm driving the pickup. That seat's only wide enough for three."

"That's okay. I'll hop in the bed and hunker down," Mark offered.

"You will not," his father bellowed. "You'll not only freeze your butt off but it's dangerous. If you insist on going, then you can sit in the front and hold one of your friends."

'One of his friends' turned out to be Red. In his mind he did his Bugs Bunny imitation, 'what a revolting development this is. Despicable. She was nothing but a hunk of soft flesh that smelled of cheap cologne. Not that she smelled all that bad. It seemed to even be in the hair that constantly brushed against his face. The worst part of the whole thing was, he didn't know what to do with his hands. Shannon sat in the middle pressed against his left shoulder and hip. His other side was firmly against the door. He put his arms around her waist letting his hands rest in her lap. She squirmed slightly to become more comfortable then rested her arms on top of his. The edge of his lower arms barely touched the bare skin above the jeans. He sighed. Come on Dad, I don't need this torture. Put your foot in it.

* * *

At the hospital, all four visitors were permitted to go to Mrs. White's room at once. In spite of the bandages and nasty bruises around her eyes, it turned out she wasn't injured nearly in as badly as the policeman, who called Shannon, had indicated.

"Oh Mom," the teenager cried.

Mark held back, watching Shannon who didn't seem to be sure if she dared hug her mother or not. Mrs. White extended her arms and they were hugging.

"You look awful," Shannon wailed. Candy stood close to her friend wringing her hands.

"Not as bad as it looks, honey. Got a broken nose and a number of cuts. Mostly I got me a pile of bruises, but unlike you, mine are on my back. They want to keep me overnight given that I coughed up some blood. He kicked me in the stomach when I was down. You'll have to watch the kids till . . . where are the kids?"

"We got it wired, Mom. Mrs. Goodwin is with them."
Mrs. White looked first at Mark then at his father. "Bless her heart. Tell your wife how much I appreciate what she's doing."

Mr. Goodwin nodded. "No problem. All we want is for you to get better. We'll keep watch over your family."

Mark looked at Shannon and was surprised to realize how sensitive he was when he felt tears on his own cheeks. Wiping them away with his knuckles, he asked, "I don't understand. What the heck made Reverend White do this?"

Ruby looked at Mark and then at his father before she answered. "It was all over something that has been building for quite a while. I should have listened to you, honey." She turned toward Shannon. "There are things that happened involving Jan-

239

ice and Rochelle, and the beating he gave Shannon last night, I confronted him today."

This was news to Mark. So that was why Shannon had been walking so funny and never sitting down.

Mrs. White continued. "I accused him of child molestation. When he claimed all these things were a form of punishment for wrong doings, I asked him why, when he was referring to your daughter, Mr. Goodwin, he used the term, 'She needed to be punished. All of a sudden he went berserk and here I am."

Mark looked up as a large boned woman came through the door, thinking that her face looked like a bulldog. Turned out she was nearly that tough.

The lady bulldog came directly to the black girl. "You must be Shannon. I'm Sergeant Seymour from the County Sheriff's Office. I would like to ask you a few questions. Would also like to have a physician examine you, if you don't mind."

Shannon looked at her mother who nodded. "I don't mind," she stood quietly.

"Would you be up to giving us a statement?"

"I uh . . . this is sorta extreme. Kinda spaces me out. It's one of those things where I hate my father, but at the same time I love him. Would what I tell you be helpful or hurtful to him? He needs some professional help."

"We know that, young lady, but our first priority is protecting the family."

"May I ask a question?" Mr. Goodwin seemed baffled. "Mrs. White mentioned something about my Laura? Sheriff Martinez already has a man in jail and a confession."

"Actually his suspect is now here in Clarksdale County Jail, but he is due to be released this evening. His mother is at the jail as we speak."

"What do you mean released? Why would he be released?"

Mark knew what the woman officer's statement meant. This was getting to be too much. He felt sick, in a daze.
"Oh my God. Do the police suspect Mr. White?"

"I've already informed Mrs. White but obviously you folks haven't been apprised of the latest news. It concerns another little girl in Dalton."

It was Candy who asked, "You mean the missing Heinz

kid?"

She sighed. "I'm afraid so. Her body was recovered from the Sandstone River late this afternoon. The Sheriff's Department is cooperating with the Dalton police and we have cause to believe Mr. White could have been involved."

"Oh my God," replied Mark's stepfather.

"Oh my Gawd," Candy murmured.

"Oh no!" cried Shannon.

* * *

The Man was also thinking, 'Oh my God!' He had no way of knowing that, in the restaurant, Mark Goodwin had been lost in his thoughts, merely staring past him and out the window. That Goodwin kid is on to me. Has to be. Where in the Hell did I go wrong? Why isn't he blowing the whistle? He's the one who found the watch, but how did he connect it to me? I didn't buy it at the local jewelers, bought it down in Clarksdale. Is he trying to find some other sort of proof? Oh my God, what am I gonna do? This is a problem I am going to have to deal with, one way or another and damn soon. Talk about needing a plan. Why didn't I shoot that punk the other night? He has to be . . . he is going to be eliminated.

CHAPTER NINETEEN

It was after eleven by the time they left the hospital. Shannon had been in with the lady cop and a doctor forever. While they waited Red explained in detail about Shannon's condition.

"Why didn't you clue me in?" Mark asked.

"She didn't want anybody to know. Had to practically drag it out of her myself."

"I guess you realize this thing about her father and the fact that there has been a second murder turns our investigation into a whole new ball game?"

On the return trip Mark found himself more uncomfortable than ever. The journey was made in total silence. His father appeared to be concentrating solely on his driving. Shannon stared straight ahead, unflinching, off in a world of her own. Candy promptly fell asleep, her face pressed against his chest, her hair against his cheek. What was worse, he had to hold her in his arms to keep her from pitching forward or falling all over Shannon. His right arm and hand rested fully on the exposed flesh of her stomach but his left arm lay directly under her breasts. Each time the truck hit a bump he could feel the softness. Couldn't understand the experience since it made him warm and he liked it.

His mind drifted off into what Superman would do. If the gal on his lap had been Lois Lane he would know how to handle it. After awhile holding the redhead felt comfortable, as though he was her protector. He didn't want it to stop.

Suspicions that the sheriff was the killer had been shaken with the introduction of Mr. White as a suspect. Facing him was a whole new set of possibilities. Could Reverend White have been the burglar? Entirely possible; same size as the burglar. Always wore black dress boots as did the intruder. With his head covered by a ski mask, and wearing gloves, there was no way to determine his color; or should there have been? Shouldn't he have been able to see some skin around the eyes? Why couldn't he remember? Shannon told us he owned a watch similar to the one they found? A watch that was missing. He also owns two pair of the Eagle Gold boots. This case is already taking more twists and turns than a TV movie. He was wondering about the Heinz child. Wanted to reach out and shake Shannon by the shoulder to ask, "Where was your dad last night?" But he didn't.

* * *

On Sunday morning Mark rolled out of bed without being called. He looked out the window. Rats, another cloudy day. Paper's here though. Wonder what they have to say 'bout the Heinz's girl? Take my shower then go out and get it.

When he came out of the shower he stood looking at himself in the mirror. Flexing his muscles he checked his chest, then the rest of his body. He and Ollie and Buzz worked out sometimes in the weight room at the fire station. Buzz's dad let them use it. Don't look too shabby there, Marcus. Screwing up his face he remembered when he stood naked in front of Red. So? She got an eyeful. Anyway, she called me a hunk. I'll take that, even from her.

As soon as he was dressed he went out to get the paper. Taking off the rubber band he spread it out on the kitchen table with every intention of checking on the Heinz story. But for a moment he couldn't look, petrified with a sickening horror as he recalled the scene out on Lone Pine Trail.

'GIRL'S BODY FOUND IN RIVER'. All he could see after that were snatches of news, phrases. 'The mutilated body of eight year old . . . Two fishermen . . . Second murder in two weeks. Then his eyes focused on a small paragraph. 'Dalton Police are concerned that a local pastor could be implicated. Police have no other suspects at this time.'

"Oh God," Mark prayed, clutching the paper to his chest. "Let me be Superman in the flesh for one day. Give me X-ray vision and super strength and the power to fly. I want this depraved monster in my fingers of steel."

He didn't even realize until his mother rapped on the door

to his room that he'd carried the paper in with him.

"Marcus, we're leaving for church so you'd better hurry it up unless you want to walk."

"I'm coming, I'm coming." Good Grief Charlie Brown. Why do we drive to church? It's only two blocks. One if you went up the alley.

* * *

At church, prior to the service, there was no other topic of conversation. Mark heard Mrs. Worthington talking to his folks. "The town's people are outraged that this could happen in our quiet city. We are all running scared. Families with small children are terrified. I'm sure this has to be terribly hard on you."

Watching his mother's face she seemed to be carved from stone, as though she wasn't listening.

"For the first time in this town's history," the lady continued, "doors and windows are being locked. Small children, particularly girls are no longer permitted out alone day or night."

Mark's father was trying to cut her off and usher his wife on into the sanctuary. Mark and his family were regulars at Creighton Baptist but he was surprised to see Candy and her brother this morning and more amazed to see Shannon and the three White children. Candy smiled his way as she walked past and she told him, "You look pretty far out in your go to meeting duds."

"Aaaaah. My one and only sports shirt and new Levis. Big deal."

"At least you polished your boots."

Looking her over he couldn't remember ever seeing her in a dress. It was a lime green sheath she'd borrowed from Shannon. The word which came to mind was . . . bitchin', but he'd never say it to her. Instead he made a face and spoke to the black girl. Hi Shannon. Uh . . . you look nice."

"Hi Mark. Don't look so surprised. I don't even want to be here, but my Aunt Bella came over and insisted me and the kids go to church with her."

"Has the AME closed up?"

"Naw, they're open but I'm never going back to my dad's church. Never. Anyhow, Aunt Bella goes to church here. She hates my dad."

"So how are you feeling? I mean, about him."

244

"I'm trying not to think about it. I hate him for the molestation stuff, but as for the murders . . . I don't think it was him."

"Nor do I." Candy was staring at her friend. "That's pretty wild. How did you get your hair to look like that?"

Shannon tried to smile, white teeth showing, "It's cornrows. Aunt Belle did it for me. Takes forever."

Mark's folks moved over to where the group stood and his mother inquired, "Well hello, Shannon honey, how is your mother doing?"

"Oh hi Mrs. Goodwin. I called down there this morning and she's a whole lot better. Of course she hurts all over. They may let her come home today."

"That's good. If you need anything you let us know."

"I want to thank you for watching the kids for me last night."

Mark saw Red's mom and dad talking to the pastor's wife. When Mr. Swanson spotted the Goodwin's, he walked over to shake hands and then gave his mother a comforting hug, patting her on the back. "We all share your pain," he told her and her reaction surprised everyone.

"You don't know about pain," his mother's eyes seemed to spit at him.

Mark wondered what triggered it. Probably all the parishioner's comments about the new murder were catching up to her. "I know about pain," she told him, "and since he has killed another child, I know it wasn't my fault. Laura's death was not my fault. There is a contemptible savage out there and no child is safe. No child. Not even yours."

Mark was surprised when Candy slipped up beside his mom and placed an arm about her waist. She was nearly as tall as his mom who turned to lean her head against the teenagers. Mark turned away, feeling tears streaming on his own cheeks.

They sat listening to the preacher and Mark wanted to leave. The morning sermon obviously had been changed to fit the occasion and sure as heck isn't what my mom needs.

"Our own dear little Gretchen Heinz, only eight years old, was last night the victim of an evil, godless monster. We agonize with the parents of this child, who are compelled to live with this terrible result of a sick society. The Heinz family is foremost in all our prayers this day, my friends, and their only consolation during this time of terrible grief is that their daughter is already in heaven."

He went on and on and Mark was glad when it was over.

In the foyer, Candy and her father stopped next to Mark and his mother. They were waiting in line with other parishioners to shake hands with the preacher. His own father was off talking to a deacon and Mark resented the attention Candy's dad was showing to his mother . . . like he was trying to put a move on her. The jerk had his hand on her shoulder and was rubbing it when he asked, "Did you hear the news? Sheriff's Department released Walter Jordan this morning."

"I hadn't heard, but it's about time."

"I tried to tell him he had the wrong man," Mark butted in.

Mark's mother turned to Red's dad and told him, her eyes following his hand sliding down her arm. "That is so sad about Walter. Once you've been arrested for a crime like that, the stigma leaves the jail with you. Things will never be the same for that poor man. Oh, here's my husband."

Mark watched as the two men shook hands. At least he'd taken his claws offa Mom.

"And there's my wife," Swanson nodded.

"Michael! Quit that. You are going to break something." Mark could see Mrs. Swanson across the foyer trying to grab the darting imp who had climbed up onto an indoor planter. She dragged him by one arm over to where they stood and rationalized to his mom, "that boy has such an inquisitive mind."

"By the way, Goodwin, I called Heinz early this morning. Told him to take two weeks off with pay, so you'll have to assume his duties. I understand you were a butcher at one time."

"At one time, but I'd be rather rusty."

"We would absolutely die," Mrs. Swanson offered, "if something like this happened to Michael."

At that moment Red's dad spotted Shannon coming up from the basement classrooms where her three charges had attended youth church and he frowned. "I'll be darned, there's the White children. Kinda surprising to see them here. I heard their father has been implicated as a suspect."

Mark's dad dropped a bomb. "For a while last night they

246

did but I guess they didn't have anything to hold him on. Talked to Mr. Frazier this morning and he says the preacher had ironclad alibis for both nights. Posted bail on the other charges. Guess he'll be back in town today."

Shannon overheard and stopped short. "My Dad is coming home today?"

"Not home per se," he told her. "Guess he's going to stay in the motel until he gets himself straightened out. The sheriff mentioned something about a court order to stay away from the house."

Candy moved over to give Shannon a hug. "I'll drop over after lunch and we can play some monopoly or something."

"Shannon looked at Mark. "You wanta come by?"

Mark's mind was in a whirl at this latest twist. It definitely wasn't Weird Walter. It might not be the sheriff. I never did think it was Reverend White. Something Shannon had said earlier, something he couldn't recall at the moment, caused him to have his doubts about the Reverend White. So who? "Gosh Shannie, I Can't. We're going down to Clarksdale to visit my grandparents. Take them to dinner tonight and all that good stuff."

"Oh, that's right." Candy seemed anxious to get going. "I forgot."

"Come on Mark," his father prodded. "We told Grandma Goodwin we'd be there by 1:30." To Candy's folks he said, "Mark's grandparents are celebrating their fortieth anniversary today."

"How nice," Mrs. Swanson was smiling. "Both of Michael's grandmothers are alive but one of his grandfathers is gone. Michael! Leave those pamphlets alone. You folks have a nice time." "By the way Mrs. Goodwin, we'll have to get together one of these days and do lunch."

"See ya later, Red. Don't trust anybody wearing black dress boots."

"You too," she replied. "See ya when we see ya."

"Teenagers." Julie Goodwin was shaking her head. "Not a care in the world."

* * *

A delegation from the AME Church went to Clarksdale to bring Shannon's mother home. As soon as she was through with her lunch, Candy came over to visit as promised. The two girls played games, listened to music and gossiped away the after-noon. About 4:30 Mrs. White took them by surprise.

"Why don't you two fix yourself some sandwiches then go to the movies? The Elders from the AME Church are coming by at six. They have promised to help us through our difficulties."

"What about the rest of the kids?"

"Aunt Belle is going to take care of them. Give you a chance to see that movie you've been waiting for."

"Far out." She gave her mother a careful hug.

"Do you need money?"

"Think I got enough, Mom. Come on Candy, let's do it." She was already checking the paper. "Here we are; Evil Destiny: 5:45."

* * *

When the two giggling girls left the theater at 7:50, Candy was in no hurry. "I'm not ready to go home yet, want to walk down to the Pit and see who's hanging out?"

"That sounds bad to me. We can get some ice-cream. You buying?"

"I take it you're . . . like broke." Candy was going through some of her cheerleading moves.

"Like you know."

"Gotcha covered. I happen to get my allowance on Sun-days."

They passed the power company and used the alley that ran between the rear of Dalton National Bank and the City Parking Lot exiting onto Palm Street. A gleaming black Mustang convert-ible burned rubber, rocketing from the driveway at Kelly's Burger Pit then braked to a stop as it cut the two girls off. Charlie Deiter, Heather's seventeen-year old brother, with a trio of other high-school chums were cruising. Charlie let out a long, low-pitched wolf whistle. "Hey Red, c'mere."

Candy moved forward and placed both hands on the top edge of the passenger door. "Nice wheels. You are soooo lucky that your daddy can afford to keep buying you tires."

Charlie grinned as all three boys smirked at the teenagers. Shannon moved up alongside her friend but didn't touch the car. "Whatcha say good lookin'? You chicks wanna go for a ride?"

"Come on," one of the boys in the back called out. "We'll

treat you gals real nice."

Candy snorted. "We prefer older men. You guys are hardly out of diapers."

"Well look who's talking. Stuffing your bra full of tissue don't make you a grown up. Screw you wise ass broads." He gunned the engine, popped the clutch and made the tires squeal for half a block before making a screaming turn onto Washington.

Shannon sighed. "Is he good lookin' or what?"

"He is. Blond and blue-eyed like Heather only not an Albino. Trouble with guys like that is, all they are interested in is one thing. Making out."

"I've got a notion to dye my hair." Shannon looked both ways then crossed the street.

"You're jerkin' me. What color?"

"Red like yours."

"Boy Shannon, you are a wire. You wouldn't like it."

"I don't know. Sure gets you nothing but attention."

"Yeah. Kind of attention I don't need."

"That's a crock. You'd be miserable if nobody paid you any mind."

Her statement was true and how well Candy knew it. She wouldn't trade ten minutes of her new life for the whole city of Montgomery.

* * *

The Man was cruising along Cedar Street as the two girls came out of the alley next to the power station. Noticing them but not seeing them as persons, his mind was way off somewhere in space, he turned left on Washington as they moved into the lighted city parking lot. The flood of light caught his attention when it flashed across her hair and he sucked in his breath. It was that little redheaded bitch, the girlfriend of the Goodwin jerk. She's with that black gal, Reverend White's daughter. The sheriff's new murder suspect. Where the heck are they going? At the corner of Washington and Palm he had it figured out. The Burger Pit. Must be a way to separate the redhead from her friend? I've got nothing against her and she's not on my list, but what the hell? Put the fear of God in that Goodwin punk. Let him know that I mean business.

A black convertible burned rubber as it left the Burger Pit

249

parking lot and pulled in front of the two girls. Crap! There's that Deiter joker and his gang of rowdies trying to hit on them. Come on gals; don't take 'em up on it. Words were exchanged, apparently not too friendly and happily the Mustang convertible roared away. Turning into the city parking lot behind Dalton Bank he shut off the engine and waited. The tension was like a coiled spring as he watched them through the window. First at the counter placing their orders, then both girls were being frisky, constantly in motion, the black one was horsing around with a couple of boys. He continued to wait.

Are they going to stay in there forever? Darned near 9:30. Been over an hour. At last! The bitches are coming out. In his mind he was trying to trace their potential course. The black bitch lives on the corner of Washington and Locust and the white broad a block away on Riverview. If I was her I would walk to the reverend's house, say good-bye, then take a short cut through the Goodwin property to her place. Makes sense. What he need-ed to do was, drive up Palm to Taylor and leave his car at the corner of Taylor and Locust, walk down and hide in the bushes at the Goodwin place. Knew for a fact the Goodwin's were out of town, probably until late tonight. His eyes were vicious, his smile satanic and he knew it.

From where he concealed himself in an area between a storage-shed and some oleander bushes next to the Goodwin house, he could see the two girls standing by the front porch at the White residence chattering away. "Come on," he whispered. "Give it a rest for crying out loud. Kids your age should be in the house by this time of night." He grinned again. "Don't you ladies realize that the streets of Dalton are getting downright danger-ous?" Gripping the roll of gray tape with his right hand he tore off a six-inch long strip with his left and held it in his palm, his right hand was holding the gun.

What could he do if she decided to go the long way be-cause of the streetlights? Have to rush on through to Riverview. Plenty of shrubbery around the banker's place and the judge's house only the judge has that damned dog. Could he get there in time to cut her off? And if she cut the corner could he get close enough? Not to worry. Here she comes, like a poor little lamb. All I need to do is wait. Shoving branches aside he concealed

250

himself between two large bushes next to the front corner. There was barely enough room to squeeze by. His diabolical mind was racing as he watched her come. Fifty more feet. Turning my way. He felt a sinful quivering in his loins. Thirty feet. Twenty. He tensed, his hand poised face high, ready to slap the tape onto her mouth. This little turkey is mine. She was there and he reached for her.

"Candy? Is that you?" A male voice called out as a hand held floodlight drenched her body with whiteness. "Where the heck have you been? You were supposed to be home by nine. I've been out walking the streets looking for you."

"Oh . . . sorry Dad. Shannon and I went to the Pit for ice-cream and I wasn't watching the time."

The Man's mind whirled and he actually sank to his knees in the darkness trying to halt his momentum. The redhead was past. Her voice had a peculiar ring to it. Like she was surprised her father cared.

"Do you have any idea how dangerous it is getting to be for a pretty young lady to wander around outside after dark?"

"Sorry." She responded, "It won't happen again." Swanson put his arm around his daughter as they headed inside.

First the Goodwin kid, now the Swanson bitch. This place is jinxed. The Man wanted to cry.

CHAPTER TWENTY

When Mark arrived at school Monday morning he was the center of attention. "Where in the heck did you get the threads," Shannon asked. "They are extreme." At least fifteen students circled him in awe.

He was wearing one of his patented black shirts but the trousers were deep red. The waist fit perfectly but the seat hung halfway to his knees and the legs appeared to be ten sizes too large and a couple of inches too long. A bright chrome chain draped down his left hip extending from his wallet to a belt loop. "Mom wanted to go to the mall down in Clarksdale. Got them at a place called Corky's."

"Awesome," Jodie seemed to be getting cozy with Shorty Carr.

"They look gross," Candy snorted. "Pretty stupid if you ask me. Looks like Bozo the clown has left the circus. You even got the big red nose."

"Well Red look who's talking. Farmer John in her bib over-alls and cow pucky boots. Where did you find those, at the Thrift Shop?"

"Maybe I did. Anyway I look cool. You look like a big city gang-banger."

"At least I don't buy my duds at the Thrift Store like some red headed bimbo we all know." He couldn't understand why her overalls fascinated him. She was wearing a flesh colored top under the bib that made her, in his mind, look like she was wearing nothing but the overalls. Crap, that's stupid, he thought. Who in the heck would want to see her in the buff?

"It's none of your business but I am trying to save enough

out of my allowance to get my hair done again. I want to get it dyed blonde."

"You will not!" Mark stood with his mouth open for a long five seconds. "I mean . . . you shouldn't. Not that I give a whiz one way or the other but . . . you just shouldn't."

The bell rang for first period and everyone scattered.

* * *

"Hey Mark," Buzz bumped up against his side as he was opening his locker. "Look what Nutt Sawyer gave me."

What he saw was two, fat white cylinders. "Are those what I think they are?"

"Yeah. Roaches."

"Jeeze, Buzz. Don't let anybody see you with them. Where'd Nutt get 'em?"

"I don't know, some high school guy. You told me you'd like to try one sometime to see what the big turn on is.

"Heck Buzz, I was only jerkin' ya around. I don't even smoke."

"What the heck, buddy?" Reaching into Mark's locker he stuffed one of the cigarettes in behind a wadded up sweatshirt. "Maybe later, if you decide you wanna try it. Gotta go. See ya at noon."

Actually he had told Buzz he'd like to try one, but he probably never would. At the moment he was concerned about his near miss Saturday night and worried there could be other events. Where the heck is my English book. Ah, there tis under the sweatshirt. He dug it out, the piece of clothing coming with it. The cigarette slithered out and rolled a couple of feet down the hall. Dean Ruggle, the student everyone loved to hate, was right on the spot and he snatched it up.

"Mr. Hernandez!" The boy practically screeched at the principal who was heading for his office.

"What is it Mr. Ruggle?"

Mark turned as the principal took a few steps his way. The bantam sized boy was holding the white object up for him to see and pointing toward Mark. With its plump center and twisted ends, the principal recognized it for what it was. Mark's face turned gray, his usually rapid mind deserted him, as he stood with his mouth open, unable to speak.

"Mr. Goodwin. I want to see you in my office! Dean, would you come and bring the evidence with you."

Once inside, with the door closed, Mark knew it didn't get any worse than this. For the first time in years his confidence totally deserted him.

"What is this?" Mr. Hernandez pointed a long finger toward Mark's new trousers.

Mark shrugged. "I'm trying to keep up with the latest."

"We are not the least bit impressed. You keep trying to push the envelope. Bringing narcotics into this school brings automatic expulsion and of course you are off the team."

His heart couldn't sink any lower.

"I am going to call your parents then I'll call Sheriff Martinez. What happens next will be pretty much up to him and Judge Elliot, but I'd venture a guess it will be Willow Creek Camp for you . . . perhaps until you turn eighteen."

Dean Ruggle was gloating, his eyes as beady as some jackal with a dead rabbit.

As though blaming the other student, Mark hissed. "Way to go, Shark Bait. Better go out and show all the students your slimy brown nose. I'm sure they'll be impressed."

"That will be enough, Mr. Goodwin. Dean will be recognized for his courage and school spirit. If there were more students in Dalton like Mr. Ruggle, this school would be the showcase of the state. He lifted the phone.

* * *

Buzz Tarmen had been listening to all the chatter among students about the new murder. He looked up as Carmelita Hoover, who had left the bathroom the moment the event went down, came in with the news.

"Listen up, everybody." She had their attention. "You ain't gonna believe what just happened. Mark Goodwin got busted for having marijuana in his locker."

"Whaaaat? Oh my Gawd." Candy stood next to Shannon's desk with her mouth open.

A clerk came to the door and summoned Mrs. Turner. Another student came in. Apparently he'd overheard two teachers discussing Mark's problem and within minutes, like falling dominos, word traveled from room to room.

All Buzz could say was, "Oh shit."

Everyone seemed to break up into groups. No less than fifteen students claimed to have witnessed the incident resulting in at least ten different versions of what took place. Buzz couldn't believe how soon the tales grew, ranging from one cigarette to a package of grass to a pound of coke. "Jerks," he snapped, knowing pupils were quite naturally prone to believe the worst.

Heather Deiter came in. She too had been in the bathroom with a mild asthma problem. When she spotted her fellow cheerleaders, she moved to join them. "I hear they took Mark down to the police department. Guess he's in big trouble."

Leaving his seat Buzz moved to where the three girls gathered next to Shannon. Leaning with his hand on the back of her seat he tried to steer them off the subject. "How's your mom doing? Don't think I'm not glad you're here but kinda surprised." He was also trying to keep his own discomfort from showing.

"Darned near didn't come this morning." Shannon told them. "Mom's kinda aching and terribly depressed. I offered to stay home, but a couple of church ladies stopped by to keep keep her company."

"Heard that your dad's coming home today too." Buzz was having a hard time to keep from squirming.

"Yeah," there was an actual sound of relief in her voice. "I knew it wasn't him. Had alibis for both nights. Posted bail on the assault charges so he'll be back in town today."

"Not exactly home," Buzz told her. "Hear he's gonna stay in the motel for a while. Something or the other about a court order to stay away from your house." This wasn't working. All he could think about was Mark and then Ollie blew it open.

"This thing with Mark is the shits," Ollie moaned.

"If I'da had any idea this sort of thing was going to come down on Mark I'd have stayed home," Jodi told them.

"I can't understand it," cried Shannon as they waited for Mrs. Turner to return. "It's hard to believe Mark is involved in that crap."

"I sure never would have thought it," Ollie sounded depressed. "We're best friends, so you'd think he'd wire me in on something like this. Not that I've ever tried it myself . . . "

"You guys are so quick to judge," Candy snapped. "Even

255

though I don't like him, I don't believe for a minute he is involved. There's gotta be an explanation. Doesn't even smoke for crying out loud. Bet there is a logical explanation for this whole thing."

"You're probably right," Jodi insisted, "but I'll bet you a dollar old Bobby Hernandez isn't listening to any explanations."

"And Sheriff Frank has to be in heaven," Shannon had covered her face with her hands.

"We ought to tie that Dean Ruggle snot into a sack full of skunks," Ollie suggested, "and dump him in the river."
Buzz, who had remained silent throughout this discussion, was suddenly standing. "I gotta cut out. Tell Mrs. Turner I went home sick."

"Buzz? Where are you going," cried Shannon?

"Gotta go take care of something." That was all he said and he was gone.

Outside, he headed down Main Street on the dead run, keeping up the pace for the entire five blocks until he crossed the bridge. Directly ahead was the Fire Department.

* * *

"I told you I'd be busting you big time one of these days, boy, only I didn't expect it to happen quite so soon. You're in way over your head this time. Soon as Judge Elliot gives me a call back, I'm going to ask for permission to hold you in a cell like an adult. You're going to do time for this one." Principal Hernandez, who had accompanied the boy to the station, was nodding in agreement.

Isn't this the pits, Mark pondered? I'm the one in trouble while the guy who killed my little sister is roaming around free as a bird.

"All I gotta do is look atcha," the sheriff continued, "Gangbanger clothes and all that hair. I ain't going to let you get a damned pot smokin' gang started in my town."
It's Ollie's turn to be Superman, Mark was thinking. Time for him to come crashing through the wall and to the rescue. Boy oh boy Marcus, you blew it this time. With my reputation, nobody will listen to any excuses. How tough would they be on him? First offense? Doesn't that mean something? What about his friends? Ollie would stick up for him, wouldn't he? So much for the Kryptonites and a murder investigation.

Roger S. Williams

"Couldn't reach his Pa at Dalton General and his Ma ain't home either. We'll keep tryin'." Marion sat looking at Mark like she wanted to cry.

Everyone turned as the front door creaked open and Buzz, followed by his father, walked directly into the Sheriff's office. Mark looked up, his eyes full of questions. He knew the Sheriff respected Lou Tarmen, one of Dalton's two paid firemen. Guy was also active in youth activities in the community.

The sheriff offered his hand and the two men greeted each other. "Lou, what brings you down here? You know Principal Hernandez, right?" He glared at Buzz. "Aren't you supposed to be in school, boy?"

"I believe Buzz has something to tell you Sheriff. Go ahead son."

The sheriff sat down behind his desk and the chair creaked precariously as he leaned back. "Okay, let's hear it."

"Yes Sir. I . . . I uh, want to make a deal."

"A deal? Like you could possibly have something worth dealing about."

"You might be surprised, Frank," Lou told him. "I believe he actually does."

There were triple chins when the sheriff bent his head and squinted. "This I gotta hear. I suppose this so called deal involves Goodwin?"

"Look Frank," Mr. Tarmen interrupted again. "I'm aware that you don't like either Buzz or Mark due to some of the boyish devilment they get into, but they are both basically good kids. It would be a good idea if you would hear my boy out."

"I'm all ears."

Buzz had the fingers of one hand locked in the other and was twisting. "The roach in Mark's locker was mine. I stashed it there. Neither one of us use weed. A kid from the high school gave it to me and I thought it would be cool and make us look like big shots to be showing one around."

Mark was fascinated. The Principal was frowning, the Sheriff clearly disappointed as he leaned toward Buzz with renewed interest. Why would my buddy do this? Could this possibly be his way out? He knew Frank had been looking forward to teaching him a lesson.

"I see," Frank seemed to be agreeable. "I'll accept that.

257

Only I'm surprised you would stick your neck in the noose to save his ass. My problem is, it was a marijuana cigarette, and it was in his locker on school property, and he had to know about it. There will be a fair hearing at the courthouse and what happens will be up to Judge Elliot. Appears to me both you boys are in trouble, so I don't see what makes you think you got a deal."

"I'm not trying to deal me for him. Happen to know who the dude is that's been peddling this stuff, mostly down at the high school, and I know you want him."

Buzz's father was nodding.

The Sheriff came right out of his seat, the chair hanging onto the rolls of fat then pulling free with a thud. "Okay boy, let's hear this deal."

"Me and Mark get our hands slapped, and that's it."

"Just like that?"

"Not entirely," the boys' father stepped in. "Buzz tells me there are some bad stories going around school about what happened today, stories blown way out of proportion. I believe Mr. Hernandez should call an assembly and use you, Frank, to talk to the kids. I've heard some of your homey little chats Sheriff, and they are always pretty clever. You should have been a politician. Anyhow, you should give them a talk on the evils of drugs and at the same time clear Mark's name. I realize the boy is a thorn from time to time, but you and I both know he'll outgrow that."

Mark listened intently, knowing what the Sheriff was thinking. Elections were coming up the week before Thanksgiving and it couldn't hurt Frank's image to make something bigger out of this opportunity.

"All right, tell me who this guy is and you got yourself a deal. I believe what you are telling me so my estimation of you boys has gone up about fifty points. Goodwin was good enough of a friend not to rat on you, and you are one hell of a friend to put yourself on the hook to clear him. That kind of friendship is worth its weight in gold. Alright, let's have the guys name."

"Grady Small."

"You're shittin' me. You mean the used car salesman down at Deiters?"

"He's the one. Keeps a small supply of roaches, baggies and other crap in a briefcase he carries on the front seat. You know? In case he gets a quick sale. But you should see what he has stashed in the trunk."

"Well I'll be a horny toad. Me and Ralph are gonna have to do some snoopin'. My boy, you do have yourself a deal. I'll let Goodwin go and tomorrow, down at the schoolhouse, I'll tell them it was all a mistake."

* * *

Mark had been considering everything going on, his mind racing. Facing the sheriff he decided he should say something. "Look Sheriff. Elections are coming up next week and you could make a heap of points with voters by making this bust. And, Mr. Hernandez, you could make a big show, you know? With the students by showing them you are tough on narcotics in school but fair when it counts."

The Principal snickered. "But I'm not running for re-election.

"What are you getting at, Mr. Goodwin?"

"I was thinking that if you guys make it look like this was all a clever plan between the school and the sheriff, and Sheriff Frank catches this smuck by using me and Buzz to help. You know . . . a set-up. You guys'll come out of this looking like the smartest dudes in town. In the meantime it will clear up all the nasty rumors floatin' 'round."

"Damn." Frank was nodding. "Boy's smarter than he looks. What do you think, Ray?"

"I think . . . " he started to say Mr. Goodwin, but changed it to, "Mark is too smart for his britches. In any case we will only be distorting the truth since the boys will be responsible for your apprehending this man."

The phone rang and the Sheriff snatched it up before Marion could reach out. "Sheriff Martinez here. Oh, hi Judge, it's you. . . . Right. This is about narcotics. . . . Yeah, well listen, Henry. Me and Ralph are going to bust someone for faulty brake lights or something and I'm gonna need a pair of search warrants. Wan'ta take a look inside the trunk of Grady Small's car and then snoop around the perp's apartment. Suspicion of drug possession for sale, in case you're wondering. . . . Yeah, that's what I said, Grady Small. . . . Right, and uh . . . thanks Judge. We'll be coming by right soon."

The Principal wisely began making plans. "I want you boys to stay out of school for the rest of today and all of tomorrow morning. I will call an assembly for 1:00 PM tomorrow afternoon which will give us a chance to prepare a program."

"Right," Frank told them, "I'll pick you boys up 'bout a quarter till. You and Mark can ride down there with me. If any of your friends call tonight . . . shine them on. Man, I'm going to enjoy this and I agree with you boys, this is the right way to handle it."

"And," Buzz's dad told him, "properly handled, your re-election could be a cake-walk. With these murders hanging over your department you could use some favorable publicity."

The fat face broke into a grin. "I ain't been too concerned, but these unsolved murders ain't helping my image."

"I'll tell you this Frank," Principal Hernandez told him, "if you could only solve these crimes, you could run for Mayor."

"Kick my brother out of a job? Working on it twenty-five hours a day."

Mark surprised Frank by extending his hand. The Sheriff looked at it as though he didn't know what it was and after a short pause he took it. "Sorry I been giving you so much of a hassle the last couple of years, Sheriff. You got a tough enough job without putting up with all our teenage crap. No hard feelings, okay? You're pretty tough, Frank, but you're okay."

Frank was nodding in agreement. "Tomorrow I'm going to 'make some points. You interested in making some points too, boy?"

Mark shrugged.

"There is something you're gonna have to do for me."

"I'm listening," Mark replied, realizing the Sheriff was getting nowhere in his murder investigation, most likely since there was no investigation. Going through his mind was, starting tomorrow, the Kryptonites and I are gonna get serious about this killer. Real serious. Buzz's dad is a cool head, might be the one we need to unload on. "What do you want me to do?"

* * *

The hot topic Tuesday morning throughout the school concerned Mark and his arrest. Since Ollie was Mark's best friend everyone was asking him what was going on. There was conversation concerning the discovery of the murdered Heinz girl, but she was already old news to the school kids and this incident with Mark hit closer to home.

Candy, Shannon and Ollie met in the grandstands for lunch as they always did but nobody was eating. "So much for the Kryptonites," she let them know.

Ollie was frowning. "Couldn't find out anything about Mark last night. His mom sounded like an answering machine. 'Beep, this is a recording. Mark is not available to come to the phone at this time.'"

"This is exactly what I got when I tried to call Buzzes' house," Shannon told them. "I don't even know if he was home."

"Maybe the Sheriff held them overnight," suggested Ollie.

Candy seemed unusually gloomy. She didn't understand the hollow feeling in her chest. "Mark was home all right. Could see the light from his bedroom window when I went to bed."

"I guess that's good news . . . maybe. I'm really pissed," Ollie snapped. "But I ain't sure if it is with Mark or with the Sheriff. Here comes my wayward sister. Bout time you showed up, Sis."

Jodi was the last of the group to arrive and there were two guys with her. "Did you hear? The Principal has called for an assembly this afternoon."

"Yeah, we heard. So maybe we'll find out what's happening."

"And what's gonna happen," Candy cried.

"What ticks me off," added Shannon, "is that I haven't been able to get a hold of Buzz either, and where the heck is he today?" For the tenth time she glanced toward the front as though expecting him to show.

"What do you suppose they will do to Mark?" Jodi wondered, sitting on one of the hard benches with a fellow on either side.

"Probably send him to Boy's Town," Candy made a face, "or whatever it is they have out here at Dulltown."

"Willow Creek," Shannon informed her. "Down towards Clarksdale. It's kinda like a boy's reform school. However, I wouldn't think it would come to that. Not on a first offense."

"You forget how much the Sheriff hates him."

"Yeah," Candy snorted. "Here we have a murderer trying to put Mark in jail for a marijuana cigarette. Figure that one.

She caught a glimpse of a black and white patrol car as it drove through the delivery entrance. Then it stopped and she could see the backs of three individuals entering the school through one of the doors to the auditorium. She grimaced. Poor Mark. They're ganging up on him.

* * *

Candy looked around, not knowing what to expect. Every pupil was there along with the entire teaching staff, the kitchen staff, the custodians and even the grounds keepers. Mark's mom and dad were there and so were Mr. and Mrs. Tarmen. She was sure Principal Hernandez would explain about the arrest then go into one of his long-winded admonishments about something and this time narcotics.

She watched them come in. First the principal accompanied by three men and she frowned when Cory Frazier, Ollie's dad, smiled and waved at the crowd. He was there representing the Dalton Union newspaper. The second man, Kim Kamamoto, a local freelance photographer who sometimes provided shots for the paper, walked in front of the stage with the third man, George Saunders, principal of Jefferson High School. As Mr. Hernandez turned to take the stairs to the stage, these three men sat in the front row with the teachers. The entire gym began to buzz with speculation centered mostly on how bad things were going to be.

Candy's stomach felt like it was full of squirming snakes.

Mr. Hernandez thumped the microphone several times until he was satisfied he was on the air. "Students. May I have your attention please?" Candy was amazed when, as though someone had thrown a switch, all sound ceased. "As you already know, there were certain events that took place at our school yesterday. In order to bring you up to date on what has transpired, and why it took place, we have with us today Sheriff Frank Martinez who wants to tell us about an exciting series of events. Sheriff, if you would."

What the heck is going on, Candy wondered? The fat man seemed to be puffing from exertion as he came from off stage. She chewed on the side of her finger and then jerked when the two boys followed him. Buzz sat in a chair to the sheriff's left and the biggest surprise was Mark who sat on his right. He was conservatively dressed in Levis and a long sleeved plaid shirt and she gasped; his long hair was gone. It had been cut and neatly combed like a nerd. That's not true. He looked sharp. Handsome? The room began to buzz again.

* * *

"Good afternoon students." The sheriff concentrated on the three men in the front row. As far as he was concerned, the principal's idea of having the press here was a stroke of genius. "As you all know, due to efforts to keep narcotics under control by your local police department, drugs have not been one of Dalton's major problems. However, over the past few months we have been aware of an increase in drug activity in the vicinity of the high school and in the last couple of weeks there have even been incidents at Dalton Middle School.

"Our department was very much on top of this problem. In this case, what we had to do was set a trap in order to apprehend this perpetrator of the plague that was getting a foothold in our community. With the cooperation of Principal Hernandez and the staff at Dalton Middle School, we have been able to do exactly that. Dalton Middle School provided us with two students who were enlisted to help us set and spring this trap. I am very pleased to have with me, right here on stage, the two Dalton Middle School students aided us in carrying out our plan. I am also happy to say, the person responsible for these crimes against society is in jail. At this time, I would like to recognize these two students, who gave us the help we needed to put a stop to drug dealing on our campuses." He looked out over the expectant faces, knowing he was handling this thing right and every one of these kids will go home and tell their folks what a great police department Dalton has.

The photographer had moved down to where he was on one knee closer to the stage.

"I wish to recognize at this time, Marcus Goodwin and Nelson Tarmen, who I am happy to have here on the stage sharing the spotlight with me. Dalton can be proud of young men like these who put their own lives in danger in order to stop this scourge trying to invade our city. If you two men will please step forward, Principal Hernandez would like to make a presentation."

The camera flashed, lighting up the three faces over and

over. Frank gave the photographer his best profile then stepped back to watch as Martinez moved to the microphone.

The Principal's secretary had created a pair of awards on her computer. These she took to Stevens General Store where she had them framed. Martinez extended his hand to each of the boys. "Mark Goodwin, Nelson Tarmen, it gives me a great deal of pleasure to present you with these certificates of appreciation for your heroic actions. Through your efforts, the perpetrator of these heinous crimes is behind bars. For that, we owe each of you and our fine sheriff, Frank Martinez a great big thanks for ridding our community of this terrible criminal element." He handed each of the boys one of the awards and shook their hands as the camera continued to capture it all.

The sheriff was bobbing his head in agreement but Mark looked baffled while Buzz was grinning. Every person in the assembly was standing, clapping and cheering.

"Here, to also offer his congratulations, is George Saunders, Principal of Dalton's Jefferson High School. George."

This is good, Frank was thinking as the high school principal, all six foot six of him, walked up the steps and to the podium where he adjusted the microphone. He shook also hands with each of the boys.

"I can't begin to tell you how much I appreciate what you young men have done to help keep our classrooms free of drugs. I very much look forward to having you both as students at my school next fall. The two of you are a tremendous asset to this community and I can understand the sense of pride the students at Dalton Middle School must feel for their classmate heroes."

Frank fidgeted. Long-winded jerk is going to talk the rest of the afternoon without one word about me.

He rambled on and on until Frank muttered loud enough he knew Mark, who was sitting next to him, could overhear, "Okay, okay already. At least you two have learned a valuable lesson."

* * *

Even Mark lost interest, looking about the multipurpose room, counting the number of ceiling tiles it took to do a room of this size and thinking about how Superman hadn't let him down, only today the Man of Steel was a small black boy named Buzz.

The happiest man in the room was coach Donnelley who

gave him an 'A-okay' with his fingers. The team could probably handle Cotton tonight without him. Not to brag, he thought, but without him they could kiss off any chance they had of making a game of it against Clarksdale Friday.

Whew! At last! Mr. Saunders wound his portion of the program up by saying, "And we again turn the program over to Sheriff Martinez who will talk to us about the danger of using drugs. Sheriff."

* * *

The sheriff knew he had the audience in his pocket and that he could do a bang-up job by dropping clever little tidbits. After half an hour of his lecture he finished by saying, "As long as I am sheriff of Dalton, I promise you I will keep this city drug free. "I'd like to spend a few minutes by opening this meeting up to questions from the audience. Anything you'd like to ask on the subject of drugs?" He paused.

A number of students responded. It was obvious that they liked their sheriff and he was proud of his ability to think on his feet.

The cute little red-headed girl stood and paused until the feeling in the room was electric, "I have a question."

The way these kids dress now days. A man's flannel shirt, way too big, jeans full of holes, should have been shit canned years ago. And a baseball cap with her hair stuffed out through the back. Hmmm. It's that Swanson's kid with the cute southern drawl that won't quit. What was her name? "Yes. And what is your question, honey?"

"So okay already. You have drugs in our town under control. And we thank you for that, Sheriff Martinez. But how come you aren't able to catch the person who is murdering this town's children?"

Her question took him so totally off guard his answers were bumbling, incoherent and foolish. He could have killed her.

* * *

The Man was sitting way to the back, out of everybody's way and well concealed from being seen by the Goodwin kid. He was pretty much pissed that Frank had arrested the kid, took him down to the station, caught red-handed with some marijuana, and then turn him loose. Loose, Hell! Politics! Turn him and the punk into local heroes. Could have put that loose cannon into

265

Willow Creek for five years and I wouldn't have anything to worry about. Kid would be like any other gangster, who'd believe anything he had to say? So I have a problem to take care of. What is it they say? Dead heroes don't talk.

CHAPTER TWENTY-ONE

The Kryptonites met briefly following the Sheriff's lecture. The Principal gave them a thirty-minute break after the assembly had taken all of the fourth period and well into the fifth. Mark, Ollie and Buzz were already sitting in the grandstands. They watched as Shannon, Jodi and Red came their way. He was concentrating on the redhead so Mark didn't notice the cute, but tiny, Deiter doll, who was so sweet on Ollie, trailing the group by a half dozen paces. Instead he was thinking how tall Red seemed compared to Jodi and how she looked, as Ollie would say, 'Foxy' in her green and white outfit. The other girls were also wearing theirs.

"Got practice?" a rather subdued Mark asked.

"Yep. We get to cut the last class." Candy made some arm movements and a high kick. "Soon as the bell rings. So Marcus, what's with the hair?"

"Not my idea. Sheriff insisted I get it cut. Part of the deal we made."

"Deal?" Candy wrinkled up her face. "What do you mean, deal?"

"Actually Buzz made the deal. He's the one who put the roach in my locker. Sheriff was ready to send me to Willow Creek till I was eighteen. Buzz told Frank he'd tell him who was selling this crap down by the high school if we could make a deal."

"You guys," Shannon told them, "are gonna fool around and hang yourselves. So the haircut was part of this deal?"

"Frank liked my idea about making it look like Buzz and me were setting a trap for Grady Small. Insisted that I look more like a gentleman at the assembly for the newspaper photographer. No big deal. It'll grow back."

Candy went through another set of moves, spun around and ended up on the bench next to him. "So what you're sayin' is, there was no big clever plan between the sheriff and the school? You guys merely lucked out."

Mark shrugged as he glanced at her and made a remark he hadn't intended to say. "By golly, Red. You're becoming a pretty good cheerleader." She started to reply but instead sat with her mouth open. Mark looked away, and there stood Heather, hands clasped in front, a strand of hip length white hair hanging over each shoulder. Wonder what she wants?

"Your hair looks better short," Candy told him. "You look older . . . more manly."

"More dorky," he replied. Red's remark made him squirm so he turned his attention to the blond. "Well hi, Heather. What's hanging?"

"I uh . . . " She glanced at Ollie and then the girls and fidgeted. "I was wondering if . . . like you know. If I could maybe hang out with you guys?"

Mark could see Ollie watching with puppy dog eyes as if the decision was totally up Mark. Probably was.

Mark knew the fact Buzz wanted to be with Shannon all the time, was a big reason this 'Club' existed at all. He could be facing the same thing with Ollie. Unexpectedly he felt devilish. "That gives us a problem, Heather. This club we all belong to is rather exclusive." The expression on her face was distressing and Mark knew it. "We call ourselves the Kryptonites."

"I . . . then there's like no room for someone like me?" She was asking Mark, but her eyes, nearly pleading, were fixed on Ollie's.

Mark was sure she had no idea the Kryptonites even existed. He knew that Heather had never been shy so what had taken her so long to approach them? "Why would you want to belong to the Kryptonites?"

"Kryptonites? Like I don't know what Kryptonites are."

"We're the toughest, meanest club in Dalton. You know, me and Red and Shannon; Jodi. Buzz and Ollie. That's it?"

"What does this club do, anyhow?"

Mark could practically tell what she was thinking, that they were just a group that hung out together at school, at the Pit and stuff like that. And if outsiders wanted to fight one of them or something, the rest would be there as back up. Maybe they gossiped and held secret meetings. Mark looked directly into her eyes, trying to appear fierce. She was on the verge of crying.

Jodi spoke up before he could reply. "Right this minute, we have one purpose. To find out who the guy is that killed Mark's sister and the Heinz girl."

"But . . . but . . . but."

"Do I hear a motor boat?" Mark asked. "You don't have to do anything if you don't want to, but the six of us have been conducting our own investigation."

"But when? At night?"

"Of course at night."

"But how do you get out without getting caught?"

"Like, you know," Candy lay back on the grass. "My parents are gone so much I don't usually have to worry about them. Anyway, I sneak out my bedroom window. Only with me, I don't even think they would care."

"Or we tell our moms that we are going over to someone's house to study," said Shannon."

"Well, I can't get away with that." Heather looked like she was about to turn and run. "Like my room is upstairs and anyhow, my folks would kill me." Then there were tears streaming on her cheeks. "I guess that means you wouldn't want me."

"Oh come on Heather," Mark jumped down from his perch to stand in front of her, a foot and a half taller than the, and he guessed; she was eighty pounds. We're going to invite you to join. What you have to do is become a member that's all."

"Oh my God. Oh my God. Like what do I have to do?"

"Hold on. First we have to put it to a vote. Guys, Heather wants to join our club. What do you have to say?"

"Why not?" Shannon was all for it. "Even things out. Three guys, three gals and Jodi."

"Okay, do we want to make it unanimous?"

There were six yeas and Heather beamed, wiping at the tears on her cheeks.

Mark studied the tear stained face for a moment, but decided he wanted to have some fun. "Only first you have to be initiated."

"Whatever you say, I'll do it."

Screwing up his mouth, he pondered what devilish prank he could come up with. There was a sudden evil thought that made his eyes sparkle. "You have to kiss Ollie." It was hard to tell who was the more embarrassed, her or Ollie.

"I . . . well . . ." She swallowed, her blue eyes wide with excitement. She moved over close to Ollie, put her hands behind her back and leaned demurely forward, even closing her eyes.

Ollie looked frantic. As far as Mark knew, the only girl he had ever kissed was his own sister, and that was a long time ago. Had to bend way down to touch his lips to hers in a quick little chicken peck.

The whole thing reminded Mark of a painting he'd noticed in the barbershop yesterday by some guy named Rockwell. It was of a tiny tot kissing her brother. "You call that a kiss? It's going to take a better one than that for you to get into this club."

Ollie took the initiative, stepping down from the stands, placing his hands on the Heather's waist and easily picking her up. Their lips came together, like a movie kiss, and slender hands came up to cradle his head. Mark, Jodi and Buzz hooted and whistled until they parted. Wow, Mark thought. That has to be a kiss those two are gonna remember their entire lives.

"What in the heck are you bawling about now?" Mark frowned.

"I'm not bawling," Heather wailed, "I'm happy."

Shannon understood and she turned to touch Buzz on the cheek and they kissed. Candy's eyes were moist and shining.

Mark had an uncomfortable feeling which was made worse when Candy asked, "Why didn't I have to kiss somebody in order to join?"

"Hey Red, if it means that much to you, come over here and I'll give you a big juicy smackeroo."

"Gross. I'd rather kiss my dog than have you slobber all over me."

"Your dog would take one look at your ugly face and barf."

"No worse than how you would make me puke." Their eyes clashed, and yet she lowered her eyes. "I'm glad you weren't in some big trouble."

"That's kind of weird coming from you, but I suppose I

should say thanks."

Mark had no idea what was behind Shannon's smile but she knew exactly what was going on and was thinking, one of these days.

* * *

"Hey Mark," Buzz gestured with his eyes. "Look who is sitting over on the stone wall all by himself."

"Well well, Dean Ruggle in person. I'd better have a chat with that faggot bed-wetter."

Mark stood in front of the lad who was studying a colony of ants through his thick glasses. Mark could sense Ruggle's eyes moving, first to the pointed toes of his western boots, then slowly up the peg legged Wranglers, past the huge silver belt buckle, the plaid shirt and ended at his face. Mark gave him an evil grin and squinted, trying to make his blue eyes seem ice cold. The alarm on the small boy's face turned to terror when he looked about. The other six kids totally screened him from being seen by any of the teachers. Mark placed his large foot in the middle of the boys lap and Dean couldn't help himself. He wet his pants.

"Hi Deano. You doing all right? Mark's five friends were in various states of apprehension, from wanting Mark to do something in retaliation to a fear that he would.

"You better leave me alone." The voice cracked. "I'll tell M-Mister Hernandez if you hurt me." The small boy was grasping Mark's ankle trying to dislodge his foot but Mark let some additional weight rest on it.

"You ought to break the little weasel's neck," Ollie told him."

"I was thinking more along the line of using my thumbs to pop his buggy eyeballs out." Mark looked at Candy. Her eyes were shining. Was she frightened, he wondered, or excited? "Not true. Ruggle's my buddy, aren't you Deano?"

The boy nodded vigorously. "I was only . . . "

"Actually, I want to thank you."

"Th--t-t-t-thank me?"

"Sure. If you hadn't turned me in, I probably wouldn't have learned this valuable lesson. I had no idea how much trouble I could get into because of a little grass. It took a pathetic turd like you to wake me up. Yep. You taught me a lesson I'll never forget." The bell for the next class jangled behind them and

271

Mark removed his foot then offered the cringing boy his hand. "No hard feelings, huh Ruggle?"

The white-faced lad took the offered hand and Mark easily pulled him to his feet although the boy dropped the notebook scattering papers all about his feet. Mark bent to retrieve the frightened lad's schoolwork. "Pretty careless there, Deano my man. Guess you spilled your coke in your lap."

* * *

"Boy, she's got it bad, doesn't she?" Candy was watching Ollie and Heather as they walked toward the gym.

Jodi was slightly jealous that her brother had a girl friend. "Yeah, saw this coming. Thought they'd start going together right after the fair. Soon as those two were done smooching Heather latched on to Ollie's arm like she'd won some sort of a prize?" Shannon had Buzz, Candy had Mark whether she knew it or not, and, can you believe it? Ollie and Heather are an item. "Can you imagine her and Ollie together? She's smaller than I am." Jodi had both hands open in front of her, palms up as though they were asking the question.

"Hey! They look cute together." Candy's grin was devilish. "Like a 200 pound gorilla and a hamster."

"Yeah," Shannon nodded. "Like Smoky the Bear and a bunny rabbit."

Jodi joined their laughter. "Right. Like Pluto and Daisy Duck."

The girls were getting hysterical.

"Hey hey. I know." Candy was tugging at Shannon's sleeve. "Like a Rotweiller and a Toy Poodle."

"A white Toy Poodle," Shannon giggled.

"Yeah," Jodi was depressed again. "A white Poodle."

* * *

The cheerleaders were going through their final practice and Candy was aware that a certain degree of tension was building at Dalton Middle School among the other girls and the boys on the team.

Before they started practice, Mrs. Turner gave them a pep talk. "Ladies, this is our second game of the season. Some things you need to know about this evening's opponent before we play. Since Cotton and Dalton are only seven miles apart, over

272

the years a fierce rivalry has been the result. It doesn't seem to matter which team has the superior abilities the competition is always intense. You girls will be faced with the task of keeping our team and fans at a fever pitch."

"I heard they were a bunch of farm kids who, like aren't very good." Heather was the one to express what most of the Dalton students thought.

Candy also spoke up. "I heard that they are mostly His-panic and a lot smaller than our eighth graders. Shouldn't that give us a big advantage?"

Mrs. Turner smiled, shaking her head. "You would think the Indians would be far superior to the Scorpions. But don't you believe it. For a reason known only to the basketball Gods, these games are always a donnybrook affair. Always decided in the fi-nal minute of play."

Candy was thinking about the way Mark, Ollie and Buzz played during the season's first game. "We'll kick their butts," she promised.

* * *

The boys came out the side door of the gym. Mark was actually looking toward the opening from which the girls generally exited.

"Looking for your sweetie?" Ollie teased.

"I guess the gals are practicing their moves. What do you mean, my sweetie? You're a complete Nerd. Gotta bug out for home. Promised my mom I'd stop by Steven's Store and bring home a couple of things for her. Barely got time to grab a bite to eat and do a couple of chores."

"Don't feel like the Lone Ranger," Ollie told him. "I got an errand to run for my old man."

"I'll walk with ya, Mark," Buzz caught up with him and they headed down Main.

In Steven's Store, Buzz wandered around while Mark did his shopping. Once they were outside Mark growled at the black lad, "I saw that Buzz. You ripped something off."

"So what?"

"So, can't you ever walk through a store without copping something?"

"What's with you? I've seen you do it lots of times? Know

273

what I'm sayin'?"

"Not any more, buddy. Some of the crap that has been going down lately is wakin' me up. First, that guy putting a gun to my head and then this near miss over the roach thing, not to mention losing my sister. There are unfeeling jerks out there that would stuff your buns into Juvi work camp till you're eighteen. There are demented monsters out there who will blow your head off . . . for a watch, or whatever. I'm starting to get the idea there is much more to life than actin' the Bad Boy, and I'm likin' it."

"Man," said Buzz. "Didn't mean to jerk your chain."

"That's okay. I've decided to chill out on bad things; anything that could put this life I'm starting to enjoy in any kind of danger. Guess I'm getting a few bad vibes, you know? Don't want to hang around Willow Creek 'til I'm eighteen. Got enough problems."

"Hey man. Didn't rob a bank or anything like that. Know what I'm sayin'?"

"Come on Buzz. We keep copping even little things and sooner or later somebody is gonna put the hammer down. If Steven's should decide to press charges, we'd be history. I like school this year. I love basketball. Things are goin' better than ever at home. And the Kryptonites, I don't want to give any of that up. So what the heck did you swipe?"

"Jeeze. Maybe I better take 'em back." His tone was sarcastic as he pulled a small box from inside his shirt. "Got a whole box of Trojans."

"Trojans?"

"Yeah, you know, condoms."

"Condoms? What are they for?"

"Man, are you ever dense. Don't you know zip? My boy let me clue you in. You take one out of its little plastic wrapper and . . ."

"I know how you use 'em, my question is, what do you need them for? Even if Shannon would let you, and I'm sure she wouldn't, you'd be mincemeat if her father found out. He'd cut you up and make hamburger out of your body."

"Wasn't planning on using them, they're only for show. Know what I mean?"

"You're weird. Shannon finds out you got those and she's

gonna gross out. You're gonna be history. Come on stupid. Let's head for home. I can hardly wait till it's time for the game."

In front of the Post Office Mark came to a halt. "Look what we got here." Dropping to his knees he spoke to the couple, "Hi Tracy. Hey man, what's happening John?" He eyed the Corwin teenagers who were hovering over a wire cage. There were five kittens, a mixture of mostly Siamese.

"We're giving them away," Tracy let him know.

"My mom hates cats. Couldn't take one if you paid me."

"We'd like to have one." Two of the Montgomery girls, seven and nine, stopped to 'Ooooh and aaaaah.' "How much are they?" The smallest one asked.

"They're free," Tracy shrugged, "but you need to get an okay from your parents first."

"No," said the older child. "It's okay. We want this one with the black ears. It's mommy's birthday. She's gonna be so happy."

"Oh boy," Mark hooted, "is she ever. Come on Buzz, got things to do." Taking a couple of steps he stopped and turned back to look at the kittens once again. A crooked grin crept onto his face as he reached into the cage and brought out a soft white animal with one brown paw and a brown splotch on the left side of its face including the ear. Looking deep into the clear blue eyes he told them, "I'll take this one."

"Hey man." It was the first time John had spoken. "You said your mom hated cats?"

"That she does, but I love 'em. Come on Buzz. Let's go have some fun."

When they reached Mark's house he crossed the street to slip alongside the Swanson residence. The Lexus and the SUV were both gone. Checking Candy's bedroom window to make sure no one was inside, he told Buzz, "This is cool man. She most always keeps her window's open a crack. Come on old buddy, take your knife and pry out the corner of the screen."
"Oh man, like you know. This is so ba-ad."

Reaching through the opening Mark dropped the small bundle of fur onto Candy's bed and Buzz pushed the screen back into place.

"Man. If I could only be a mouse."

"Bad idea, Dude," Buzz was grinning. "That baby is the world's best mouser. Know what I'm sayin'?"

* * *

The basketball game between Dalton and Cotton was over by 8:00. It was no contest. The Indians were taller, faster and more aggressive than the Scorpions. Superman led the way with thirty of Dalton's sixty-eight points, overwhelming Cotton by exactly thirty.

Except for Heather, the Kryptonites headed for Ollie's garage after the game. Buzz had agreed to join them and the three boys meant to continue working on the motorcycle. Buzz and Mark had expected a reaction from Candy about the kitten but it turned out she and Jodi didn't go home after practice, going instead to the Pit for a sandwich then back to the school in time for the game.

"Gotta cut out at ten," Shannon told them. "My curfew."

"Don't feel like the Lone Ranger," said Mark looking at a black SUV parked in the drive three doors down and across the street. "Mrs. Gages' son musta drove down from Monterey for a visit," Mark took a guess. "Nice wheels, huh?"

Jodi was in the garage being a pest. She taunted them over the fact she was sure the Harley would never run again.

"Look what I got." Ollie was waving a grease-stained book over his head. "Sam, down at the junkyard, found it for me. Actually, he told me I could look through a whole pile of automotive manuals he had stacked in a storeroom."

Mark took the well used, soft cover book and read the title: Harley Davidson Motorcycles
Repair Manual
1942 to 1948
Illustrated

"Oh boy," Buzz was excited, "we got it wired."

The book turned out to be a tremendous amount of help as piles of parts fit snugly into place. Even Jodi found herself working at the puzzle while her two friends were looking through a stack of old National Geographics.

"It's nearly ten," Shannon said. "Me and Candy are heading out. No use pushing our luck."

Buzz was quick to agree. "It's time I cut out too and it

looks to me like we are right on the edge of having it running. Hey Shannon, wait up. I'll walk you home."

"I'd better hit the road too," Mark shrugged. "Maybe tomorrow night we can try firing her up. What I better do is stop by Five Points and pick up a can of that either stuff farmers use to start balky tractor engines. See you guys at school in the morning."

The two girls and Buzz left first but Mark simply had to tinker for an additional fifteen minutes. "Man, I gotta shag ass. I was supposed to be home at ten too. Should'a brought my bike."

"Hey man, take mine. You can ride it to school in the morning."

"Thanks a heap buddy. See you in the AM."

* * *

As he straddled the old bike he looked up at the heavy concentration of clouds covering the full moon painting feathery splashes of yellow and white around their edges. Awesome, he thought as he pedaled along in an oppressive sort of darkness. A creaking sound caused him to glance back as Ollie pulled down the door and there was a yellow frame around the perimeter until it disappeared. He was not aware of the dark SUV, its lights off, slinking out of the drive down the street and onto the road behind him.

Peddling easily he covered the two blocks to the Y at Riverview Drive and Old River Road. At the last instant he elected to ride down Old River Road. Along the left, thirty feet past the town flagpole, the road climbed steeply for half the length of the Banker's Estate. It had always been called Baker's Hill. He needed to shift to the lowest gear then stand and pump with all his strength to make the climb. Lot of guys would have to get off and walk their bikes up but it was worth it. The gap between him and the unseen vehicle was slowly closing. As he paused at the top to catch his breath, the darkness seemed to shrink in about him, gripping his flesh. There was a gust from a cold breeze that seemed like a premonition of something bad.

At the bottom of the grade he'd have to cut through the Swanson's property even though it was quite a climb hauling a bike up the bank behind Red's house but since there were no lights on Ollie's machine he'd avoid the traffic. Of course there could be traffic on Riverview Drive where he lived, but there was never anyone on Old River Road at night.

The hidden moon found a gap between the clouds at the instant he pushed off, casting eerie shadows on the steep bluff on his left, running nearly eighty feet high for a half a block, dropping off in a steep slope down to the water on the right. The clouds were more green than gray in color as the full moon crept behind them again leaving a luminescent glow that slowly disappeared and yet enough light remained to turn the river into a wide ribbon of glittering silver. Werewolf moon, he was thinking, letting the bike freewheel as the wind streamed through his hair, feeling a sense of exhilaration flowing through his veins.

The thought, werewolf, left him with a peculiar sensation and he shivered, turning to look back. There was a growling sound and he saw a dark shape, with its lights off, looming only yards away, accelerating rapidly. The first thought in his mind, as he pulled as far to the right on the shoulder as he possibly could without going over the bank and into the murky water fifteen or twenty feet below, was . . . the killer? No way. That would be stupid. How would the killer know he was going to be at Ollies?

The black beast was roaring, coming straight at him. "Holy shit," he screamed, diving headlong over the embankment, hearing the horrible crunch and scream of metal under the monster's wheels. Sliding, rolling and tumbling, he was unable to halt his momentum, crashing through some thorny growth next to the river's edge. The spines raked his arms and face and punctured his legs through his trousers as the cold liquid grasped him, sucking him under the water, gasping and flailing, his mind not yet catching up with the events.

Finding himself about ten feet out, with the slow moving current tugging him along, he swung his head about to get his bearings then began to take long overhand strokes toward the shore. Without a doubt, someone who thought he knew more than he did was trying to kill him again. As it was, he was lucky to be alive, but how lucky was that? Tomorrow the guy was going to know he wasn't dead. On the other hand, he reached out for the bank, perhaps the killer was merely trying to frighten him off. Whew! Made it.

There was a sharp pain as something struck his neck and

278

the forked end of a branch went by on each side of his throat. A shadowy figure held the long pole, driving him back into and under the murky water. Fighting and struggling, grasping at the pole, panic welled in his gut as he was forced deeper, his face pressed into the murky bottom. A strange notion entered his mind. What would Superman do? Use his powerful hands of steel, and that's what Mark did, twisting his body as far as he could without breaking his neck. He threw one leg over the pole effectively jerking it momentarily from his assailant's grasp. Before the man could recover he had pulled free. Guy musta got the branch again because as he scrambled along the bank he was struck between the shoulders by two sharp prongs. Then he was in the water and pushed under again. Rolling free, he once more surfaced only to be struck again with the fork straddling his face. He was in deeper water now so he dove. Underwater he reversed directions and began to swim upstream against the current. Would the guy suspect? He swam and swam, his lungs ready to burst but continued to swim. He reached a point to where there was no choice and he did everything he could to surface without a ripple.

The Man was thirty feet away watching the river downstream. Mark quietly pulled himself behind some brush and waited. Time crept along into what seemed to be an hour as the dark shadow stood without moving for a long time. Finally he lit a cigarette. The flare of the match made the black ski mask appear gray. For an instant, small circles of skin around his eyes appeared. He tossed the empty match folder aside, and Mark could see the glow when the Man sucked in the smoke. After a few minutes, he flipped the cigarette out over the dark water in a trail of orange sparks. Then he turned to scramble up the embankment. A door slammed, a starter snarled and a set of headlights penetrated the gloom. With an effort Mark dragged himself up on the bank where he sprawled, shivering. Merely frightened out of his wits while in the water, on land he was terrified. He was also angry. Bastard had ruined Ollie's bike.

* * *

The Man was feeling quite content. That last time had done it; I got the stupid punk. Pushed the kid right down into the muck and held him there. He had seen the bubbles come gurgling up. Sure wish the body had come to the top. Wouldn't get a chance to use his knives on this one, nor would he have the opportunity to leave his trademark by removing some legs. But I'm glad that's over. I can go ahead with the rest of the list and nobody will know who's involved. Nobody!

CHAPTER TWENTY-TWO

The kitten was sitting on the foot of the bed happily washing its face. There was a mild scene the previous night when Candy showed it to her mother, but by promising she would take care of it, she convinced her to let her keep the animal. It required her to make a wobbly trip on her bike down to Steven's General Store to pick up kitty litter, a cat box and cans of cat food, but she managed. The deal was sealed when it jumped up into her Dad's lap and started rubbing its face against his hand and he had to love it. How smart is that? Stayed clear of Michael.

When she came out of the shower she picked up a brush to run through her slightly damp hair and turning, she caught sight of her naked body in the full-length mirror that her dad had fastened to the back of the bathroom door last evening. She nearly was overwhelmed by what she saw. It was caused by something Mark had said yesterday afternoon. She'd been wearing a pair of Jeans, one of her dad's flannel shirts, Rebocks and a baseball cap. Stopping Mark in the hall she felt she should personally, away from the group, tell him she was actually pleased that he wasn't in trouble after all. Before she could open her mouth, Mark had joshed, 'Hey Red, you look more like a boy than I do.' She glared at him for the remark touched a sore spot, and this time it wasn't the 'Hey Red'.

Looking back at her from inside the mirror was a tall, slim, strikingly lovely female, a fully developed young woman. Is this a magic mirror? Where is the short, plump, ugly carrot top? She turned left, then right, then back to full face. This didn't happen overnight, so I haven't been seeing myself. I'm . . . I'm kinda pretty. I am pretty. No wonder I am beginning to have these strange thoughts. A teenage Ann Margaret, that's what I am.

She grinned and spoke to the mirror. "Yesterday I couldn't even spell woman, now I is one. Marcus Goodwin, don't you forget it." She began to hurry with her wardrobe, putting on a pretty, flowery, printed mini-skirt, which she hadn't worn for over a year since it had been too big for her. Now it fit rather snugly and was several inches above her knees. She completed the outfit by slipping into a mint green, sleeveless pullover that had a crisscross trim that emphasized her bust line, matching green socks and a pair of black pumps with two-inch heels. Again she looked at her reflection in the mirror and added, "Okay, Marcus the Monster Goodwin, tell me I look more like a boy than you do."

* * *

Mark woke up shortly after daylight. It had been a restless night. Couldn't get what had happened out of his mind and his shoulders ached. To top it off there was a heck of a crick in his neck. A new day, and he wondered if he would live to see another one?

Quickly he was out of bed and dragging himself into some sweats. Pulling on his boots without any socks he grabbed a light windbreaker and slipped silently out the side door. Crossing the road, he took a shortcut through the trees and bushes surrounding Red's house. Ducking behind one bush his eyes peered at a lighted window. Was Red up already? Maybe she was leaving a light on for security. Couldn't blame her.

Hurriedly working his way down the bank to Old River Road he located the spot where Ollie's bike had been crushed. Last night he'd dragged it up the hill and stashed it in the garage. Slipping and sliding down the embankment, he found himself standing next to the wild brush growing along the river. Looked different in the daylight. What he needed was some clues.

He began to search stumbling through an area of scattered, broken tree branches. Probably tossed on the shore during last year's high water. There it is, 'bout twelve feet long, with no limbs other than the fork at the end. How did the Man find it in the dark? The fork was pointing to an opening between bushes. That's where he'd gone into the water. Gravel everywhere. Wouldn't leave any prints. Oh boy. Look what we have here. In the muddy area right next to the river was a pair of prints. Water stood in each depression. It was clear. The water hadn't been there long enough to destroy the two marks. A pair of eagles.

Mark looked at his watch. Guy had stood there for a long time taking a smoke then pitched a match folder off this way. There it is. He snatched it up, turned it over and muttered, "Yeah, Sheriff Frank, gotcha." In gold, on the purple surface were three words. 'The Lucky Lady'.

* * *

"Gawd Mark, what happened to you?"

Gonna be hearing this all day, he thought. First my dad, then Red. Who's next? And that's why this morning he dreaded meeting Candy in front of his house. Lately she seemed to show up the instant he came out the door and as much as he detested it, he ended up walking to school with her. Could have been worse but they met Shannon every morning down at the corner. This didn't explain the fact it had been his habit to leave by the rear door where he parked his bike. Be easy enough to ride his bike like he used to or even make some excuse, but he took the easy way out and let her tag along. Darned if he would carry her books. At least he had a bike so what was he going to tell Ollie? This morning he was wearing a black turtleneck pullover to hide the red and purple stripes on his neck.

Man! This gal actually looks nice this morning but he certainly didn't intend to say so. He did say, "So, Birdlegs. You decided to be a girl today, huh?"

She smiled slightly.

Around the corner on Washington, Shannon waited for them in front of her house. As though she and Candy were on the same wavelength, she too was wearing a mini, actually a black skirt with a Hawaiian print blouse. Mark was wondering how much he should tell them about last night. Was also wondering about the kitten but it was up to her to bring that up.

"Hi Shannon." It was a duet.

"What the heck happened to you?" She was staring at Mark's face and the exposed portion of his neck.

"I rode home from Ollie's last night on his bike. Ran off the road. Crashed through some thorny bushes."

"Some of us are clumsy, I guess," Candy put her foot up on a stone wall to tie her shoe showing Mark a great deal of leg.

"Man, did you ever get scratched up."

"So, do you want to play doctor again?"

"Sure. I'll show you mine if you show me yours."

"Funny ha ha. Not that kind of doctor."

"Are you gonna clue us in as to what happened? There aren't any thorny bushes on Riverview," Shannon informed him.

"Wasn't on Riverview. Last night, after I left Ollie's, I rode down Baker's hill and . . . "

"And the killer tried to get you." Shannon was making a joke.

"How did you . . . no, no, nothing like that. Don't be so suspicious. And that's not funny." He was dying to tell them the truth, but didn't think he should.

"You're the one who told us to be on the alert for anyone suspicious."

"You know what's funny?" Candy extended her arm much like a mother does to her children to halt their progress as an older model convertible approached on Main. "In a small town like this, every man you see seems suspicious."

"Boy Red, you got that right. I'm even looking over my shoulders at all my male teachers."

Shannon started laughing. "Me too. Been keeping my eye on old man Witherspoon, the custodian, and he wears cowboy boots."

"Yeah," Mark laughed with her. Never can trust these octogenarians."

Candy continued with the joshing. "Is that the same as a vegetarian, only he eats nothing but octopuses?"

They were all laughing. "Let me tell you about Monday evening. Went to the barber. Darned near did a job in my jeans when he put the straight razor to my neck. I'm looking all around to make sure there are witnesses. Especially since he was wearing dress shoes. Black."

Candy was becoming serious. "Wow! That is spooky."

Mark remembered the burglar's shiny black shoes. "How many guys in this little town wear those Eagle Gold boots?"

"One of my teachers does," replied Candy. "But his feet are a lot smaller than the killers. Even Steven's down at the store wears boots. Don't know if they are Eagle Gold." Shannon winced. "This thing is totally killing me. We all know that my dad does and his alibis seem awfully thin to me."

"Anything happening since he's out of jail." Mark bumped Candy's hip with his knocking her off the curb.

"He's staying at the Ezyinn Motel until he and mom can work things out. He's refusing to get professional help and I heard my mom tell Mrs. Snodgrass that the marriage is over. She's been talking to an attorney. God, I hope not. I want things back the way they were a year ago."

"They'll work it out." Candy shoved Mark off the other side of the walk so that he had to do some acrobatics to keep from falling into a planter. "My dad wears black dress shoes too, only I know he isn't the killer. Wasn't within 3000 miles of Dulltown when your sister . . . " she looked guiltily at Mark.

"It's okay." Mark pursed his lips before he continued. "I've learned to deal with it. My dad wears dress shoes part of the time, only most of his are brown. Got some black ones but none of them are boots."

"Could be Digger Jones the mortician."

"Or, as Mark keeps saying, the Sheriff."

"Well look who's here," Mark turned as Jodi came trotting across the Green Spot parking lot to join them.

"Oh wow!" Shannon was staring at Jodi's feet. Where did you get the combat boots?"

"Mom found them at Clinton's Shoe Store. I guess he bought a ton of them from Army Surplus. Aren't they extreme?"

"Your mom actually bought them for you?"
"Well she actually bought them for Dad to wear fishing, but I put the move on them this morning. They're too big for me, but . . ."

"They're bad. Shannon knelt to check them out. "I want some. Wonder if he has some in smaller sizes? They are drop dead awesome."

"I get caught up in some of the teenage fads," Candy told them, "but personally, those don't wire me. 'Bout ten sizes too big."

"Got paper stuffed in the toes and two pair of socks. What the heck happened to you, Mark?" Jodi did a double take at the cuts, scratches and bruises.

Mark had been glad about Jodi's boots. Took their mind off

his problems. "I crashed Ollie's bike through some bushes," he told her.

"Were you hurt?"

"Maybe a few broken bones. I'm feeling great today." He wasn't. His stomach felt like someone was squeezing it and he had all he could do to keep from looking left, right and to the rear. "Here I am, Marcus Goodwin, completely surrounded by beautiful women."

"Must think you have money," Candy smirked. "Certainly isn't for your charm."

"Hey Red. I wasn't including you. You have a face that would make a toilet barf."

"Come on you two," Shannon admonished. "Kiss and make up."

"Blaah! I'd rather kiss my brother." Candy eyed him. "While we're on the subject of total jerks, you're the one who did that last night, aren't you""

"Did what?"

"Don't act so innocent. You put that kitten through my bedroom window."

"Moi? What makes you think I'd do anything like that?"

"It pooped on my bed."

Mark grinned. "So do you, so what's the problem."

"Mark put a kitten in your bedroom?' Shannon was walking backward in front of the group. "What did your mother say?"

"Lucky for me, she likes cats, but it's my responsibility to see that it was taken care of."

"What did Funny Face think?" Jodi asked.

"Funny Face doesn't know how to think, do you Red?"

"That crazy dog wants to mother it."

"What did you name it?" Jodi agreed with Shannon about Mark and Candy.

"Marcus. What else?"

Jodi was grinning. "You mean you get to sleep with Mark every night? Ooooh, naughty naughty."

"Don't let it get out at school, Jodi. I'd be known as the stupidest kid in Dalton."

"Hey," Mark was frowning. "Let's drop this subject."

"You embarrassed?" Candy was laughing. "Wait till you

guys see it. I totally love it."

"Speaking of sleeping with somebody," Jodi asked. "Did you hear about Carmelita?"

"No," Shannon shrugged. "What's Hoover up to now?" "I heard that she and Buster Grimes actually did it."

"You're kidding," Candy pretended astonishment. "How can you be sure?"

"Buster was bragging about it to Ray Lopez who is a good friend of my brothers."

"Ain't none of our business," Mark grimaced.

"Doesn't surprise me," Shannon stated. "She is such a tramp. The way she dresses and all. Nothing but an airhead."

Candy blew a huge bubble with her gum. "Can you believe they would actually do that? It's so gross."

"Probably get herself P.G. and have to drop out of school." Mark had always liked Carmelita and her wild ways but not in a romantic sense.

Jodi was eyeing a group of boys walking the opposite direction heading for the High School and she frowned when they seemed to be eyeing Candy's legs. "Carmelita's a slut. You know what else I heard?"

"Jodi," Shannon admonished, "you are such a gossip." "I'm a wealth of information. I heard that Corky Barnes is going out with Frenchy Farquharson. Can you imagine?"

Shannon gave a mock look of shock. "I can't imagine what someone as cute as Corky can possibly see in a dweeb like Frenchy. Like they are totally opposite."

"Well here we are, ready for another day in paradise." Mark was looking about for Buzz and Ollie, wondering if he should tell them about what actually happened last night. Ollie's bike was the problem. Have to make something up. He was angry and he was scared and there was a bigger problem. The Kryptonites would be meeting again at lunchtime and to be honest with them he needed to tell them about his near miss. Needed to let them know how dangerous their investigation was becoming. Needed to tell them about something new he had learned. What he needed was to get the killer off their backs . . . actually off his back . . . but how?

* * *

The Man pushed open the door, made an immediate left and began looking over Clinton's stock of running shoes.

The owner and his wife were busy with the overwhelming task of restocking the shelves. Apparently they had received a new shipment. Clinton looked up and gave him a wave, said something to his wife and moved toward The Man, grinning as he approached. "Thinkin' 'bout taking up jogging?"

"Oh I might. I'm getting out of shape." He nodded toward the stacks of boxes. You moving out or moving in?"

"Got a big buy out on a store over in Cotton that went out of business."

"What the hell is this? Reeboks with lights that flash when you're walking?"

"Some of the teenagers like 'em. Can't keep enough of the smaller sizes in stock. Big hit with the youngsters. It's okay by me at fifty bucks a pop."

"Folks now-a-days can't to seem to get their priorities straight."

"How's your boots holding up? Got a new shipment of Eagle Golds."

"Actually looking for something that would be comfortable for hiking. Those damn boots are good. Wear like iron."

"Want to hear something funny? Becky . . . that's the high school gal we have working here evenings, was telling my wife that a couple of middle school girls came in the other night and were asking a whole bunch of questions about that brand of boots."

The Man stood with his mouth open, his eyes startled. "Whatever for?"

"They had a pencil tracing, you know, like you'd make from a plaster cast of a foot print. Told her they were working on a pretend criminal investigation. School project, they said."

"Did Becky say who these girls were?"

"Ummm. Don't think so. Why don't you try a pair of these on? These have comfortable insoles and are less than fifty bucks."

The man was obviously in a hurry. "Got a pair of these in elevens? If so, wrap them up."

"You don't want to try them on? Oh, by the way, she did mention that the one of the teens was Reverend White's daugh-

ter. He buys Eagle Golds. Probably where they got the idea of using them as a clue. Couldn't even guess who the little one was."

I can find out, the Man was thinking. What the Hell is going on? Has that Goodwin punk got his whole gang helping him?

* * *

Ollie had been so late Mark didn't see him until the group met as usual during the lunch period. He and Ollie were the first ones at their meeting place with Heather close behind.

"Hey Dude, what the heck happened to you? You look like you tangled with a wildcat. Thought you were going to bring my bike to school this morning."

"Uh . . . wrecked it."

"Whatcha mean, you wrecked it? You wrecked my bike?"

"Yeah . . . I uh . . . Here comes Red and Jodi." Mark plopped down on the wooden bench lacing his fingers together behind his head. "Wonder where Shannon and Buzz are?"

"How the heck did you wreck my bike?"

"Tell ya 'bout it later. Here's Shannon."

Shannon's first concern was, "Where's Buzz?"

"Never fear, Buzz is here," Mark jerked his thumb toward the side entrance to the gym as the black lad came their way. "Hey Buzzard, what's goin' down?"

"Coach asked me to help carry in some boxes from his van. School bought us a dozen brand new basketballs. Last night was awesome, so are you dudes ready for Clarksdale   Friday night? What the heck happened to you, Mark?"

Mark repeated his story, this time telling him, I lost control, got to going too damn fast and ended up crashing into some bushes and then rolling down the bank all the way to the water."

"Are you gonna be up to playing basket ball. I hear Clarksdale is pretty tough."

"Are you kidding? I'm scratched up not crippled. Anyway, we could beat Clarksdale if I was on crutches."

"Uh, uh, uh," Ollie told him. "You know what Coach Donnelly said? Getting over confident is a sure way to get our butts kicked."

"What I meant was we should beat them since Superman is ready to fly again."

Heather made herself comfortable in the crook of Ollie's arm. Man-o-man, Mark thought, cuddling like a couple of love-birds. Red was unusually restless, going all the way to the top of the wooden bleachers then jumping, two footed, from board to board. Candy was standing on the bench above where he sat. He had no idea that from her position one of the purple stripes showed over the edge of the turtleneck. Felt her fingers touch his skin, pushing the soft material down. Turning to glare at her, needing to lean way back, he looked up. To his surprise, from where she stood he could see her long legs under the short skirt including her bikini panties and he looked away feeling guilty. Her fingers were warm on his flesh.

"Like wow Mark, you must have taken some kinda tumble. Both sides of your neck look like you have forty hickeys."

"Jodi is the only one to ever get hickeys," joked Ollie. "She probably even has hickeys on her butt."

"You're jealous," Jodi puckered up her entire face. "Any-how, that's something you will never know. Better check out Shannon and Buzz. They probably got plenty."

"Plenty of what? Hickeys?" Shannon asked. "That'll be the day. Golly Candy, you look great today. Hardly ever see you in a skirt. Doesn't she look awesome, Mark?"

"Yeah, awesome. The skirt Red is wearing today looks like she crashed her bike too . . . into Mrs. Crow's flower garden. What a mess."

Candy felt this farce had gone far enough. "Mark?"
He didn't answer.
"Mark," she stared at his back. "Why are you lying?"

He leaned back to look up at her again, wondering why his eyes seemed to be drawn to again look under her skirt since look-ing made him feel so uncomfortable . . . like warm? He realized that she had no idea she was showing him everything she owned. "Hey birdbrain. Where do you get off calling me a liar?"

"Well, you are. You're not telling us the truth about last night. Those marks on your neck aren't from a thorny bush. Something happened last night that you are not telling us."

"Like what?" With a half smile he shook his head in dis-belief. "I'd hate to be married to you. Mind readers scare me. Okay, Red. I keep trying to protect you guys, but you've opened up a can of worms. Since we are all in this together, I'll clue you guys in . . . " The bell sounded. Lunch period was over.

"We ain't got enough time right now, but for your own good you guys should know the truth. Why don't we all meet over at Ollie's garage right after dinner? We'd better talk, seeing that we could all be in a heap of danger." Looking back at him were a half dozen startled faces.

As though someone had turned on a water faucet, Heather was crying. "I want so desperately to be part of this, but my folks practically keep me in jail. I can't make it."

"Darn it all, Heather." Mark was disgusted, telling himself, this little cookie isn't going to be of any use to us. "Why did you want to join the Kryptonites if you couldn't participate? If we meet right after school could you come for an hour or two?"

Ollie looked like he wanted to rap a few heads.
"I know, I know what," she was jumping about, her long hair dancing about her shoulders. "You said after dinner. Why don't we meet at my place? You guys can bring your swimsuits and we can hold the meeting out by the pool. I'll call my mom to set it up. Say about seven."

"Are you kidding? Asked Mark. "As cold as it is?"
"Our pool's heated and on the patio we got some of those over-head gas heaters. Come on you guys. It'll work. Please?"

"Out of sight," said Ollie.

"Hey, works for me." Shannon turned to Buzz who was nodding.

Mark was remembering something Red had told him yesterday right after Heather joined the group. She had mentioned that if houses were rated, the banker's mansion would be number one, Judge Elliot's number two, and the Deiters number three. Then she told him that Heather's house was right next to theirs only their place sits further back from the street than ours. "If you look out the window from our den," she said, "you're looking right into their pool. I practically drool every time I see it. Sure would like to see inside their place."

Red didn't even hesitate as she told Heather, "Count me in."

"Okay," Mark agreed. "I'm cool with that. I'll fly home right after school, grab a bite to eat and change into my suit. See you guys there."

* * *

The Man went from the mountaintop of elation to the valley of total depression. It was like being on a roller coaster. All morning long he was gloating about disposing of the Goodwin kid, then was plunged into despair when he saw the boy, big as life, walking home from school with that little redheaded quail. How in the Hell did he manage to get away? Why hadn't he called the police? Mighty strange. All he could figure was, the kid didn't know as much as I thought he did. Otherwise, after last night, he would have gone straight to the authorities. That damned kid was a definite threat that had to be eliminated. Next time I catch up to this s.o.b. his charmed life is gonna be over.

CHAPTER TWENTY-THREE

"Elaine, where in the hell have you been?" Ray Coquillard snapped.

"You knew I was going to a Tupperware party at Margaret's after work. You don't listen to anything I say."

"So, where's my beer?"

"Oh crap. I forgot."

"You'd forget your head if it wasn't fastened to your shoulders. When I called you at work I specifically asked you to fetch me some beer."

"Well Mr. Free and Easy Raymond Coquillard, if you wouldn't have all your beer guzzling buddies in here sponging off us while I'm out busting my ass to keep groceries on the table, we'd have plenty of beer in the house."

"Oh sure. Like maybe it's my fault I'm out of work."

Elaine pressed a hand to her forehead, closing her eyes, heaving a deep sigh. "It sure ain't mine. As near as I can tell, you aren't even looking anymore."

"Got my name in at a dozen places. Trouble with Dalton is, there are so few places that pay worth a damn."

"What was the matter with that job Viking offered you over in Cotton?"

"I ain't working for no twelve bucks an hour haulin' vegetables. That's half what I was knocking down at DGF."

"Well, even twelve bucks an hour would be better than what you are making setting on your duff. At least we'd have money coming in until you found something to meet your high standards. You ain't working for DGF anymore and don't tell me that wasn't your fault."

"I don't feel like arguing about this again tonight. Get your fanny down to Five Points and pick up a couple of six packs of Bud."

She knew there was no use getting Ray riled up. He'd only smack her around again. Lucky for her she hadn't told him about the substantial raise she received when Swanson gave her the new position. She planned on stashing most of that away and was reaching a point from where she was desperately wanting out of this relationship. But how? Why was she one of those women who insisted, 'even a bad man is better than no man'? She headed for the door.

"Pick me up a carton of Winstons while you're at it, will you Hon?"

"Deadbeat," she muttered under her breath.

* * *

The Sheriff always considered himself to be quite the ladies man, which was a carryover from his high school football days. He retained a grudge against the rest of society when no college picked up his talents, never considering the fact all his teachers had given him 'Cees' by order of the head office to keep him on the team and he flunked the entrance exam at five different colleges.

"What do you say, Doc? The fair is over and our little town has quieted down again." The two men were sitting in the Lucky Lady tipping a couple of brews and shooting the breeze.

Doc Snyder was aware of the fact Frank was having a fling with the Lucky Lady barmaid, Rosalie Sanchez. She was cute, although on the plump side, and he couldn't begin to picture her making it with the sheriff. In fact, most everybody in town knew about the affair . . . perhaps even Frank's wife.

Frank snapped his fingers and beckoned to the mini-skirted waitress. "Bring us another pitcher, would you Hon?"

"What's the plan, Frank? Our wives go to San Diego on the church bus for that choir contest thing and you're all over Rosie, as usual."

"While the cat's away," the waitress teased then went to fetch another pitcher.

"What the heck, Doc? Won't be home till Friday afternoon."

"I'll tell ya what, Frank. If you don't be a little more discrete about this thing between you and Rosie, your wife is gonna whack your balls off."

"I ain't worried. Like I tole ya, she cut me off after our last child was born. Doesn't care where I get it as long as I leave her alone. All my wife does is bitch about how marriage to me is having someone to wash my socks, cook my meals and listen to me bitch about her relatives. Sure don't need her crap. Have enough on my mind trying to solve these two murders."

"Speaking of these two crimes, last time we had a murder in Dalton was when Josh Hoover killed that guy right here in the Lucky Lady over a pool game several years ago."

"That was a bad one all right. Opened up that guy's throat with a broken beer bottle. What we're working on is a different matter. Have no idea what this guy's motive is and yet he seems to have a purpose. If I could figure that out, might have someplace to start."

"Does he simply hate little girls? M.E. says it doesn't seem to be a sexual thing."

Rosie returned, dark eyes laughing at the sheriff. "I'm surprised, with your old lady gone, that you ain't hitting on me tonight. Too much for you last night, huh?"

"Are you hinting?" He asked.

"Maybe."

"Actually I was thinking about hangin' 'round till closing time, then take you home for an all-nighter."

"You couldn't handle it." She playfully hit him on the shoulder and moved away.

"Haw, haw," Doc gloated. "Guess she told you.

Frank nodded. "All I gotta do is show her some money. You know Doc; like I was sayin', if it was a sexual thing for this man I might be able to get a handle on it. You know, known sex offenders and that sort of thing? Can get all that crap out of the office computer but this thing baffles me."

"Been five days since the second murder. What about the forensic evidence Bill got at the scene? Did the M.E. learn anything from that? You know, those little things they pick up; pubic hairs, stuff from under her nails? What do they call it? Trace evidence?"

The sheriff spread his hands. "Between me and Ralph and

Bill we couldn't find anything of importance. Bill says the time of death was sometime between eight to twelve p.m. last Friday night. So she'd been in the water sixteen to twenty hours. Not much trace evidence left."

"So 'bout all you got is the fact it was the same M.O."

"That's it. With the Goodwin victim he cut a piece offa her leg, the section between the knee and the thigh. Who knows why? If that's what he did to the Heinz victim, then the rest of her legs probably floated way down stream somewhere. What's got me in a pickle is, he either had to do it someplace like in a bathtub or there would be a great deal of blood somewhere."

"Yeah, bathtub. That's where I'd probably do it," Doc explained.

"The other thing is, both girls were naked. So where are their clothes? Can't flush them down the drain."

"Did you see the Lost and Found ad concerning a watch somebody picked up out on Lone Pine Trail?"

"Actually Marion called my attention to it. However, Lone Pine Trail runs for eight miles all the way up to the lake. They didn't say where so it coulda been anywhere."

"I would have thought you'd call whoever placed the ad to check it out. Could have been at the scene of the crime."

"I'm going to have to give you a job as an investigator, Doc. Was so busy with the new murder I didn't get a chance to call 'em."

"Well, I guess if anything happens around town tonight, all I need to do is call Rosie's house?" Doc chuckled. "Want me to float you a loan?"

"I don't need a loan. She's the one who always needs money."

"In other words, if you didn't take care of her financial needs, she wouldn't give Sheriff Martinez the time of day?"

"Eat your heart out, Doc. Rosie likes what I got. Anyway . . . it's Wednesday evening. All we ever get on a Wednesday is a drunk or two, maybe a domestic dispute. Ralph knows how to handle that sorta crap."

* * *

Heather was busy in the patio getting everything ready. An outfit from Clarksdale had professionally landscaped their rear

yard and she knew it was a showplace. There were exotic orna-
mental shrubs and trees, boulders and a waterfall, a brick path-
way winding among beds of colorful flowers. From about midway
it sloped down toward Old River Road providing a spectacular
view of the river and the green ranches beyond. Her mother
didn't mind showing it off even to a group of teenagers.

Heather was so thrilled she could hardly stand it. It was
hard for her to understand why she had such difficulty in making
friends. She tried her best to have a pleasing personality . . . at
least she thought it was. To her, being an Albino was nearly as
bad as being black. You were different and people seemed to shy
away from someone different.

Mom was as thrilled as she was when she told her that six
of her friends were coming. Mom's in her late thirties but could
easily pass for an older teenager herself. Way she is dressed tonight, she wants my friends to know it. Lot bigger boobs than me
but she's ten times as old. Maybe she's trying to compete.

Ollie and Jodi were the first to arrive. Jodi had brought a
friend, Shorty Carr. "Hi Ollie," she was aware he was looking right
past her and at her mom who was wearing, of all things, a bright
red bikini with a knee length cover up open down the front. Her
straight blond hair, nearly as white her daughter's, down about
her shoulders. Heather was glad to see Jodi and Leroy Carr together and introduced them individually. Shorty was a member
of the basketball team who'd had his eye on Ollie's sister ever
since he'd first spotted her among the cheering squad.

"Oh my," Heather's mother seemed curious as she took Ollie's hand.

Like she'd probably noticed the look that passed between
me and Ollie when he came in. Like what the hey? She was
young once.

"My, aren't you a handsome one? Are you a football player?"

"Pop Warner," he grinned. "Basketball this year. Next year
in high school . . . both for sure."

The doorbell rang again. "I got it," Heather dashed into
the house, returning with Buzz and Shannon who she also introduced.

"So this is Buzz? Rumor has it that you do some handyman work around town."

His smile showed his perfect white teeth. "Yes ma'am. Been pickin' up a few extra bucks. Layin' it away, like for, you know what I mean? College."

"Good for you. We'll talk later. Maybe you'd like to tackle our attic."

At that moment the doorbell rang for a third time. It was Mark and Candy.

When her mom took Mark's hand, she spent a long couple of moments looking into his eyes and didn't let go. "I understand you are Dalton Middle School's new heros."

"Not me. Just one of the team."

Her eyes crinkled. "How on earth did you get those bruises?"

He shrugged. "Crashed my bike into some bushes."

"Lucky you weren't hurt." She continued holding his hand in both of hers. "Sorry about the misunderstanding regarding my husband's concrete. The sheriff actually discovered who did it."

Heather knew this was news to Mark and several of the Kryptonites moved closer to hear. "Oh yeah? Who was it?"

She still had his hand. "Some high school lad named Martin Gilmore."

"Marnie?" Ollie was grinning. "Now the whole thing makes sense."

She was making Mark uncomfortable with his hand in her grasp. "Well I'll be darned. He's such a dork. Wears those great big round glasses about an inch thick. I'm the guy who tagged him with the name, Marnie Google, you know, after the comic strip character."

"I guess his nickname is what led the sheriff to him. That and the fact the boy was angry when he bought a used car from our firm. According to my husband the engine blew up. Kid was upset that we wouldn't guarantee it. I mean; it was a twenty year old car." She gave his hand a squeeze and released it. I'm certainly glad it wasn't you."

"Yes ma'am. Me too."

Like enough is enough, Heather was thinking, becoming slightly jealous of her own mother. The fact she held Mark's hand so long was unnerving to her. Worse, she could tell it also made

298

him feel uncomfortable, only he kept checking out her body. Men!

"Well, I'll leave you bunch of wild Indians alone. Enjoy the pool and if you need anything give me a holler." Eight pair of eyes watched until she disappeared.

"Your mom's a babe," Ollie offered.

"Gets it from me," Heather giggled. "Come on guys, like let's get wet." Heather was removing her beach wrap, revealing a tiny white body in a fluorescent lime bikini. All four of the girls were down to their swimsuits before the boys made a move.

* * *

As he turned off Park Street onto Main, his head snapped around to stare out the window of his Lincoln. Couldn't believe his eyes. Been wondering how, with all this other activity in town, he was going to accomplish his next 'punishment' and now I discover all my planning is wasted. Opportunity has come a knocking. There was no mistaking the green Trans Am. It was that bitch Elaine Garcia pulling into the parking lot at Five Points. All he needed to do was cut her off on her way home.

I'll make a right on Cedar, pull into the City parking lot, get that portable red light he'd bought out of the back, and then slip over to Taylor Street and wait for her. Lives way out in the toolies, at the end of Taylor.

Hadn't been planning on doing her until later, but don't look a gift horse in the mouth. In truth it had been his plan to make her his final conquest of the five, his final revenge. The one he would punish the most severely. He knew from the past two he'd better take them as they came. Since it was all her fault anyway, she shouldn't be too surprised he'd want to make her pay for the grief she had caused him. An evil grin moved snake-like across his face. I can worry 'bout the Goodwin kid later. I know I'm gonna have me some fun with this sweet thing, and then I'm gonna make her pay and pay dearly for everything.

* * *

Mark found himself staring at Red. She looked different and yet she looked the same. He didn't know but what the brief, dark blue bikini was new. It was actually a year old but she had developed so much since the last time she'd had the thing on, it was rather tight, and a tad revealing.

Mark had to work at removing his western boots so Ollie

was the first boy ready and he turned towards Candy. "Wow! Look at you." Mark frowned as he watched Ollie cupping his hand in front of his mouth as though to shield what he was saying from the others as he told her, "nice bod."

"Ollie," she squealed and slapped his shoulder, but not in anger. Then she gave him a mighty shove and he performed some acrobatics, losing his balance and fell into the pool. "At least," she joked, thinking of what Heather's brother had said, "I don't have to stuff my bra with Kleenex."

Mark frowned again as he watched the exchange, sensing a strange feeling he'd never had before. Jealousy? The 'nice bod' remark also made him aware of another feeling. As far as sex was concerned, Mark was running slightly behind his peers. Unlike most teenage boys, it was not the all consuming, sixteen hour a day thought process. Knew what sex was but thought of it more as a matter of reproduction than recreation. Other than looking at some Playboy magazines Buzz seemed to have access to, he paid little attention to the female body. He did remember the nude pictures and how he had felt kinda wicked looking at them. "Man," Buzz had exclaimed, "look at the bazooms on that one." "Wow," he had answered. "If she fell down she'd never hit her nose." If truth be told, Candy's bazooms weren't too shabby.

That was until today. In something new for him, he found himself checking out the 'bazooms' on the four girls. Jodi didn't have anything more than a couple of bumps. As tiny as she was, Heather looked good in a bikini, like a miniature woman. Red and Shannon were both . . . what was the word Ollie used? Stacked? Well built, crossed his mind. Shannon was skinnier than Red but the so-called 'Girls next door' in Playboy had nothing on these gals.

Then he got a very strange feeling. The redhead was checking him out. He didn't understand why. Looking at them turned on some juices he didn't know he had. Made him feel like he was blushing all over, so he dove in, cutting the water smoothly. When he surfaced he shook his hair like a dog does. His eyes focused on the scattering of freckles that covered Red's shoulders and peppered the whiteness showing from under the bra. Wonder why Candy isn't jumping in, standing there like she was afraid of the emerald water?

"What's with you?" he asked. "You got chicken pox or something?"

"They're freckles, stupid."

"Well, I sure hope they ain't catching. What's the matter, Red? Afraid of the water." Mark was doing a backstroke while looking up at her.

"For the first time in my life, I had my hair done. I'm afraid the pool water will ruin it."

"Won't hurt it at all," Heather shouted up at her. "Come on in."

"Are you sure?"

"Been over three days hasn't it?"

"Two weeks today. So how do you know it won't hurt it?"

"Like, my mom does it all the time. Check it out. Only if it's dyed it will probably turn green."

"That's what she needs," Mark teased, "to go with her evil green eyes."

With a deep sigh she extended her arms and her body knifed into the tepid water an inch from Marks.

They were soon frolicking in the pool. Someone suggested king on the mountain. There were three obvious pairings leaving Mark and Candy looking at each other.

"Come on Marcus," she dared him. "We can take 'em."

Diving down he came up with his head between her legs. She wriggled to get comfortable on his shoulders. It took some time, and a great deal of screaming and grunting, for the jostling to complete, but it was a mismatch from the start. Buzz, several inches shorter than Shannon, had trouble keeping his own balance with her on his shoulders. Jodi and her friend Shorty were more interested in wrestling each other than winning a competition. Ollie, with his size, would have been a shoo-in with a larger and stronger companion than the four foot two, seventy-nine pound blond. Even then, they finished second.

Mark had his muscular arms wrapped tightly across Candy's thighs while the redhead fought like a tiger, pulling, shoving, jerking and twisting. The couple eventually emerged from the pool victorious. "Told you we could take em." She slid off his shoulders and down his wetback and when he turned to face her she gave him a hug.

301

There were the strangest stirrings as he stood with his arms hanging uselessly, feeling her softness against his chest. Then she was gone. He could see Ollie wrestling with Heather and at one point they stole a kiss. Wonder what it feels like to kiss a girl? "Man, this is wild," Mark was moving toward the edge of the pool. "Hey guys, come on out and gather 'round. Need to talk about some things."

The entire group, except for Ollie, came out of the pool and stood toweling off. Mark squinted and asked, "you coming, Dude?"

Ollie waved him closer and Mark went to one knee. "Give me a couple of minutes, Marcus. Confidentially, watching a couple of gals built like Shannon and Candy while making out with Heather has given me a boner."

"Man, are you ever weird." Looking at Candy he muttered, "She doesn't do a thing for me."

"And you call me weird."

At that moment Mrs. Deiter came out but the red duster was buttoned down the front. She was carrying a cake, paper plates and utensils. "Hi guys. Thought you might like some refreshments." Sitting the cake on a glass-topped table she told them, "there are plenty of soft drinks in that fridge over there. Help yourselves." She began cutting the cake.

Mark shrugged, moved to the refrigerator and opened the door. "Hey gang, name your poison. We got cola, lemon lime, root beer, orange and grape."

"I'll take a root beer," Jodi grinned, "and bring Ollie a diet Coke. How bout you Leroy?'

Shorty also grinned. It was obvious the diet remark amused him. "Coke's okay by me."

Mark was under-handing the cans to each person and nobody missed. "Shannon?"

"Grape."

It was the first time he'd checked Shannon out. Was thinking about the beating her father gave her. He understood why she wore a simple one-piece suit. Everything was covered except for a couple of dark stripes on the back of her right thigh.

"Buzz?" he called out.

"Root beer for me too."

This one he arched way up and Buzz had to back pedal to catch it. "What about you, Red?"

"I'll have whatever you're having."

Looking at the lower shelf he called out, "Great. I'm having a Miller Lite."

"Over my dead body," snapped Mrs. Deiter. "We can't have the sheriff charging in here to break up your little party, can we?"

"No Mrs. Deiter, we sure can't."

"Call me Carolyn."

"Mark shifted uneasily "Okay . . . Carolyn. That jerk would drink all the beer." He was wondering if this meeting at Heather's was going to be a bust for the Kryptonites. When Mrs. Deiter left them again everyone except Mark seemed to be in a festive mood. Their meeting had turned out to be, as Carolyn had called it, a party. Lifting his Coke can he sat reading the label, what it contained, the nutrition facts. Sodium, Calcium, Protein and he wondered why he cared? If he didn't do something about Frank, this could be his last party. Maybe the Kryptonites would have some ideas.

"Hey guys." His voice was loud, demanding attention. Seven heads turned. Seven pair of eyes looked into his. "I'd better clue you in on exactly what happened last night because we may all have a problem. I mean big time."

* * *

As Elaine Garcia passed the corner of Taylor and Mulberry a car turned behind her and followed but there was nothing unusual about that. So why was there such a strange feeling as though something was clutching at her stomach? The sudden flash, flash, flash of the red light took her by surprise. She was certain she'd made a complete halt at the stop sign on Main after leaving Five Points. Not being in a grand hurry to get back to the house, she was poking along, so what had she done? And why would the Sheriff wait until she was half way down Taylor Street before he stopped her? Or was it the Sheriff? God forbid that it was Ralph. Man thought every woman in town should be in love with him. Maybe she had a taillight out. Pulling to the right she rolled to a stop next to some vacant land.

The Man walked up to her open window, a bright flashlight shining directly into her eyes.

"Sheriff? What on earth are you stopping me for?"

"Would you mind stepping out of the car, ma'am?"

She heaved a huge sigh. "Do you want my license and registration?"

"Yes ma'am."

Fumbling in the glove compartment she located the current registration then reached for the door handle but it swung away from her touch. "Frank? What the hell is this all about?" She felt a sudden unexpected chill. This man didn't sound like the sheriff . . . or Ralph. The voice was peculiar, guttural, muffled. Then her knees went weak. When the light left her eyes she saw the ski mask, the black SUV and the glint of steel as he pressed the muzzle of a huge gun against her breast.

"Walk ahead of me." The gun shoved her in the middle of the back and she let out an anguished squeal. "Get into the SUV and do as I tell you and you won't get hurt."

"You're not the sheriff. Who are you?" Her heart was throbbing in her chest, her mind racing, trying to comprehend.

"Try to remain patient my dear. You're about to find out."

His laugh was something evil. It turned her blood to ice.

CHAPTER TWENTY-FOUR

"Listen up guys," Mark was standing under one of the heaters, sucking on his coke. The bruises about his shoulder and neck were highly evident. "Here's the skinny 'bout last night. Someone, and I'm pretty sure it was Frank," he paused for effect, "tried his damndest to kill me."

"Like oh my God," squealed Heather.

"Oh my Gawd," cried Candy.

"Holy shit," added Ollie.

Shannon squirmed uneasily, "I was only joking . . . I mean, about it being him."

"Yeah it was him. Last night I wanted to get home as quick as I could so I borrowed Ollie's bike. Then, of all things, I decided to go down Old River Road. Had no idea he was following me. Had his lights out. Looked back and here he comes. This jerk forced me off the road. Ran right over Ollie's bike. Was driving a big black SUV. I crashed through the brush and ended up in the river. That's where he tried to drown me and that's why all the bruises on my neck. Held me underwater with a long branch that had a fork on the end."

There was a chorus of gasps.

"I was darned near history, I'll tell you that." Their leader had everyone's attention and, with the exception of Shorty, it wasn't necessary to explain who he was.

"Well . . . ?" Candy spread her hands. "My Gawd. You got my stomach doin' flip-flops. How did you manage to get away?"

Even though the memory terrified him, Mark was relishing the attention his tale was creating. Didn't even have to add any thing to it. Their faces looked like a bunch of Cub Scouts listening to their leader tell ghost stories around the campfire. He lowered his voice. "Once I thought he had me for sure, but I got a hold on the branch and twisted my body and actually pulled it out of his hand. Only I made a mistake. Was so keen on catching my breath I let the branch go. Guess he grabbed it 'cause next thing I know I'm pinned again. Fooled him though. Dove under the water and swam upstream. Held my breath 'til my chest hurt and then held it some more. Man was watching down the river. Stayed behind some bushes forever until the guy left, he kept watchin' and watchin' the river. Reckon he thought I was a goner. Probably waiting for me to float up."

"Mark!" Shannon was appalled. "This is getting serious."

"That's what I've been tryin' to tell you guys. Ask me if I was scared? Half out of my wits, and you know why? 'Cause probably by now he knows I'm not fish bait."

"What are you gonna do?" Heather asked.

"I can't believe you keep insisting it's the sheriff," Buzz glared at him. "You never offer us a dime's worth of proof. Know what I'm sayin'? So this time, did you see him?"

"Yes and no, mostly a dark shape, ski mask and all that. Could see his eyes and the skin around them when he lit a cigarette. Man was white."

"Where's my wrecked bike," Ollie asked? "Leave it down there?"

"Naw. Drug it home. It's in the garage and I'll have to do something 'bout that for ya. But listen Dude, early this morning, 'bout six fifteen, I cut across past Red's house and went back down there to look around."

"I was awake," Candy told him. "Why didn't you let me know so I could help?"

"Saw your light. Figured you were in your Pjs. I don't go round rappin' on peoples windows at six a.m."

Her grin was cute. "Probably a good thing. I was naked."

Something about her statement made him look at her intently, like she was a different person. "Hey! Turnabout is fair play. That would be gross! That's the last thing in the world I'd want to see first thing in the morning." Looking at her tiny bikini, all the exposed white skin and her softly rounded shape, he tried to imagine what she'd look like with 'em off. Probably like some sort of freak. There was another voice way back in his mind. 'She's a fox,' it said.

"I found some footprints in the mud. Perfect match. Also found the broken branch he used to hold me under. Remember seeing him light up and toss a folder away. This morning I found a match book From the Lucky Lady."

"One of Frank's hang-outs," Buzz shrugged. "Everything you've got is purely circumstantial. What it amounts to is . . . we got nothing. Know what I mean?"

"I've got some ideas," Mark continued. "Didn't even tell my folks. I am gonna have to explain why I have Ollie's wrecked ten-speed. Sorry 'bout your bike, Dude. I'll let you have mine if you want. I don't much use it anymore. Looks like my biggest problem is what will he do once he finds out I'm not dead? I am gonna watch for a chance to snoop around his place when he's not home. I want to look under his Explorer. See if there are any scratches or marks like maybe red paint from where he ran over Ollie's bike."

Ollie snorted. "Red paint? Don't think there was enough paint left on my ole bike to leave a mark."

"You better not get caught," offered Candy. "Wouldn't surprise me one dang bit if the sheriff saw you, he'd shoot first then ask questions."

"We gotta do something right away," said Ollie, "or the sheriff is going to get away with another murder. We need to spread the word all over town that we think it's him. That way if anything happens to any of us . . . . You're sure it was the sheriff? Was this guy fat? Would think you could tell that much."

"No moon. All I could tell was he wore that same ski mask as the guy who robbed our house. I don't know why he wore one, you know, if he intended to kill me."

Shannon was sitting with her face in both hands looking at Mark through her fingers. Her black skin had a peculiar, rather chalky cast to it. "I'm pretty much getting' scared. What if it isn't the sheriff? You sure he was white? What if it was my dad? He wears those boots. He lost his watch. We have a black SUV. He was out of the house late on those nights. He's here in town with nothing to do. Oh God," she wailed. "It can't be him. It can't be. This whole thing makes me feel sick."

307

For Shannon's sake, he was thinking, it has to be the sheriff. "I'm telling you, Shannon, the man was white. Seems to boil down to this SUV. We know the killer has a big black SUV. Frank has a big black SUV. The White's have a black SUV. Who else around town has a black SUV? Must be a zillion of them."

"We have an SUV," Candy shrugged. "Candy apple red."

"Red looks like it's black in the dark,' he let her know.

"Guess it's a macho thing, same as them good ole boys in Alabama and their big pickup trucks. All these guys with their SUVs need is a gun rack."

Mark shivered. "Wash your mouth out, Red. By the way, how come you're being so quiet? Let's hear what you think."

"Got so caught up in the story of your ordeal . . . Hey, it isn't what I think that's important and I'll tell y'all why. Shannon's dad is not the killer and neither is the sheriff. You wanna know why?"

* * *

"So here we are batching it with our wives both down for the State choir competition again?" Doc would sit with a beer and turn and turn the mug, always adjusting its position but seldom taking a sip. "I'll say this about your wife, Frank. She has one hell of a good voice."

Frank held his beer gut in both hands like it was something he was proud of. "It should be since she gets so much practice yellin' at me. Maggie said she thought they would win first place again this year like last time. Kinda puts little old Dalton on the map since they go up against some rather big church choirs." He squinted at Doc who was one of those guys that would nurse each beer until it got warm. Frank always called him a cheap date.

"Yep, they won the thing last year with that Republican song."

"Battle Hymn of the Republic." Doc corrected.

"Yeah, that one. Heard them do it at the Fourth of July picnic and it flat ass gives you goose bumps."

"Sure does, Frank. Sure does. That guy Kelly can take a few housewives, a handful of farmers and some teenagers with fairly good voices and make them sound like the Mormon Tabernacle Choir."

"Maggie tells me that they don't practice a song by going

through it and through it. The man takes it apart, piece by piece, note by note and lets them know how he wants each word sung, how he wants it to sound, where to put in, what he calls, a sting. Guy's a friggen genius they tell me."

"Yeah, Frank, that's the way you should treat these murders. Take them apart piece-by-piece, item-by-item, person-by-person like one of these forensic experts do. Wife tells me this director is so good, they are thinking about moving him to the high school next year. I don't see what a man with his talent is doing in a backwater town like Dalton. Perhaps he has some ulterior motive. Tell me this, have you thought of the possibility this Brad Kelly fits your profile of a serial killer?

"Damn it Doc, you're getting bad as me. Getting to where anybody looks at me cross-eyed, I wanna lock 'em up. Way I hear it this guy's wife and two children were killed in an armed robbery when he lived in Chicago. At least that's the story. Never caught the guy so that's when you start wondering if maybe there wasn't some hanky panky going on? Maybe one or both of them was foolin' around. Guess he moved out here to get away from it all. Couldn't handle the big city anymore, I'm uh thinkin'."

"Well, he's a single guy, early thirties, a loner and possibly with mental problems. They never caught his family's killer so maybe he's the one who did it."

"I hear what you're saying, Doc, and I intend to look into it."

The waitress walked past with a tray of beers for the four men playing pool. On her way back, Frank reached out to stop her. "What do you say, Rosie Honey. 'How bout you and me getting it on tonight?"

"Tell you what, Frank. I'd have to pay Mary Lou for keeping the kids the rest of the night . . . and I need some bread pretty bad for my car payment. Way I look at it is, an all-nighter ought to be worth a hundred bucks."

* * *

Everyone's eyes fastened on Candy's face. Shannon gasped. So did Mark. Her eyes were steady, an emerald green, as she looked into his and he looked away and then back. "And tell me how, Miss Smarty-pants, do you back up such a wild statement?"

"Pretty simple,' Candy explained. "My computer program says neither man is guilty. Mark already verified it wasn't Reverend White. The Man who dumped your sister's body smoked Winstons. To top it off, Shannon tells me her dad's boots are a size eight and a half. The size we put into the computer after checking the plaster casts was a size eleven."

"So? Your point is?"

Turning to Shannon she said, "Your dad doesn't smoke, does he." It was a statement, not a question.

"No." Shannon's eyes seemed to light up. "Never has."

"Okay. We established that the killer was smoking out where we found Mark's sister. And Mark tells us that last night he saw the killer light up, throw away a match folder and stood watching the river. Also, Mark told us the black SUV was humongous. My computer eliminated your dad after the first entry. Think about it. You guys have a small SUV. Toyota or something."

"Honda CRV," Shannon agreed.

"I've always said it wasn't him," Mark growled. "So that takes us back to the sheriff. Everything points to him. He smokes Winstons. He drinks Bud. He used to wear a watch. And he wears the black shoes with an eagle on the heel."

"Boots with an eagle on the heel," Buzz corrected.

"Wore a black ski mask," Mark nodded, "and uses gray duct tape on all his victims."

"All circumstantial," Candy said. "But I have found out a dang sight more. Y'all been so busy lately with everything I forgot to tell you guys what I discovered about the price tag. Checked around a couple of places and guess what I found?"

"That Turner Lumber sells nails by the pound?" Mark prompted.

"I'm sure they do, but Steven's sells meat by the pound."

"Will wonders never cease?" He was trying to be flip. It was obvious he didn't feel flip.

She glared at him and then looked about. "Let me tell y'all why it isn't the sheriff."

Mark squinted, pursed his lips and studied the redhead. He was trying to keep his mind totally focused on their investigation. On what Red might have to tell them, but something else about her was starting to bother him. She was standing like she was posing, like one of those fashion models, one hand out in front, palm up. The other was resting with her knuckles on her hip and her legs were crossed at the ankles.

He continued to watch her slim white body and the feminine curves, as she moved to where her swimsuit cover-up was hanging on a chair. What's the heck is goin' on he wondered? Keep trying to see her as a Playboy centerfold. Naked. Boy is that stupid.

She began digging into a pocket, pulling out a plastic sandwich baggie. I brought these along since I figured we'd be talking about clues. These are price tags from the meat department."

"How did you get those," Buzz asked, "rip them off?"

"All I had to do was flirt with the stock-boy and he went and got me some. These are the same as the one we found."

"You flirted with the stock boy?" Mark asked uneasily.

"Yeah and guess what? Asked me out."

"Asked you out? Whatever for?"

"Maybe he wanted to make mad passionate love to me. Why do you care? I had to tell him, 'No way. Can't date till I'm fourteen and in high school.' He's a junior and I think he's cute. His name is Brian."

Mark licked his lips and asked, "What I'm wondering is, how do you connect this price tag to the killer? Who the heck works at the store that would make a good suspect? Mostly women. Stevens wears those boots. Maybe it's Brian, the cute guy."

"No, no. Wait. There's more. Remember the blue garbage bags? I also found out about them"

"You're kiddin'." Red's investigative abilities were beginning to fascinate Mark. "You mean where it came from?"

"You got it. My dad carried one home last night from DGF. Had some stuff out of Sam Dalton's old office he wanted to sort through. I asked him why they used blue. Told me they're not garbage bags. Have a special thermal quality that helps keep meat cold when they truck it out. And get this. Brian told me DGF puts the original tags on the meat. Machine printed. Steven's keeps some spares in case they want to mark something down."

"Or up," put in Ollie, "the way things go now days."

Candy ignored him. "We need to check out people who

work at the meat packing place. I remember reading in the paper that the legs seemed to have been removed with a surgical saw. What if it's a butcher who works at DGF? He would have access to meat saws."

"Great," Mark snorted. "That narrows it down a bunch. Everybody in town works for DGF."

"I'm only telling you what I learned. Gotta start somewhere. They don't all work in the meat packing part. What we need is a list."

Shannon was nodding, "At least we're on the right track." She sighed. "Thank God, Candy, you've eliminated my dad. Since we're pretty sure the sheriff is out, and we know it wasn't Weird Walter, so who else can it be?"

"I've eliminated my dad," Mark tried to laugh. It didn't work.

"What?" Candy was astounded. "You suspected your own father?"

"Heck no I didn't suspect my father, but sometimes he wears black dress shoes. Doesn't have any boots at all, and nothing in the Eagle Gold brand. Plus, he doesn't wear aftershave with the aroma I remember."

"That's pretty funny," Buzz told them. "I checked my dad's closet since I knew he wears boots on his job. The black boots he wears to work are not those expensive kind. Think he buys them down at K-mart in Clarksdale. I knew he was clean but I was curious if he might own some of those. Know what I mean? He don't."

"Doesn't," Shannon corrected.

"Whatever."

"So what's our next move?" asked Candy. "Turn everything we know over to the police?"

Mark growled. "To Dumbo and Jumbo? Not hardly. Let me think on it tonight. Maybe I can come up with some sort of plan by morning. My dad works at DGF so we may have to ask him to help. In the meantime, we gotta keep out of dangerous corners. Especially me. Most of all we need to keep our cool."

* * *

Elaine was plotting. The Man had driven down Forest Drive right on past Main and then turned on Lincoln, which meant he

312

wasn't heading for the quarry or Lone Pine Trail. Nor was he heading for Lover's Lookout or Wild Canyon Road on the other side of the river. Lincoln dead-ends at Park, so when he slows down to make the turn onto Park I'm out of here, even if I get hurt. Trying to move without him being aware she felt for the door handle. Her gut began to churn. There was no handle. Her fingers were frantically moving, forward, back and up and down. There was a smooth panel covering everything. I am not going to cry. Whatever he wants, I aim to cooperate. Last thing I need is to get myself hurt. He turned right on Park then sped up, driving out toward the Interstate. What the heck is this? Guy is turning into the DGF driveway.

Too late, she realized she had made a mistake. When he walked around to open her door, she should have dove out on his side and ran. The door jerked open and he had his hand in her hair, dragging her from the seat. They seemed to be at the rear of the building. The Man had a key. Once they were inside, The Man didn't waste any time. He used a roll of wide gray tape to secure her wrists behind her back. His fingers were working at the snap on her jeans, then the zipper. There was no way to stop him as he dragged the garment down and off her legs. When he picked up a sharp boning knife she felt sudden warmth and knew she'd wet herself. There was no cut. He used it to slice the material of her blouse and bra in order to by-pass her secured arms. He removed everything, even her shoes. She shivered, and not due to the fact it was cool. He began removing his own.

When he pulled off the ski mask she shrieked. "My God! It's you!"

"Thought you would be happy to see me." He was pushing her down onto the cold concrete where he forced her legs apart then fell on top of her. "Way I got it figured you owe me this."

She cringed from his fowl breath and made mewling sounds, but there was no stopping him. It went on and on for what seemed like hours. After he was through, she was grateful he didn't hurt her, but she looked up curiously as he stood obscenely over her, tearing off another strip of the tape. A horrifying thought permeated her mind as he reached down to slap it over her mouth. Two little girls were dead. My God. It could be him? Now he's going to kill me.

* * *

Heather's mother again came out onto the patio. "Heather. It's time for you to say goodnight to your friends. School night, you know. I don't know about the rest of you, but my Heather has some homework to do."

"Oh mom."

"You heard me, Honey. Say your goodbyes." She smiled at the rest of the Kryptonites. "I'm so happy you could all come. You are welcome to use our pool anytime you get the urge. If you don't mind it's my turn. I get my twenty five laps every evening rain or shine." She striped off the red duster.

Gal's doing that on purpose, Mark thought. She knows us guys are looking and she likes it. "Thank's Mrs. uh . . . Carolyn." Calling her by her given name embarrassed him. "We had a wonderful time and thanks for the treats. Come on guys. My homework is done, so I for one am going to wander over to Ollie's and goof around with the Harley for a while." He shook his head. Ollie and Heather kissed and behind them Mark saw Mrs. Deiter watching, but she smiled.

* * *

"A hundred bucks?" Frank's voice was so loud everyone in the place was looking. "Are you out of your mind woman? I ain't 'bout to plunk out a hundred bucks for some loving."

"I'll bet Doc Snyder would. Wouldn't you Doc?"

"Well I . . . " he smirked. "I probably would only I'd have to borrow the money from my wife." He began to guffaw as though he'd made an extremely funny remark. "But honey, I'll bet you'd be worth it. Frank thinks he's such a stud women should pay him. Right Frank?"

"Hey man. When you got it you got it."

Rosalie shook her head. "Here's another beer, Frank; on me. I guess I'll see you next Tuesday as usual. If you don't need me I'd better make the rounds."

Doc was shaking his head as he stood. "Guess I'll head for home, my friend. Sounds to me like your plaything doesn't need the money."

"Playin' hard to get. She makes out real good on her tips. Some of these jokers get a few drinks under their belts and all she has to do is flirt with them. Tells me they often leave her a couple of bucks for a beer and once in a while as much as a fiver. Rosie's problem is, she doesn't know how to manage her money. Guess I'll down this beer then go back down to the station and check up on some things. Maybe I'll call that phone number and see what they can tell me 'bout the watch."

"Gonna say this one more time, Frank. Get some outside help. The county sheriff has that mobile crime lab and trained professionals to operate it. Even I have enough sense to call in medical experts when I've got a problem beyond my scope of knowledge."

"Been thinking about that very thing, Doc. I reckon Monday I'll give them a call."

* * *

Mark and Ollie left the Deiter place, leading the way with Shorty and Jodi taking their sweet time. At the pool party he had felt kind of out of place with everyone else paired off. He was an outsider and he felt it. Maybe he needed to find a girlfriend. Wonder if Carmelita would be . . . ? Naw. Not her. She's playing with those senior high guys. There isn't a babe in the whole eighth grade worth a second look. One thing for sure, Red didn't fit the bill. She's cute enough, I'll give her that, but she's nothing but a royal pain. Cold day in hell.

As they turned into Ollie's drive Mark threw out both arms halting the foursome in the shadows cast by a row of oleanders. Jodi was pressed right up against his back. "Holy shit, it's the black SUV coming down Lincoln."

The teenagers discovered they were holding their breath until the dark car cruised past.

"Is it him?" Jodi whispered.

Mark heaved a huge sigh. "Looked something like the one from the other night, but I don't guess it is. There was a man and a woman in this one."

Ollie's eyes followed the black Navigator. "Looked like a black man and a white woman. They're turning onto Park."

"Heading for the freeway, said Shorty. "Probably from out of town."

Mark blew out a big puff of air. "After what I've been through, I'm getting freaked out by everything that moves."

Ollie touched his arm. "You gotta pull yourself together

man. Can't go around looking over your shoulder for the rest of your life."

* * *

It was around eight thirty when Candy left Heather's. Since it was a school night both Candy and Shannon had been ordered to be home before nine.

"So long," Candy pursed her lips, watching as Buzz walked along with Shannon hand in hand. He gave her a quick kiss then crossed the street as she turned toward her house. The Swanson residence was right next door to the Deiter home. Candy draped her towel about her neck and trotted inside wearing her damp suit. She quietly slipped in through the kitchen door and headed for her room, coming to an abrupt halt when she spotted the silhouette of her father in the den standing in front of the window. There was only a dim light next to the leather sofa but the window seemed to be shimmering like blue neon and it made her suspicious.

Moving until she was nearly beside him, she looked out at the Deiter's swimming pool. Heather's mother was doing laps. At last she came up out of the pool and stood for several seconds under the lights, water following the curves of her white body.

Candy's father sensed her presence and turned, his eyes filling with guilt.

"I was . . . uh . . . .."

"Checking on the weather, right Dad?"

The feeling of guilt caused him to be angry. "I suppose you're going to squeal about this to your mother?"

"Hey Dad. It's cool. None of her business and anyway I understand. It's a man thing."

He looked curiously at his daughter. The towel around her shoulders didn't conceal the bikini. He was amazed at how much she had changed.

She grinned. "Not only that, but she's got a shape to die for. That I could be that lucky."

He glanced back at the woman who was reaching up to do something to her hair, emphasizing her figure, and then he looked at his daughter again as though seeing her for the first time. "You're getting there, Candy," he said softly, moving away from the window. "Without a doubt baby, you're getting there."

316

She couldn't believe her ears. It was the first nice thing he'd said to her in ages . . . and . . . and he'd called her 'Candy' . . . and 'baby'.

* * *

Inside the garage Jodi had a hard time pulling Shorty away from the motorcycle. If he had any idea how near they were to being done he probably would have balked.

"Come on Leroy, let's go up to my room. I got some new CD's. It's okay with Mom as long as I leave the door open." Reluctantly he followed her, leaving Mark and Ollie to their task.

"Well that's it, the last piece." Ollie gave the wrench one last tweak then began wiping the grease spots off the transmission with a red mechanics towel.

Mark's eyes shined with excitement. "Great. It's time to see the results of all this labor. Where did I put that can of either? Ah, there tis."

"Batteries fully charged, even though I understand it will run off the magneto alone . . . if you kick the starter hard enough. Too bad it doesn't have an electric starter." He turned the key. "Here goes nothing."

Mark gave the carburetor intake a small shot of either and Ollie stepped firmly on the kick-starter. All they got was a whomp, whomp, whomp. He kicked again and again. "Crap!" Mark gave it another shot of either.

This time, with a sound like a cherry bomb, it backfired and both boys jumped.

"It fired." Ollie's eyes were filled with wonder.

"Yeah, let's hit it again." Another shot of either and another step on the starting lever. Putt, putt, wham, putt. Mark pursed his lips. "It's trying. Acts like it isn't getting enough gas."

Ollie looked sheepish, then reached under the gas tank and turned the shutoff valve. "What can I say? Too excited I guess."

Mark sprayed the carburetor again. As soon as Ollie put his weight on the lever, there was a slight pop, a puff of black smoke and the motor roared to life, and two boys stood grinning as broadly as possible, giving each other high fives.

Instantly the door between the garage and house opened and Ollie's father came out, grinning nearly as much as the boys. Walking around the machine he reached out to grasp the throttle control on the handgrip, revving it up a couple of times. In about ten seconds, Shorty, Jodi and Ollie's mother pushed through the door and crowded around.

After a few minutes of ooohs and aaahs, his father shouted over the noise. "Okay boys, let's shut her down. You're filling the garage full of poison gas. It's after ten so it's time to break this party up. You'll have plenty of time this weekend to try it out."

There was a deathlike silence when Ollie turned the key to shut it off.

Mark had heard Mr. Frazier. Ollie hadn't. "Did you say this week-end?"

"That's what I said. Saturday morning I'll take it out to grandpa's ranch. All I ask is, after we haul it out there . . . or maybe I'll ride it out. Keep in mind when you boys are riding it be extremely careful. I don't want to have to waste my time visiting you guys in the hospital . . . or the morgue."

* * *

The Man was inside the building executing the rest of his plan. The sex had relieved one need but not the other. First, a strip of the duct tape was used to cover her red painted mouth. Since her hands were already taped together behind her back he did the same to her feet at the ankles. Gal weighs in at about hundred twenty-five pounds, he figured, and yet he easily lifted her onto the huge metal work area. Her eyes widened in horror as his index finger pushed the red button and there was a 'Wooooommm' followed by a continuous whine as the giant bandsaw came to life.

Stroking her smooth thighs with his callused hands, he told her, "This never would have happened if you'd been nice to me, you rotten bitch. It's all your fault. I lost everything because of you. Lost my wife, lost my kids, lost my job. It's time for you to pay the piper. Revenge can be a very sweet thing, don't you think?"

Elaine tried and tried to scream from behind the tape, squirming frantically as she felt her skin slide on the slick metal. She fainted.

CHAPTER TWENTY-FIVE

Another couple of hours like this, Rosalie was thinking, and I'll be outa here. Frank could stuff it. She looked toward the paunchy sheriff and he motioned to her, so with a grimace she made her way back to the table where he sat finishing his beer. Doc was standing, ready to leave, talking down to him.

"C'mere Rosie. Want to tell ya something."

She stopped directly in front of him, smiling as she always did. "Tell me what?"

Reaching out with a folded piece of green money, sticking it down her neck, he pushed it into her bra as far as he could with his index finger. It was a hundred.

"Got to get my lazy ass out of here," Doc Snyder was nodding knowingly. "Keep your beeper on, Frank. No telling who may be calling in the middle of the night." He was doing the horselaugh again.

* * *

Twenty minutes later the Man was grinning and humming to himself, breaking out in a raucous laugh, more nearly a cackle. The packaging machine nearly did it all. It wrapped in plastic, sealed and weighed while printing out a tag with prices provided by vendors. All he had to do was clean up the leftovers, shove them into the bin under the steer bones and next week they'll be fertilizer. He hadn't bled her out like they did when they butchered a cow or a pig, so he spent a great deal of time hosing down the work area.

When he was satisfied the place was in order, he carried the two plastic cartons of wrapped meat into the freezer, knowing where he was going to place them. "This stack of breaded veal cutlets we put in the bin labeled 'Green Spot Cafe' and the box of hamburger is going to 'Steven's General Merchandise'. Gonna want to be eating out myself the next several nights."

Humming to himself he lifted the rest of the body down. Don't weigh nearly as much as she did. These women who want to lose weight ought to come see me. Sliding the torso into a fifty-five gallon plastic bag he took off the rubber apron which he dropped into the hamper with a dozen others. After he retrieved his clothes he threw hers inside the bag, then swung it onto his shoulder like a sack of feed, pausing for one last look around before he turned out the lights.

The bag was carefully placed in the back of his SUV. Learned my lesson from doing the Goodwin twerp. Laid her body on a plastic drop cloth and in spite of it ended up with some spots of blood on the carpet. His plan with the little tyke had been to hide the body and he had thought this had been accomplished, certain he'd picked a spot where no one would ever find it until it was a pile of bones . . . unless some animals carted parts of it off . . . for dinner.

When the body was discovered he realized the excitement and terror it generated throughout the town was too much of a turn-on to resist. From here on he wanted them all to be found. If they weren't discovered, what good was it to do the thing?

With both the little girls he'd taken their clothes home. Souvenirs. The heck with Elaine's duds, leave them with the body. What I'll do with this bitch is drive up route 61 north of town, and dump her in the river so she'll float down toward the bridge. Don't have any idea how well she might float . . . in her condition, but wouldn't it be a joke on them if she ended up where the river curves past the Main Street bridge or perhaps behind the boathouse pier. Man, that would be awesome.

Passing Owens's place he continued across the Turtle Creek Bridge to the northern most entrance to Shoemaker Park and pulled in behind some heavy brush. Carrying the bag to the top of the embankment he dumped it out. Using the toe of his shiny black boot, he shoved the corpse over the edge, waiting until he heard the splash then tossed the plastic bag down the slope.

It was the first time he'd worn the watch since he'd recov-

ered it from the Goodwin punk. Pushing the button on its side to light the dial, he told himself, "Eleven bells. I'd better get the hell out of here. Only been gone for a couple of hours, but I feel good. As Richard Simmons would say, 'I feel simply mahvalous'."

* * *

After leaving the movies, Ashley Wolfe and Ramon Villar-real, two seniors from Dalton High School, drove down to a spot behind Judge Elliot's house known to the locals as Dalton Beach and to the teenagers as Lover's Lookout. At this time of year, when the water level was down, there was a quarter mile long, fifty foot wide, strip of sand where the river completed it's 'Ess' curve. They sat in Ramon's, souped up, Ford truck for a while making out.

"Darn you Ramon, look at the time. I was supposed to be in by eleven and it's midnight."

"Hey Babe, don't blame it all on me. I can't help it if you are so exciting I lose track of time. Anyway, you are the one who insisted we drive down here after the show." He was combing his long hair. "Tell them we had a flat."

"Yeah. You know what they'll say? 'That's what cell phones are for.' I don't know why they bug me so much. I'm the only kid in the senior class that has to be home by eleven. You'd think I was a child."

Ramon started the powerful engine and pulled on the lights that seemed to skip like a flat stone across the black water as he began the turn. "I'll tell them the truth. They should understand. It should be cool. After all, they were young once."

"Oh yeah. You should hear the lectures I get from my mom about teen pregnancies and disease."

Burning rubber he whipped the truck around in a skidding arc, then slammed on the brakes. "Did you see that?"

She was kissing his neck. "See what?"

Putting it into reverse he backed up and turned until they were facing the water. Driving slowly forward, peering into the gloom, letting the white glow sweep along the sand, there was nothing in sight except the yellow beach and murky water. "Guess I was seeing things." The engine shuddered to a stop when he forgot to push in the clutch. Thirty feet away was the stark white-ness of a naked woman laying at the river's edge, flat on her

321

back, her arms and black hair spread over the sand, her lower body floating in the water. Ramon was opening his door.

"Oh my God, Ramon, don't! Let's go for the sheriff."

"She might be alive. I gotta to go see."

"Oh my God Ramon. It looks like she's dead. Come on. Let's go."

He ignored her pleas and she reluctantly followed him as they cautiously approached the lifeless form, their hearts beating like drums. Moving aside so his shadow wouldn't fall on the woman, his eyes were drawn to the cuts all over her chest, upper arms and her stomach. Her chest was so severely lacerated they no longer looked like breasts. He accidentally touched her shoulder with his toe and the torso rotated as his eyes adjusted to the glare from the headlights.

"Holy Mother of God, somebody has cut off her legs."

Ashley was being sick in the bushes.

* * *

Midnight. The sheriff was sitting in the Lucky Lady shooting the breeze with a couple of truck drivers. They were all three watching Rosalie as she moved about doing her final chores before locking up. The three men had been making bawdy talk about women in general and Rosie in particular and Frank was thinking, "Eat your heart out, drivers. This little filly is all locked up. In his mind he was plotting on how he planned on getting his hundred dollars worth. Something about giving her that much money had turned his thoughts to the stud he'd been back when he was in his twenties.

"This sure is a quiet little town," one of the truckers told him. "Wonder why someone doesn't build a decent motel here?"

"Yeah," the second trucker added, "the EZY INN is clean enough, but it must be a hundred years old. 'Stead of a shower, got them old cast-iron tubs that stand on feet with claws."

"You guys should feel lucky ole Mattie Crow don't furnish you with a galvanized laundry tub like I had to use when I was a kid." Frank was one of those men who could drink beer all night as long as there was a bathroom nearby and never show the effects.

"Come on sheriff," the driver with the cowboy hat joshed. "You're not that old."

322

Frank laughed. "No, but from some of the tales my grand pappy tells, that's the way it was. Once a week, Saturday night, the tub came out. He and his wife would go first and then the six kids. One tub of water and . . . " His beeper went off. "Now what?" He growled.

He called out to the bartender, "hand me the phone, Gary. Gotta make a call."

"Sure thing, Frank. This time of night, probably a damned accident." The bartender plopped the tan instrument on the end of the bar.

The sheriff studied the red numbers on the end of his pager as he punched them in. "Better not be anything that takes much time. I got me some plans for tonight. Hello! This is Sheriff Martinez here. Who didja say's callin'?"

He listened, his eyes closing to slits, his lips forming a firm line. The bartender leaned forward, curious. There wasn't the usual, 'who? What? Where?' Abruptly he hung up and snapped, "I'm on my way."

"Whatcha got, Frank?" the bartender asked. "Accident."

"We got us another body," he snapped.

"Oh shit! Another little girl?"

"Not this time. This time we got us a woman."

* * *

The Man wandered aimlessly among the new cars in front of Deiter Ford paying no attention to style, color or price stickers. "What the heck am I going to do?" The Man muttered aloud. "Why are a couple of schoolgirls interested in the Eagle Gold boots? Could it actually be, as they had told the clerk, 'A pretend investigation'? Clinton informed him the tracing had probably come from a pair of boots owned by the black broad's father. Is it merely a coincidence? Could be."

That stupid Clinton found the whole thing amusing but it wasn't to me. Especially, when he asked Clinton, in a joking tone, if the clerk had mentioned his name.

"Not yours. The girl, Becky, had told them to check out Sid Turner, Reverend White, Banker Elliot or the sheriff." Isn't that a laugh? As if ole butterball Frank could come up with a plan as carefully thought out as this one of mine.

Some kids found Elaine's body last night. Lot quicker than

323

I expected. Floated nearly straight across the river from where he'd dumped it. Ended up at Lover's Lookout. Medical examiner came up from Clarksdale but so did a couple of guys from the county sheriff's department. Frank is in so far over his head they're gonna be trucking in a whole batch of outside help. Not going to do any better than our local police department. No way they can trace this thing to me.

The service center at Deiter's was open, but it was too early for any salesmen to be on the job. He felt safe acting like he was interested in the new models. Gave him a perfect opportunity to keep an eye on the front entrance to Dalton Middle School. Doin' my own 'pretend investigation'. Need to know who the person was with the black bitch.

Here they come. All four of 'em. Goodwin, his little red-headed gal pal. Then we have Reverend White's daughter . . . and . . . the Frazier brat. Uh huh.

I could have a bucket full of problems. They may or may not suspect it's me, or if they do they don't have enough proof to take it to Frank. Started with that damned watch. Knew exactly where out on Lone Pine Trail the Goodwin kid had found the thing. I'm sure that jerk suspects me and that's why he is always staring. The clincher was the deal at Clinton's. Clinton had told him the drawing looked like it had been made from a plaster cast by placing a piece of paper on the cast and than using a pencil lead. Where in the Hell had he left a footprint? Alright, so the two girls were practicing doing a crime scene investigation as a school project. Sure they were.

Footprint? Oh hell. It was obvious. Down by the river where he'd thought he'd done away with Goodwin. But what in the Hell else had happened to make them suspect him? Somehow or the other I gotta get them to back off. Better yet, I need to catch them all together, like in the middle of a street. There's gotta be a way to set it up. Terrible accident. I never even saw them. Too bad. Killed them all.

* * *

By ten a.m. Frank and Ralph, along with Doc Snyder and a group of his cronies, were in the barbershop. Mrs. Shipman was doing a dye job on one lady while another waited her turn. Jeff Shipman was giving Ralph a haircut and Doc was waiting to have

324

his trimmed. The small shop was near to overflowing. The sheriff's crime lab came up from Clarksdale and their men had taken over. He understood several FBI investigators were also on their way. The only reason Frank was there was that he didn't want to miss out on whatever they might be saying about him.

"Well Frank," Doc told him, "looks like you got your tit caught in the wringer this time. Whole town's a buzzin' with all these outside law people nosing around."

Frank was feeling pretty low. "Hey, I'm glad to get the help. No way me and Ralph can go it alone anymore 'cause we gotta third murder done by the same psycho." I made a couple of mistakes out at the scene last night. The coroner and the M. E. came up along with a couple of guys from the county sheriff's. Should have kept his mouth shut 'bout how the Dalton police were making significant progress on these cases. That he expected to make an arrest at any moment. Made him look bad when they began asking questions and he had no ready answers.

Ralph was leafing through a Sport's Illustrated. "Not only that, Frank, but I see the county mobile crime lab is parked over by the court house so I reckon they're gonna hang around. One of the county guys said even the FBI is on the way."

Jeff was sharpening his razor on a leather strop. "This is only the beginning. You see all those copters over at Frazier's ranch?"

"Sure did," said Doc. "Way I hear it, ole man Frazier is charging them ten bucks a pop to ferry them into town. Some reporters from the Clarksdale Clarion and the rest of them are from TV stations. Some from Clarksdale, one from L.A. and one all the way from Las Vegas."

"Look what's goin' on as we speak." Jeff used the razor to point out the window. A television van pulled into the parking lot at the Green Spot. "I'll bet the café is suckin' in the business this morning."

"Getting out of hand," Frank told them and he didn't mean the visitors. "We got us a serial killer right here in Dalton."

"What makes it so bad," said Jeff, the young barber, "is that it could be anybody. Getting to where I'm eyeing every customer suspiciously. If I should be so lucky to get him in my chair, this old straight razor would turn him into a female."

Ralph squirmed. "I hear ya, but for sure it ain't me so quit waving that thing around. With all these men from the sheriff's department, the FBI and TV reporters, me and Frank might as well go on vacation."

"Not me," Frank was bobbing his head. "I want that psycho as bad as they do."

* * *

Four blocks away, in the Lucky Lady Bar, two-dozen patrons were getting an early start with their drinking problems. "Why do you suppose this maniac cuts off their legs?" Bill Stevens, who owned the lumberyard asked.

"Beats me," the mailman replied. "Did you hear what Ralph told Frank?"

"Sure didn't. Ralph can come up with some zingers."

"He says the guy probably makes a stew and eats them."

"I could actually see him doing that," added Sam the junkman, "with the small pieces he cut off those little girls legs, but Elaine had some mighty fine stems. Heard on the news where he amputated both of hers clean off at the hips. Take a guy a year to eat that much meat."

"They had a case like that a couple of years back in New York or Chicago didn't they? Jeffrey Daummer or some such?"

"Hannibal Lector," Bill enlightened them.

"That's right," Sam shook one finger in the air. "Hannibal the Cannibal."

"It was in Cleveland. Made a movie about it with Jodi Foster. Silence of the Lambs. She won an Academy Award."

"Maybe," the postman started laughing even before he finished the statement, "he ground them up into hamburger and sold it to Kelly's Burger Pit."

"Haw, haw, haw," Kelly laughed. "Gotta get my ass back over to the shop. That place is swarming with customers this morning. Is that why you always order a double-double?"

* * *

At Dalton Middle School, the teachers were having trouble keeping the student's attention. They seemed to keep breaking off into groups to discuss the events of last night and the past week. To a person they were more excited than frightened.

When the Kryptonites met at noon, there was little conver-

326

sation. They sat like seven mannequins, merely picking at their lunches, staring blankly into space, with the exception of Ollie who ultimately broke the spell. "Guess what's coming to town?"

Mark grunted, "I don't have a clue. Wal-Mart?"

"I wish. We won't see one in our lifetime. Dad had these people in the newspaper office yesterday asking about advertising. They're going to put in a Pizza Parlor."

"You're jerking us," Mark looked at Ollie who seemed ecstatic. "Where?"

"On the other side of the river right next to the fire station. They bought some land from Traster's Farm Equipment."

"Cool." Buzz was showing his white teeth. "Also right across from the cemetery. Know what I mean? That's probably where they're going to get their meat?"

"Man," Candy snorted, "are you ever gross."

"You guys got any ideas?" Mark looked without interest at a sandwich, dropping it back into the bag. "You know, about these darned murders?" When he said this, he shuddered. It was a feeling he'd had before, the feeling like the ground moved.

"Don't know," shrugged Candy. "We were certain all he had was this freakish thing about killing little girls. Garcia woman was an adult."

"I got one," said Shannon. "Since we are making about as much progress as Frank and Ralph are, we may as well let the FBI and the crew from Clarksdale handle this thing and get on with our lives."

Mark let his eyes drift from face to face and was unhappy with what he saw. "Is that the opinion you all have?"

There was some muttering and squirming.

"Well, not me. I made a vow to my little sister that I wouldn't rest until the psychopath that killed her was behind bars. You guys do whatever you want, but I'm in this 'til the bitter end."

Candy moved down a row to sit beside him slipping her arm through his and pulled it close. "Count me in . . . to the bitter end."

"And me," Buzz agreed.

"I'm with you Marcus," Ollie slapped him on the back.

"Me to," Jodi and Heather spoke in unison.

"Make that seven." Shannon put her arm around Buzz.

"Wherever Buzz goes I go."

"All right, how many can make it to a meeting this afternoon right after school?"

Five hands went up. "Like I can't." As usual, Heather looked like she might cry. "With all these killings, my mother drove me to school this morning and she intends to pick me up right after. From now on, I guess."

"At least your mother cares about you," Candy stated bitterly. "I doubt if mine would even leave her TV if I was a victim of this deranged madman."

"We need to hold a club meeting," Mark told them. "My house is out. My Dad is having some sort of gathering there this evening, and Ollie's mom is having a Tupperware party."

"We could meet at my place again." Heather was hoping. "Like Dad won't be home and Mom is having her bridge women there."

Remembering how it went the last time Mark was thinking up an excuse. "We wouldn't want to disturb your mom's hen party."

"No problem. Like they meet in the game room. It's in the front of the house. Like they wouldn't even know we were there."

Mark stood and started to walk toward the school. "Okay. We'll make it work. Let's get this day over with. I might have a plan."

* * *

Mark had his history book open rapidly scanning the bold headings on each page. Often this was enough to help him pass one of Guy William's tests. He had a feeling, a premonition, and looked up at the wall clock, 2:37 exactly. It began as a deep rumbling in the distance along with a sound like rushing wind. Then with a wrenching shudder the undulating, jerking, jolting seemed to go on forever. Somewhere in the distance a bell clanged and clanged then stopped. Fifteen of the seventeen students in Mr. Williams' history class, following years of drills on this subject, moved in unison to dive under their desks.

Candy, frozen in shock, was leaning over hers hugging the top, her face a white mask of terror, watching the crazy dance of books and furniture. All in one motion, Mark first went to his knees, and as he glanced up toward the ceiling he spotted a sign

328

of danger. Like a catapult he threw his body in her direction, his momentum carrying both of them into the aisle between the rows of desks as a thirty pound fluorescent fixture tore loose and crashed down, its sharp corner imbedded two inches into the wood surface. Celotex tiles from the suspended ceiling rained all about them. Mark, without realizing he was doing so, protected her body with his.

After an eternity, lasting forty three seconds, the erratic motion stopped and there was a silence so total it was spooky. Mark struggled to get off the prostate form and discovered he was clutching a fistful of Candy's blouse, so he pulled her to her feet at the same time.

She surveyed the damage to her desk and gasped, "My God! You saved my life! Mark! You saved my life. I don't know what to say."

"I can't believe anyone can be that stupid," he snapped, his adrenaline pumping. "You sat there like a dunce."

His caustic remark was more than the terrified teen could handle and she burst into tears, but in his alarmed condition he didn't notice.

He was aware that Mr. Williams rushed outside and at first Mark thought he was so panicked he was bailing out, but then he could see the teacher's eyes sweeping the face of the building and when he returned he told them, "Class, I want everyone to remain calm. Starting with the back row, I want you to rapidly exit to the outside. Stay away from the walls and go directly to the athletic field. Josh, would you lead the way."

Mark milled about with the rest of the students. Principal Hernandez, after making a rapid evaluation of the building's condition and making sure there were no injuries, addressed the students. "Those of you who walk to school are free to head for your respective homes. I must admonish you to avoid the fronts of any buildings that are made of brick due to the danger of crumbling facades and the danger of after-shocks. In other words, stay off Main Street, and be alert for downed power lines. Do not, under any circumstances, attempt to move them. The school will be closed possibly into next week while an assessment is made of the damage. State inspectors will have to examine our buildings to make sure they are safe. It may be a few days or it could be several weeks before classes will resume. You will be notified."

He no sooner finished than Mark was running.

* * *

The Man was frantic. This was his first earthquake experience. He'd been taking a stroll west along Main Street from Rosie's Bar for a couple of block to the parking lot behind Steven's General Store where he'd left his car. The initial shaking had knocked him down onto his hands and knees and he found himself scrambling, not to get up but to find a safe spot. As he looked back the way he had come, the entire brick front of the second story above the TV store crashed down onto parked cars and all the way across the street toward the Post Office.

The shaking was so fierce he had difficulty even crawling but he hunkered down under the bed of a delivery truck parked in front of the clothing store. Glass was all over the sidewalk as the huge windows of the clothing store, the real estate company and the insurance place exploded. And then it stopped and it was deadly quiet for a moment until sirens began to wail.

How bad was it, he wondered? He'd torn up the knees of a brand new pair of jeans crawling across the concrete. He wondered about the schools, particularly Dalton Middle School. That building is entirely brick and was built way back before they were requiring earthquake measures. Maybe, and one can only hope, it collapsed, and had crushed the life out of some very deserving punks.

Looking toward Cedar Avenue, he saw a kid running like a bat out of Hell. Son-of-a-Bee, it's that Goodwin bastard! Damn, there is nothing I can do. If this had only happened at night, I might have had a good chance to have bashed him over the head and toss him into a pile of rubble. Life isn't fair.

CHAPTER TWENTY-SIX

Vince Swanson left DGF before the shaking stopped and drove as swiftly as the rubble littered streets would permit. Main was blocked in front of the Post Office. There was a pile of bricks and debris extending from sidewalk to sidewalk. The entire front of the second story from the McDougall building, which housed the TV and Appliance Store, collapsed into the street, so he drove on down Riverside to Washington. The Marquee at the theater was hanging at a forty-five degree angle but both the Baptist and Catholic churches looked untouched, except for the long time landmark, the free-standing bell tower at the corner of Washington and Palm. It was nothing but a pile of rubble.

Turning onto Palm, his heart leaped. Huge pieces were missing from the front of the Elementary school and his eyes frantically scanned the crowd of children in the playground. Oh, thank God. There were about fifty kids and several teachers out on the playground, well away from the building, which had sustained significant cosmetic damage. And there was Michael, playing on the swings, the child seemed to be taking the whole thing in stride, laughing and waving like it was an ordinary day when he noticed his father driving up. Vince talked to the teachers before picking up his son, and was informed that the school would be closed for several days. Once they were in the Lexus, he continued on down Forest Drive toward the Middle School. Candice was nowhere in sight. A very foxy looking lady spotted him and walked over to see who he was looking for.

"Hello. I'm Mrs. Turner, one of the teachers here. Who are you looking for?"

"Vince Swanson. Looking for my daughter, Candice."

"Candice? Oh you mean Candy. She already left for home. Should darned near be there by this time."

"Everyone alright?"

"Got some minor damage but no injuries." She saw Michael in the Lexus. "How do things look up at the elementary school?"

"Building has significant damage to its facade," Vince told her. "However I have no idea what the inside looks like. No injuries there either, I'm told, but the lady I talked to thought it would be closed for a couple of weeks. I was really happy to see that my son was okay."

She looked through the window at the boy bouncing around in the back seat. "Hey young fellow? Were you scared of all the shaking?"

"Heck no. I'm making me another earthquake. I ain't a fraidy cat."

Vince smiled. "I'm glad to hear that." Wow, he was thinking, eyeing the woman's long legs under a red mini. "I'd better move on and see how we fared at home. Thank God everyone is alright."

* * *

Candy had actually walked down Main as far as the Burger Pit. At Palm there was already a city truck and men placing a barricade and Main looked like a war zone. Rubble everywhere. Cutting through the City Parking Lot to Washington she was looking everywhere, intently curious. Baptist Church looked okay from the outside but several of the older houses along Washington were missing their chimneys. One of them, next door to Shannon's house, had fallen inward and smashed through the roof. Wow! Movie took a hit too. Their big . . . whatever it was called . . . marquee? . . . was hanging at a funny angle. That's quick. There were barricades all round there too.

As she started up her driveway she heard a sound and turned to see her father arriving home at the same moment. He stepped out of the car and she was surprised when he asked, "Everything all right with you, honey?"

Did he call me honey? She didn't tell him about the horrifying near miss with the light fixture. "Lots of minor damage,

332

you know. Mostly falling ceiling tile, broken windows and some loose bricks. Principal says the school will be closed for the rest of the week until State inspectors check it out and for cleanup."

"Michael wasn't even scared. Did it frighten you, honey?"

There it was again. Honey? Not once in her life had her father called her honey. It gave her some strange feelings she didn't understand. Did it take an earthquake to turn her into a person as far as her father was concerned? "It scared me plenty, but I knew right away what it was. To me hurricanes and tornadoes are a lot scarier."

"I see the Goodwin's lost their chimney but ours is standing."

She hadn't looked that way and as they walked up the drive she glanced back. There was Mark, already busy with a wheelbarrow removing the bricks and mortar. He didn't look up.

"Glad you're all right. Phones are out so I couldn't call home." They were standing in the driveway. "Oh oh! I see we have some damage to the front porch. Aside from that the house looks sound from the outside. Our fireplace looks intact. Had major damage at the warehouse. We probably have a weeks worth of work getting everything off the floor and back onto the racks. Thought I'd come home and check on you guys, then go back down and get things organized. Let's go in and see how your mother took it."

Her dad was talking to her, just like she was a real person. It was the most she could remember her father ever saying to her and it felt good.

Inside, the house was a shambles. Her mother was a collector and a pack rat. She liked pictures, plants, bric-a-brac and porcelain dolls. None of these fare well in a major earthquake.

"What's going on here?" Vince's brow furrowed when he saw what his wife was doing.

"I am packing mine and the kids things. We're going home."

"Oh no!" Candy was frantic.

"What do you mean, home? This is our home. Where do you expect to live in Montgomery?"

"With Grandma Swanson, if need be. I'm not going through another one of these." As she was speaking an aftershock rattled dishes and caused the dining room chandelier to sway. She screamed, "we're having another one. Oh my God! Michael? Where's Michael?" She was hysterical.

"Bette, get hold of yourself. Michael is right here . . . somewhere." He looked around. "We are safer in a wood framed house than we ever were in a Bama hurricane. We are home and we are not going anywhere."

"At least you know a hurricane is coming. Don't try to talk me out of it. I'm taking the kids and leaving."

"You can't do this to me," Candy exclaimed. "For the first time in my life I got all these friends and I got all these wonderful activities at school. I'm getting good grades. I'm not going. I'm staying here with Daddy." She moved to stand next to him and received a further surprise as he put his arm around her and gave her a squeeze.

"You two can do whatever you want. Michael and I are leaving on the first flight out of Clarksdale."

Michael came trotting in carrying a cage. "Hey Dad, look at my pet rat. Ain't even scared. Is the big shaking all done?"

"Yeah son, I believe it is. We will have a number of little ones, but nothing like the big one."

"Michael, get your things together. We are leaving."
He hadn't been part of the argument so he didn't understand. "Where we going, Mommie?"

"You and I are leaving. We are going to grandma Swanson's. Your sister and your dad are staying here."
"I don't want to go to grandmas. I want to stay here with Candy and daddy." He moved over to stand next to his sister, his arm about her waist. She put her arm around him and her father extended his arm to include them both.

"We'll talk about this later," her father gave both kids a squeeze. "I want you to take a sedative and lie down until things have calmed down. Candy and I are going to take a ride down to the plant to see how bad things are and get the cleanup process started. Come on, honey. Ride down to the plant with me. At least you were born with some good sense."

"I wanna go too," Michael was jumping up and down. "I wanna go too."

"You can't leave me here all alone," her mother cried.

Her father let out a long sigh. "All right Bette, here is what we'll do. You ride down there with us and after you'd had a chance to sort things out you'll feel better. Things won't seem so dire after you calm down."

"Oh dear God," she wailed, "I can't stay here."

* * *

Mark was surprised to hear the phone ringing and tripped over some loose masonry and stumbled through the front door. "Hi. Here's Mark. What's up?"

"Marcus, it's Ollie." His friend was so excited he could hardly talk.

"How 'bout that? Phone was dead not ten minutes ago. What's up Ollie? You got a bunch of damage over there?"

"Heck no, hardly a scratch. Grandpa Frazier lost his chimney though. It fell all over his driveway and he can't get his cars out of the garage. Dad said if we would go over and clean it up, after he gets through with all the newspaper stuff, he'd ride the Harley over there and we could practice riding it. Can you go?"

"Lost our chimney. Been cleanin' up the mess. Man Ollie. We just had an earthquake and your dad is going bike riding?"

"Hey man. It was just an earthquake, not the end of the world."

Looking out the window at his own pile of rubble Mark was thinking, what the heck? Just tell my folks what the problem is. This crap isn't in anybody's way. "Tell ya what, buddy. Better'n what I was gonna do. Was gonna wander 'round town and look at all the damage but that can wait. I'm outta here. Only a mile, so I'll change into my Superman threads and fly right over. Meetcha there."

Mark ran all the way and actually beat Ollie. Ollie's grandfather was standing out front surveying the missing chimney. That's when he heard a wonderful sound, a motorcycle's roar on the bridge. To his surprise Ollie was riding the bike with his dad driving the car right behind him.

"Oh man," Ollie said as the machine spluttered to a stop. "Oh man!"

"Hi Mark," Mr. Frazier said. "Thought I'd just follow Ollie over then head on back. There's a great deal of news to gather and a paper that needs printing so I don't know when I can return. You two get your job done, and then you can putter around for a while. And I mean, putter. These machines can be danger-ous even in the hands of an experienced rider. See you latter, Ollie. Probably at home."

Mark watched Ollie's dad talk to Grandpa Frazier for a while and then he backed out and drove away. "Gee Ollie, I didn't know you knew how to ride."

"No problem. Pretty much like a heavy bicycle with a mo-tor. But oh man what a rush!"

"Come on Ollie. Let's see how fast we can get this crap moved. I want a turn on that mother."

* * *

"I'll say this," said Troy Valimar, owner of the Green Spot Café who was talking to some of the local business owners. "That was a dandy. Frazier, down at the paper was telling me it was a six point five. I hear there are many sections of the town without power. Thank goodness ours is not off."

"So's mine," Carly Stevens from the market next door told them. "Strangely enough, most of the downtown has electricity. Guess it's 'cause we're adjacent to the power station.

"Got any damage in the store?" Troy asked, pouring coffee for the three men in the booth. Stevens, Turner and Deiter."

"Are you kiddin'? I shouldn't even be here. Every aisle in the store is blocked with canned goods, boxes and broken glass. Thought I'd check around to see if I can round up some high school kids to help with the restocking."

Ken Deiter was looking out the window. "Hear the entire area north of Washington Street is blacked out from the river to the mountains. No problems at the agency except we lost nearly every window in the showroom. None at home either other than no phone, no electric. Goodwin's lost their chimney. So did the McAlister's." He nodded towards the parking lot. Looks to me like most of our residents have ventured downtown. No cooking facilities at home so they're looking for a place to eat. I'd say you're gonna inherit the whole bunch, including my family who, as we speak, are on their way."

Troy grinned. "Bad enough I got all these media people here." He nodded toward five men and a woman in the large booth toward the back. One of them was reading something in-side this morning's Dalton paper and the front page was fully in view. The black headline stated: SERIAL KILLER STRIKES AGAIN.

"Boy this is all we need," Ken Deiter was shaking his head. "Kinda puts little ole Dalton on the map."

Peggy, the waitress stopped next to her bosses shoulder. "Got an idea, Troy. Why don't you have someone go over to the Baptist Church and borrow some of their tables and chairs from their activities center? We could put a couple in the lobby and a couple in the open space in front of the kitchen. You guys discussing the quake or the murder?"

"At the moment we're talking 'bout both. You got a great idea there, Peggy. I'll get the boy right on it. Those tables seat eight. Four of 'em would give us room for thirty-two more. Five-o'clock. Be dark pretty soon. Ummm. Our phones are up so I'll call home and see if the girls can come in. Gonna be more than we can handle."

As Troy stood he remarked, "Understand Frank has picked up Elaine's live-in boyfriend as a suspect. Turned him over to the county sheriff."

"Doesn't surprise me," Carly sighed. "Raymond Coquillard. Never has amounted to a tinker's damn. I guess he used to knock her about on a regular basis. Sheriff had to go out there a couple of times last month. Damned out of work hippie nogood-nic. Got fired from DGF several months back. He's the kinda of guy that doesn't want to work. Content to sponge off some hard working woman."

"Beyond me," Peggy was curious, "why someone as attractive and as smart as Elaine would put up with that kind of abuse."

"Low self esteem, I guess. Well, will you look at this; here comes the Swanson's. Talk about pretty women and abusive men. Although I don't reckon that applies to him."
Troy agreed. "Way I hear it, Elaine gave as good as she got. That damned f . . . "

Peggy nudged him, "Watch your language, boss. We have children present."

"I was going to say, He deserves whatever he gets."

* * *

"Man I can't believe this is happening," Mark stole another look at the Harley. "If I was only Superman I'd be able to move this pile of crap in two seconds."

"We're gaining on it," Ollie told him; sweat streaking through the dust covering his face. He looked up at the sky. "We're fast runnin' outta daylight. Should get through in time for a ride though."

A half-hour later Mark was grinning. "Hey buddy. We musta set some sort of record for moving . . . who knows how many tons of stone and crap." They were sweeping the drive clean when Grandpa Frazier walked up, smiling broadly.

"Good job. Here you go boys." He handed each of them a twenty-dollar bill.

Ollie stood with his mouth open, "Heck Grandpa, you don't need . . . "

"I don't want to hear it." He nodded toward the motorcycle. "Let's see what you guys can do. Wasn't for my bum leg, I'd be on that hog myself."

For over an hour the two boys took turns riding alone, then rotated from front to rear as they rode in tandem. It was pitch dark so they were using the headlight.

When Grandpa Frazier called it to a halt, all Mark could say was, "Man oh man oh man. What a hawg.'

"You got that right," Ollie moaned. "Gonna be a hundred years before I'm sixteen and can legally ride it on the streets."

"At least," Mark agreed.

* * *

Candy was enjoying every minute of the time she was spending with her father at DGF. She'd never been near the place. He was giving his family a guided tour of the entire operation and as he had promised, everything was pretty much of a mess. They began in the offices, accounting, scheduling, and all that good stuff. The plant was in operation in spite of the quake. Nearly half of the employees remained on the job. Those worried about their families had been sent home. Those working were either doing their normal tasks or were busy trying to get the scattered merchandise back on the shelves.

There was the weirdest feeling in Candy's stomach as she passed a desk with a huge spray of flowers lying on it. Not in a vase or anything, merely lying next to one of those brown and white plastic name things. Elaine Garcia was printed in gold. Oh my Gawd. She was glad when they moved on and out into the plant itself. All the automated equipment used to load trucks with a jillion items for maybe twenty-five or thirty supermarkets each fascinated her. DGF had everything. Produce, house wares, cases and cases of canned stuff. And then they were in the meat department.

Place was neat and clean and yet it had a peculiar smell. Blood, she thought. The huge saws, the grinders, sharp knives everywhere. Cows, cut in half, hanging from metal hooks on rolling tracks. Watching a man cutting inch thick steaks from a slab of beef on a powerful meat saw made her shudder. There it was, she thought. A saw large enough to cut off somebody's legs, and one of the half-dozen men working there today could be the killer. Strange thought, for that is what she had suggested to the Kryptonites. Yuck!

Michael, as usual, was snooping into everything. Even her mother seemed interested in the tour and was much calmer although in no hurry to return to the house.

"The electricity is off so we can't even cook," she told them.

Her dad looked at his watch. "Been here an hour and a half already. Well, no problem, Bette. When I came through town earlier, the Green Spot is operating. We'll have to detour down to Lincoln since Main is blocked at Locust. I'll treat." He sighed. "Little early yet, but let's head downtown."

"Oh goody," Michael jumped down from where he had climbed on top of a stack of pallets. "I wanna hangaburger and a coke. Want a hangaburger anna coke."

All the way out to the car and during the entire drive to the restaurant he kept it up until Candy wanted to scream. As they entered the overflowing restaurant, Michael continued chattering. "I want French fries and lots of catshup."

Candy snapped. "If you don't shut up, I'll give you catsup all over your bratty head."

"Good evening folks." The restaurant owner offered his hand. "Since you're here, I guess the plant must have survived."

"Evening, Troy. Pretty much but we have lots of cleanup. There is little structural damage other than a few loose bricks and some broken glass. Looks like it hasn't done your business any harm. How long is the wait?"

"Shouldn't be too long. Sent my handyman down to the

church for some extra tables and chairs. With a dozen out of town officers and all these media people from all over the place and half the town without electricity, busiest we've ever been. We made it through the quake all right. Lot of stuff fell off the shelves in the storage and would you believe it? Grease actually slopped out of the deep fryer. Here comes John. Got some space up front and at the back and with some rearranging we'll get everybody fed. It'll only take a few minutes set up."

Candy's father took her completely off guard when he told Troy, "I'll give your man a hand. How 'bout you, Candy, want to carry some chairs?"

"Cool," she replied.

* * *

The Man's expression was dour. Even this early in the day his favorite spot next to the window was taken. Had to sit on a stool at the far end of the counter. His face brightened when he saw the Swanson's walk in. All these weeks and he hadn't met the man face to face. Pimp suit and a tie. Guy looks like a Mafia hit man. Since that rotten old man Dalton is gone, wouldn't hurt to plant a few seeds, let him know how much he knew about the meat packing business. Wonder where Troy's gonna seat 'em. Place looks packed. Well, well, well. Guy's got it covered. Here comes John with a truckload of tables and chairs. What's all the gesturing? Must be talkin' 'bout it. What the hell? Swanson of all people is going out to help unload. So's the teeny-bopper. Maybe I should volunteer. Naw. Best not. Little redhead is part of that Goodwin gang. I'll wait till they're seated; maybe get their orders in. Patience my man.

* * *

As soon as the Swanson's were seated, Peggy made her way over, bringing a tray with water, silver and napkins. Mr. Swanson winked at the pretty waitress. "So where are all of these out of town people staying?"

The waitress shrugged. "Other than the Ezyinn, we don't have any lodging here. Way I hear it a lot of them rented cars from Deiter. Plan to drive up to the lodge at Sandstone Lake."

"Guess the earthquake threw a monkey wrench in their plans."

"At least it takes their minds off the murders for a while."

"That was a shock. The Garcia woman I mean. She was my personal secretary out at the plant."

"No kidding? How horrible. Well . . . the sheriff pulled the Garcia woman's lover in for questioning. Guy's a worthless, lazy and abusive type, so who knows? Could be it's him. The newspaper and TV people hightailed it right over to the jail." She looked around at the crowd then sighed when she saw Troy's two girls come in. "Would you like to order now? Running a special tonight. Breaded veal cutlets, choice of potato and fresh vegetables, with soup or salad."

"Mmmm. Breaded Veal. One of my favorites." Vince told her. "I already know I want a green salad with blu-cheese and a coffee."

The waitress turned to his wife but she waved her away, studying the menu.

"Honey mustard on my salad," Candy was looking around to see if any of her friends were there, "but I'll have the stuffed pork chops, with baked potato, and a chocolate shake."

"And how 'bout you, young man?"

"I wanna hangaburger and a Coke and French fries." Michael emphasized each item by pounding the table with his spoon with each word. "And lots of catshup."

Bette looked up from the menu. "Michael! If you don't stop that I'm going to turn you over my knee. You're giving me a headache."

Her father saw the surprised look in Candy's eyes and he understood. "'Bout time, Bette. 'Bout time," he mumbled under his breath. Partly my fault but that kid is getting out of control.

"How 'bout you ma'am? Would you like a salad?"
"Please," she said lamely, "with Ranch and I believe I'll also have the pork chops." She sighed, and looked at her daughter. And a chocolate shake."

Candy turned at the sound of a familiar voice when someone called out. "Oh, hi Candy." It was Heather Deiter. Mr. Deiter was looking at Candy's father as he eyed the four remaining seats at the long table. "Mind if we join you?"

"Our pleasure," her dad told them.
Heather plopped down next to Candy. Charlie sat catty cornered from her and he smirked her way and then winked. First time

she'd seen him since the encounter over by the Pit. Man! Is he's good lookin' or what. She turned to Heather and the way they went at it one would think the two girls hadn't seen each other for months.

"Be right back to bring you set-ups, and menus," the waitress told the Deiters.

* * *

It's time, the Man was thinking. Sliding off the stool he pulled his shoulders back and moved confidently over to where the family sat. The little redhead didn't even look his way; too busy discussing important teenage crap with the albino bimbo. It's possible they don't suspect me since they gotta know I'm here. "Excuse me, Mr. Swanson. I don't believe we've met." *He extended his hand but eventually let it drop when Swanson didn't move.*

"I know who you are," *the slim man growled.*
"I realize, with the earthquake and all that, this might not be a good time, but if you ever need any help down at the plant, I'm one of the best butchers in Southern California. Be glad to give you my number."

"Don't hold your breath. Was reviewing your personnel files. From what I read, you're nothing but a slime-bag."

What did he say? The Man stood there, unbelieving. A horrible anger quickly boiled deep inside. "My file? Those records are supposed to be confidential. How did you . . .?"

"Be that as it may, old man Dalton had filed them away in the Past Employee's drawer. Something my new secretary has mentioned made me curious. You're a real piece of work. Good day, sir!"

If I had one of my meat cleavers I'd chop this S.O.B up into stew meat. He turned abruptly and returned to his stool.

* * *

"How you doing, Frank old buddy? Got one table left. You better grab it. Where's the misses tonight?" Troy was directing the sheriff and his three kids to their seats.

"Looks like you got more business than you can handle." Frank was waving at some people waiting to be seated. "Maggie's in San Diego on that church choir thing.

"Business I can handle, sheriff. I guess you and Ralph pretty

342

much have your hands full, what with another murder and an earthquake?"

"Yep, we do. Got the whole town barricaded off. Thought I'd bring the family down here for dinner. Even if the Missus was home our electric is out. 'Course the Misses can't cook anyway. Haw haw haw."

"Looks to me like she's been doing pretty well by you." To the sheriff's two sons, 10 year old Rick and 11 year old Frank Junior, he asked, "how you boys doing tonight? Keeping your dad in line?"

"Yeah," the older one joked, "it's a tough job but somebody has to do it."

Frank glanced at his thirteen year old daughter who was trying to catch the Goodwin girl's attention. She made a face. He knew she'd much rather be spending the evening with her peers but until this killer is caught she's gonna be on a short leash. "What's tonight's special, Troy?"

"Breaded veal cutlets. One of your favorites, Frank."

"With mashed taters and gravy?"

"I better check and see how many are left. Got a carton of them today fresh from DGF and they are nearly all gone. Since most of the town is without electricity, we've had an overflow crowd in here. By the way Frank, is there anything to the rumor going around about problems at the dam?"

"That's all it is, a rumor. State is sending a couple of Geologists up there to check it out. All I need is for the dam to let go, as if three unsolved murders and an earthquake isn't enough." He glanced up as Peggy came with menus and Troy went to the kitchen.

Joyce ordered without looking at one. "I'll have the western, bacon cheese burger with fries and a large coke."
"Might as well of taken her to the Pit." Frank grinned.
Peggy nodded and smiled. "Since you've got all this outside help are you and Ralph making any headway on the Garcia case?"

"Got four left," Troy called from the kitchen pass-through.

Frank looked at his two boys who nodded. "Put a hold on three of 'em."

"You think Elaine's boy-friend is the one?" Peggy asked.

"That's what we're thinkin', sweetie. So does the county

sheriff and so does the FBI. Might even be our serial killer."

* * *

The arrival of the sheriff and his teenage kids only diverted the Man's attention for a minute then he returned to glaring at the back of Vince Swanson's head, watching as the waitress brought their salads. Peggy gushed over them. *The man's wife seems terribly unhappy. Husband's probably an ass. Could hear the man and the teenager talking and laughin, probably about him. What do you expect from a pig and a sow.*

The Man's glare intensified. *Swanson's were chattering away, talking to the Deiter's. All assholes. They don't have any idea who they are trying to put down. Too bad that jerk doesn't know how close I came to snuffing out his daughter the other night.* He grinned. *If he had, Troy wouldn't have to worry 'bout running out of cutlets. They're asking for it. What was it he called the little twerp? Clarice or something?* The girl's auburn haired mother refreshed his memory.

"Candice," he heard the woman say, "you are such a pig. Stop eating with your fingers. What do you think forks are for?" Mr. Swanson snorted in agreement. "She even stabs food with her fork then picks it off and eats it. I suppose when she starts dating and her beau takes her someplace nice to eat, she'll be eating with her fingers."

"Girl has no manners at all. Doubt she'll ever have a boyfriend. Look at what a gentleman Michael is."

"Piggy Wiggy," was Michael's response, dumping so much catsup on his fries it poured off his plate onto the table.

The Man watched the cutie who seemed to be way off in a private world of her own, but then she was quite alert, eavesdropping on the conversation coming from the next table. He too was instantly curious.

* * *

Ordinarily Frank wouldn't discuss such a thing with a civilian, but with all these college educated, wannabee cops in town, he no longer cared. "Tell ya what, Peggy. We're making some progress. Ole man Frazier was fishing earlier today at that hole where Turtle Creek leaves his property and empties into the river. 'Bout an hour before the quake hit. Right there on the bank he found what was left of a ladies blouse, some pants and a bloody

344

pair of panties. To me the biggest clue was a blood stained blue plastic garbage bag. Goodwin kid told us the guy who robbed their house was using one that color. I've seen those blue ones before but I don't recall where from. Turned all these clues over to the big boys from Clarksdale. They seem to want to run the show, so let 'em. I'll have a coffee, Sweetheart."

* * *

The Man smirked when he heard the sheriff list his so called clues. So what if they traced the bag back to DGF? Give them a couple of hundred suspects. What I got my mind set on is that pretty little piece of jailbait. Way her folks rag on her, she ought to tell the jerks where to stuff it. 'Slime bag' huh? Sorta glad I didn't get to her the other night. Kinda like dating. Thrill of the chase. Shouldn't be too tough. See her all over the place. He sat for a while longer, steaming. At length he took out the small notebook. There was a list of names followed by captions that explained what he thought of either the person listed or her parents.

1. Gretchen Heinz - 8 years old
Foreigner   Father's a Kraut talking S.O.B.
2. Eugenia "Pepper" Morris - 11 years old
Old man's a Black S.O.B. do-gooder
3. Laura Goodwin -8 years old   Eric's a bullhead-
ed S.O.B.
4. Jenny Lou Horiwitz - truck drivers wife   Blind
as a dog turd
5. Elaine Garcia - Pretty little Wetback   Cast iron pussy
She's gonna be my toy.
6. Mark Goodwin   Knows too much   He's next

Glancing toward the Swanson family, the man took out his pen. Very slowly he clicked the ballpoint then added another name to his list. *Well, Mr. High and Mighty you can join the list of those I intend to punish. Maybe later on I'll do the little boy,* he wrote:

7. Candice Swanson   Pretty little jailbait. Looks good enough to eat.   Dad's a prick.

CHAPTER TWENTY-SEVEN

Vince was happy to find Bette much more tranquil on Friday morning than she was following yesterday's quake. Probably some of the things Reverend Johnson from the Baptist Church had told her when he stopped by their table last night at the Green Spot to say hello, knowing they were newcomers, wanting to get in a plug for his church. When Bette expressed her panic and desire to leave the area, he pulled up a chair and had a very reassuring chat with her and it seemed to work. She looked frantic each time there was an aftershock, but there was no further talk of leaving.

Wonder if we have a Friday morning paper or did the quake shut down the presses? Pulling open the heavy, hand carved oak door he had so lovingly restored, he stepped out into the crisp early morning air. There it was like death and taxes, in the middle of the drive. He bent to pick up the paper and hearing a sound from across the street, he glanced up. The Goodwin boy was alongside their house hauling away the last of the debris from the fallen chimney with a wheelbarrow. Hard working lad. Damn if that doesn't give me an idea.

He tucked the paper under his arm and crossed the street. "Mornin'."

Mark looked up and grinned. "Howdy. What's shakin'?"

"Not much I hope. Looks like your house came through the quake okay."

"Pretty good. Except for the chimney. We got a few cracks, genuine lathe and plaster, you know. Mom lost some of her china when the cabinet fell over on the dining room table. A few things like that. We're lucky the chimney fell into the yard instead of through the roof."

Vince was taking stock of the tall, muscular lad. "We didn't have much damage. Lot of my wife's knickknacks fell.
"Looks like you got some problems with your porch, the footings sort of crumbled."

"Yeah, I have. In fact it's worse than I originally surmised. Been watching you work and I was wondering, are you any good as a handyman?"

"Hey man, I'm good at everything I try."

"Is that a fact?" Vince admired a person who was confident. "Then I take it you've done some carpenter work?"

"I've done a little. Enough to know what it's all about."

"What I need is to have someone jack that corner up and replace the footings. The problem is if it isn't taken care of at once I'm going to lose part of my attic. Maybe even some of the roof. I figure with all the quake damage in town, it's going to be hard to find a contractor."

Mark glanced across the street at the damage and made an appropriate face and a sound with his mouth.

"I've been concentrating on the inside but I'd like to work on the outside at the same time. This quake gives me an excuse to jump right on it." And, he was thinking, I am sure there will be some insurance money. "Thought maybe I could hire you on weekends and evenings, whenever you have some free time, to give me a hand. I want to restore this old house to its original condition. Could pay you . . . maybe seven bucks an hour."

That got Mark's attention and he looked more closely at the rundown structure.

The boy's calculating a great many hours, Vince was thinking, turning at a sound. Candy came out the front door also looking for the paper. She was in her pajamas.
Spotting the two men she walked across to join them. "Hi Mark."

"Hi Red. You always run around town in your PJ's?"
Mr. Swanson placed his arm about her and she snuggled to him. It didn't register that she was taking advantage for as long as this wonderful stage lasted. "You're up awfully early, aren't you Sugar?"

"I woke up and wondered what the paper might have to say 'bout the quake. You know, the damage and all that stuff. I guess they couldn't print . . . Oh! You got it already."

"Yeah, I got it." Turning back to Mark he continued. "I've decided to go ahead and restore this house. Was going to lease it till we could buy or build what we wanted as we first planned. The more I see of this one, the more I want to rebuild it. Things got touchy right after the quake. Bette wanted to take the kids and go back to Montgomery."

"No way!" Mark looked at Candy.

"You mean you'd actually care if I left Dulltown?"

"Who the heck would miss you? Don't care if you stay or go. Was just thinking about the club. Shouldn't be too hard to find someone to replace you."

"It would take three people to replace me, but knock yourself out."

Mr. Swanson grinned, knowing what was going on, remembering when he used to torment Bette the same way. What has it been? Fifteen years? Already? "As I was saying, I was trying to make a deal with . . . uh . . . Mark? . . . to help me paint and remodel."

"Oh? Can I help?"

"Can you paint?"

"Of course. I can swing a pretty mean hammer too."

"What do you say, Mark, think you can handle it?"

"Cool. When do you want me to start?" Again he looked across at the damage. "Better do something to that porch right away. Can see from here that the attic gable is already sagging."

Candy was watching and listening, obviously fascinated.

"Okay Mark. Let's go across the street and so I can tell you what I have in mind."

* * *

As the trio started to cross the street, a white Camaro cut them off, nosing into the curb. At first Candy didn't recognize the driver until he called out.

"Hey Mark." It was coach Donnelley who hollered through the open window. "You're the man I'm looking for." Stepping out of the Dodge sedan he stood with the door open. "The game with Clarksdale is on. Even though they had some shaking down that way, there was no damage to the gym. The phone at my place is out but they got through to the school office so I'm making the grand circle early, trying to catch all the players."

"Cool," exclaimed Mark. "I'm raring to go."

"What about the cheerleaders?" Candy noticed the coach looking at her father and in an instant corrected the situation. "I'm sorry. Mr. Donnelley, I'd like very much for you to meet my father."

"My pleasure. Charles Donnelly." The coach extended his hand, purposely-embarrassing Candy by saying, "You sure do have a good looking daughter."

"Vince Swanson." The two men shook hands. "We like to think so, but don't tell her or she'll get a bighead."
Mark was smirking at her and Candy knew she had the type of fair skin prominent with redheads, which could turn nearly as red as her hair and she could feel it. Such a happy glow and her father had no idea an earthquake had turned her world inside out.

"I hadn't thought about the cheer-leading squad, but Candy's right, they should be there. I'll look up Mrs. Turner and have her contact the others. She probably doesn't even know the game hasn't been canceled. The bus will be at Riverside Park at 5:30 instead of at the school. I'll see you there, Mark . . . and Candy. Nice to have met you Mr. Swanson.

* * *

Standing in front of the house, Mark was shaking his head. "I'll tell ya, Mr. Swanson, looks like right here is where we need to start."

Candy remembered her dad calling the porch a lovely work of art. It extended across the entire front of the house and had four pair of two-story tall columns supporting the porch roof and overhanging attic. There was a banister with a carved handrail and small turned spindles. Everything in desperate need of paint, some needed to be repaired or replaced. The biggest problem was the column supports had been made from stone and mortar with no actual footing. These were deteriorating and the one at the left corner had disintegrated during the earthquake permitting the corner of the roof to sag nearly eight inches. She wondered if Mark had the smarts it took to fix it. Acted like he did, but, knowing how cocky he was, that could be an act.

"Want me to start on it today?" the tall lad asked. "I got all day till the team bus comes."

Turned out her dad was smart enough to question Mark's abilities. "Just for my own information, how do you propose to lift up that corner and save the columns?"
Mark was fascinated, itching to dive in. "I'd better jump right on it or that corner is going to give way. I'll have to anchor those two columns to the structure or they'll be laying in the yard."

"Got any ideas?"
"Yeah. I know a guy, house mover. Morrie Stanowitz. Think he'd let me borrow one of his jacks. Could raise that corner back up till it's level then pour some new footings. Problem is . . . your old porch floor, especially on this end, has a bunch of dry rot and should be replaced. I remember watching the Norman Brothers when they redid the rotten porch on the Banker's house. They used jacks and four by fours on two by six pads. Heck, I can do that. First I'd prop up the roof beam, pour some footings, rebuild this end of the porch and put the columns back."

Mark glanced at Candy. She watched and listened, fascinated. Why should he care what she thought?
Vince cocked his head. "Are you certain you can do all that?"

"Heck yeah. Like I told ya, I can do anything. I try to figure out how to do things and have them done while other people stand around arguing about where to start."

"Looks like I've found the right man. So? Can you start right away?"

"I'm going to need some tools and material."

Candy was staring at her neighbor, her eyes filled with surprise. "Man-o-man, Mark. You got it wired."
He made a face.

"Take a look in the garage. I believe old man Clayton had similar plans before he passed away. It looks to me like he planned to replace the entire porch. There is enough tongue and groove fir in there to do the whole floor and there's also a pile of lumber stacked inside; floor joist, beams and the like. Might be a tad hard to work with since it's been stored in there for who knows how many years? Anything else you need, make a list and we'll have Turner Lumber bring it out. I'll set up an account so you can pick up the paint, nails and things like that. You know how to use power tools?"

"Damn betcha. Dad has all kinds and I use them all the

time. Got another problem today though, electricity is off."

"Allright. I have to go down to the warehouse for a while, but you go ahead and start however you think best. I'll try to get a generator from the rental yard. Think you'll find every kind of power tool you can imagine out in the garage. Just be careful is all I ask. I'd say, for appearance sake, I'd like to get the entire front shaped up before we take on the rest. Bill Turner down at the lumberyard has ordered some special paint I like to use. I'll check because it should be in. It is actually an epoxy that goes on like a thin coat of stucco. All we have to do is wire brush any peeling paint, fill any big cracks or depressions and then spread this stuff on with a brush and a plastic trowel. But first things first, I'll go see about that generator."
As soon as her dad left, Candy timidly inquired, "What do y'all want me to do?"

"First, go in and get some clothes on," Mark growled. "Then if I need ya I'll letcha know."

* * *

Mark felt slightly silly pulling the red wagon along the sidewalk, but it was the only way he could think of to transport the fifty-pound jack. Too bad he couldn't call on his Superman powers and lift up the corner. Couldn't remember the last time he'd pulled the wagon. It had been Laura's. This too gave him a funny feeling. Had to walk all the way down to Pine. Seven long blocks, right out in the open. Then come back. Made him feel like a target.

Getting a jack from Morrie turned out to be a good idea. He threw the jack and Mark's wagon into the bed of his pickup and drove it over to Swanson's house. Gave him a few pointers and tips, even drew him a diagram of how it might be done. When Morrie left, Mark heaved a huge sigh, studying the drawing and thinking, it was just about the way he had planned on doing it. Man! I'm smarter than I thought I was.

Candy was sitting on the steps holding the kitten, which had its head up against her cheek. "Are we having fun pwaying wiff our widdle wed wagon?"

"Stuff it Red. Just stay out of my way. This is a man's job."
"I hope one shows up, otherwise nothing is going to get done."

Before he began any construction he went across the street

351

to fetch an extension ladder. Standing it against the gable next to the two unsupported columns he could see a four-inch gap between the top of the columns and the sagging roof beam. In the garage he discovered what he needed, an unopened plastic package of six large metal screw eyes. Using a hammer and a long screwdriver, he turned these into each side of the beam directly above the columns. Then he wrapped a length of rope round and round the columns and secured them to the metal eyes.

Candy watched, spellbound. "Wow! You go up and down that ladder like a monkey."

"Superman," he told her. "The ladder is just for looks."

"So, Superman? Do you think that little piece of rope is gonna hold those big heavy posts if you can get the roof jacked up?"

"Rope is to keep them from falling. I'll get them propped up." She had pointed out a problem that had nagged him. How could he prop them up until the footings were replaced?

She giggled. "I know. Superman can hold them up while I build a new footing."

Ignoring her he dragged a twenty-foot length of four by four from the garage. Scrambling up the ladder he dropped the end of a metal tape down to obtain a measurement from the ceiling to the top of the jack. Then he used a handsaw to cut the four by four to the right length, nearly eighteen feet. Standing it on the jack he discovered he had a problem. No way to hold the post in place and operate the jack. "Uh . . . Red?"

"Don't look at me," Candy was cuddling her kitten, stoking the soft fur. "I'm doin' what ya told me. Staying out of your way."

"Aw come on. Sometimes my mouth gets me into trouble."

"All right, let's hear you say it."

"Say what? That I'm sorry?"

"No. That you are a jerk."

"Hey, I'll tell you I'm sorry but I ain't gonna say that."

"Then hold the pole yourself. I'm going to walk over to Shannon's and see how their house survived." She started down the drive.

"Wait. Come on Red. So I'm a jerk."

"What did you say?"

"I said . . . I . . . I'm a jerk."

She had one of those smiles he loved to hate, but he continued to hold the post in place.

"Okay. Let me put Marcus in the house then I'll help. When she returned she stood with her arms folded. "So, what do you want me to do?"

"I'm gonna hold it steady and you stick that metal rod through the hole in the jack and turn it. It'll screw up and push the post up. Morrie says one of these would lift twenty tons."

She had to kneel with her torso against his leg as she followed his instructions. Glancing her way he frowned but she began to turn the screw using the steel rod made for that purpose.

"Did you see all that damage downtown?" she asked.

Something was going on that he didn't understand. She rocked forward and back as the metal rod passed in front of her chest and with each motion the softness of her breast pressed against his leg. It was causing a reaction in his own body and he was forcing himself to think about other things.

"Yeah." He told her. I ran all the way down Main to Park on the way home right after the quake. Some of those old brick buildings took a jolt. Mc Dougalls' is a heck of a mess."

"The worst part is the quake has taken everyone's mind off the murders."

"I know. The newspaper was full of page after page of articles and pictures of quake damage. All I saw was an item on page three 'bout the Garcia woman."

"Garcia? Saw her desk yesterday when we were down at DGF. And then my dad was talking about her the other day. I guess he had a run in with your dad over the fact my dad wanted her for his personal secretary."

"Yeah. She worked for my dad ever since Dalton died."

The timbers of the attic creaked and cracked and groaned but the entire corner rose an inch, then two and three. He didn't really want her to stop, but when they had gained about six inches he told her, "better stop there for the time bein'. We're going to build a temporary wall to prop it up while we tear apart the porch. We'll worry about leveling the top beam when we get this end of the porch rebuilt."

He didn't catch the look on her face when she picked up instantly on the word, 'We.'

* * *

The Man was driving up and down nearly every street in town. It was interesting, seeing the aftermath of yesterday's quake. Nearly everybody who had an un-reinforced chimney had lost them. Fortunately most of them fell away from the struc- tures. Sidewalks were humped up in a number of places and there were a great deal of open cracks, some several inches, in the streets. City workers had another problem repairing several waterlines and Community Electric men were pulling new wires every place he looked. Several houses were off their foundations and there were two on the hillside west of town that had slid twenty-five or thirty feet down the slope.

"Pisses me off." He liked talking to himself. "Everybody's mind was occupied by the quake. Nobody is saying a word about the Garcia bitch. Out of town investigators are probably working the case, but even they had to have other things on their minds.

"Heard Carly Tarmen say that the Goodwin's lost their chim- ney. Take a drive past and see what it looks like." He smiled. "Couldn't happen to a nicer family."

When he turned off Washington onto Riverview he slowed nearly to a stop. Two people he recognized were doing some- thing in front of the Swanson place. "The Goodwin kid and his plaything. What the hell are they up to. Tearing apart the front porch?" He could see the jack and the two columns. "Man, if only there was only some way to jerk that jack out of there. Whole damn roof would come crashing down on those twirps."

The two kids never looked his way and he held his breath until he was past.

* * *

"Okay," Candy told him, "see how much help an Indian Princess Warrior can be?"

"There isn't any such thing. If you're determined to help, you can fetch me about five of those twenty foot two by fours, and two eight footers from the garage while I get some tools. All you need to do is drag them around one at a time."

"What's a two by four?"

"Oh boy, are you gonna be a big help. It's a piece of lum- ber two inches thick, four inches wide and twenty feet long."

"I'll do it, but white man speak with forked tongue."

354

"Yeah. That too." Together they constructed a very sturdy wall four foot wide and twenty feet tall with a one by four diagonal brace. For support he placed a six foot long piece of two by eight flat on the ground for the wall to sit on. First Mark went up the ladder to nail a couple of two by four stops on the back of the beam to keep the wall from falling. Using a rope over the top rung of the ladder, together they raised the wall into position and wedged it under the attic support beam to the right of the jack and post. Then Mark held the post while Candy lowered the jack so that the beam rested on the wall.

They both stepped back to look at what they'd accomplished. "Pretty impressive, don't you think?" Mark grinned "I'll say. You're smarter than I thought you were," Candy actually reached out and punched him in the shoulder.

Her remark wasn't much but it pleased him. "You ain't doin' so bad yourself.' He punched her in return. "But if I am so damn smart, why can't I solve this murder thing?"

"That reminds me of something. I was lying in bed thinking about it this morning. Your father and Mr. Heinz work for DGF. Yesterday I find out the Garcia lady worked there."

"What's your point?"

"Is this a coincidence or what?" She was chewing at her lower lip.

"What are you thinking, that this dude with the high class boots works there too?"

"Either does, or used to. I'm thinking about the blue garbage bags that came from down there. Dad gave us a tour and that included the meat processing plant. You should see the equipment they have in there. Saw a worker, a butcher I guess, cutting inch thick slices of round steak off a piece of cow. That's one big saw! Big enough to saw off Elaine Garcia's legs."

"You think there's a connection? C'mon Red, help me lower this post." When this was done he eyed the two columns hanging by the rope.

Candy looked at them uneasily, and yet asked. "What do we do? I mean if I'm right?"

As Mark studied the two columns his mind was on two subjects; murder and construction. There was over two inches clear under the columns. "Hold on a minute. Got an idea." In the garage he found what he wanted. It was a five-foot long, heavy metal rod, sharpened on one end for digging. "Here's what I want to do," he told her, laying the four by four on the porch so the bulk of the piece of lumber rested on the part that was solid. A couple of feet extended past the edge of the porch.

"So what do you think about my idea?" she asked.
"I'm getting some bad vibes, that's what. I'm thinkin' you could be right." Using the metal bar he discovered he could lift the two columns one at a time up against the roof structure. "Quick. Shove the end of that post under." She grabbed and pulled. It easily slid under and to the middle. "Right on." He relaxed. "Whew. Heavy mother. Let's get the second one up."

"You're pretty clever, you know that?"
He again felt a warm glow and was thinking, darned if Red isn't almost human. "Don't want to brag but I like to think so, but we still got a problem. Need to use the jack to lift them up and at the same time swing them 'bout a foot clear of the porch."

"Too bad we don't have some way fasten them to the beam."

"Hot dog! That's it. I knew you were good for somethin'." Back into the garage and this time he returned with an eight foot long piece of two by twelve. Using the handsaw he cut it into four two-foot pieces. "Okay," he told her as he positioned the jack under the cantilevered end of the timber. "I'm going to take this pry-bar and lift the end of the four by four on the porch until the column on the right touches the beam. When I get it up, you slide these scraps of wood under the four by four. Then we'll jack up the other end. Once they are both up tight I'll go up the ladder and nail these pieces of two by twelve to the top of each column, inside and out and then to the beam."

"Bitchen," she was nodding. "Can see where this is goin', only will nails support them?"

"You'd be surprised how much one nail will hold. It exactly as he had hoped. He let the jack down and removed the four by four. The columns stayed in place.

"It's amazing what a half-dozen sixteen penny nails will hold. However, Red, to answer your question, I been thinkin' this over. If they canned someone for something the killer did involving my dad, Mr. Heinz and the Garcia woman, then he is trying to get even."

Candy agreed. "Your dad's one of the bosses so he might know who it is."

"Might be able to find out, if I can think of some way to steer him onto the subject. "So let's get to work. Gonna tear this whole end apart."

"Where did you learn how to do all this stuff," she asked.

He shrugged. "I've always been interested in construction, so when I see some going on I watch to see how it's done. If I can see it done then I can do it. Lot of times me and Ollie will ride our bikes out to where Guy D'Angelo is building a bunch of houses, Dalton's first tract. I'm getting wired on how this stuff is done. Who knows? Maybe someday I'll be a contractor."

Candy was dragging the rotted boards to one side and stacking them as he worked with a hammer and crowbar. "I hope you don't ever plan to get married. I got an uncle in Montgomery who is a small time contractor and they are rich and poor, rich and poor all the time. Uncle Walt and Aunt Vera have gone bankrupt twice."

"I never said anything about being a small time contractor."

"Oh? You plan on being a big shot, huh?

He stopped what he was doing. "You know what, Red? We need to find out two things. First off who this guy is, and more important, if anyone else was involved he might be gunnin' for? What we actually need to do is find some way to get a look at the DGF employee records."

Employee records? She wondered. Why does that ring a bell? "Oh my Gawd."

"What?"

"I'm trying to remember. We couldn't cook at home last night so we went down to the Green Spot for dinner. Some guy came over to our table and talked to my dad. I wasn't paying all that much attention. I was talkin' to Heather Deiter who was sitting next to me."

"This guy. What did he look like?"

"Mark, I don't remember. He was standing behind me and I never even looked back. Man was bragging about being a hot-shot butcher or something like that. All I remember is my dad called him a slime-bag. I have no idea why."

"Then my dad has to know him."

"I suppose. You know what?"

"No I don't know what. I wasn't there and if I had been, I'd have been a lot more intense than you were."

"Wonder if it's this guy who was living with the Garcia woman? Paper says he was unemployed. Don't remember the guy in the restaurant but I do remember something. He was wearing black dress shoes. Shiny. Might have been boots."

* * *

About noon Candy asked, "You hungry. I can go in and make us some lunch."

She no more than finished speaking than her mom came out the door with a tray. On it were grilled ham and cheese sandwiches, packages of chips, lemonade and some cookies. "I have no idea what's going on, but it sure looks impressive. Thought you two could do with a few refreshments. You guys must be working awfully hard with all the noise going on out here." She placed the tray on the porch next to the steps.

Mark was looking at his grimy hands. "Gosh, thanks, Mrs. Swanson.

"Anytime," she told him. "Candy, why don't you take Mark in and show him where the bath is so he can wash up and you too, Missy."

"I can do that, and thanks Mom. You're a life-saver."
They ate the food and did away with a whole pitcher of lemonade. Then they went back to work. By about two thirty an eight by ten-foot section of the old porch was gone. Most of the northern section of town continued without electricity and Mark was surprised when he looked up to see Mr. Swanson driving a DGF pickup truck carrying a generator.

"Right on," yelled Mark and he rushed into the garage, returning with a roll of electrical wire. Without even asking if it was okay, he opened the house meter panel, pulled out the main breaker and proceeded to connect the generator to the house wiring. "That'll work," he called out. "Fire that monkey up and your refrigerator and other appliances will come on line."

Mr. Swanson stood back, looking at their handiwork, shaking his head. "I'm absolutely amazed how you know all this stuff?"

Mark shrugged, feeling pleased. "That's what Red asked

me earlier. I told her I've always been interested in construction stuff, so when I see guys building something I hang around and watch. I got this thing where if I can watch something being done then I can do it."

"Well I'll tell you this, I am impressed by the way you are handling the porch. Amazed actually. How can you get this much done in one day? Unbelievable, and to top it off you give us electric in the house."

"That generator is only a two K so don't try to use any appliances like your toaster or electric skillets or the microwave. Not enough juice. Check the gas about every two hours."

"I wanted a bigger one but they were all rented out. Okay to run the TV?"

"TV, lights, fridge, that sort of thing. And you, Red, don't go running no hair dryers. Hey, if it's okay with you, I gotta cut out. Need to get me a shower and catch a bite to eat before heading for the team bus."

"Me too." Candy looked at her dirt stained hands. "Okay if I walk down to the park with you Mark?"

"Probably be a good idea," Vince told them. "Getting to where it isn't safe for a good looking gal to be out alone anymore."

Yeah," Mark snickered. "We gotta watch out for Ann Margaret."

* * *

Candy and her father went inside where she heard him tell her mother, "We have electricity for tonight as long as I keep that machine full of gas. I'm totally overwhelmed with what that young man has accomplished in one day. Going to be worth every penny he is getting."

"I helped," Candy let him know. "How much am I getting?" She was fixing herself a peanut butter and jelly sandwich.

"I guess we can up your allowance a few bucks."
"I've been watching how hard she's been working," Candy's mother said, "I hope we can do better than a couple of bucks. What are you doing, Candice?" Her mother was straightening out things in the kitchen cabinets. "You'll spoil your dinner."

"I'm not all that hungry and I won't be here for dinner. Got to get ready to go."

"Go? Go where? You haven't been home one night this week."

"We got a game tonight. In Clarksdale."

"Clarksdale? And how do you propose to get there?"

"Team bus. They're leaving at 5:30."

"I would think with all these murders, you'd want to stick pretty close to home."

"She's a teenager," Vince laughed. "They live in a different world than we do. They think they're indispensable."

Candy was waiting for an opportunity to ask a pertinent question. Mark had prompted her on what to say. The moment came.

"I've nearly got the house back together," her mother said. "Without any help from your daughter, I might add. Reverend Wickerly stopped by and promised me that earthquakes only occur in the same area every thirty or forty years so I am going to be all right. Did your people get everything picked up at the plant?"

"Faster than I expected. Gave me a chance to review the personnel files. Our home office in New Orleans wants me to streamline the operation."

"Oh? Are you going to have to let some people go, I mean two months before Christmas?"

"It's unavoidable. We are carrying some deadwood. I also need to shift some individuals around since we are running top heavy in some departments and paying overtime in others."

Candy jumped at the chance as she asked, "That man you were talking to in the restaurant last night that said he was a butcher? Wasn't he fired from DGF?" It was a guess and Candy held her breath.

"That jerk. He was a department head who was asked to resign. Couldn't keep his hands off the female employees. Used his position to force women to accept his advances."

Bingo, she thought. Bingo, bingo, bingo. "What was his name?"

"Young lady, I don't think that is something you need to know. I've already told you more than I should. It's company policy not to jeopardize his future if he left voluntarily."

Darn, close but no cigar. In her mind she could hear the man's voice but couldn't bring a face into focus. It was like a curtain, that if she could draw it aside she would know who he was.

"Bette, why don't we drive down to Clarksdale and take in the basketball game?"

"Since when have you become interested in basketball? Clarksdale is forty miles away."

"I'd kind of like to see our daughter perform. After the game we can go out for a late dinner. Pizza maybe. Take Candy and her boyfriend."

"He's not my boyfriend. That's totally off the wall."

* * *

The first part of the basketball game with Clarksdale was, as Old Grandpa Frazier, who never missed a middle school or high school game, put it, "A real stinker." Clarksdale was leading 14 to 4 three minutes into the game. Dalton came out flat and even easy shots failed to go in. At the half, Clarksdale led 35 to 24.

When the teams returned to the floor for a few minutes of practice prior to the second half, Mark looked toward the cheerleaders and frowned. Two Clarksdale players were hitting on Candy and Heather. Jodi was flirting with two guys in the stands while the other three watched in awe. Not that he was jealous it was simply a matter of not being friendly with the enemy.

In the second half, Dalton couldn't get it together and the six cheerleaders sat glumly to the side. The Trojan's gradually built their lead to thirteen points.

* * *

With three minutes and twenty seconds left in the contest Coach Donnelley called time out. His face showed how thoroughly disgusted he had become.

After last week's play he began to have a dream. Coach Madison was retiring from the High School and he intended to apply for the position. A respectable season could put him at the top of the list. To cap it off, the seven best players on this team would be over there with him.

"What's with you guys? I've been on top of this thing for thirty minutes and I can't believe what I'm seeing. You guys are a better team than these clowns. They aren't beating you; you're beating yourselves. And you, Goodwin, where is the Superman we saw last week who wanted to kick ass against Citrus? I still see the war paint, so why are you playing like a sissy? I don't mind losing if we give it our best shot and are simply outplayed, but I don't like to see players give one away. If you guys can't handle it, I'll put in all our subs. Get your butts out there and at least make the final score look respectable. We get these guys again next month at home."

* * *

Mark took the in-bound pass from Buzz, dribbled across the mid-court stripe, made a spin move on his defender and drove the lane. The entire Trojan team sagged in on him so he made a blind pass out to Shortie, who promptly canned a swisher for three points. As the Trojans brought the ball up the floor, Mark appeared to be leaning left and the Clarksdale player tried to dribble past on the right only to have the Indian slap the ball away. It went skittering down the court with both players in pursuit. Mark won the footrace and made a lay-in with number 22 hanging all over him. The free throw was good and with two fifteen remaining, it was only a seven-point game.

The Trojans went into a time killing four-corner offense. There isn't enough time for this crap, Mark was thinking as he purposely hooked his opponent's arm. The boy missed the first and canned the second. Eight points. The lead was insurmountable.

Four quick passes, Romero to Buzz to Shortie to Mark who again drove the lane, this time snapping the ball out to Ollie in the corner. The big lad took everyone by surprise by firing from long range. The coach groaned and Mark said, "Oh no!" The ball hit nothing but net. Three more points and it was 69-64 Clarksdale, with thirty-three seconds on the clock.

Without the coach even telling them to do so, Dalton came out in a full court press. The Trojan player was having difficulty inbounding the ball and in desperation tried a long pass. Mark, with his long arms and leaping ability, picked it off and all in one motion, pump faked his defender then put it up from way outside the three point circle. It was a miracle. 69-67. Time-out Indians. Twelve seconds left.

Mark could see Candy leading the way as the cheerleaders tried to whip the meager group of Dalton fans into a frenzy. Mr. Swanson, of all people, was standing, waving his fist in 'Go, Go, Go' fashion. Candy's mother was seated, her elbows on her knees, her chin resting on her knuckles, but he could see the tension written on her face.

He waited as the coach wracked his brain for a plan. All he could tell them was, "get the ball, get the ball, get the ball. 'Bout the best we can do," he said, "is open it up to where they have to pass to number twelve, then foul him instantly. He is their poorest free throw shooter. I want both Mark and Ollie under the basket for the rebound, and Shortie, I want you at mid-court ready to take the outlet pass and drive for the basket. We gotta hope the Trojan player misses both. We have the momentum so go for the tie."

The five boys played the pattern exactly as Donnelley had laid it out. The second number twelve touched the ball; Ollie fouled the smaller boy hard. With the Clarksdale fans screaming encouragement, the player took the two shots. He missed the first and there was a massive groan. The second hit the back of the rim, bounced high but Mark mistimed his leap. The six foot one center for the Trojans came down with the ball and made a serious blunder, as he turned to the right with the ball in his outstretched hands. Mark simply snatched it from his grasp. The clock showed six seconds. Like a race horse he flashed past defenders, going the length of the floor, then made one of his floating, hanging, scoop shots, trying to make sure, even if he missed, to draw the foul. The basket was good. The foul was called. Oh wow, he thought. Awesome. All tied up and time-out Clarksdale.

Mark wasn't listening to the coach. Instead he was looking at six young women in short green skirts and tight sweaters with pleading looks on their faces. The girls were holding hands so tightly their knuckles were white. Ain't this something? We've gone through a colossal earthquake, we've had three murders and a maniac killer remains on the loose, and at this point in time this free throw is the most important thing in the world. Who can figure?

When he was at the charity stripe, he took a deep breath and looked at the girls again. Candy was holding a glittering gold pom-pom on each side of her face, her green eyes locked onto his as though he was some sort of a God. Mark grinned and called out, even though there was no way she could hear him, "Hey Red, this one's for you." 70-69. The Indians were undefeated. All six cheerleaders were trying to hug him at once. Was he embarrassed? Heck no. He was in heaven.

* * *

At the time, both Mark and Candy would have preferred to return to Dalton on the team bus, but when her father said, "Hell of a game, Mark. Hell of a game. Come on you two, I'm going to buy you the biggest steaks in town."
Even Michael got into the flow when he told them, "I'm going to be a basketball player . . . just like Mark."

They went to a place called The Hickory Smokehouse where they were shown to a booth. Her folks took one side so she was compelled to squeeze in between Mark and Michael. She cringed, then made phony goo-goo eyes and acted like a spastic as she said, "My hero," and bumped him with her hip.

He made a face at her, for the first time seeing close up the paste on Indian tattoo she had on her cheek. He liked it. Taking her dad at his word he said to the waitress, "I'll have the Chuck-wagon cut . . . medium rare."

"I want a Chuck-wagon, just like Mark," Michael said.
Vince grinned. "Sure Mike. What you can't eat we'll take home in a doggie bag."

"Funny Face and the cat are also gonna to be livin' high on the hog." Mark nudged her in the ribs.

"Is it okay if I have the prime rib?" Candy ventured.
"Baby, after the way you performed order two if you want. You were the best cheerleader out there."

"You were," her mother told her. "And so graceful. I guess you have at last outgrown your awkward stage."
"And," her father said, "by far the best looking. What a combination. Your red hair and that green skirt."
Candy flushed. The heck with the team bus, this was awesome.

While they were eating salads Mr. Swanson was rehashing nearly every play in their last minute comeback and Mrs. Swanson said, "I'm so glad we came." Then she smiled. "Of course this is better than trying to cook at home without a microwave."

Once their main courses arrived Candy made a face as Mark dug right into his huge steak, then noticed he was looking at her plate.

"So that's prime rib? I've never . . . uh . . . can I have a

364

taste?"

"If you don't get your germs all over it."

"I'll lick my fork off before I use it."

"Oh yuck."

"Can I have a taste too? Asked Michael who had hardly made a dent in his steak.

Candy sighed. "If you guys wanted prime rib why didn't you order prime rib? Go ahead. Knock yourselves out." She was thinking how Shannon would hold a treat in her lips and let Buzz take it with his. "Disgusting," she said aloud.

"Awesome," Mark licked some juice from his lips.

"Awesome," echoed Michael.

This whole day has been unbelievable, thought Mark. I hope I live to enjoy it.

CHAPTER TWENTY-EIGHT

Sometime Friday night, while they were in Clarksdale, the electricity was restored. On Saturday morning Mark hurried through his breakfast and then was back on the remodeling project cutting lumber and building forms for new concrete footings. The redhead surprised him . . . twice. By showing up as early as he did and by wielding a pretty mean hammer.

"I gotta take my wagon down to Turner Lumber and pick up a couple of sacks of cement. We got plenty of sand and gravel behind the garage but nothin' to mix it with."

"Won't they deliver?"

"I called them early this morning. Told me they were booked up nearly all day. S'okay. I don't mind."

"Okay if I tag along?"

"Hey, knock yourself out. You can pull the wagon if you wanta."

"Not me. I stopped playing with wagons when I was six."

As they walked, Mark was constantly looking left, right and behind them.

Candy squinted at him and asked, "With all these news and TV people and out of town cops all over town, you aren't worrying about the killer are you?"

"After what's happened so far, it's hard not to."

"Only he'd be taking a heck of a chance trying anything with all that's goin' down. 'Specially after the quake."

"I know you're right, Red, but . . .. We're here. Cement is down in that lean-to."

Turner's was a madhouse of activity. Dozens of patrons

were looking for earthquake repair materials, lumber, plumbing, plywood for temporary window covers, glass and patching plaster. Mark found the bags of cement. Candy tried to help but he snapped, "I got em," and easily lifted the ninety-four pound sacks onto the wagon, which sagged under the weight. He could tell by her eyes she was impressed. Was always pretending to be Superman . . . and maybe he was.

Back at the house he used the wheelbarrow and a hoe to mix cement. It was strenuous labor but the sort of activity Mark loved. Candy was right in the middle of it and full of questions.

"How do you know how much of each to use?" She asked.

"For something like footings you don't need as much cement as you use in flatwork.
One shovel of cement, two sand and three of gravel is the starting formula, but for footings and considering the size of the gravel, you can make it with four and even five shovels of gravel. With the gravel we're using, two bags of cement will make close to a half-yard of cement. Twelve or thirteen cubic feet."

"How much are we making in a wheelbarrow?"

"'Bout three cubic feet. Wheelbarrow will hold six but we couldn't handle it."

"How many feet do we need?"

"I calculated it out last night and we'll need to mix about five batches today."

She had been using the hoe to mix the heavy material and she handed it to him. "Whew! Aching muscles tomorrow."

"We just need to pace ourselves. Hey Red, you're a mess. You got cement on your blouse, cement on your knees and a big splotch of cement on your cheek."

"At least it proves I'm doing something. Dad's gonna give me an increase in my allowance for helping."

"Yeah, bout ten cents an hour."

"Hey! I'm worth darned near as much as you are."

"Not even on your best day." The first couple of loads he dumped directly into the 12x12 inch base footings. Then using a galvanized pail he began filling the 6x12 inch portion that was formed up out of lumber. He had found plenty of rebar in the garage and a heavy duty bolt cutter so he was placing a short upright bar every two feet and four rows of horizontals exactly as he had seen it done several times. They were on a third batch when Michael came out and horsed around throwing fists full of dirt into the newly mixed cement.

Candy pushed him away. "Michael, don't do that. What a pest."

"Hey Mike, come here." Mark held out the hoe. "You want to help."

"Oh boy, you bet."

"Okay, you take the hoe and mix the cement." It was already thoroughly mixed. Mark was looking around for a suitable container when he spotted a small sand bucket. "Okay, that's enough. What I want you to do is," he filled the bucket half full and tested it for weight, "carry this over and dump it into the forms. See like this. Right in here."

Michael was absolutely elated.

"When we get it full, I'll show you guys how to trowel. Got to be all the way to the top."

"Towel?" Michael asked. "We gonna use a towel?"

Mark showed him one of the metal tools. "Trowel."

It took the three workers nearly two hours of strenuous toil to mix and carry enough cement to fill the corner footings. "Boy, you sure figured out how to handle Mr. Nuisance," she whispered.

"Kid has some smarts but too much energy. All he needs is someone to shove him in the right direction. That does it, Mike. We got her poured full. It's time for me to show you how to finish cement." They took turns using the wooden float to prepare the surface, then he got Candy started on running the edger while showing Michael how the trowel worked.

"This isn't actually necessary," Mark told her. "I always want to make sure it is perfectly flat and level because we will be bolting a wooden two by six plate on top." As he was telling her this he was forcing a ten-inch long anchor bolt into the wet concrete about every four feet.

The two teenagers looked up at the sound of a diesel engine. Parked at the curb was a king-cab Dodge pickup with lettering on the door, which stated Guy D'Angelo Construction. A sun bronzed Italian man climbed out and walked toward the pair.

"Hi Goodwin. Whatcha got going?"

"Yo, D'Angelo," Mark replied. "What's shakin'." The two

men exchanged high fives.

Guy eyed the temporary framework and the concrete work. "Looks pretty good so far. You sure you're not getting in over your head?"

"Hey, I had a good teacher."

Guy grinned. "One of the best."

"I hope you ain't pissed over me stealing one of your jobs?"

"Naw, that's cool. With Cottonwood Hills in full swing and all sorts of calls about quake damage, I got more than I can possibly handle. I stopped by to see if you need any advice. You gonna introduce me to your good lookin' girl friend?"

Mark was sheepish and apologized. "This is Red Swanson. She lives here. Red, this is a friend of mine, Guy D'Angelo. He's Dalton's one and only big time contractor."

"Nice to meet you, Mr. D'Angelo. I don't like being called Red; my name is Candy. That's just Mark." She extended her slim hand and he grasped it in his, nodding that he understood.

"I do have a couple of problems," Mark told him. "I have no idea how we are going to tell if we have the porch roof level once we get it jacked back up. As you can see, we got this one jerry-rigged temporarily."

"The answer to your first question is; water level"

"Water level?"

"Yeah. You use a garden hose and two ladders. Take one end up and attach it to the other end of the porch beam. Measure how much of the hose protrudes past the bottom edge of the beam. Okay?"

Mark nodded. Already his mind comprehended where this was going. "Right. Then I take the other end up to the beam over here and fill it full of water. Right."

"You got it. Once the water is up to the top on both ends you are dead on level. Works best if you use two people on the ladders. Of course out on the job we use a transit and a story pole."

"Man, I got it wired."

"I gotta go check on some of my jobs, Mark. If you need any advice just hop out to the job and I'll fill you in. Keep up the good work, man . . . and by the way, when school is out in June, if you are looking for a summer job, drop by and see me. Nice to

369

have met you Candy. Hope to see you again."

Mark was glowing and so was Candy.

After the contractor drove away Candy prodded, "Thought you already knew how to do everything."

"That's not what I meant. Actually I know how to figure out a way to do things. Anyhow, if I don't know, I'm not afraid to ask someone who does."

Mrs. Swanson came out with three glasses and a pitcher of raspberry iced tea. "Would you look at Michael? That boy is so clever." The boy had a short twig in his grasp and was scratching the new cement. "Oh my," she began laughing as Michael dropped the stick and rushed over for a glass of the tea.

Mark looked at the scratches. "Over my dead body," he snorted.

Candy also looked. Scratched in the smooth surface was a heart. Inside were the letters, M.G. + C.S.

"My my," laughed Red's mother. "From the mouths of babies what we can learn."

"Oh man!" Candy acted horrified. "That is so gross."

But no one rubbed it out.

Mark turned out to be one of those individuals who could have a half dozen projects going at once. Since the cement would have to cure for at least a day, he scurried up the extension ladder to start preparing the front of the structure for painting. Candy worked on the lower part from off a stepladder. Michael was given a wire brush, which kept him occupied until he tired of this unproductive chore and left for parts unknown.

They scraped and sanded and filled holes and cracks. "We have some areas," Mark told her when they were taking a break, "where the paint is peeling and flaking off so much, I'm going to get some paint remover and strip it down to the bare wood."

"This is a tough job, I'll bet'cha that."

"Anytime you wanta quit . . . "

"Not on your life. I'm as tough as you are."

"You wish. You're okay though, considering you're the weaker sex."

"Is that a compliment?"

He shrugged. "We got some cracked glass other windows that need new putty. I'll check with your dad and see if he would like to replace these with duel pane. This is the west side of the house so it takes the worst beating from the sun. I'm anxious to try that special paint your dad is talking about. Turner is going to deliver it Monday."

"Have you thought anymore, you know, about what we talked about yesterday?"

"Yeah. After you told me what your dad said about the guy who got fired from DGF, I've thought about it so much I can hardly concentrate on what I'm doin' here. Got some ideas though. We need to have a meeting."

She was nodding. "Probably at Heather's again, huh?"

"That would be keen. We need to keep right on top of this stuff."

By the middle of the afternoon, Mark was ready to start cutting pieces for the porch even though the cement was not ready to support the lumber. He wanted to get it laid out and ready for Monday, since the word was, no school till Wednesday at the earliest.

"Hey Red, "Gonna be able to work on this thing the rest of today and every day till school opens again. Seven bucks and hour! Gonna have a small fortune by that time."

"Wonderful. Should give you enough money to buy me something nice for Christmas."

"In your dreams. I only wish I was sixteen so I could buy a car." He actually grinned when she forced out her lower lip in a phony pout. Soon as we get most of the pieces cut to size we'll call it a day. With some of the new things we've discovered, when I get home I want to see if I can round up all the Kryptonites for a meeting this evening."

"How 'bout I call all the gals and you do the guys?"

"Good idea. Then call me and clue me in. Oh oh, here comes Mike again.

For the next hour it was, "Here Michael, hold this board for me. Michael, see if you can pound a nail in this board. No Michael, you may not use the power saw."

"Can I try it?" Candy picked up the tool.

"Yeah . . . I guess. Let me show you how to hold it and how to place the lumber so it won't kick back on you. By the time I get done teaching you how to do all of this stuff, we could build a house together."

"No kidding? Does that mean we're going to get married?"

Mark choked on that one. "When hell freezes over. I'd rather marry Miss Radish."

"Miss Radick is exactly your type. Face like a horse, laugh like a donkey and a rear end like an elephant."

"Don't knock it. She outshines you in every department."

"You can stick it. I'm going to take a shower."

"Good idea. You smell like something that crawled in a hole and died." He watched her go up the steps. "Don't forget to call me."

She stuck her tongue out at him and went inside.

Hate to admit it, but that gal is a whole bunch of help. Don't know what her dad is paying her, but whatever she's worth it.

* * *

As he finished putting away the tools and started across the lawn toward his place Mr. Swanson turned into the drive.

Stepping from his Lexus he held up his hand to stop the boy. "Holy shit," he exclaimed, surveying the front of his house. The two columns were hanging by the four cleats. The once sagging roof was propped up on a tall, four-foot wide support. There were forms with new concrete. A ten-foot by twelve-foot section of the porch was gone. Off to one side was a sizable pile of lumber, cut to size and ready to be installed. Even the front of the house appeared different where wire brushes had been at work and fillers applied.

Mark stood quietly. He was the type of individual who always worried he wasn't doing as much as was expected. Looking back at the house he waited.

"This is totally beyond belief. I mean absolutely fantastic. You are a wonder worker. A regular wizard."

Mark's face glowed. "I uh . . . I'm glad you like it. Made better time than I figured and Red worked with me all day. Even Michael helped."

"It's Saturday night. Let me pay you for the time you've put in so far."

"Oh, well, let me think. Yesterday we didn't get started till 'bout 8:30 and we worked till you came home at 3:00 or so, with probably an hour off for lunch and breaks."

"What about the hour you spent wiring in the generator?"

"Well you know, I was just doing that. Anyway, you bought me a big dinner last night. Then today we started at 8:00 and I'm right this minute putting everything away. And of course we took a couple of breaks and had lunch again. Mrs. Swanson made us sandwiches. Oh . . . and I spent maybe half an hour talking to Guy D'Angelo, you know, the contractor, about a couple of things I wasn't real sure about. So maybe five hours yesterday and six today." Wow, he was thinking; seventy-seven bucks.

Vince opened his wallet, extracted a bill and shoved it into Mark's shirt pocket. It was a hundred.

"Uh, I don't have any change."

The man held up his hand. "You don't owe me any change. If I had to pay a contractor for what you have accomplished today, it'd be triple that or more. You are doing a great job."

Mark was in high spirits. "Well gee I . . . what about Candy?" It was the first time he'd ever called her by her name. "She worked nearly as hard as I did. I'd better share some of this with her?"

Vince laughed out loud. "Mark, you're one of a kind. I'll see to it that my daughter is taken care of. See you Monday, I guess. Way I hear it the school will be closed several days."

* * *

As Mark walked into the study he was happy to see his dad hang up the phone. He wanted to use it to call all the Kryptonite men. They needed to talk, and as Red said, probably over at Heather's.

"Hi Mark. How's the job coming?" His father was mixing himself a drink.

"Fantastic . . . so far. We're getting' a handle on it."

"Looks pretty good from what I can tell. Actually quite impressive."

"Thanks. Mr. Swanson paid me for yesterday and today." He didn't tell him how much.

"You should make a pretty nice piece of change by the time you get that monstrosity in shape. What you need to do is open a savings account at Dalton bank. I was talking to Frazier down at the paper and I guess they have electricity restored to most of the town. City rented a front-end loader from one of the ranchers and has removed the huge pile of rubble on Main Street in front of McDougall's. Things are rapidly returning to normal. Frazier seems to think your school will reopen about Wednesday."

The phone rang and Mark leaped to snatch it up, waving a hand toward his dad. "It's for me, Dad. Hi Red. What's the scoop?"

"I actually talked to Heather, Shannon, Jodi and Ollie. It's all set for Heather's place at seven. Shannon's gonna call Buzz so we got it covered."

"Jeeze. You guys don't even need me."

"'Bout time you were finding that out?"

After dinner the Kryptonites again met at Heather's house to discuss where they stood on their investigation. Even though the pool was heated, they didn't come to swim. It was a chilly November evening and the teenagers were wearing sweats and even jackets. Mark wondered why the redhead seemed so happy, so he asked, "what are you grinning about? Cat poop on your bed again?"

"Heck no. Sent him over to your place. Wanna hear something awesome?"

"Anyway I can stop you?"

"Dad gave me fifty bucks for helping you." She was in high spirits. "Gave Michael five."

He didn't know if it was due to what he had said to Swanson but felt pleased. "What the heck? You earned it. Hey guys, like to bring you up to speed on what's going on with our investigation. Between Red and I, we've found out that the killer used to work at DGF. Red has actually seen the man but has this mental breakdown as to who it was."

There were murmurs and questions. "Where? Who? When? Do we know him?"

"It's one of those cases of someone standing two feet away and not actually looking directly at them." Candy's discomfort was obvious. "It was right after the quake and I was so wired my mind wasn't with it. So when my dad talked to this guy, I buzzed him off without looking."

Shannon was cuddling close to Buzz for warmth. "So what's the plan?"

Heather was sitting on Ollie's lap but she quickly slid off to sit beside him when the rear door opened.

"Hi gang." Mrs. Deiter took them by surprise as she came out with a heaping platter of store bought cookies and a steaming pot of hot chocolate. As she handed around Styrofoam cups, she had no idea of the nature of this meeting, thinking it was merely a kid's type of club. "Don't you think it is getting rather chilly out here? You kids are welcome to use the family room if you wish. Our bridge club is using the entertainment center."

"Thanks Mrs. Deiter . . . uh, Carolyn." Mark was helping himself to the cookies. "We'll be all right for tonight."

"Suit yourself, and enjoy." She paused. "I'll turn on the overhead heaters." She did and then was gone.

"Your mom's okay," said Ollie, who wanted to put his arm around Heather but was not only shy, but also worried her mom might be watching. He moved slightly so that his hip was touching hers.

Heather shrugged. "She's all right I guess. Watches over me like a hawk."

"Better that," Shannon reminded them, "than finding you someplace with your legs cut off."

Jodi shuddered noisily. She was with Shortie Carr again and Mark had to explain to him what they were up to.

"Cool," the boy said. "I'm willing to help."

"Like I told ya, what we need is to get a look at the personnel records at DGF. I don't think they have a night-watchman, do they Red?" Mark was back in charge.

"They sure don't. We could sneak down there and see if we can find a way in."

"Any chance you could swipe your dad's key?"

She made a face with her mouth. "Don't see how. He keeps them in his pants pocket day and night. I'm sure not going to try sneaking into their bedroom."

"Bummer." Mark rubbed his lips, pondering his options. "Okay, here's how it works. Since it will be easier for me and Ollie and Buzz to sneak out at night, I thought the three of us would go over to DGF . . . let's say midnight tonight, and see if we can find a way to get inside. We have to get a look at those records."

"We may as well meet down there," suggested Buzz. "You

375

know, on the backside, behind the meat packing plant."

"Uh . . . " Nothing had been done about replacing Ollie's old bike. "Wish we could use the Harley. I guess Ollie and me will have to ride double."

"Works for me," said Ollie. "I'll ride it and you do the double. Meet me down at the bowling alley at a quarter to."

"That's cool. Once we find out who this guy is, we'll go from there."

* * *

The Man was inside the offices of Dalton General Foods. It was a few minutes after ten and he was angry. The door to Goodwin's old office was locked. The lettering had been change in gold on the glass:
VINCENT SWANSON
VICE PRESIDENT
GENERAL MANAGER
What to do? Couldn't very well break the glass. He wondered? Didn't that bitch Elaine keep extra keys in her center drawer? At least that wasn't locked. In the desk drawer there was a brown clasp envelope stuffed with keys. He dumped them on the polished surface. Each had a round, hand lettered tag. 'Electrical Room. Computer Room, Storage, Supply Cabinet, Pharmaceutical Products', and there it was. Name hadn't been changed. 'Goodwin's Office.'

There it was, bigger than life; Dalton's old filing cabinet. Looked out of place in the room with all the new furnishings. Middle drawer is labeled; Old Employees. It took him less than two minutes to locate and remove the file from the cabinet then he was out, the door locked behind him, and he placed the envelope of keys back into the drawer. "Home free," he exclaimed aloud. "I'll show those slime-bags."

* * *

It was already midnight when Mark and Buzz met Ollie at the corner of Lincoln and Park. Due to his size it was agreed Ollie would pedal. Mark perched precariously on the handlebars. It was a three-mile ride from Main Street to the plant and they made the trip in fifteen minutes. Hiding the bikes behind some shrubbery they quietly sneaked along the north end of the building heading for the rear, drawing up short at the corner as Mark

376

held out his arm to halt the others.

"There is somebody back there," he whispered, his heart pounding.

"What are we gonna do?" Buzz wondered.

"That you Mark?" Asked a female voice.

"Red? What the heck are you doing down here?"

"I told you, I'm in this all the way. Aren't we girls?" Out of the shadows the rest of the Kryptonites appeared. Heather sidled over to be next to Ollie.

"Heather? How the heck did you manage to get out?"

"Went out the window, just like you guys do. Like I crawled out into the Mulberry tree and climbed down. Only I hope I can get back up in the dark."

"Unbelievable," said Mark as he watched Buzz give Shannon a small kiss. Not to be outdone, Ollie then did the same to Heather.

"You guys are late," Jodi let them know.

At least, he thought, Shortie Carr isn't with her. "So? You guys working by the hour?" Mark was already checking doors and windows. Everything was secure.

"All metal doors," said Buzz. "Deadbolts. You know what I'm sayin'? I don't do too hot with that kinda lock. Only one worth a try is the fire door, but all it's hardware is on the inside."

"No use breaking a window," Ollie was examining the heavy metal mesh covering each of the lower windows.

"Wait." Mark was looking at a row of small awning type windows about eight feet above the ground. Several were cranked open. "If we could hoist somebody small, like Jodi, up to one of those windows, she could probably crawl through."

"Extreme." Jodi was bouncing like she was keeping time to some unheard music. Actually she was cold. "But who is going to hoist me down on the inside?"

"Uh . . . " Mark stood studying the opening.

"I know," Candy's eyes shined even in the darkness. "You guys take off your shirts and tie them together. Then Jodi can tie one end to a window hinge. Should make at least a six foot rope."

"Candy, you're all right," said Ollie, "only why don't you gals take off your shirts too and we could make a ten foot rope?"

"Dream on, big guy," Buzz joked. "Come on men, let's do

it."

"Good idea. Guess that's why we pay Red the big bucks," Mark chuckled. "We'll freeze our cookies off, but let's do it." After they made the rope from their shirts, he and Ollie easily lifted the tiny girl to their shoulders where she teetered as each held a leg and then she placed her palms against the building. Mark was the only one of the three who never wore undershirts and his skin seemed to glow in the darkness.

Jodi's shoulders were even with the opening. "The windows are covered with screen."

"Regular window screen?" Mark asked.

"Yeah."

"Give her your knife, Buzz."

It took her a few minutes to saw away the screen and then she was inside. A moment later and the fire door opened.

"Your dad has my dad's old office, so I know where it is." Mark was leading the way. "We go through this section, which I guess is used to store packing boxes, then on through the meat processing section." They began moving stealthily past the eerie shapes of meat saws and grinders and even though he was certain there was no one around, he cautiously opened a door giving them access into a long hall leading past the produce department and to the main offices.

"Crap!" Mark tried the knob. "Your dad has the door locked. Dad never locked the door."

"Step aside." Buzz was looking the door over. "No dead bolt. Know what I mean? Watch this." Using his plastic covered student card, he wiggled the lock, rocked the card and the door was open.

"Where did you learn to do that?" Candy's eyes glowed in amazement.

"In reform school."

"You've never been to reform school," stated Shannon.

"No, but if I had been, that's something I would have learned."

Mark shined his flashlight about the office. It was plush. Everything smelled new; the floors, the furniture and the paint. The only old piece of equipment in the room was a greenish filing cabinet standing away from the wall as though it was not permanent. Without looking he knew it was the one. The drawers were labeled, 'A to I, J to R, S to Z'. "Oh boy. Center drawer is standing open. Got a bad feeling about this. Hold the flashlight for me." Candy took the light, directing it into the open drawer as he surveyed the folders. About midway two were pulled up slightly. "I hate to tell you this, but someone has beat us to it."

"How can you tell," Ollie asked. "There must be a hundred in there."

"There is a fresh gap, right here." The tabs on the two folders caught his eye. "Between Pinkerton and Powers."

"Well that's a clue then," Red told him. "Man's name starts with a 'P'."

"Well," disappointment showed in Mark's eyes. "At least that's something."

"Wait." Candy was aiming the light toward her father's desk. There was a manila fold lying in the center. "Maybe that's it."

Shannon was the first one to move to the huge oak desk and Mark and Candy bumped into each other in their haste to get a look.

"Is that the one we're looking for?" Mark couldn't keep the excitement from his voice.

Shannon moved it slightly. "No. The name on this one belongs to someone named Garcia."

Jodi drew away as though the folder was labeled poison. "The murdered woman?"

Mark reached out to take the folder and directed Candy to shine her light on it as he went through the file page by page. "Hmmm. Got her original application form, insurance papers and a sheaf of quarterly evaluation reports covering about five years. Not much help." Pawing through them, pausing once in a while, he continued his search. "Nothing. All kinda repetitive. They keep using words like dedicated, cooperative, works well with co-workers. All these tell us is she was a super employee." He stopped. The one he was reading seemed totally out of place. "Listen to this one. Lists her as unqualified, as insubordinate and . . . get this. 'Suggest immediate demotion or termination.'"

"Isn't that strange?" Shannon touched the folder as if it would give her a sign. "Here we have a perfect employee who all of a sudden gets a bad performance report."

"So?" Said Ollie. "She probably had a bad month."

Heather, who had shyly been staying to one side spoke up. "Who signed them? Like I mean that one and the one before and the one after."

"That could be the answer." Mark looked at all three reports. "My dad signed the one previous and the one after but this one is signed by another person."

Candy was looking over his shoulder. "Oh my Gawd!" She dropped the flashlight and the jolt broke the filament in the bulb, plunging them into total darkness.

"How stupid can you be?" Mark snapped.

"I'm sorry." She clicked the light on and off several times without success.

"So? Who signed it?" Shannon asked.

"That explains the missing folder," Mark was whispering. "The negative report was signed by someone whose name begins with 'P'."

"Who?" Asked six voices in unison.

"Our deputy sheriff, Ralph Powell."

CHAPTER TWENTY-NINE

Shannon hadn't seen her father since the night of her 'punishment'. It was her understanding that the AME Deacons had sent him to Los Angeles for counseling. Today she felt obligated to go to church Sunday morning since their Family Care Department was providing food and assistance to her family.

While she was getting dressed the phone rang and she snatched it up. "Hi Shannon, it's me, Mark. How 'bout meeting us at the Pit right after church? We need to talk."
"Uh . . . okay, I guess, only I don't have any money. Not getting any allowance since Dad left."

"Don't sweat it. I'll spring for lunch. I got a job."
"No kidding? Where?"
"Doing some repairs on the Swanson house."
"Cool. That way you and Candy can be together all the time."
"Yeah. Job does have its drawbacks."
* * *

As soon as the church service concluded, Mark and Candy met the rest of the Kryptonites at Kelly's Burger Pit. Sunday school and church was the furthest thing from his mind. It was filled with everything from excitement to terror. While they were eating, they quietly discussed last night's findings.

Heather brought up a question. "Like shouldn't we tell somebody about Ralph, like maybe the sheriff."

"Who's going to believe us? We don't have any evidence."

Mark was wearing one of his black, tough-guy, outfits, which caused Jodi to remark, "You guys look like twins. Candy's dressed all in black too."

"Yeah," Candy joked. "Identical." She and Mark were last in line at the order counter. "What we need to do is get some proof."

Ollie bought Heather's lunch even though she insisted on paying. Buzz ended up buying Shannon's and they shared a six-piece box of chicken and a giant French fry.

Candy was checking her purse and even going through the pockets of her jeans. "Oh heck. The fifty bucks Dad gave me is lyin' on my dresser. Told me to buy some new clothes. Hey Mark, I'm a little short. Could you loan me a couple of bucks?"

"Heather is a little short. You're a beanpole. What the heck? I'll buy."

"I'll pay you back."

"You will not. I told you I was buying."

"Oh? Is this our first date?"

"Dream on. I don't hang out with scarecrows."

"Better to be a scarecrow than a vulture."

They all sat in the large corner booth, Heather cuddling with Ollie, Buzz and Shannon in the middle, leaving Mark on the end scrunched up against Candy. Jodi had left for parts unknown right after church.

"Okay Marcus," Ollie prodded. "You acted like you had some sort of a plan."

"You know what we need?" Candy was talking with her mouth full of hamburger.

Mark mimicked her sound. "Whug oof we weed?"

"Dork. We need to lay our hands on that folder the killer took from DGF last night," she told them. "Then we would have some solid evidence."

"Where do you think he would hide it, at his apartment?" Ollie asked uneasily.

"Could be," Mark, making screwed up expressions with his mouth, was trying to think like Ralph would. "Actually I wonder if he wouldn't take it to his office. Why the heck did Jodi cut out to so quickly?"

Shannon shrugged. "Rusty Elliot asked her to go bowling."

"Rusty?" Heather put on her most horrified expression. "Like he's in high school . . . a junior or a senior and the Judge's son. I can't see those two together. What in the world does Jodi see in him? Like they're so totally opposite."

"He wears pants," Candy told her. "That's all that matters to Jodi, and he has a car and money to spend."

"Well, I thought she had the hots for Shorty Carr."
Candy shrugged. "There's something mysterious about an older man, you know."

"Ollie was busy teasing Heather with some French fries. "You got a plan, Marcus?"

"I will in a minute 'cause I've been thinkin' 'bout it."

"One thing for sure," Shannon was adamant. "We have to do something. That maniac is dangerous and he seems to know who we are."

Mark was leaning with both arms on the table. "Of course he does. I'm lucky he didn't find some excuse to shoot me. In the line of duty, you know. Could make up some cock and bull story about thinking I was stealing or something. There are only 'bout four places he could hide the folder, at his place, in his SUV, in the patrol car or at the police department. I'd make a bet that it's at his office."

"How come?" Candy stretched to reach for the catsup, her soft chest firmly pressed against Mark's upper arm.

There was that weird feeling that has happened several times lately. She moved away and he wondered why he didn't want her to. "Uh . . . Here is how I see it. Since Ralph is on duty from three till midnight, and he was out to DGF before we went out there last night, he was in the police car. Probably got in with keys he kept from when he worked there."

Candy had flooded her fries with catsup. "So? The folder is probably in his patrol car. Ain't no way we can get it outta there."

"I doubt it. Has Wally's Car Wash go completely through it every couple of days. That means it is either in his office or he took it home."

"So, what do you propose?" Shannon was munching on a chicken drumstick. "That we break into the police station?"

"A couple of us should go there tonight and look it over. It might not be all that hard."
Heather was wheezing slightly, excitement obvious in her eyes and she used her atomizer and it seemed to produce immediate

results.

"I'll bet he took it home, know what I'm sayin'?" Buzz held a long French fry out toward Shannon, jerking it away when she snapped at it.

Mark frowned. "Come on you guys. This is serious business. Here's what we'll do."

Five teenagers leaned eagerly toward him.

"Oh my Gawd! There he is!" Candy was fiercely grasping Mark's arm.

"Who? Ralph?" He turned to look, as did all the others. Ralph's black and white unit was pulling into the Green Spot parking area across the street.

Ollie licked his lips and squinted. "Had to park it way down at the end . . . next to the store. Think we could get a look inside."

"Not in broad daylight in front of God and everybody. Anyway, I'm sure he keeps it locked. Carries a shotgun in a holder right on the dashboard."

They watched The Man walk casually toward the entrance, greeting a couple that was leaving. "Sure don't look like a killer," Shannon was hugging herself like she was cold.
Mark shivered, his whole being tensing up. "He does to me. And we gotta stop him."

"You mentioned having a plan?" Candy asked.

"Okay. Listen up. Guy spends his whole shift cruising the streets or hanging out at Five Points or The Green Spot. Tonight . . . let's say about 8:30, we'll meet in the theater parking lot. From there we'll split into two groups. Buzz and Shannon and Jodi can go to Ralph's apartment. Think you can get inside, Buzzard?"

"Hey! Is the Pope Polish?" He laughed. "Not that I need it, but people of my race seem to learn these things, know what I mean?"

"Right. Okay, we got that covered.' Turning to Heather who looked like she might cry he asked, "Can you get out? Say 8:30?"

"I doubt it." She was bitter. "Like they won't be in bed yet and ever since that man killed that woman . . . it's like I'm the prisoner."

384

"Bummer. Well, me and Ollie and Red will check out the police department. I'll take a quiet walk past Ralph's car and see if I can see anything through the windows. Doubt it though. Give you guys a call later."

* * *

At dinner that evening Mark was plotting. If all this stuff was in the Powell personnel file, then his father must know most of the details. What he needed to do was pry this information out without letting Dad know how involved they were. An opportunity reared its head soon after his mom finished placing all the food on the table.

"Are you and the new general manager hitting it off any better," she asked.

"That jackass is purposely trying to irritate me. First he steals my office, next he steals my secretary. Today he is talking about reorganizing and moving our entire staff of workers around."

Mark decided to take a stab in the dark. "I heard from somebody that the woman who was killed was part of the reason our deputy sheriff no longer works there. Something about sexual harassment."

"Where did you hear that?"

"From our neighbor across the street. I guess she overheard her father talking about it."

"His resignation was supposed to be privileged information. That Swanson jerk has no morals whatsoever. But you're right, even though Ralph was a good worker, he couldn't leave the booze or the women alone."

"I guess he went on the wagon . . . AA even," Mark's mother put in, "after he lost his whole family in that terrible accident last February. Finally got his life back together and a new job."

Marks hair stood up on the back of his neck. A motive. He vaguely remembered the accident.

She handed him the platter of pork-chops and he took four. "Mark, don't be such a pig. You can always have seconds."

"Save time this way. Nobody makes pork-chops and gravy like you do, Mom. Getting fired probably ticked Ralph off though, didn't it?"

"Most of Ralph's problems were of his own creation, particularly at home."

"Then Candy's dad was right, he was involved with the Garcia lady?"

"Well, since the cat is out of the bag, I'd better give you the straight story to overcome any rumors you might hear. Ralph was the foreman of the meat-processing department. He used his position to get favors from some of the female employees. Man was constantly touching Miss Garcia, using suggestive remarks, threatening to demote her if she didn't give in to his manly charms. Promised her a raise if she complied."

"Typical sexual harassment," added his mom. "Some men are such pigs."

"The company got all this information from Elaine when she filed a report. But things came to a head one day when he had her cornered in an alcove next to the ladies room. Actually had his hand inside her blouse. Chuck Morris, he's a black man, pulled him off and then hit him."

Oh oh, Mark was thinking. Mr. Morris has small children. Their daughter is what? I'm thinkin' ten or eleven.

"Elaine went to Heinz, the head butcher, who in turn brought her to me. I reviewed the man's record and gave him the option; resign or be fired."

"I guess his life went down-hill from there," Mark's mother picked up the story. "Everyone knew he would get drunk, beat on his kids and abuse his wife. I guess he came home drunk, actually bragging about why he was fired . . . or so a neighbor woman told the police. Guess she was visiting with Mrs. Porter when he came home. They lived right next door to the Frazier's. She left when he started slapping his wife around. Looked like she threw some clothes into a suitcase, herded the three children into the car and headed for her mother's in San Jose."

"Oh yeah, I remember the wreck," Mark was nodding. "Drove right out onto Park Street in front of a truck and trailer. Killed 'em all instantly."

"I'm surprised," his dad was helping himself to another portion of mashed potatoes and gravy, "that he didn't try to sue DGF. Truck was driven by Dennis Horiwitz who was known to have a heavy foot."

Bingo, Mark told himself. Plenty of motive and the Kryptonites better get some concrete evidence darn soon or either the Horiwitz or Morris child could be his next victim. After dinner he slipped into his room and quietly made some phone calls.

* * *

Buzz was clearly in charge of the three Kryptonites who planned to break into Ralph's apartment. They held their meeting behind the middle school at 8:10. Each of the Kryptonites was required to do some story telling about who they were going to visit in order to get out. Since there was no school Monday, most of them were ordered to be home by ten. There was no moon and the teenagers were practically invisible. As suggested by Mark, they all wore dark clothing and Jodi, to be as inconspicuous as Shannon and Buzz, had covered her face with charcoal. Moving like a trio of cat burglars they crossed the street heading for the Hightown Apartments.

"Do you know which one is his?" Jodi was more frightened than she let on.

"Of course," Buzz hooked his thumb to indicate the one on the end, not nearly as relaxed as he let on. "This one right here on the corner next to Mulberry Street. Miss Radish lives right next door. Let's work our way around to the back yard. Know what I'm sayin'?"

He led the way as the trio moved from bush to bush until they were next to the rear door.

"What have we got here?" Using a penlight he was checking the lock. Looking up he was excited as he told them, "This is going to be easier than I expected. Lookie there. Bedroom window with the slider standing open 'bout three inches." In ten seconds, he pried out the aluminum screen with his knife blade, shoved the window to full open and easily climbed inside, reaching back to give the two girls a hand. With the beams of three flashlights bouncing from spot to spot, they began a systematic and thorough investigation of every possible hiding spot, starting in the bedroom, the closet, the living room, the entry closet and every nook and cranny in the kitchen.

Jodi was hopping about. "Oh man, I gotta pee."

"Good grief Jodi, why didn't you go before you left home?" Buzz aimed his light toward the bedroom. "Go use The Man's bathroom, but hurry it up. I don't believe this." He and Shannon completed the search of the kitchen, not actually expecting to find anything out there.

"Crap," groaned Buzz. "We've covered every inch of this place. Know what I mean? What we have to show for it is zip." Jodi returned from the rear.

"Everything come out all right?" Shannon had her hand on a cold knob. "Where does this door go?"

"Oh my God," Jodi whispered, "someone's coming." Shannon had the door open. "Quick. It's the garage." She and Buzz moved as one, but Jodi stood petrified with terror until Buzz reached back to frantically drag her out of the kitchen.

"Behind the SUV," he whispered as he heard the creak of the front door and he bumped into the grill of the black Lincoln, using his hands to feel his way, brushing against something on the wall and it fell to clatter on the concrete floor. All three tensed, holding their breath, working their way along the sleek metal sides until they were behind the huge vehicle.

In the morgue like silence they could hear The Man in the kitchen, muttering to himself. There was a sudden flash of light when the kitchen door opened followed by a flood of white from an over-head fluorescent fixture. Three teenagers crowded close together to become as unnoticeable as possible. The Man was laughing and talking to himself.

"Time for me to punish another one. I'm gonna get them all and I mean every damn one. Right after work I'm gonna start with that little bitch." He opened the passenger door while talking to himself. "Hah! Checked out her house. Even in this crappy weather she sleeps with the window open." Placing something on the floor of the vehicle he continued to mutter. "Bed is right next to the window. All I gotta do is reach in and take her and I will, right after midnight. Witching hour for our little redhead."

The door slammed then for a terrifying, heart stopping few seconds he came around to the front. On the side wall was a row of box-end wrenches hanging on hooks from a tiny quarter inch size all the way up to one and one quarter inches. The largest of these was missing. The Man bent down to retrieve the fallen tool. "Damn aftershocks." If he had glanced to his left he would have spotted six terrified eyes. Turning back toward the kitchen he opened the door but stopped as though listening. Buzz held his breath for an eternity. It was like the Man was trying to re-member something, and then they were plunged into a crypt like darkness.

The three teenagers began to breath again, waiting and waiting until at last the pencil thin strip of light at the bottom of the service door disappeared followed by the front door slam-ming. A few minutes later they could hear the sound of an engine starting, then fading into the distance.

"Whew! My heart is beating again. Know what I mean?" Buzz snapped on his flashlight. Jodi was trembling so violently he wondered if he ought to slap her, but didn't. "I thought we'd bought it."

Jodi was clutching his arm, and yet she said, "good thing I used the toilet before he came."

"What do you suppose he put in the van?" Shannon wondered.

"One way to find out." Opening the door he had to stand with his arm around Shannon as all three crowded into the opening. On the floor sat a portable red spotlight and a shoebox. Shan-non reached out for the box then hesitated, before lifting the lid. Buzz felt her shudder. Inside was a leather butcher's pouch, which held several wickedly sharp knives, a meat cleaver, a metal sharpening shaft and a small, fine toothed meat saw.

"What does it mean?" Jodi seemed to be recovering.

Buzz knew. "Mark's sister and the Heinz victim each had legs missing and the Garcia woman, according to the news lost both of hers. It's his personal butchering tools."

Shannon also had her arm about Buzz's waist. "What are you suggesting?"

"I'm suggesting that our ex-butcher hasn't stopped butch-ering. Know what I'm sayin'?" Buzz was picking up the box.

"What are you doing? You gonna take em?"

"Well, they could be used as evidence. You know what? I better not. Be better if the police picked up this stuff with a warrant." Shining his light into the rear he paused. "What's this? Couple of   Blue plastic bags? Wonder what's in 'em?"

"Oh my God, I wouldn't open those for nothing. What if it's body parts?" Jodi was nervous again.

Buzz had to look, and then he was shaking his head. "This one is full of the loot from Mark's house. DVD player, jewelry, and

stuff like that. That cinches it. We know we have the right man.
Let's see what's in the other one. Doesn't look like loot. Reaching
into the bag he pulled something out.

"What is it?" Shannon was terrified.

"   Clothes," he told them. "Little girl's clothes." Stuffing the
items back into the bag, he took it with him. "Let's go. I say let's
give the sheriff a ring or wake up those two FBI guys staying out
at the Ezyinn."

"Wait a minute," Shannon screwed up her face. "What did
he mean about tonight and someone's bedroom window?"
Buzz had a horrifying thought, remembering the words, 'Witching
hour for that redhead'. "Oh God. I know about that window. Me
and Mark dropped a kitten through that same window Tuesday
night."

"Candy?" Jodi was horrified. "He's going after Candy."
Shannon became rigid. "Buzz. We have to let her know."

CHAPTER THIRTY

"**G**otta be home at 10:00 sharp," Candy told him as she met Mark at the corner. "Told my folks me and Shannon had some things to do."

"That's cool. I sure hope this works. We get enough evidence, we can take it straight to the sheriff."

"Or, if he doesn't believe us, according to my dad, there are a couple of those FBI men from Clarksdale staying down at the Ezyinn."

"You told your dad?"

"No I didn't tell my dad, it was something he mentioned."

They had planned to meet in the parking lot behind the bowling alley but Mark changed that plan, stopping his friends as they rounded the rear corner of the building.

"There's Ralph's car," he pointed to the cruiser parked in a handicap spot. "Let's get going. This is great. We won't have to worry about him for a while." He glanced about to make sure they weren't being observed by anyone else. "Nobody in sight and I'm getting' good vibes."

"This is one those places where we could have used Buzz and his knowledge about locks," Candy sighed.

"Yeah, but in this case, the less people involved the better. Isn't every night a group of kids break into the police station."

"If somehow we manage to actually do it. Where the heck is Ollie?" They waited an agonizing three minutes before the big lad showed up and within moments Heather appeared. It was obvious she had been running and she was making scratchy gasping sounds.

"You okay?" Ollie gave her a one armed hug and she placed

391

her head against his chest and nodded.

"Took an asthma pill just before I left. It'll like kick in most any minute."

"Ain't love wonderful," Candy was already moving. "Let's go."

As they crossed Locust, Mark asked Heather, "how did you manage to get out?"

She grinned. "Would you believe? Like my folks are gone. Went to Crown Ford down in Clarksdale for some promotional thing. Something about a dinner and looking at a preview of some sort of brand new model. Lucky for me, my brother is out cruising. Keeping Ralph busy, I hope. Like this is so totally cool."

"Yeah it is and I've got a feeling 'bout tonight, like we're gonna find something to bring this to an awesome conclusion." Mark was leading the foursome past the courthouse, which was barricaded off while some repairs were being made.

Walking along behind the building, scanning the rear wall Ollie tried a couple of lower windows and the door. "I sure don't see any way in."

Mark was studying a telephone pole that had metal climbing pegs starting about seven feet above the ground. "Ollie, give me a boost. I'm going to check out the roof. Might be a vent or a roof hatch or something. We gotta get in even if we have to break the glass out of the door."

Once he was on the roof, he had to pause for a moment. His adrenaline was cranking it up. Okay, let's see what we got. Twin-Pac. Huge thing. If I had some tools might get in through the ductwork, or if I had a cordless drill and a saber saw, could cut a hole in the roof. Walking over to the front parapet he looked down into the street. Hardly anything stirring. Looks pretty hopeless. Darn it. Front door is probably our only choice. As he returned to the rear he heard the muffled sound of his name being called.

"Mark?" Ollie's face was a white mask looking up at him.

"No way in from up here without tools."

Ollie was pointing. "Think I see a way in. Bathroom window. 'Bout nine feet up, same as it was out at DGF. Doesn't even have any screen over it."

"Let's give it a try. If it's not unlocked, we'll have to break

392

it." Mark was looking around. "Only how do we get up there?"

* * *

Officer Ralph Porter didn't realize he was doing exactly as Mark had suggested to the group. Hung out at the bowling alley for a while, but that was boring so began cruising. He felt confident. Things were quieting down around town even though there were a half dozen out of town lawmen present. Maybe more. Those two FBI guys hadn't left. The county crime lab was sitting in the courthouse parking lot and those guys were staying up at the lake. What a charge it was going to be to do another one right under their noses.

By my way of thinking, if he did the little redhead it would let the Goodwin kid and his group of followers know whoever was doing these things meant business. Was pretty sure they were conducting an investigation on their own. The watch, the ad, the shoeprint and all that good stuff. None of it was proof of anything.

He licked his lips, feeling the growing warmth at the thought of using his tools on the Swanson chick. In a few more hours she'd be history and no way anyone else suspected him. Weren't even looking for him. He was a respectable lawman, for crying out loud. He grinned. They were looking for a psycho. That's what they figured it took to do the kind of things he'd been doing.

* * *

Candy stepped between Mark and Ollie. "You two guys boost me up like you did with Jodi." She had been holding a flashlight that she stuffed inside her shirt.

"Good idea. You're light enough and small enough it should work." Mark and Ollie made a saddle with their hands, then stooped so she could step in, then raised her high enough to step off onto their shoulders where she teetered unsteadily supporting herself with a hand on each of their heads until she felt comfortable enough to lean against the wall.

"Cool. A slider; left half is open and it looks big enough for me to squeeze through." By stretching she managed to stick her arms and head inside then pulled herself up. "No screen. Bet they get plenty of flies."

There was a slight amount of light coming in from somewhere up front and it was enough to make out the fixtures. Men's room. She wrinkled her nose. Now what? Have to go in head-first. How could she do it without getting hurt? If she let her body hang forward as far as she could it was still a six-foot drop. If I hang by my knees, tuck my head under and roll. Gotta do it. Maybe they could do the shirt thing again. Too small for her to turn around and nothing to tie it to. Why didn't that stupid Mark think to bring a rope? Wait. Her eyes were adjusting to the dark-ness. She could see the metal compartment walls. If she could catch the top of the closest one she could swing herself down. Maybe even land on top of the toilet tank. Stretch as she might, her fingers barely missed.

"What's happening?" Mark prodded. "You need our shirts?"

"Gonna go for it." She put her palms on each side of the window frame and pushed off, grabbing the top of the wall, but her feet collided with the tank, kicking off the lid, which crashed to the floor. "Thank God," she breathed, "I'm all in one piece."

"Holy Crap," gasped Ollie. "What was that crash."

"You okay, Red?" Mark strained to hear any sound.

Using the toilet as a step stool she wasn't tall enough to see out the window but she called out. "I'm okay. Heading out front to take a look."

"Can you open the back door?"

"I'll check it out."

"Okay," Mark's heart was beating furiously, "but hurry it up."

Stopping at the solid rear door she winced. Keyed dead-bolt. No way. Moving into the front office she was confronted with three desks and there was enough light from the street lamp she didn't need the flashlight. Which one? Can eliminate the one in the middle. Computer screen, Roll-O-Dex, obviously belongs to the secretary. One of the others had a framed picture of a fat woman and three kids. Leaves me one choice. Moving to the third desk she started through the drawers. Lips pursed, she screwed up her face when she found the first three of the six were empty. A fourth contained part of a package of cookies, some change and an empty holster. The remaining two were filled with paperwork in hanging folders, but not a single manila file. Rats. Hope those guys found something in their search of the Man's apartment. Whoa, what have we here? Pulling open the shallow

394

center drawer, there it was.

On top of the folder was a small spiral bound notebook and she simply had to open it. It was nothing. On the first page were the words; 'Police Business.' He apparently kept a log of his daily police activities. Turning one more page she gasped. There were seven names, three of which were crossed off. The sixth and seventh names made her tremble. 'Marcus Goodwin and Candice Swanson'. Snatching up the two items she hurried to the bathroom, stepping up onto the rim of the toilet tank again so she could shove them out the window. "I don't see how I can get back out the way I came in. I'm going to check the front door."

"Oh boy, you did good," Mark called back to her. "This looks like exactly what we need."

Thrilled and excited she moved back into the office, past the desks, she didn't hear The Man open and close the front door. Only one thought was in her mind. Get her butt out of there. It had an old fashioned dead bolt with a turn latch and as she reached for it a hand covered her mouth and a cold gun barrel pressed against her cheek.

"Hey baby. I'm as surprised as you are. Ain't got a clue how you found a way to get in, but I ain't complainin' 'cause I planned on looking you up later tonight. What the hell are you doin' in here?"

No way she could answer with his palm pressed firmly against her lips. Candy was horrified. Never in her life had she felt such terror. If he had just grabbed her, it might have been possible to use some Karate. Then cut and run. The gun changed everything. None of her Karate training had involved a gun.

"Gonna take my hand away. You make a sound and I'll blow your head off. You understand me?"

She nodded frantically. He'd moved the gun barrel down to the soft flesh under her chin and used the pressure to force her toward the door.

His laugh was like nothing she'd ever heard. "You and me are going to go play some games, sweet thing. Let's move it."

"Hey Red," came a muffled voice from outside the alley door, "can you open it?"

Ralph cocked his head like he was not sure if he was hearing things or not. He frowned and opened the front door, pushing her out into the cold night.

* * *

"Come on Red. Quit fooling around." Mark shouted, the sound echoed in the alley.

"Like what's going on?" Heather sounded nearly hysterical.

"Don't know. Either something is wrong or she has gone out the front."

To his surprise Heather was running, dashing past the rear of the post office to peer around the corner at Locust Street. She screamed. Mark was beside her as a black and white car flashed past going east on Main, the head in the passenger seat turned away from the window. All he could see was a mass of red hair.

What are we going to do?" Wailed Heather. "He's has her in the police car. My God, like he's going to kill her."

Ollie was holding on to Heather, his face so pale it was starkly white even in the darkness. "Where could he be taking her?"

"Pipe down a minute." Mark was so tense he was actually shivering nearly out of control. "I gotta think."

Ollie was shifting from foot to foot. "Back out Lone Pine Trail?"

"I don't think he is going very far. This is one time the sheriff is right. Killed the others someplace else then dumped their bodies in different places. Where the heck would you take her if you were an ex-butcher?"

"To the meat packing place," Heather screeched. "Like that's how he cuts off their legs."

"Oh my God," Ollie exclaimed, "and then he eats them."

"No way," Mark's voice cracked. "Heather, you get to a phone, probably at the bowling alley. Call the sheriff. Call my dad, then call Candy's dad. Tell them where we're going. Then go to the Ezyinn and see if those two agents are there. Ollie, let's run to your house. We gotta get there fast so that motorcycle better start. That ghoul isn't going to eat my redhead."

* * *

Heather had never been more excited or more frightened. She was totally surprised that her asthma wasn't acting up. Like a startled rabbit, she darted from the alley and across Locust.

396

There was a young man inside the Texaco station but she didn't slow down as she passed it, crashing through the double barroom doors at the Lucky Lady. A dozen startled men, including the sheriff, looked at the tiny ghost of a girl.

"Help," she wailed, going directly to the sheriff. "He took Candy. He's going to kill her."

"Hold up there a minute, sweet thing." The fat man was actually grinning. "What are you ranting and raving about?"

"He has Candy. He's gonna kill her." Tears were streaming on her cheeks.

"Who are we talkin' 'bout, little lady?

"Talkin' 'bout Ralph. It's him. He's the killer. Put Candy in the police car. He's gonna kill her."

"Come on sweetheart, calm down. Ralph's the killer? Boy, that's a good one. He's probably giving her a ride home. Not very safe out on the streets for . . . "

"You stupid, incompetent, fat pig," she screamed. "I'll go talk to somebody who is smart enough to listen."

She was out the door heading for the Ezyinn. Ignoring the office, she spotted a white sedan with buggy whip antennas and a government license plate in front of unit six. Banging on the solid door with both of her small fists she was screaming, "Please, please, open it up."

The FBI man who opened the door was wearing a white tee shirt, which displayed his brown shoulder holster and the black weapon. "You gotta come, she screamed. The killer has my friend. He's taking her to the DGF Packing House. Like he's going to butcher her."

"What?" The man stood there, bewildered. "Who are you?"

Heather didn't faint; she merely slumped to her hands and knees, sobbing out of control.

"Her remarks clicked with the second agent in the room. They had already established that the blue plastic bag was the type used in the DGF meat department. Tomorrow they planned to start an investigation out there. "My God," he called out, grabbing his coat. "Did you hear what she said? Let's go!" He didn't know what to do about the girl so he easily picked her up and carried her to the car.

* * *

397

Candy knew where they were. In her mind she could see a person, flaming red hair, white body and bloody stumps where the legs had been. He was clutching both her wrists behind her back with one hand as he reached up to turn on a single, hanging, overhead light, then produced a roll of heavy gray tape. First he placed a strip across her mouth. Next he pulled her up by first one arm and then the other, wrapping tape around and around her wrists as he secured them to a pair of meat hooks hanging down from a metal track. Her feet no longer touched the floor. Selecting a ghastly appearing knife from a rack he approached her and she cringed in horror, sucking her stomach away from the gleaming blade, but he used it to systematically slice at her clothes. First, up the front of her sweatshirt and the flashlight fell out.

"What have we got here? A flashlight? Rats. Here I thought you were a freak with three tits. Guess I'll have to be satisfied with two. Let's see whatcha got." Using the knife he cut the cloth out to each shoulder. The material slithered down her back. Sliding the blade between the cups of her bra, he easily severed the narrow band of cloth.

"My, my. Ain't that about the prettiest things I ever saw. Perfect as those are, I believe I'll cut 'em off and keep them for souvenirs . . . after I take care of other butchering." A couple of strokes at her shoulders and the bra dropped to the floor. He was pulling down her jeans and panties all in one motion. There was a sudden coolness. She was naked.

"Wow! Ain't nothin' in the world pretty as a teeny bopper. But . . . I'll tell ya, honey, man's gotta do what a man's gotta do. It's damned near a crime to have to cut you up. If you've been eating at our local diner, you already know that human flesh tastes pretty much like veal, or didn't you try the breaded veal cutlets at the Green Spot the other night?"

She was going to be sick. She was going to choke to death on her own vomit. The Man was putting on a rubber, wrap around apron.

"I don't have much free time tonight. On duty, you know. I'd like to cut up your tender young body into veal chops, veal steaks and make up some veal patties." He cackled as he sat a freezer box on the counter next to her hip.

She could make out the red and white label. 'Kelly's Burger Pit.' Out of the blue, like the gripping of a powerful hand, the terror hit her. Pulling an evil appearing tool from a leather holder, he touched her chest with the razor sharp boning knife, letting it slide, making a two-inch long gash between her breasts and she tried so hard to scream behind the tape the pressure hurt her ears. Her bladder hurt. Her bowels felt like they were about to let loose.

He continued to talk to her in a fatherly sounding tone. "Best I can do on short order is to turn out twenty five or thirty pounds of prime hamburger. Folks in Dalton are going to think they have died and gone to heaven."

Placing his face right up close to hers, his breath rancid, he snarled. "Slime-bag huh? I'll show that slime-bag." Pushing a black button a meat grinder began to snarl and groan, then he pushed a huge red button and the giant meat saw again screamed in agony until the blade stopped slipping and it settled into a continuous wail.

Candy's mouth behind the tape was drawn in a grim line, her eyes pressed tightly closed. There was terror but also a feeling of intense anger, with herself. This big mistake was all her fault. She was the one who kept pushing Mark and the Kryptonites to continue with the investigation. She tried to force everything out of her mind because, for her, it was all over.

* * *

Mark was furious with himself. They had made a serious mistake and he knew it. Trying to do this thing on their own had been stupid. Even if no one believed them, they should have taken their knowledge to the sheriff, to their parents, to the news people, even confronted Ralph himself. Then he would have had to stop. Candy was going to be killed and it was all his fault. They were going to have to go it alone. They were her only hope.

In Ollie's garage Mark automatically leaped into the driver's position, reaching to turn on the gas cock with his left hand, turning the key with his right then stomped on the starting lever. Nothing. Again and again and again. "Oh God, please."

"Wait." Ollie crawled off, snatching up the can of either. This time it fired on the first kick.

Ollie's dad opened the house door and stuck his head out

and shouted. He was in his pajamas. "What the hell are you boys doing out here this time of night?"

"DGF Packing house, Mark yelled and the motorcycle leaped into the darkness. He nearly laid it over making the turns onto Lincoln then onto Park. It leaped again as he went through the gears, the red needle on the speedometer inching past 100 miles an hour. In less than three minutes they roared into the DGF parking lot. Mark jerked up on the front wheel while gunning it and it jumped the curb, crashing through the brush and around to the back of the building. He shut it off.

As quietly as he could he pushed it to the spot under the same window they had hoisted Jodi through the previous night. He leaned the bike against the wall. By standing on the seat, he could reach the sill. Using the toes of his western boots on the heavy wire mesh that covered the lower window to gain added leverage, he pulled himself up.

There was light coming over a dividing wall from the room next door and it illuminated the metal framework supporting the roof. He whispered loudly, "Come on Ollie. Window's about eighteen-inches clear I think you can get through."

Mark heard the unmistakable sound of a band saw starting and all at once he had a basketball-sized lump in his chest. Not bothering to wait for Ollie, he spotted an eight-inch wide plank catwalk going through the trusses and he was on it, nearly running, not even aware of the dark twelve-foot void below him.

Ollie was grunting and puffing, but he made it through. Mark was faced with a five foot difference in roof height between where he stood and the next level so he used the metal framework to climb up into the higher trusses then looked back when he heard Ollie cry. His friend lost his balance on the catwalk and fell sideways. He would have gone all the way down but a flailing hand caught a metal tension rod in the next truss and he landed on his hands and knees. Like a white gorilla he came crawling across without rising up, and then he was beside Mark and they were both looking down into the meat-processing department.

In the dim light of a single hanging lamp they could see a white figure with red hair streaming about her shoulders, a piece of gray tape covering her mouth and her arms stretched high above her head, her wrists secured to some metal meat hooks with the same gray tape. The hooks were hanging from a track that ran from an outside door, past the meat saws and on into a huge cooler. Ralph was wearing a rubber or vinyl sort of covering that protected the whole front of his body.

Ollie swallowed loudly and whispered. "She's naked."

Other than the pictures in Playboy, and one time a pornographic magazine Buzz got from somewhere, Mark had never seen an unclothed female. Even in his terror, he couldn't help thinking about what he was seeing. She is actually pretty good-looking. Pretty good? She is the most beautiful thing I've ever seen.

They could hear the Man say, "Well honey, it's time we get to work." Reaching out he pushed her along. Rollers supported the wicked meat hooks and he was taking her to the saw.

The meat hooks? A horrible thought went through Mark's mind. 'Raped with a foreign object' the papers had stated. It was easy to understand why Laura had the round hole in her belly. This demented creep hung their bodies on the meat hooks. He whispered, "we have to stall him until help comes. I'm going to yell out."

"Are you crazy? Guy has his gun. He'll blow us away. Let me try something. See what I brought." Ollie produced a Whamo slingshot from his hip pocket. It contained fifteen metal balls in its handle.

* * *

Ralph was lifting Candy's legs onto the saw table. Picking up a long, thin, razor sharp blade, he reached out to touch her throat, chuckling in something more near a growl as she cringed away. "Ah huh huh huh, I love this work. "I have to bleed you first, then gut you. Doesn't that sound exciting?"

Her eyes reminded Mark of those of a deer he'd once seen in the headlights of his father's car. They had missed the deer by inches but he recalled those eyes.

"As soon as I've drained off your blood, I need to cut you into quarters, like a side of beef. Make it easier for me to . . . Yeow!"

* * *

Mark jerked his fists in satisfaction. Ollie had stretched the rubber bands and let the slingshot snap. The quarter inch metal ball caught Ralph in the middle of his back. The Man yelled, jerked and howled, letting Candy's legs drop off the table. They could see her cowering in terror with no idea they were there. Ollie was reloading. Ralph was swinging his head left and right in an effort to determine what hit him and from where it originated. "Where are you?" He screamed, bending down to reach inside his jacket, which was on the floor, producing his revolver from its holster. Ollie shot again, this time aiming for a stack of metal trays about ten feet behind the saw. KAWHANG!

Ralph whirled and pulled the trigger, the explosion echoing off the metal roof.

"Keep him busy," Mark whispered. It's dark enough up here that he can't see us. I'm going to work my way over till I'm directly above him. Only 'bout thirty feet from here."

"Go for it." He let another shot go; actually aiming at the Man's head but it missed and broke a window.

Ralph whirled, thinking he could sense someone overhead and took a shot at a shadow. He was holding the gun in both hands like he was a TV cop, waving it back and forth as he was looking up into the rafters. "Where are you?" He screeched. "Come on down from there or I'll blow your damned head off."

Mark was halfway. The next pellet struck Ralph in the chest and he clutched at it in pain and fired a random shot into the darkness. Wood splintered directly behind Mark's feet. He gasped but kept crawling.

The Man spotted the powerful flashlight he'd found inside Candy's clothing and snatched it off the counter. Crawling up onto a worktable he began panning the light back and forth through the trusses. Ollie broke another window and the Man fired again. Mark was ten feet away, inching forward, the sound of his movements covered by the crunching sounds of the grinder and the whining of the saw. Thank goodness, he was thinking, for his heart was beating a hundred miles an hour and throbbing like a drum. Five feet to go. Ralph screeched when another pellet struck his arm, but this time he was able to calculate the direction of the projectile and fired another shot. The bullet bounced off a steel support, singing ominously above Ollie's head.

The Man realized what he had to do and brought his gun down even with his waist and pointed it directly into Candy's ear.

"All right you son-of-a-bitch. Whoever you are. Come on out or the next bullet is directly into her head." There was no movement. "Don't mess with me. I mean what I say. I'll blow her head off."

Mark recognized the sound of the hammer as it cocked and he wanted to scream. Candy's eyes were sweeping the darkness, imploring, pleading.

"Don't!" Ollie cried as he stepped out onto the catwalk between trusses.

An evil grin sprang to Ralph's face as he slowly swung the gun toward the boy. Mark told himself, all right Superman, if you ever needed to fly, this is the time. He leaped. His feet caught Ralph on both shoulders propelling him backward off the table. The revolver sent a random shot, the bullet creasing Mark's shoulder before twanging off the sides of metal locker walls. The weight of Mark's body carried both of them about five feet off the table and through the air until Ralph's head struck the concrete floor nearly knocking him senseless, and yet he shook it off. Managing to hold onto the gun he rolled over to scramble shakily to his feet.

Mark had landed on his rump, the pain in his upper arm smarting fiercely, and he was frantically trying to regain his feet as the gun moved around until he was looking down the barrel. The muzzle of a Colt 45 is an awesome sight.

"Hope you said your prayers, punk." The Man pulled the trigger.

The click of the hammer falling on the empty chamber was a sound the young man would never forget. Ralph screamed in anger and swung the empty revolver at the boy's head. Mark's own terror turned to a raging fury, which exploded his body into action. Ducking under the wild swing he felt the heavy metal part his hair as he lashed out with his western boot, managing to catch the surprised man directly in the groin and as the screaming figure bent forward to clutch himself, the teenager slammed his knee directly onto the point of the Man's jaw. The killer's body hit the floor with a thud and then except for the saw, the grinder and the nearby wail of a siren, it was silent.

Mark had no idea what he was doing as he leaped onto the killer and buried his fingers in the The Man's throat, shutting off the windpipe as he exerted more and more pressure. Ralph's eyes popped open and seemed to be glazed.

Ollie climbed down from the rafters by using a stack of wooden meat boxes, riding them down as they collapsed. Locating the buttons to the saw and the grinder, he shut them down. Whirling, he grabbed his buddy by the shoulders. "Mark! C'mon Marcus, let it go." He was prying at Mark's fingers buried deep in the neck flesh. "C'mon, Mark. Hear those sirens? The cops are coming." The gripping fingers came free.

Mark shook and shook his head to clear his mind. "Ollie, there is a roll of duct tape on the counter. Wrap up the guy's wrists." Scrambling to his feet he turned to look at the redhead. Her eyes fixed on his, her slim white body, slowly rotated, swaying slightly in the dim light.

CHAPTER THIRTY-ONE

Moving to stand in front of Candy, Mark reached out, pulling tenderly at the strip covering her mouth. Try as he might to be gentle, it wasn't working so he jerked it off. Then with one arm about her waist he supported her weight as he used the other hand to unwrap the tape from her wrists. She gasped as her wrists came free and the lovely creature was in his arms.

Looking past him at the prostrate form of Ralph that was being guarded by Ollie, his wrists secured by turn after turn of gray tape to a metal table leg, he felt her shudder and he turned to see what held her attention. There was something obvious showing, a pair of polished black boots with impressions of eagles on the heels. Then he heard her crying.

"It's going to be all right," he whispered in her ear.

She looked and saw the blood streaming down the right arm of the man holding her. "Oh Gawd, Mark? You're hurt! How bad is it?"

"It's nothin' but a scratch. Candy?" he nuzzled her ear with his nose and she squirmed tighter against him. "Oh Candy, I thought I had lost you forever."

"Mark. My Mark." She continued to cry. "It's okay if you want to call me Red."

The strangest feeling coursed through his chest, one of super-human strength. The Man of Steel? He's a nobody. This is how it works in the real world.

He felt something grip his heart as she looked up into his blue eyes, hers a deep green, tears of gratitude and happiness streaming on her face, and something else. Something pure.

He held her more tightly, feeling the silk of her bare skin under his hands. "No way. I'd much rather call you Candy." With his cheek against hers, she felt perfectly natural in his arms. Her green eyes were glistening with moisture as she looked up into his and yet he had no idea what it meant.

So he kissed her.

THE END

Some Other Publishing with Passion Authors

Daveda Gruber
My Blonde World
Magical Moments
Bruised but not Beaten
Death of a Daughter
Cling to the Magic Mere Mortals
Tales of a Tiny Dog
Steelers Cheers
Red Barn and Other Short Stories
A Blonde View of Life
The Blonde Who Found Jesus
Castle of Ice
More Tales of a Tiny Dog
Snapshots ...a Blonde View
More Snapshots from My Family Album

Joree Williams
Lost Childhood
Journey to Eternity

Helen McManus
Widowed Dreams

Joe Hartman
If I Can't Finish

Mary Ann Harring-Duhart
Poetry with a Twist
Remembering Mama's Prayers
On Broken Pieces Sweat and Tears
In The Midst Of The Storm

Tayna Campos Gracia
With Silver Wings and a Golden Quill

Arthur Tugman
Adages for Life
Pick a Pun and Make Success Fun
Be Smart with Art
Give SUCCESS a Head Start with Art
The Key to Success

Poetry with Passion Global Poets
Poetry with Passion Global Book 2010

Daveda gruber and PWP Poets
Poetry with Passion Global Book 2911

Nancy Childers
Granny's Book Box

Helen VanEck Holub
The Peanut Butter Caper
Beloved Companion
Touched by God

Dorian Petersen Potter
Praising Through Poetry

Daveda Gruber and PWP Poets
Laugh with Us Poetry with Humor

Michael Duane Small
A Letter to the Class of 65'
From the Shadow of My Smile

Carol A. Eckart
The Protector

Some Upcoming PWP Books

J. Elwood Davis
Unpaid Bills

Arthur Tugman
Make the World a Better Place

The Butcher's List

Roger's Website

http://publishingwithpassion.com/RogerSWilliamsbooks.html

CPSIA information can be obtained
at www.ICGtesting.com
Printed in the USA
LVHW041107160820
663324LV00001B/91